Milledgeville Asylum

Ann O'Leary

Milledgeville Asylum

Copyright © 2023 by Ann O'Leary. All rights reserved.

No part of this book may be reproduced in any form or by any mechanical means, including information storage and retrieval systems without permission in writing from the publisher/author, except by a reviewer who may quote passages in a review.

All images, logos, quotes, and trademarks included in this book are subject to use according to trademark and copyright laws of the United States of America.

ISBN: 979-8-3915592-6-9

FICTION / Mystery & Detective / Cozy / General

Cover photo by Ann O'Leary
Cover design by Dominic Garramone
Map illustration by Caroline Rose

This is a work of fiction. Names, characters, businesses, places, events and incidents are either the products of the author's imagination or used in a fictitious manner. Any resemblance to actual persons, living or dead, or actual events is purely coincidental.

All rights reserved by Ann O'Leary.

To the estimated 25,000 patients who died at Milledgeville Central State Hospital between the years 1842 and 2010, their bodies buried unceremoniously in shallow graves in the surrounding woods.

And to caregivers everywhere.

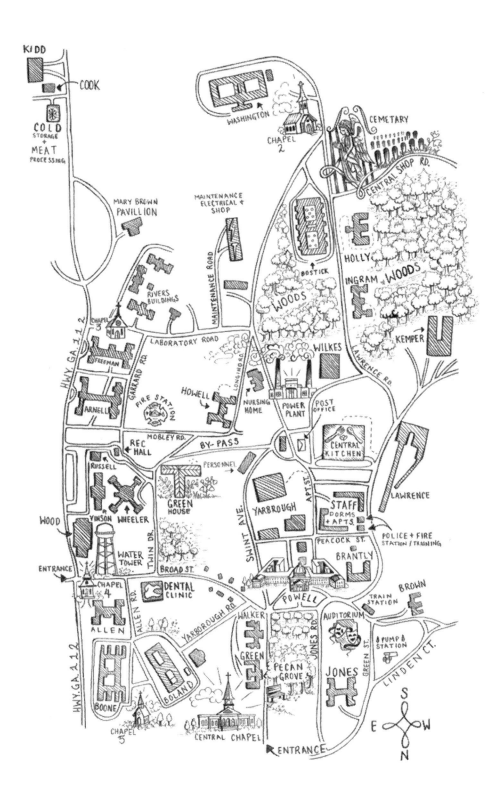

Chapter 1

Heather

July 9, 1976
Rivers Building, Ward A
Milledgeville Central State Hospital

Dr. von Brimmer interviewed me today. First time. He's the psychiatrist heading up the new Crisis Stabilization Unit I heard they're opening in the Walker building. He said, "Heather, I'd like to do an evaluation of you. We're trying to target some higher-functioning female patients who might benefit from being moved to the Freeman building. It's a less restrictive environment. You'd have some intense therapy, and you could join in the activities. Would you like that?"

I didn't answer.

He has no way of knowing if I'm a higher-functioning patient or not. I keep a low profile, try to look confused most of the time.

I have no desire to leave Ward A, but I'm not much worried. My permanent record is against it—too many black marks, starting with my teeth. I figure if I don't talk, Dr. B. won't notice my front teeth are missing. As soon as I open my mouth, I'm labeled. Violent patient. Bites. Teeth removed. Most people shy away from me.

He thumbed through my chart, lifting the metal cover and letting the pages of my life slowly fall back down. The facts, as the staff knew them, were in front of him. I took my time, looked around the office. The room was neat. No scraps of paper on the floor, no spots on the beige carpet. The floor-to-ceiling bookshelves held medical books of all sizes, some of them bound in leather. Journals in a tidy pile on the floor. A photo of him with a pretty woman, brown hair blowing in the wind, on one of the shelves. It looked like it was taken by the seashore, maybe down the Georgia coast somewhere. She was holding a toddler. Little boy in blue short pants and a blue cap. I wondered where that woman was now, who she was. When it was taken.

I walked over and picked up the photo. "Is this your wife?"

"Yes." He came and took the photo out of my hands and put it back on the shelf.

"Her name?"

He didn't answer. Gazed at the photo for a moment, then turned away.

Today was an okay day. I marked it that way on my calendar, the one I made out of toilet paper. The TP here is thick enough to write on. Four squares equal one month. I stuck it on the wall right above the iron headboard on my bed. Used some already-been-chewed gum that I found under a bench on the grounds. My little girl, Matilda, used to call it ABC gum. Already been chewed. I laughed the first time she said it because I didn't know what she meant. I told her ABC gum was all germy and not to touch it.

I've been a patient on Ward A for eighteen years. I mark off every day on my calendar. Before I made the calendar, I used to collect little pebbles from the grounds and keep them in piles under my bed, one for each day, seven for each week. I felt like Robinson Crusoe on a desert island marking off the time, trying to keep track of the days. (Sometimes I wish I *were* Robinson Crusoe on a desert island.) I get real anxious if I don't know what date it is, but I don't know why it matters.

Some of the attendants think it's important for us to know the date. Today, Bruno put six of us into a circle. We sat on chairs he took from the dining room. He told us, "This is 1976. Who knows what's special 'bout this year? No need in raise yo' hand; just speak right up."

Silence.

"This is the bicentennial year. Somebody here knows what bicentennial means?"

Silence.

He smiled his big, toothy, wall-to-wall smile. "Anybody knows what month it is?"

Bruno is black. Some of the younger attendants wear their hair in an Afro, but not Bruno. He keeps his cropped close to his head, and he dresses smart. Today he had on his blue plaid shirt, and he always presses his jeans real neat. When Bruno smiles, you can see a gap between his front teeth. His teeth are white like polished marble. His face is perfectly round, and his eyes are kind. Yep, that's the first thing you notice about Bruno: kind brown eyes. He's about my age, I figure. Around fifty.

He looked around our little group. No one gave him an answer, so he filled us in. "Today is July 9, 1976," he told us. "We done finished now. Head on back to your cots."

Lucinda's a patient like me. Her cot is right next to mine, and she helps me watch over my stuff. Another patient might stop by my bed and try to steal the trinkets from under my pillow. If you try to hide any big stuff under there, you can see the outline because the pillows are so thin. Today I hid a piece of yellow, hard candy. It's still got the wrapper on it—Brach's Lemon Drop. I'm saving it for a special occasion. And I hid a ring I found outside. It looks like a real diamond, but I'm sure it's fake, like me.

Where to start? First, I've been two people in my life. Not everyone can say that. Not everyone would want to say that. I started out as the trusting, proper little Miss Heather Edwards. Pampered little Heather. I went to Miss Elizabeth's Private School, and I was a member of the Savannah United Methodist Church. Neighbors and relatives all said I was the perfect child. What they meant was I was a compliant child, did as I was told, never grumbled. Obedient. Appreciative.

I was a daddy's girl. How I loved my daddy. He taught me to ride a bike and tackle long division. Momma. What can I say about my momma? She bought me white gloves and debutante dresses. Told me my life would be beautiful if I would learn to cook my future husband's favorite dishes, the ones his momma made for him. And she said I should always have myself fixed up pretty for him when he walked in the door after work.

My parents rented one of the small ballrooms at the DeSoto Hotel on Liberty Street and gave me a sweet sixteen party. That was the night I met my future husband, Clive. Clive McAllister. I think my daddy knew his people, which was how he got an invite. Clive's great-grandpa made money bringing supplies down from Dublin, Georgia, to Savannah after the Civil War. He thought to use horses and wagons because the train line was destroyed by the Yankees. I think it's more likely he was a gunrunner. Clive's grandpa made moonshine back in the hills. Invested his money. Got rich.

Clive asked me to dance, and I knew right away he was the one. The fix-yourself-up-pretty-for-him one. He was Mr. Charm. Called me Miss Heather. I flirted, batted my eyelashes like momma taught me.

Daddy gave his approval, and next thing I knew I was eighteen, getting married in the big Methodist church around the corner.

Daddy must be dead by now; I have no way of knowing. Momma too. I'm sure she looks down at me from up above and shakes her head. "It's hard down here, Momma," I whisper sometimes. I don't want to say it too loudly or someone might report me for hallucinating, and they'll put me back on that medication that makes my stomach twitch.

Sometimes when I'm lying in my bed at night, and I can't sleep because someone is talking to their voices and someone is peeing in their bed and someone is fighting with the attendant or trying to turn on the lights, I think about that little girl, her daddy pushing her high up on a swing, then letting it go. I hear her laughing at the circus clowns, and I see her eating ice cream on her birthday. I watch her sitting on the curb, waving at the brightly colored Fourth of July floats as they pass by.

I see her in my mind's eye and wonder, where did she go? My other self. Then I turn over and put my head into the flat piece of material they call a pillow and cry myself to sleep.

Dr. von Brimmer told me during our interview today that he's going to schedule me to see him every few weeks. Not sure why—this must be the longest evaluation in history.

He asked me, "What is the most challenging experience you have had while a patient on Ward A?" Who the fuck comes up with such questions? I think he wanted me to talk about the time Clive came to visit—the only time he ever came to visit—but I'm not anywhere near ready to do that. So I decided to tell him about the head-stomping incident. It's still fresh in my mind because it took place last week. I guess you could say it was a challenge or a nightmare from hell—whichever you prefer.

My version goes something like this. Bethesda is a large-boned, big-mouthed attendant who took a fancy to my best friend, Lucinda. I think Bethesda figured it was an okay thing to hanker after Lucinda since she's black and so is Lucinda.

Lucinda could tell Bethesda was attracted to her; so could I. We talked about it—what to do? We decided the best course was to let it play itself out. Our plan was that Lucinda wouldn't make eye contact with Bethesda and would basically just stay out of her way. Didn't work. Bethesda found ways to be around Lucinda, freaking Lucinda out. Bethesda would appear from nowhere and take a seat at our lunch table. She would be lounging around in the bathroom when Lucinda went in to pee.

Every patient gets a shower once a week. On shower day, the attendants herd us into a long line. A real long line—there are ninety patients on the ward. Then the attendants spread out. Two of them stand by the shower-room door. When we reach the doorway, they tell us to strip. Two more attendants wait inside the shower room. They help as needed. There are eight showerheads pouring out water. Patients are told to soap themselves down and then step under a showerhead to rinse off. A staff member stands at the exit to hand out towels and assist with the drying process if necessary.

On Tuesday, shower day, Bethesda was standing inside the entrance to the shower room, ready to help patients strip. This was unusual because Bethesda was never assigned to shower duty; she was supposed to help with lunch preparation during shower time.

Lucinda was standing in line right behind me. She noticed Bethesda leering at her. I turned around and whispered, "Take it easy. She won't try anything, not with everyone watching. Think of your kids. You could get an ice pick in your eyeball if you don't watch out. Believe me, she won't try anything."

Lucinda knew exactly what I meant. Our friend Pattie got the ice pick above both her eyeballs. It took them about ten minutes to hammer it in and move it around in her frontal lobe. After her lobotomy, she was a total vegetable.

I was wrong about Bethesda. She did try something. First, she took her time pulling off Lucinda's worn housedress, then followed her to the next station and "helped" her soap down, moving her hands up and down over her breasts and abdomen. Next, she went and stood near the shower spray, her beady eyes watching the soap bubbles flow over Lucinda's body and down the drain.

Lucinda's eyes shot fire, but she made no move to stop Bethesda. Her jaw was clenched, her mouth shut tight. She was shaking like a bowl of jelly, with goose bumps sticking out all over her trunk. I could only imagine she was thinking of her kids and how they would manage with one parent dead and the other a zombie.

I was almost at the exit. I grabbed an extra towel from the stack, walked back to Lucinda, and threw it to her. She wrapped it around her body and nodded her thanks. Bethesda gave me the evil eye.

The next day around noon, two Milledgeville police officers came on the ward. They were in uniform but didn't carry guns. The police have to leave their guns in a metal box outside our door because it would be dangerous to have loaded firearms on the ward.

The patients crowded around near where the policemen stood. One of the policemen said, "Your attendant by the name of Bethesda was walking across the grounds back to her car last evening." He paused. The patients stood still. Listening. Waiting.

"We have witnesses who say a bunch, maybe a gang, of colored teenagers from the male ward threw her down and stomped on her head. Does anyone know the names of those boys who done this? Com'on now, I know y'all have connections with the male ward. Speak up. Give me some names. Who done this to what's-her-name?"

He looked at his notes and said, "Who done this to Bethesda?"

The room stayed silent. The patients looked up at the ceiling, down at the floor; they were careful to not look at Lucinda. No one said a word.

I glanced over at Lucinda. She caught my eye and gave a slight nod. A shiver ran down my spine.

We never talked about it.

Chapter 2

Mattie

July 1976

Mattie McAllister slammed on her brakes in time to prevent her Chevy from rear-ending a white Buick station wagon, which had slowed down to a crawl in front of her. She watched the passenger in the front seat of the Buick roll down his window and toss a small brown puppy onto the shoulder of the highway before speeding away. The puppy landed with a thump on its right side. Mattie could see him struggling to regain his feet.

Oh my God! Mattie thought. *How could anyone do that—throw a puppy out on the side of the road in this hot July sun? Should I look for a phone booth and call the police? But I didn't catch the license number, and that poor little dog might get run over before I get back.*

She parked her car on the shoulder and rushed over to where the bundle of matted fur lay panting and whimpering with fright.

"Com'on, pup," she said, picking him up. "We'll figure out what to do with you after we get to my Aunt Tess's house—she's making one of her special Sunday brunches."

Mattie carried the puppy to her car and settled him in the front passenger seat. She took a good look at her newly acquired canine companion. Light-brown coat with mahogany streaks. Squashed-up coal-black face. Perky ears. Fat puppy tummy. She started the car, reached over, and gave the little pup a perfunctory pat on his head. "We can stop and buy you some doggy food and a dog dish on our way. And a leash. What do you say to that?"

"*Woof!*"

"I'll take that as a yes. And we have to work on finding you a good home. I'm sure sooner or later something will turn up," she told him. "Hey, that's it. How about we name you Sooner or Later?"

She pulled back out onto the busy highway. "We'll ask Aunt Tess if she can keep you, or maybe we'll ask my brother, Wilson. You'll love Wilson. He's been an animal lover since we were little kids. Matter of fact, he's studying to become a veterinarian."

Mattie was wearing the short-sleeved coral linen dress that her Aunt Tess had bought her for her recent twenty-sixth birthday. It made her feel like sunshine. She ran her hand through her crop of sun-streaked, light-brown hair; her new pixie cut still surprised her. She had wanted a change, any change.

She had her mother's clear blue eyes and lightly freckled skin. From her father, she had inherited bushy eyebrows, a fact she lamented each time she plucked them into two natural-looking arches. The remainder of her beauty routine consisted of taking a wet washcloth, slathering it with a bar of Dial soap, and scrubbing her face until it took on a rosy glow.

Aunt Tess's house—a redbrick, Federal-style mansion located at 455 Washington Avenue in Savannah—was similar to other houses in the Ardsley Park neighborhood. Black shutters framed the leadedglass windows and wrought-iron window boxes overflowed with Moroccan ivy and red Dragon Wing begonias.

Mattie parked her car under Aunt Tess's wisteria-covered carport and walked up the curved cobblestone path to the front door, which had been painted glossy black and adorned with an antique brass lion-head door knocker.

"Oh, my goodness. What kept you? I was just about to call the police," Aunt Tess said the minute Mattie stepped inside. Mattie loved Aunt Tess's voice. She had one of those slow, soft, distinct Southern drawls. She was wearing an ivory blouse with a single strand of perfectly matched pearls, a beige mid-length skirt, and brown pumps. Nylons, of course. Mattie knew that Aunt Tess never felt properly dressed without her nylons, even in the blistering July heat. Wilson stood behind Aunt Tess, grinning. He was aware this was Aunt Tess's customary greeting when they were a few minutes late.

Mattie laughed. "You say that every time I come home, Aunt Tess. Everything's fine. Matter of fact, I have news. Good news. Central State Hospital is advertising for a nurse counselor to work on their new Crisis Stabilization Unit, and I've got a job interview next week!"

"Central State Hospital? That's the fancy name for the Milledgeville asylum, right, Sis?" Wilson said. "That's good. A job interview. Time to get back out there into the world."

Mattie agreed. "I know. I've just been lying around moping, feeling sorry for myself, but not any longer."

Wilson ushered Mattie and Aunt Tess toward the dining room. "If you get the job, Sis, you'll be able to meet a bunch of new people," he said. "You can tell us more about the interview while we eat. I'm starving."

Aunt Tess had prepared a champagne brunch: white linen tablecloth; blue delphiniums poking out of a Waterford vase; fresh blueberry waffles with clotted cream; hollowed-out, homemade bread boats filled with Creole gumbo; orange marmalade scones; and a romaine and pecan salad with homemade blue cheese dressing.

"Wait. Before we sit down, I want you both to meet a new friend of mine," Mattie said. "He's waiting in the car, and he's probably hungry. I'll be right back."

"How nice," Aunt Tess said, turning to Wilson. "It's wonderful Matilda's meeting some new gentlemen after that nasty business with her boyfriend. We have plenty to eat."

Mattie ran out to the car, scooped up Sooner or Later, and returned to the dining room. She lowered the little dog onto the cherrywood floor. He bounded away, slipped, rolled over on his side, and got up and tried again.

"And here I thought you were bringing a new beau to meet us," Aunt Tess said.

"I want you both to meet Sooner or Later. You can call him Sooner or, if you prefer, you can call him Later. He doesn't answer to either one. But he's housebroken, I think. At least he was when I left him in the car."

Aunt Tess smiled. "I have to admit he looks mighty precious."

Wilson reached down and picked up the wobbling pup. "I think you're going to call him confused if you don't decide on a name. Why don't you just call him Sooner and forget the Later?"

"That's a great idea. Sooner it is. Can you believe this adorable mutt was thrown out of a car window?" Mattie asked.

"Sis, you called this pup a mutt, but I think not. The truth of the matter is, this dog is a wonderful find. He's a Belgian Tervuren. Here, let me show you a photo of the breed." Wilson walked into the living room and returned with a color photo book of all the breeds recognized by the American Kennel Club. "Here, take a look. The Tervuren's face looks like he's wearing a black mask. When Sooner gets older, he'll have a long brown coat with mahogany overtones, just like in this photo. Says here he's a herding animal, and he'll get about the same size as a German shepherd."

"Now just to be clear," Mattie said, "you're telling me this unattractive little bundle of matted fur is going to turn out to look the same as the elegant dog in this photo?"

"Yes. I'd stake my life on it. Very intelligent animal, and he'll make you a good watchdog too."

"But I'm not planning on keeping him. I don't need a watchdog, and I've got too much going on right now."

"Then what are you going to do with him?" Wilson asked.

"I guess I was hoping y'all could help me out—that maybe you or Aunt Tess could take him."

"Can't happen. I live in an apartment with three other students, remember?"

"And I have Albert. One dog is about all I can manage," Aunt Tess said. As if on cue, her drastically overweight English bulldog lumbered out of the kitchen, ignored the puppy, and lay down in his familiar spot under the dining room table.

"I'll think about it tomorrow," Mattie said, plopping herself into an antique dining room chair.

"Good plan, Scarlett," Wilson said.

"Aunt Tess, these orange marmalade scones look delicious. You made them?" Mattie asked as soon as they were seated.

"I did, child. Now, Wilson and I want to hear all your news. When are you driving up to Milledgeville for the interview?"

Wilson reached for a waffle. "Hey, that's pretty far from here— the asylum's about a three-hour drive northwest of Savannah. It'll be a long commute every day."

"If I get the job, I'll check to see if they have housing available."

"I'd be delighted, of course, if you got a position you want, Matilda, but heaven knows I'd miss having you here," Aunt Tess said.

"Oh, Aunt Tess. I'd be back often. I thought I'd never get over Allan, but, now, if I get the job, well, helping those less fortunate will give me something else to think about besides myself, won't it?"

Aunt Tess shook her head. "Why anyone would want to work in a state mental hospital, I will never understand."

"Hmm... If you get the job, you're going to be working with the crazies," Wilson said, pouring a generous amount of pure maple syrup on his blueberry waffle. "Why would you want to do that? Couldn't have anything to do with our mother, could it?"

"Yes, please tell me why a beautiful, sane young woman would want to waste her youth and beauty going to work with the insane," Aunt Tess said.

"It's kind of hard to explain."

"It's about your mother, right, Matilda?" Aunt Tess asked, her voice quiet.

"Yes, to be honest, it's about her. I just want to find out what her life was like in the hospital before—well, you know, before she, before she..."

Aunt Tess nodded. "Before she died. To tell you children the truth, I've always wondered what ever happened to Heather. Why did my brother Clive take her to that appalling place? I don't mind telling you, I was shocked when I learned he'd committed her. I only met your mother once. She seemed to be such a lovely, gentle person. And at the time she was in full possession of all her faculties, I might add. I thought they were getting on well. They seemed to be a happily married couple."

Mattie shifted her weight in her chair and bit on a corner of her lower lip. "Two weeks after Father took her away, he told us she had died. I begged him to tell us about how she used to be. I wanted to talk about her. I didn't want to start forgetting how she looked, the way she smelled. Like lavender, like roses. He said, 'Don't ever bring her name up again. She's buried in the cemetery at the Milledgeville asylum, where she belongs. I don't want to ever hear another word about her.' I never asked about her again—it felt like she just faded away from me."

"Why don't you just take a tour of the hospital?" Wilson asked. "I understand they take groups through twice a week. A couple of months ago, one of my friends from my class in animal husbandry went. Said it was real spooky. He told me they were trying to transfer a bunch of regressed patients out of the older wards. Maybe shut some of them down forever."

"I did think of that, Wilson," Mattie said, her words tumbling out. "I thought of just taking the tour and calling it a day, but somehow that didn't seem to do it for me. I want to *really* experience what her life was like, what she ate, where she slept in the short time she was living there. I want to walk on the same wards she walked on. I want to find out if the staff was nice to her. Did she have any friends to talk to? And of course, most important, what happened to her? Did she have a fall or some sort of accident? Did she catch a disease? Or maybe she had some genetic problems we know nothing about."

Wilson got up, stood behind Mattie's chair, and put his hands on her shoulders. "I know, Sis," he said. "I still miss her too." He returned to his chair and reached for the romaine and pecan salad. "If it gives you some peace of mind, then go for it. Right, Aunt Tess? Mattie should do what makes her happy."

Mattie felt tears sting her eyes. She was so proud of Wilson, the way he'd turned out. So caring, so supportive; nothing like their father Clive. "And I want to find Mother's grave," Mattie said, looking at her aunt. "If I find it, maybe we can arrange to have a proper headstone put on it."

"Yes, of course," Aunt Tess said, "we'll see to it she has a fine headstone. Clive indicated to me that they buried her with nary a prayer in the old cemetery at the asylum. That was not proper. Not proper at all. She should at least have had a Christian burial."

Aunt Tess appraised Mattie from across the table. "Now, Matilda, I think it's high time for you to contemplate finding yourself a husband. Would you rather be pushing a patient in a wheelchair or pushing a baby in a baby carriage? Wait, don't answer that."

Mattie chuckled and reached for some clotted cream to spread on her scone.

"I have good news for you children—your father is coming for a short visit this Saturday," Aunt Tess said. "I would like you both to come for dinner. I'll make jambalaya and key lime pie, Clive's favorites."

Wilson and Mattie exchanged a glance.

"Now, you two, don't be giving each other that look. I know you have some problems with your father, but remember, he is my only brother and he is your father, no matter what you think of him."

"Father always seemed so distant," Mattie said. "So unapproachable. Like he resented me—and Wilson, too, for that matter."

"Be that as it may, I would like you both to be here," Aunt Tess said. "He's driving all the way down from his new house in Atlanta just to spend time with us. And he's bringing a guest. I believe her name is Baby Bun. He wants you to meet her."

Yuck. Another catch from his long line of catches, Mattie thought. *Why doesn't he get a job like other fathers? He could sell used cars or something. Why does he have to sell women's lingerie?*

"Apparently, this lady works for your father at Darling Dainties," Aunt Tess said. "She is one of their top models, I believe. I do hope she likes jambalaya."

Aunt Tess appeared to think it was settled, but Mattie said, "I'm so sorry, Aunt Tess. I've already signed up for a CPR class. I want to get recertified before my job interview."

Aunt Tess raised her eyebrows. "CPR?"

"Cardiopulmonary resuscitation," Wilson said. He placed his left hand over the back of his right. "You hold your hands like this and push up and down on someone's chest if they're having a heart attack or something."

"Yes," Mattie said. "And you have to breathe for them right into their mouth. I hope I never have to use CPR on a patient, but just in case, it's good to know."

"I'm tied up, too, Aunt Tess," Wilson said. "I promised a couple of my friends I'd go river rafting with them. Tell Father we're sorry to miss him and Baby Bun. She sounds interesting…"

"He used to make Mother cry about his shirts," Mattie said.

"What shirts? Whatever are you going on about, Matilda?" Aunt Tess asked, not unkindly.

"The shirts. His shirts. After Mother ironed them, he used to look them over. If they weren't ironed the way he wanted, he would go in his office and slam the door. Give her the silent treatment. He wouldn't forgive her until she said how sorry she was and started to cry."

"Doesn't surprise me," Aunt Tess said. "Augusta, our father, was a lot like that. And the apple doesn't fall far from the tree."

Make that a rotten apple, Mattie thought.

"He wouldn't even let her go to the women's Bible study class at the United Methodist Church by herself, for heaven's sake," Mattie said. "He would drive her there and wait for her in the car."

"I heard Father tell her she was going crazy," Wilson said. "He yelled, 'You're loony.' I distinctly remember that word."

"Well, Wilson, that part was true: our mother did go loony," Mattie said.

"She seemed perfectly normal to me," Wilson said. "I remember she made cupcakes for all the kids in my kindergarten class for Christmas. They had little green and red sparkles on the icing. Could a crazy person do that?"

"Enough. Clive is my brother," Aunt Tess said. "I plan to welcome him and Baby Bun—or is it Honey Bun?—to this house on Saturday. You children were too young to understand what was going on."

"But Aunt Tess, I was already eight when Father took her to Central State," Mattie said.

"Yes, and I was five. We remember a lot," Wilson said.

Aunt Tess put her fork down on her plate and looked across the table at Mattie. "There is something else, Matilda. One of my friends in the Savannah bridge club told me her sister lives in the town of Milledgeville, which is only two miles from the asylum. She said her sister's part-time cleaning lady, Bethesda—or was it Bermuda?—had also been working part time as an attendant on one of those awful women's wards. One of the really difficult ones, where they put all the worst patients. I believe my friend told me it was called Ward A." Aunt Tess shuddered. Her hand reached up to her neck and she fingered her pearls. "Anyway, that poor woman was recently stomped on the head by a bunch of colored boys from a different ward. They jumped her when she walked behind a building on her way to her evening shift. I cannot imagine in my wildest dreams why those patients would act like that."

"You said 'recently.' Do you know how long ago?" Wilson asked.

"I think it happened only last week," Aunt Tess said.

"Did the employee die?" Mattie asked.

"No, but she'll never be right in the head again. The sister of my friend in the bridge club is quite miffed because she has to look for a new cleaning lady. I don't know anything else about it. But what I do know, Matilda, is that you should be very careful. Promise me now. You don't have any idea what goes on in that place."

Chapter 3

Mattie

July 1976

Mattie shifted her weight on the uncomfortable oak bench in the empty waiting room of Central State's Human Resources office. She glanced at the room's only adornment, a lopsided poster tacked to the wall directly across from her. Two lines of bold red, white, and blue letters stretched across the top: *Celebrate 1976: The Year of the Bicentennial, the 200-Year Anniversary of the Signing of the Declaration of Independence*. Beneath the caption was a print of *Washington Crossing the Delaware*. A dozen Revolutionary War soldiers were aboard a strong cargo boat, crossing the icy Delaware River to make a surprise attack on a garrison of Hessian soldiers, who had joined forces with the British troops.

When Mattie could no longer resist the urge to straighten the poster, she walked over and faced the scruffy-looking heroes. *Hi there*, she whispered as she leveled the tipsy poster. *Thanks a bunch —great job!*

The office door opened, and a beaming, five-foot-three, somewhat-rotund female figure emerged. "Hi, I'm Annie Able Anderson, director of Human Resources." She grabbed Mattie's hand and shook it vigorously. "Please come into my office. How y'all doin' today?"

"Just fine," Mattie answered, following behind her.

"Sit right over there, honey," Annie Able said, pointing to a chair across from her desk. "I think you folks who work with the mentally ill have a special calling, don't you know? Can you believe how hot it is? But then it's July, right?"

Mattie could see beads of perspiration appearing on Annie Able's forehead, causing her vintage cat-eye glasses to slide down the bridge of her nose. Her auburn hair was cut short on the sides, long and wispy in the back. Two quarter-size spots of Love My Pink blush adorned her cheekbones.

"Now I want you to tell me all about yourself," Annie Able said, plunking herself into her desk chair and reaching for a truffle out of a red plastic bowl. Her more-than-abundant bosom skirted the desk's surface as she pushed the bowl of candy toward Mattie. "Help yourself. I made 'em. Cooking's been a hobby of mine since I was a young 'un at my momma's knee. My momma—the patients called her Miz Max—worked at this hospital for thirty-four years."

"These are delicious, Miss Anderson," Mattie said, nibbling on one of the round chocolate morsels covered with ground pecans.

"Call me Annie Able. Everyone does. Able was my momma's maiden name. I just love the way it goes together—Annie Able Anderson. I think it's called *il-lit-eration*. Something like that."

Why can't I be more like her? Mattie thought. *She's so open. Says whatever comes into her mind. No filter. I bet she doesn't walk around thinking disaster is about to strike at any moment.*

"Well, Annie Able, I grew up in Savannah," Mattie said. "I got a Bachelor of Science in Nursing from Emory University in Atlanta. My boyfriend, Allan, and I met in college and moved to his hometown, Memphis, after we graduated. I took a position in the Intensive Care Unit at Saint Joseph's Hospital. We treated patients involved in automobile accidents and industrial accidents. Also stroke patients and coronaries—stuff like that. I worked a lot of extra nursing shifts so I could pay Allan's tuition at the University of Tennessee College of Medicine."

Allan, she thought, fighting back the tears that came whenever she remembered. *How could he have packed up and left without even saying goodbye? He thought I was great as long as I was paying his tuition. Then not so great. Said I was boring. Too focused on my job. What if he was right? I haven't felt much joie de vivre for a long time. Wonder if he found himself a fun-loving blonde.*

Mattie's voice had faltered when she mentioned putting Allan through school, but Annie Able took no notice. She asked the routine question, pen poised to jot down the answer. "And y'all left there because…?"

"I left St. Joe's Intensive Care Unit because my charged defibrillator pads hit Dr. Lions in his butt."

"Tell me more," Annie Able said, her head bobbing.

"Well, I was working the p.m. shift," Mattie said. "Our only patient was an eleven-year-old boy named Bruce. He had a brain tumor, a high-grade cerebellar astrocytoma. I was working with Daleta, a wonderful patient care tech, and we were determined little Bruce was going to make it through our shift. I readjusted Bruce's IV and checked his vitals. Everything seemed okay. But a few minutes later, when I reached over to brush his hair out of his eyes, I could see he'd stopped breathing. No pulse. Daleta grabbed the defibrillator and pushed it close to Bruce's bed. I called out to Dr. Lions, our pediatric intern, who was sitting on an empty bed reading the stock market reports. At first, he ignored me. A few moments later, he got up, walked over, stood by Bruce's body, and stared down at him. I think that's when he froze.

"I pressed the on button, which charged the paddles with three hundred volts of electricity. I held them carefully out in front of me and yelled 'clear.' Dr. Lions was supposed to move sideways, out of the way. But he didn't budge; he just stood there. Then he took a step backward without looking, and my live paddles hit him in his backside."

Mattie felt Annie Able would have a better understanding of the situation if she were to demonstrate, so she stood up and pantomimed Dr. Lions backing up into the paddles.

Annie Able was right there in the moment, her mouth agape. "No! Do tell. What happened next?" she asked.

"I'm happy to report I did go on to defibrillate Bruce, and he lived another two weeks," Mattie said. "But as soon as Dr. Lions could think straight, he went right to his father, the CEO of the hospital. I got the boot."

"Well, you might be just the person our new Crisis Stabilization Unit needs," Annie Able said. "Someone with a bunch of medical expertise to interface with the staff."

"That's great, Annie Able."

"Now I'm goin' let Caroline know you're ready. She'll be your supervisor—if'n she likes you, that is."

"I'd enjoy meeting her," Mattie said.

Annie Able raised her eyebrows and gave a little chuckle before dialing Caroline's extension. "Hey, Caroline, I've done found you a perfect candidate," Annie Able said into the phone, her loud, lilting voice reverberating in the office. "Can you interview her and give her a tour of your new facility?"

She hung up, looking pleased. "Caroline wants me to take you over to the Walker building. They're making the wing facing Broad Street into the new state-of-the-art Crisis Stabilization Unit. Doin' lots of remodeling—trying to make it safe for patients having a crisis. Like they might want to hurt themselves right there on the unit. That space used to be Ward G. They kicked out the psychotic males who used to live there. Most of 'em had shock treatments and lobotomies and such. Said they were going to relocate them, probably send 'em to some of the other male wards in Walker."

Annie Able shuffled some papers and grabbed Mattie's resume. They exited the Powell building, walking past the white Greek Corinthian columns, and descended the wide concrete front steps. Annie Able said, "Some of the Milledgeville town folk refer to this here Powell building as the White House on account of it's painted all white, and it's 'bout as big as the White House in Washington, DC. But if'n you include the wings attached on both sides, it's a way lot bigger. Afore Powell got built in 1857, there was a patient's dormitory building standing right here on the exact same spot. They knocked it down to build Powell."

At the bottom of the steps, Annie Able pointed toward Broad

Street, the main road leading to Powell. "This is where they brung the first patient back in December 1842," she said. "That poor ol' gentleman was a professor. Name was Tillman Barnett. He come tied up in a horse-pulled wagon, his kinfolk aside him, all the way from Macon."

Mattie stared down the long road. She could picture Tillman bouncing along in a wagon, all strapped down, crazy as could be. *Poor Tillman. I bet he was so miserable. Someday I'll go search the woods and find his grave. Bring flowers and say a prayer.* She turned and looked at Annie Able. "This place is enormous. There seems to be so much land here."

"They started out with only forty-eight acres, but now it's a lot bigger—more than seventeen hundred and fifty acres," Annie Able replied. "Twelve thousand patients. We got everything we need to make them patients comfy right here on the grounds. We got a giant laundry building, two fire stations, a police department—that's where all them security officers are located—a power plant, a post office, and a central kitchen. Don't forget five chapels; the mental folk like to pray a lot. Visitors like a place to pray too. And there's a pretty pink-brick railroad depot near the auditorium. It's got them fancy gingerbread cutout things fixed to the edge of the roof. The steam engine train used to come out from Milledgeville twice a day and brung visitors and workers and such. Stopped running lots of years back, but we still got the depot."

"It's like a regular small town."

"You got that right, honey. A small town. And there's a big cemetery, way out over yonder in them woods. I hear told it's mostly neglected. Overgrown with tons of weeds and vines. Most poor souls who died here during the past 134 years had medical stuff like dysentery and typhoid, but the records show a lot died of 'maniacal exhaustion.' I'm not sure what that is 'xactly. Way back then, wasn't much record keeping. When a patient died, the ward supervisor told the attendants to go dig a hole and bury the body out in the woods. They etched a number into an iron marker and stuck it on top of the grave."

"You said they put a number on the markers—did they engrave the patient's name also?" Mattie asked.

"Nope, no names," Annie Able said. "Just numbers. Probably some big shot thought it was a violation of the patient's confidentiality. Like a dead person could care, don't you know."

"Is it possible to find out where a patient was buried?"

Annie Able paused for a moment and took a long look at Mattie before answering. "If'n you need to know who's buried in a particular grave and the number's still readable, there's ways of finding out the name of the deceased."

"Oh no, I was just curious."

"As for what happened to Tillman, he didn't last long once he got here," Annie Able said. "Died the next spring. He was the first patient to be buried in the cemetery in them woods."

"Poor Tillman," Mattie said. "Buried out there all alone."

"They engraved 'Number One' on his marker," Annie Able said as they made their way to Walker. "I heard tell you can still read the number, plain as day."

"What year did you say they opened Milledgeville, Annie Able?"

"It opened in 1842. I been doin' a little studying on the history of this place, but I don't like to bore people 'bout it."

"Oh, that wouldn't bore me at all," Mattie said. "If I'm going to work here, I'd love to learn more."

"Okay then. This here is what I know: When the asylum first started out, there was thirty patients all told, some of 'em was epileptics, some was schizophrenics, and some was what they referred to back then as feebleminded. The bigwigs in the Georgia Assembly bought the land. It come with an orchard and a well and a vineyard. There was two tall wooden houses on the property. They had to light the place with kerosene lamps and torches on account of there weren't electricity back then. The houses was divided up into dormitories. The men patients slept on the first two floors, and the females had to sleep on the top two. A matron, plus two slaves, cared for all them sick, disturbed folk. They made the slaves sleep in the kitchen in the basement."

"I read in one of my psychology magazines that in the 1850s people believed that all schizophrenics were possessed," Mattie said.

"Honey, you're so right on 'bout that. If someone in the town of

Milledgeville, or anywhere else in Georgia, acted funny, then their kinfolk would be 'fraid they was possessed. They would first take 'em to a doctor. The doctor would send 'em in front of three judges, who was in charge of deciding if'n they was crazy. More times than not, the judges would say that the funny-acting person done lost their mind. Then two Georgia peace officers would come and put chains on 'em and cart them off to the asylum."

"No one back then had running water or inside plumbing. They must've been miserable."

"I think they used the rainwater they collected in cisterns for drinking and bathing and the like," Annie Able said. "The big problem was that they had to feed a lot of folks—the workers and the patients—so round about 1855, the slaves and the patients joined up together and raised hundreds of chickens. Plus, they started tending a herd of milk cows and dozens of pigs."

"I had no idea. Sounds like the hospital became self-sufficient very quickly."

"It sure did," Annie Able said. "They planted tons of crops—okra, corn, and soybeans."

"That must've been one gigantic farm," Mattie said. "I wonder if the people here at the hospital interacted with the townspeople. Maybe they traded goods and stuff. The town of Milledgeville is only two miles away. I've visited the town. Such a neat place. Lots of historical charm. And I was amazed at all the beautiful antebellum houses."

"Yep, it's a mighty purty town," Annie Able said. "It was the capitol of Georgia from 1808 till 1868. Nowadays the capital is Atlanta. As I recollect, they put the Old State Capitol in Milledgeville on the Registry of Historic Places round 'bout six years ago, in 1970. But nope. Weren't no love lost between the townsfolk and the asylum. The townspeople didn't much like the asylum being so close by. They called it the 'City of Crazies.' Besides, back then, afore the automobile, you could only get to town by oxcart or carriage and when it rained there was big ol' ruts in the road."

"You know an amazing amount of Milledgeville's history, Annie Able. Both about the town and Central State."

Annie Able nodded. "Like I said, I've been studying up on it.

Lydia, the librarian, knows a bunch more. She told me she's done found out a whole cartload about the asylum, and she's fixin' to write a proper history. She's the young lady who got me interested. Y'all gotta go meet her sometime—she's a mighty fine person."

"I'd love to," Mattie said.

They passed the circular pond in front of Powell, crossed over Broad Street, and arrived at a park the size of a football field. Over fifty pecan trees dotted the area, spaced thirty to forty feet apart, affording shade to the numerous patients who wandered beneath their branches. Squirrels scampered here and there, collecting the pecans and burying them. An evergreen hedge bordered the area, which was decorated every Christmas with homemade ornaments crafted by the patients under the watchful eyes of the hospital activity workers.

Some of the patients, who had been given a pass by their doctor to go outside without an escort, wandered up and down, puffing on cigarettes. When they finished, they tossed the butts on the grass or under the pecan trees. Other patients followed the smokers, picked up the butts, and smoked what was left, up to and including the filters.

A stooped-over but agile elderly patient dressed in tatters ran up to Mattie. She stuffed part of an old dirty rag into her hand and said, "It's a million dollars. I will bring you more tomorrow." She folded Mattie's hand over the rag.

Annie Able seemed happy to get out in the fresh air, and she chatted as they walked. "Back in 1840, when they was building this place, the State of Georgia insisted on calling it the Lunatic, Idiot, and Epileptic Asylum. It's not considered nice now to call crazy people lunatics and idiots, so we just say Milledgeville, and everyone knows where you mean. When I was little and I didn't get an A on my report card, my parents would always threaten to send me to Milledgeville. And, honey, here I am." She laughed at her own joke.

Mattie's head swiveled side to side. There were patients everywhere—it looked as if school had just been let out. They came up to Annie Able asking for cigarettes and surrounded Mattie like a bunch of beggars from a Third World country.

An old man was holding up his dirty brown corduroy pants with one hand and trying to touch Mattie's hair with the other. A teenage girl wearing a long green-wool sweater over a pair of baggy Levi's sweated in the July heat. She hit out at the air, barely missing Annie Able's head, the whole time yelling at her voices. The smell was staggering, a mix of unwashed bodies and cigarette smoke.

Mattie wondered if maybe she should tell the friendly HR director to look for a different person with medical expertise to interface with the staff.

Annie Able sensed her discomfort and laughed. "Y'all get used to the population in no time. They're really very nice folk once you get to know 'em. Now, listen up," Annie Able said to the disheveled old man. "You need to stop that monkey business. Leave Mattie's hair alone. Go back to your ward and put some shoes on your feet afore you get ringworm."

To the hallucinating adolescent girl, she said, "Go tell that nurse over yonder you're in dire need of medication."

Mattie watched as the patients dispersed.

They continued their walk across the park unhindered. Blue skies, not a cloud to be seen. The heat of the day was nearly upon them, but a slight breeze made walking pleasant.

"We're 'most there," Annie Able said. She stopped, turned, and gazed at Mattie over the top of her glasses.

"Mattie, honey, you're gonna find it's a lot quieter here. Nothing hardly ever goes on around this place. I'm afraid it's gonna seem mighty uneventful to you here on account of you being used to working in a busy hospital."

That's just what I need, Mattie thought. *I need to spend time in a quiet place where nothing happens. I'd like to be able to sleep again and maybe even laugh and love again.*

"The truth is, I think I'll really enjoy working with mentally ill patients," Mattie said. "I believe it's important to develop a therapeutic alliance with them and try to help them cope with their problems."

Annie Able nodded her head, content with Mattie's response. "Know what?" she said. "If'n Caroline hires you, there's an empty apartment available right next to mine in the staff apartment complex behind Powell. And ol' Annie Able here just happens to be the apartment manager, so I could show the place to you. Pets are okay.

You've gotta pay your own utilities. Two bedrooms, and the kitchen's got a big harvest gold refrigerator and a matching stove."

"Thanks, that sounds good—it sure would be convenient to live on the grounds," Mattie said.

Annie Able pointed to a three-story-high redbrick, Gothic-style building with two tall turrets on either side of the center front section. "Looky—we're here already," she said. "That's the Walker building."

"It looks like a medieval castle," Mattie said.

They walked past a bronze plaque that stated the building had been built to serve as a male admission building and that construction had been completed in 1884. Once inside, Annie Able pointed to a cardboard sign that said "This way to the Crisis Stabilization Unit." There was a black arrow on it, pointing down a long hallway. They made their way across the well-worn linoleum floor and followed a series of arrows until they came to an oversized steel door. Over the top of the door was a metal sign with an inscription: "Crisis Stabilization Unit. Press buzzer for assistance."

As soon as Annie Able followed the instructions, an annoyed-sounding female voice responded via the intercom. "Who is it and what do you want?"

"It's me, Annie Able Anderson from HR," she said, her mouth right up to the speaker. "I have your candidate here for an interview."

The steel door swung open. Mattie's potential new boss, Caroline, stood in the doorway, hands on her hips, tapping one of her red patent-leather boots. She snatched Mattie's resume out of Annie Able's hands and dismissed her with a sweeping gesture that said "Get lost." Mattie gave a quick wave goodbye to Annie Able and trotted off after Caroline like an obedient schoolgirl.

As soon as she entered the unit, Mattie could smell the fresh paint. She glanced down the main hallway and noticed two men wearing paint-splotched overalls diligently applying a semi-gloss coat of dusty-rose paint to the bland gray walls.

Caroline walked into the first room on the right side of the hall, Mattie close on her heels. "This is the nurses' station," Caroline said. "Look through that window." She pointed to a four-by-six-foot shatterproof glass window flush with the wall. "You can see right into the seclusion room from here. My staff can spy on any patient who's locked up in there for a time-out, or any patient who's dumb enough to get themselves strapped down into full leathers."

They exited the nurses' station and headed down the main hallway at a fast clip, passing empty patients' rooms as they did so. "The patients' rooms have all been remodeled," Caroline said. "Sixteen rooms on the unit, two patients assigned to each room."

Some of the empty rooms had their doors ajar, and Mattie could see barren, sterile spaces sparsely furnished with two single beds, one desk, and two straight-backed chairs. No drapes. Shatterproof glass windows. A bathroom connected every two bedrooms. Four patients of the same sex would share each bathroom.

Caroline pointed out more details as she walked. "Every last feature of the unit has been scrutinized for any device or material that might facilitate a patient's death wish," she said. "Or homicidal wish. The windows have all been replaced at great cost to prevent a patient from breaking the glass and using the pieces to slit his or her own wrists, or to stab a fellow patient or staff member. The beds are bolted to the floor."

Their walking tour ended when they came to a sunny, seventy-foot-wide room with windows stretching across the entire south-facing wall. "This is the solarium," Caroline said, stifling a yawn. "This is where patients will congregate when not in their rooms. It also serves as a dining room. The patients will eat here morning, noon, and evening."

Caroline turned abruptly, left the solarium, and started back down the hall toward her office. Mattie followed a half step behind. She could see Caroline's hips gyrate in her tight, black-linen skirt, which constricted each of her steps. When they came close to where the two painters were finishing up their work, Caroline stopped so short she nearly pitched forward out of her boots.

"What do you think of this awful rose-color paint?" she asked, turning around to talk to Mattie, demanding an answer.

"I like it. Makes a cheerful background for the patients. Studies have shown that warm-colored paint..."

Caroline ignored her response. She walked over to the two brawny painters who were finishing up the last of the hallway and told them to change the paint color from dusty rose to pea green, the traditional color for hospital walls.

"Pee green?" one of the painters asked. "I know this is a hospital, but pee green? Pee is usually yellow."

"No, you idiot," Caroline said. "Pea green like the soup."

While this conversation was taking place, Mattie walked into one of the bathrooms. Over the sink, the potentially dangerous glass mirror had been replaced by a fake aluminum mirror, the kind used in carnivals to cause distortions in the House of Fun.

Mattie couldn't resist the urge to make a goofy face into the pretend mirror. "Mirror, mirror on the wall," she whispered, "who is the biggest halfwit of all?"

She could have sworn she heard the mirror whisper back, "Caroline."

The painters slammed the lids down on their buckets of rose-colored paint, told Caroline to find another painting company, and stormed off the unit. Caroline continued on her way, unperturbed. When she arrived at her office door, she turned to Mattie, who was still tagging along behind her, and said, "See those three offices over there in that alcove across the hall from my office? They belong to the Mental Health Management team. I can't believe Central State Hospital gave them a quarter-million bucks to start up this Crisis Stabilization Unit."

Caroline walked into her office, took a seat at her desk, and instructed Mattie to sit in the chair across from her. Caroline leaned back and peered at Mattie. "Even though my husband's a radiologist, I don't want you to think for a minute that's the reason I got this supervisor's job," she said.

I have a feeling that's the only reason you got this job, Mattie thought.

Caroline had an eleven-by-fourteen-inch photo of the doctor on her desk, and she turned his almost life-size face toward Mattie to admire. "He's a radiologist," she repeated, gloating. "Weekends off, you know."

Mattie took a brief look at his beady eyes and tight-lipped smile before trying to get Caroline back on track. "Exactly what kind of patients will the new unit accept?" she asked.

Caroline recited her canned information: "We will have thirty-two patients. All diagnoses, including major depression, schizophrenia, manic depression, borderline personality disorders, obsessive-compulsive disorders, and dementia."

"And the age groups?"

"We will accept patients twelve years old through ninety-five."

Caroline opened Mattie's resume, glanced at it, and tossed it back down on her desk. "And what exactly *is* your previous psychiatric experience?" she said, enunciating each word.

"I've been working for the past two years on an ICU in Memphis, but I have a good foundation in psychiatry because I did my undergraduate psych training at St. Louis State Asylum and I…"

While Mattie was talking, Caroline moved the radiologist's photo around on her desk, trying to find the perfect spot for it. She took out her emery board and began shaping the nail on her left ring finger.

"Well, I think you'll fit in well here," Caroline said, her tone upbeat. "I'm going to give you full-time days. Forty hours a week. You'll be scheduled to work every other weekend and every other holiday. Can you be here at eight o'clock on Monday, July 19, for a two-week orientation?"

"Definitely," Mattie said. "I'll be here. And, um, thank you."

Caroline stood up, walked around her desk, and extended her hand to Mattie. As soon as she had Mattie's hand in her grasp, she placed her left hand on top of her right, letting it linger long enough for Mattie to enjoy the sight of her solitaire marquise diamond engagement ring and matching wedding band.

Mattie walked back to the Human Resources office and knocked on Annie Able's door. "I got the job!" she said. "Caroline hired me for full-time days, starting next Monday."

"Well, that's wonderful," Annie Able said. "I was hoping you and Caroline would get along. Now I've got all kinds of employment forms for y'all to sign, and then we can walk over and take a look-see at the apartment if'n you want."

Mattie said, "Sure do."

The vacant apartment was located on the second floor of a nondescript redbrick building just south of the fire department.

Mattie took a quick look at the two bedrooms before lingering in the living room in front of the picture window. She fixed her gaze on the dense woods in the distance, stretching right across the horizon.

I'll be close to the cemetery here. I can almost see it over there, hiding behind the trees.

"This is just perfect. Since I'll be starting next Monday, do you think I could move in on Friday?"

"You betcha," Annie Able said. "Welcome, neighbor!"

Chapter 4

Mattie

July 1976

When Allan walked out of Mattie's life, she moved in with her Aunt Tess, her father's younger sister, who insisted Mattie stay with her in Savannah until she could figure out a direction.

In 1946, Aunt Tess had married Uncle Albert, a big-time stockbroker. She watched with dismay as her husband turned into a bigoted, controlling geezer, who often bragged he could skin a live rabbit in five minutes flat. He provided the money; Aunt Tess cleaned, and cooked all the meals. In time, she became a proficient chef, taking great pride in her newfound abilities.

Uncle Albert refused to allow Aunt Tess to have anything to do with her brother Clive. He was strictly off-limits to her. No visits. No phone calls. But in January 1950, a few months before Mattie was born, Aunt Tess decided she could no longer live without a visit to Clive. She was dying to meet his wife, Heather, and was willing to risk the wrath of her husband to do so. However, she knew she would be much happier if Albert were not to find out.

The day after she made the decision, she put on her shawl, long gray skirt, and walking shoes. She took her empty shopping basket and told Albert she was on her way to the market. She sent a prayer upward asking that Heather be home but figured the odds were in her favor. She suspected her brother would never allow his wife to work outside of the home.

Aunt Tess walked the four and a half blocks from her house on Washington Avenue to Heather and Clive's house at 3002 Abercorn Street in record time. She hurried up the steps and made her way across the wide porch.

Heather answered her knock. She was wearing a billowing yellow chiffon top with embroidered butterflies and a plain beige skirt. Her long, chestnut-brown hair was piled high on her head in a neat updo, and a few loose tendrils framed her face. Porcelain skin. A faint touch of blush. *She is so pretty and fresh,* Tess thought. *Even lovelier than I imagined.*

Aunt Tess said, "I'm Clive's sister. I can only stay a few minutes, but I felt like I had to meet you."

"Welcome to our home," Heather said, embracing Aunt Tess. "I've always thought of you as my sister. My missing sister. Come sit in the parlor. I'll bring tea and we can talk. I'm so happy you came to visit today."

After Heather returned with her best china cups and a steaming pot of Earl Grey, Clive joined them. Tess attempted polite conversation. "Are you working from home now, Clive? Or are you taking a day off from your place of employment?"

Clive gave Tess a brusque nod. "I do work from home now," he said. "I've started a woman's lingerie business." He took a sip of tea and wasted no time in criticizing Heather's efforts. "My dear, this tea lacks substance." Then he spoke directly to Tess as if Heather were not in the room. "Apparently, my wife cannot even boil water." He turned to Heather. "Whatever will we do with you, my dear?"

Heather's face went taut. Tears sprang to her eyes, and she hung her head. Her hand shook, and she put the delicate rosebud china teacup she was holding back in its saucer.

"I'm going to take my leave now," Clive said. "I have important business matters that need my attention."

The demeaning manner in which Clive spoke to Heather made

Aunt Tess uncomfortable. *Oh no,* she thought. *How disappointing. Clive hasn't changed a bit—he's still sarcastic and rude, just like he was when we were children.*

After Clive left the living room, Aunt Tess decided it was a good time to let Heather know her husband's true character.

"Heather, dear," she began. "When we were children, our father often called Clive names. He told him he was short and fat..." Aunt Tess floundered. She didn't want to bring up any dirty laundry; she just wanted to warn Heather about her brother. She tried again. "Clive was always self-centered and uncaring while we were growing up unless he wanted something, and then he would become charming. For instance, when I was nine, Father bought me a new Madame Alexander doll for my birthday. Clive begged to hold my doll, 'just for a minute,' he said. He bought me two Hershey candy bars and played nicely with me until I said okay. Then he took my doll into his bedroom and cut off her beautiful blonde curls."

Heather took a sip of her tea. "It's a good thing Clive isn't like that anymore. He's not short and fat now—why, he's almost five feet, nine inches tall. And he's just wonderful. He takes such good care of me, and I know he will do the same with the baby."

"A baby? Why, that's wonderful news," Aunt Tess said. "I had no idea. When are you expecting?"

"About four more months," Heather replied, smoothing her chiffon top over her abdomen. "If the baby is a girl, we'll call her Matilda—Mattie for short. Matilda McAllister. Don't you think that's a beautiful name?"

"I do indeed," Tess said. "And may I ask you to do me a favor?"

"Anything," said Heather.

"Will you tell me when the baby arrives by sending me a note? Albert never checks the mail. That's my job."

"Of course, I will, dear Tess. Of course."

"I need to get back," Aunt Tess said. "The tea was perfect just the way it was, and so are you, my dear. You are just perfect."

Clive came out of his office long enough to say goodbye.

Aunt Tess said, "Clive, promise me you'll take good care of Heather."

"I wouldn't dream of doing otherwise."

On her way home, Aunt Tess stopped at Ma's Food Pantry, a small market on the corner of Habersham and 48th Street. She purchased a pound of green beans and four Granny Smith apples, which she popped into her empty shopping basket. She made it back home before Uncle Albert could become suspicious.

Heather sent a note to Aunt Tess when the baby, Matilda, was born. Three years later, another note came announcing that Heather and Clive had just had a son, whom they named Wilson.

In 1959, a year after Clive had Heather committed, Uncle Albert began suffering from hypertension; his blood pressure frequently topped 190/96. According to Aunt Tess's understanding, salt in any form would send his blood pressure through the roof. It was forbidden under pain of death. His death.

The evening before Uncle Albert died, Aunt Tess took out her new hammered-copper cataplana pot and attempted a special recipe: *ameijoas na cataplana*, a clam, sausage, ham, and tomato dish much loved by the Portuguese. Since Uncle Albert was of Portuguese descent, Aunt Tess figured he would approve of whatever she cooked in her new pot.

She mixed strips of yellow onion, smoked sausage, ham, and tomatoes together, added the wine and clams, fastened the cataplana lid as directed, and simmered the mixture without peeking for exactly twenty minutes.

Still standing at the stove, she unfastened the cataplana before bringing it to the table, where Uncle Albert sat waiting for his dinner, holding a knife in his right fist and a fork in his left, each pointed upward.

Oh dear, thought Aunt Tess as she took a quick bite of her masterpiece. *This is so bland. Albert will not approve.* She quickly added a teaspoon of salt and closed the lid. She brought the pot to the table, opened the lid with a flourish, and ladled a generous amount of the *ameijoas* into Albert's empty bowl.

The next morning, Aunt Tess found Uncle Albert dead in his bed, and she believed, albeit mistakenly, that the teaspoon of salt had killed him. She wasted no time in hiding the half-full box of Morton Salt in the bottom of the trash. Aunt Tess realized that a coroner's inquest would be inevitable since her husband was a relatively young man of forty-two and had died at home. Two days later the coroner issued a report stating Uncle Albert had died of natural causes—no postmortem would be required. Aunt Tess breathed a sigh of relief.

She arrived at the funeral home shortly after Uncle Albert's body was delivered and asked to speak to the funeral director. "Please cremate my husband's body, and put his ashes in this container," she said, handing the director a plain black box. "I'll put it in a special spot."

Two days later, Aunt Tess retrieved Uncle Albert's ashes from the funeral home, drove straight to the Chevis Road garbage dump on the outskirts of Savannah, and gave the black box a big heave-ho right into the middle of the heap. When she got home, Aunt Tess dialed Clive and Heather's number from her wall phone in the kitchen. She wanted to tell them how much she missed being part of their gatherings, and that she wished to invite the family over for Sunday dinner. She got a recorded message in response: "This line is no longer in service." She tried to phone three more times, always getting the same message, before deciding to go to Abercorn Street and knock on their door in person.

When she arrived, she saw the house was in a state of disrepair—paint chipping off the clapboards, shutters drooping, grass a foot high. Worst of all, there was a "For Sale" sign in the front yard. She made her way to the front steps, maneuvering around the strewn trash, and knocked on the door. No answer. She walked across the porch and peeked in through the dirty glass. Nothing. She went back down the steps and stood in the front garden next to the sign.

A young woman carrying a baby emerged from the house next door. Aunt Tess waved and called out to her, "This is my brother's family's house, but I've lost contact with them. Do you have any idea where they might be?"

"Honey," the neighbor said, "they've been gone for about a year. Don't know what happened exactly. I heard Clive moved to Atlanta, and no one knows what happened to Heather and the children. Cute little kids. I watched them play in the yard."

Tess hired a private detective who discovered Clive had deposited Heather in a mental hospital and had made his children wards of the State of Georgia. According to the detective, the children had been placed together at a sharecropper's farm just south of Dexter, Georgia.

Aunt Tess wasted no time. Two days later on July 12, 1959, a Sunday afternoon, she drove to the farm where Mattie and Wilson had been staying for more than a year. Wilson was six and attending to one of his many chores: feeding the chickens. At age nine, Mattie was old enough to slop the pigs. They both looked up at the same time and saw a beautiful lady dressed in a white lace blouse with a long, purple flowery skirt. She was holding a lavender parasol to protect herself from the hot Georgia sun.

Wilson and Mattie stopped what they were doing and stared.

Aunt Tess gasped at the sight of Wilson's skinny, dirt-splattered legs, and Mattie's ragged, brown dress with pig slop all over the front of it. She held open the door of her brand-new white Cadillac.

"Jump in, children," she said. "Your lives are about to change for the better."

"I forgot one thing," Mattie said. She ran over to a far corner of the pigsty, grabbed a shovel, and dug up a small wooden box. "Our mother's locket," she said, holding up her treasure.

Aunt Tess took them home to Savannah and cleaned them up.

Mattie and Wilson found it comforting having Aunt Tess there for them, all dressed up in her finery, teaching them manners, arranging for tutors, offering them a yummy array of her homemade goodies.

Aunt Tess wanted Mattie and Wilson to have the best education she could provide. She was thrilled when Mattie earned a Bachelor of Science in Nursing degree from Emory University and equally thrilled three years later when Wilson graduated from the University of Georgia and was accepted into their prestigious College of Veterinary Medicine.

Whenever Wilson had a few days free, he would drive down to Savannah and spend time with Aunt Tess. He was there helping with some yard work when Mattie arrived back from Memphis, a totally defeated woman. He saw her get out of her beat-up, rusty old Plymouth and try to lug her sole piece of luggage into the house.

"Hey there, Sis, let me carry that," Wilson said, smiling. "You look like one of those carpetbaggers who came down from the North right after the Civil War."

Mattie burst into tears. Wilson walked over and gave her a hug. She was his big sister, the one who used to give him hugs, kiss his bruises, and make him peanut butter and jelly sandwiches for his school lunches.

Aunt Tess, Wilson, and Mattie sat for an hour in Aunt Tess's elegant living room while Mattie explained to them how her boyfriend, Allan, had used her to pay his way through medical school.

She started to cry again. Sitting with stooped shoulders and a tear-streaked face, she told them how Allan had rented a U-Haul and moved out in the middle of the night while she was still at work, taking most of her worldly possessions with him.

Chapter 5

Heather

July 21, 1976
Rivers Building, Ward A
Milledgeville Central State Hospital

Saw Dr. von Brimmer today. I combed my hair for the session. Not of my own volition. Attendant Bruno told me to. "Miss Heather, fix yo'self up. Comb yo' hair."

I like Bruno. Not because he calls me "Miss" so much, but he treats us like we've got normal-human-being sense. Some people believe being crazy means you're stupid. As if they go hand in hand. Almost everyone talks to us like we're five years old. Time for you to go to the shower room now. Time for you to go for your walk outside now.

We don't divide on racial lines here—more on crazy lines. The hierarchy goes like this: The patients labeled catatonic are on the bottom rung of the pyramid. Useless. Next are the lobotomies, also useless. Next come the shock treatment patients who are totally disorientated. Permanent brain freeze. After that are the shock treatment patients who can't remember what they ate for breakfast but can remember who won the World Series in 1960. You can carry on a conversation with them, sort of. Next step up are the depressives who could talk but don't want to bother, and on the top of the pyramid are the manic-depressives. Be wary of them because most of them are brilliant, but you never know when or where they will strike out.

Lucinda and I both fall into the depressive category. We put ourselves there. It's a good spot. If you don't want to participate in a walk, you just shuffle around, look depressed, and mumble that you can't. With ninety patients on the ward, the attendants are more than ready to take that as a no. Labels are good; they give you a sense of identity, let you know where you fit in.

The attendants are just like the rest of us—some good, some not so good. They don't want to be called "attendants" anymore. Seems like a bunch of them got together and voted. They want to be known as psychiatric technicians. Psych techs, for short. A rose by any other name, etc.

Bruno will always be a favorite of mine. He brought a hairbrush over to my cot this morning. God knows where he found it or where it's been. Doesn't matter; it should do the trick.

The best attendant of all times was Maxine. When she died in March, I cried for two days. (Depressives can get away with staying in bed that long.) We called her Miz Max. She worked here all her life. I think she saw it like a calling, like God ordained her. She could have gone to Africa, been a missionary, but she stayed right here at Milledgeville, caring for us society misfits.

Maxine was on duty the day they brought me in. Etched forever in my memory. Clive, my husband of ten years—the conniving Clive — had gallantly offered to take me for a drive in the country. He was so charming about it. I can still hear his voice. He bowed from his waist. "Would the lady of the house like to accompany her husband on a ride in the country on this beautiful spring day?" I'd just finished cutting a few gardenias to take inside. On days when one of the schizophrenic patients smears feces on the wall, I try to remember the lovely smell of those gardenias.

Conniving Clive said to me, "You look so beautiful today. That sundress suits you well."

He had been less critical lately, which pleased me to no end. And he even found a few kind words to say to the children. Looking back, I remember he had started to pick up his dirty clothes off the floor, and he even took the garbage out once or twice.

Me (all excited): "Can we take Matilda and Wilson?"

Clive: "No, this time it will be just for the two of us. Matilda is eight years old now, for heaven's sake. She's a responsible young lady. She can keep an eye out for Wilson for an hour or so, right, Matilda?"

"Yes, Daddy."

I got in the car. Clive took a blanket and wrapped it around my knees, all solicitous. Wilson said his much-loved stuffed bear wanted to go for a ride with me. He handed Brownie Bear to me through the window, and we were off.

When we left Savannah, I was all smiles. Twenty minutes later, it was obvious to me our drive was not an idle ramble in the country. We seemed to be heading in a very decisive direction—west on Route 16, to be exact. When I brought this to Clive's attention, he smiled. "Oh, my dear, I thought you would enjoy seeing the carriage house where my granddaddy kept his horse-drawn wagons he used to bring the supplies down to Savannah right after the Civil War. They're going to declare it an historical building."

"But Clive," I said, "that's in Dublin. I don't want to leave the children that long."

"You worry too much, Heather. Just relax and enjoy the drive. The kids will be fine without you there fussing."

"Clive," I said, "you just drove right through Dublin. We must have missed your granddaddy's carriage house. Maybe we should turn around."

"Now Heather, I know where I'm going. The building is a little out of town. I've been there before—can *you* say that? Can you say you've been there before?"

"No, Clive, you know I've never been there before."

"Then just trust me and let me do the drivin', ya hear?"

"Clive, we just passed a sign that said 'To Milledgeville.'"

I'd never been to the town of Milledgeville before, but I knew the Milledgeville asylum was only about two or three miles away from it. I'd heard references to the asylum all my life. Loony bin, nuthouse,

Milledgeville Asylum

snake pit. Everyone in the state of Georgia knew about the Milledgeville asylum.

Poor dumb me. I was getting uncomfortable but didn't know why. Something was amiss. I should have jumped out of the car right then, but compliant Miss Heather would never think of that. I'd think of it now. Now, I would've made a grab for the wheel, hit him over the head with my pocketbook, but I did nothing. I just froze as mile after mile slipped by.

Clive spoke for the first time in what seemed like ages. "As long as we're in the neighborhood, I figure I might as well stop and say 'Howdy' to my friend Olsen. He got a job in the maintenance department at the Milledgeville asylum and told me if we were ever up this way to look him up."

"But Clive, can't we do that another time? I want to get back home. Matilda and Wilson will be waiting."

"This won't take long," he said.

We turned off Route 441 onto Hardwick Street, then drove along Broad Street until we came to a massive white antebellum structure — the Powell building. Four white columns, each about three feet wide and three stories high, reached from the veranda to the roof with two long wings stretching out on both sides. A hammered-copper dome sat on the top of it, looking like a giant upside-down bowl.

Clive stopped the car in front of the steps, ran up to the oak double doors, and rang the bell. He had a hurried talk with one of the attendants. "They're going to go look for Olsen," he said when he came back to the car.

Within minutes, two burly attendants dressed in white tops and white scrub pants approached my side of the car. They swung my car door open. One of them reached in and grabbed my arm.

"What are y'all doing? Let me go. Stop, you're hurting my arm. This is a mistake—you can't touch me. Clive, help me! Someone help me."

One attendant—the one with the bald head—pulled me out of the car and pushed me to the ground. I landed—*thud*—hitting my head, still not understanding. Was this a robbery or something? A big mistake of some kind? Why were the men targeting me? Why not

Clive? I curled up in a ball on the ground, afraid they were going to kick me in the stomach.

When I looked up, Clive was standing three feet away, looking down at me. "Enjoy your new life," he said. He got back into the car and took off, tires screeching. I raised myself to my knees and screamed, "Noooooo! You can't do this."

The attendants pulled me up the front steps and into the gigantic front hall. Tears of frustration poured down my cheeks. "He can't do this! He must be playing a trick on me! I'm not crazy!" I screamed.

I must have looked crazy. The neat pompadour hairdo I fixed every day because Clive liked me looking like a Gibson girl had come undone. My hair was loose, twirling around my head in a cloud. Wild woman stomping her feet, pulling at her hair. Yelling, screaming, "My children—who'll take care of my children? I'm not crazy!"

I ran around inside the huge, dimly lit space, my feet pounding on the marble floor. I pulled the oil portrait of Georgia's first governor, John Adam Treutlen, off the wall and smashed it on the floor. Ran over to the long counter and began banging my head on the surface. The receptionist crouched down behind it, afraid of my wrath.

I had no idea I could ever be so angry—no rational thoughts came to my mind. I was possessed with a total blind fury. I stopped head banging and tried to calm myself.

"I'm not crazy I tell you. Whatever my husband told you isn't true. I'm just a housewife. I love my family. I'm sane. My husband did this to me. Please let me go." Sobbing, begging.

The bald-headed attendant held me up, while the other one put the white straitjacket on me. "Noooooo!" I screamed. "Don't put that thing on me!" They forced my arms into the long rough sleeves, no place for my hands to stick out. They tied it in the back, dumped me into a wheelchair, and pushed me over to the Rivers building, a big, ugly structure near the highway. Inside Rivers, the bald attendant opened the steel door to Ward A with a long metal key attached to a ring of keys. He shoved me in.

"She's all yours. This one's real crazy. Wild woman. You might need to put her into one of your cribs," he said. I heard the steel door slam shut as they left.

Two Ward A attendants half dragged, half carried me to the "Baby Room." No babies, but it was full of cribs—steel cribs with bars all around, slats close together, too close to push your head through. Only unlike regular cribs, there were also bars across the top, attached to a horizontal frame. The attendants lifted off the top and threw it—*clank*—on the floor. They dumped me into the crib and replaced the top frame, locking it in place before leaving without a word. I was, for all intents and purposes, a caged animal.

There were three other cribs in the room, but I was the only person in one. I screamed until I was hoarse, banged the cage with my fists till they hurt, then just lay there and sobbed before falling into a deep sleep. When I woke up, there was a woman sitting in a chair next to my crib. "I'm Miss Maxine," she said. "Thought you might like to have this. One of the attendants found it in the driveway in front of the Powell building." She brought Brownie Bear out from behind her back and squeezed him through the bars.

I grabbed Wilson's bear and said, "Get out. I don't want anything from you. I just want to go home."

"Have it your way," she said, "but remember, you catch more bees with honey than with vinegar." An hour later she was back, this time with food. I told her what she could do with it. This was the first time I had ever expressed displeasure by using a potty mouth. I have practiced and perfected this skill over the years.

An older man with a beard and white jacket came and stood by the crib. He told me he was a psychiatrist and wanted to examine me. I screamed at him, "Get out. Leave me alone!" I turned over, scrunched up into a fetal position, and faced the wall.

For the next week, I drank sips of water but refused to eat. When the attendants let me out to go to the bathroom twice a day, they always asked, "Are you in good enough control that we can let you go out on the ward?" My answer was to throw myself on the floor, kicking and screaming obscenities, cursing Clive and his entire family. The attendants would pick me up and put me back into my crib. "Let us know when you're ready to behave," they said as they left the room, locking the door behind them.

Eventually I became weak, refused to get up, and peed on the mattress. Miss Maxine stopped in every couple of hours; I always turned away from her, hugged my bear, and pretended to fall asleep.

At the beginning of the second week, Miss Maxine marched into the Baby Room, bringing Lucinda with her. "Look here, yous," Lucinda said. "Look at me. You done feel sorry for yo'self 'cause you can't see your young 'uns. Better you stop scratching and biting and get yo'self out of that cage and come join with the others and me. I know what it was did to you by that rotten man you married. Mine so bad I had to go stab him, so I's knows what I talk about. Now you sit up and let Miz Max help you out. No hitting, no scratching. We's all friends here. We all can help yous."

I sat up and looked at Lucinda. She stabbed her husband? She looked like someone who could help me. Maybe we could escape. I said a weak "Okay."

Between them, they unlocked the set of top bars on the crib, lifted it up, and helped me climb out. I walked between them into Ward A. I stood there, my feet dug in. Before me was a gargantuan dormitory, feces on the walls, windows boarded up. Women shuffling around wearing all their earthly clothing layered on scrawny bodies. An elderly catatonic woman standing on one leg, her back to the wall, wearing only panties and a bra, the dirty straps looking as if they adhered to her skin.

I felt woozy. I turned and looked at Miz Max. "Have I landed in hell?" I asked.

Miz Max pulled me forward; Lucinda pushed me from behind. My new life had begun.

Chapter 6

Mattie

July 1976

The solarium in the newly remodeled Crisis Stabilization Unit was abuzz; orientation for the twenty-one new hires was about to start. People were mingling, sharing credentials, munching donuts, and downing their morning coffee.

A six-foot-tall young man walked up to Mattie and held out his hand. "Hi, I'm Dave Vickers, one of the psych techs," he said in a high-pitched voice. He wore a fashionable powder-blue leisure suit, pants flared at the bottom, with a navy-blue turtleneck under his jacket. His light-brown hair was parted neatly to the side, and the wave in front looked as if it had been battened down by a hefty dose of hairspray.

He should be a model, Mattie thought. *No guy should be that good-looking. Dimple right in the middle of his chin. Baby skin, looks soft. But wait—I think he's plucked his eyebrows.*

Dave chatted for a few moments before excusing himself, intent on shaking hands with everyone in the room before the social time was over.

Mattie looked around the sea of unfamiliar faces and spied a lost-looking staff member sitting in a chair off in a corner by himself. He

.ced Mattie approaching and stood up, tucking his white polo shirt ack down into his jeans. Mattie could see he had forgotten to shave his stubble, and there was a piece of masking tape attaching the arm of his glasses to the rim. His right eye was veering off to the left; his left eye looked directly at her. *He's got a wandering eye,* Mattie thought. *Strabismus. I wonder why his parents didn't get it fixed. Some exercises should help; tighten up the muscle. Maybe I'll suggest he see a specialist when I get to know him better.*

"I'm Ben," he said, his voice hesitant. "I can't believe I got this job. I can't believe they're going let me take a lot of classes and learn a lot of new stuff. Like about all the problems people have and about all the paperwork and stuff."

"I'm Mattie, and I'll be happy to help you, Ben. It'll be easy once you get the hang of it."

"What I really need to know is, what do I say to the patients? I'm afraid I won't say the right thing—I'm afraid I'll damage them more."

"You won't damage them. Just be yourself. The patients know when someone's sincere. I have a feeling they're going to take to you right away."

Ben took a deep breath, exhaled, and sat back down.

"You'll do just fine, Ben," Mattie said, patting him on his shoulder. She excused herself and looked around. She noticed a tall, slender woman standing in the middle of the room, chatting with those around her. Her lilting laughter drew Mattie over; her name tag read *Sophia, Social Worker.*

"Hi, I'm Matilda, but I go by Mattie."

A tall, rugged-looking psych tech with brown eyes, thick eyebrows, and dark leathery skin stood next to Sophia. His golden-brown hair was collar length in back, and in the front a few locks fell over his eyes, which he pushed back into place with a quick motion of his hand. His wiry frame had not an ounce of fat on it. He wore a Hawaiian-style shirt, decorated with brightly colored palm trees and tropical waters, under a tan leisure jacket with matching bellbottoms. There was a half-smile on his face, as if he were going to break out into a big grin at any moment. "Like in 'Waltzing Matilda,' eh, mate?" he said, extending his hand. "I'm Mark," he added.

"You sound Australian. And yes, Matilda like in the song. It was my mother's favorite," Mattie said.

"Well, no, I'm not Australian, but I just spent six months there. Great country. I did some sheep shearing, and I traveled in the Outback a bit. I miss the Aussies. Maybe someday I'll go back. In the meanwhile, I'll work here until I decide on a career."

"What brought you home?" Sophia asked. "I bet you missed the pizza."

"Not exactly," Mark said. "I got a letter from my dad saying my mother has non-Hodgkin's lymphoma. I came home to help out with my eight-year-old twin brothers."

Mattie sensed Mark had said all he intended to about his mother's illness. She turned toward Sophia. "What kind of work did you do before you took this job at Milledgeville?" Mattie asked.

"I was born and raised in Milledgeville, but after I graduated from Florida State University College of Social Work, I spent four years working for the Florida Department of Corrections at the state prison in Raiford."

"It must have been a challenge working with that population," Mark said.

Sophia reached up to corral a few wisps of her light-blonde hair that had escaped from her ponytail. Her hazel eyes were accentuated by a touch of mascara. "Right. I had ten years' worth of experience during my first month. I led groups for muggers, rapists, and homicidal maniacs."

Mattie wanted to ask Sophia more about her prison experience, but she noticed Caroline stepping up to the podium.

"Welcome," Caroline said. "Each one of you should consider yourself lucky to be hired for our new state-of-the-art Crisis Stabilization Unit. Why do we need a crisis unit? The answer is simple, but in case you can't figure it out, the State of Georgia picks up the tab for the care of every crazy patient admitted to Central State. It costs them megabucks to house each patient for their entire lifetime. Our unit will accept patients who are having a crisis, and we will make them all better. So instead of a patient ending up on one of the long-term wards, the patient will have a short stay on the crisis unit. Our mandate is to save the State of Georgia a lot of money. Clear?"

No one requested a more detailed explanation, so Caroline moved on to the next item on her agenda. "A firm called Mental Health Management has been hired to facilitate our start-up. The team consists of the director, a wonderful gentleman named Bernardo Bellini; Pam Abbot, the activity director; and Dr. Guy Grant, PhD, a renowned psychologist. However—and I want to make this clear—I don't want to hear about anyone fraternizing with the Mental Health Management people, especially not with Bernardo Bellini," she said, attempting, but failing, to pronounce his name with an Italian accent. She looked around the room, her gaze settling on the attractive, newly hired social worker, Sophia. "Or you might find yourself working the night shift."

Lots of fidgeting and chair shuffling while the staff absorbed this new information.

"Any questions?" Caroline asked, glaring at her audience.

One of the new hires, Gosia, stood up and inquired in her thick German accent, "Tell me, what is proper to wear here in this place? I can wear like this?" She looked down at her plain white blouse, black cotton slacks, and sensible brown laced-up shoes.

"The rules are no sandals, no jogging pants, and no T-shirts," Caroline said. "And nothing dangling around your neck, no necklace of any kind. We don't want a patient to be able to sneak up quietly behind you and tighten your necklace around your neck so your eyes bulge and you can't breathe, now do we?" She flashed a broad smile, looking amused at the prospect.

Caroline's tone turned syrupy sweet. "It's time to introduce you to Miss Gwen from the Georgia Mental Health Institute. She'll be giving you a detailed explanation of two different methods of signing a patient into our Crisis Stabilization Unit, using either the Voluntary Admission Form or the Petition and Commitment Form."

During the first week of orientation, sessions were jam-packed with information regarding specific hospital policies pertaining to mental health, interspersed with classes on how to handle psychotic behavior. The second week moved ahead at a very fast clip. On Friday, the last day of orientation before the staff started their new jobs, Caroline scheduled a full-day workshop. "I want you people to be prepared for a day of intense instruction in the art of subduing a violent patient," Caroline said. "You will come to the workshop on time and wear comfortable, loose-fitting clothing."

At nine o'clock Friday morning, head trainer Andrew Armstrong from Physical Takedowns Inc., a business dedicated to teaching mental health workers how to subdue violent patients, stood with his arms akimbo in front of the assembled group of new employees. Mattie could see the bulge of his biceps under his long-sleeved, coal-black T-shirt, which sported a red dragon on the front. He wore a baggy pair of olive-green camouflage trousers.

"Gather round everyone," he said. "I want you to observe me when I give my demonstration on what you should do if you have the misfortune to be attacked by a violent patient. This here's my assistant, Marlene. She was a sergeant in the United States Army. She joined Physical Takedowns last year." Marlene's demeanor exuded confidence. She wore blue jeans and a long-sleeved white T-shirt, topped with a fishing vest loaded with sharpshooter medals and an array of archery patches.

"In every wolf pack there's only one alpha wolf," Andrew scowled. "Same goes with dogs. Same goes with humans. Them patients are part of the human pack. You guys are in the same pack with them patients. But when yous are with them patients, yous gotta be the alpha. Yous gotta be in charge, dominant-like. Alpha dog, alpha dog. Let me hear you say it. Say it! Louder. I am the alpha dog! Now let me hear you growl. Louder. I can't hear you!"

After a deafening roar from the class, Andrew said, "Okay, listen up. I want each of you to choose a partner; talk to 'em, get to know 'em. Me and Marlene here, we're going for coffee. Back in ten minutes."

The class scattered in different directions, seeking out coworkers to interview. Mattie spied psych tech Ben pivoting in the middle of the room, looking confused. Ben had easily met the job requirements for a psych tech position, which consisted of two things—being of the male gender and finishing four years of high school. Caroline preferred hiring male psych techs. She believed the patients would be able to relate better to males because the male techs would become like father figures on the unit.

Mattie had a hard time imagining Ben in the role of a father figure—he looked as if he could use a father himself. He was wearing the same white polo he had worn on the first day of orientation, but red stains, which Mattie guessed were from spaghetti sauce, adorned the front. His glasses were still taped at the side.

"Would you like to be partners?" Mattie asked him. "You could tell me about where you live and about your family. Then I'll tell you about myself, and we could get to know each other, which will make our instructor happy when he gets back from his break."

"Sure, okay, here goes. I live at home with my mom and dad. Dad's a mechanic at Pepe's Garage. My mom stays home and takes care of me and my brothers and sisters."

"How many brothers and sisters do you have, Ben?" Mattie asked.

Ben paused for a minute. "Um, five. Should I count myself? Then it would be six if you count me as a brother or sister. I'm the oldest. My mom and dad are very proud of me because I found a career. Oh, and my mom and dad told me to tell people they don't want me to get my eyes fixed. They told me having a wandering eye makes me special."

"That's great, Ben," Mattie said, moving her position so she would be in his left eye's field of vision. "Now, about myself: I live here on the grounds in the hospital apartments near the fire department. I have one brother; his name is Wilson."

"And are your parents proud of you that you got this job?" Ben asked.

Mattie avoided the question. "I came back to Savannah about a month ago, and I'm happy I found this job. I think I'm going to like it a lot," she said.

When Andrew and ex-army sergeant Marlene returned, they lined everyone up in two rows, each person facing their chosen partner. Mattie stood across from Ben, who was looking at her for support. She could see beads of perspiration forming over the freckles on his forehead.

Andrew's eyes narrowed as he searched each row for a volunteer.

Gosia, the German nurse, was standing at the beginning of the first line. Andrew read her name tag out loud: "Go-si-a. Come up here. Stand next to me, Gosia. I wanna demonstrate the right way to handle the situation when a patient tries to strangle you with their bare hands. First, I will show you how to get out of a choke hold; next, everyone will do a return demonstration. Now play like Gosia is the staff person, and I'll pretend to be a patient. Watch me. I'm sneaking up behind Gosia and putting my hands around her throat," Andrew told the group as he walked around and approached Gosia from behind.

"Gosia, when I start doing the choking, you put your hands up underneath mine from the inside while I squeeze on your neck. Then quick drop down to the floor. The patient who's choking you will likely be caught off guard, and they'll let go of your neck."

Gosia was not flexible enough to drop down to the floor, but she could put her hands up under Andrew's hands and dislodge them from her neck. She accomplished this with a great burst of strength, breaking out of his grasp and snapping the bone in his left index finger.

Andrew yelped, clutched his finger, and shouted at Gosia, "See, *Go-si-a*, what you did? See what you did? I think you broke it. You're not supposed to break my finger." Andrew's voice was wobbly, and he started to squeal like a baby pig.

Gosia muttered a token "Sorry," but she didn't look very sorry. She looked ready for more combat.

Everyone took a break while Andrew headed over to the Medical Acute Care department in the Jones building. Marlene prepared to conduct the rest of the workshop. She asked everyone to sit on the floor in a semicircle around her.

"I think that covers what to do if a patient is trying to choke you, but what should you do if a patient is, say, having a psychotic episode? For example, they're tearing up the ward, throwing things, threatening the staff."

Ben was sitting next to Mattie, trying to avoid the ex-sergeant's eyes.

"Tearing up the unit..." Ben said.

"Yes, Ben," Marlene said, reading his name tag. "Tearing up the unit. Throwing coffeepots, throwing food trays, overturning beds, screaming profanities, threatening staff with bodily harm."

"I can tell you how I would handle it," Mattie said, trying to take the pressure off Ben.

Marlene pointed a finger at her. "Yes, and what would *you* do?"

"Restraints," Mattie said. "I'd put the aggressive patient into full leather restraints."

"Good," Marlene said. "Very good. Does anyone know any drawbacks to using full leathers?"

"Drawback? What is this thing?" Gosia asked.

"A problem, Gosia. A drawback is a problem," Marlene said through gritted teeth.

"Yes, I know about these drawbacks," Gosia said. "Restraints make much extra work. You must give water for patient to drink every hour and take restraints off every hour so the patient, he can get up for going to bathroom. And sometimes the patient, they give you big smack across face before you try to put restraints once more on."

From the pained look on Gosia's face, Mattie guessed Gosia had gotten her fair share of smacks.

"Not exactly what I was getting at," Marlene said. "The big problem is that when a fire breaks out on your ward, the patient in restraints will burn to death unless every staff person knows where the restraint key is kept. You need to be able to release the patient in case of fire. Now, I want each of you to put your hand on your heart and repeat after me, 'I will always be aware of the exact location of the restraint key on my ward.'"

The new staff chanted the mantra not once but three times.

Class over.

Marlene packed up her gear and made a quick getaway. She was last seen jogging over toward Jones, trying to catch up with her fallen hero.

By the time the last orientation class ended late Friday afternoon, even the most dedicated had had enough. "Would you like to go to The

Brick this evening?" Sophia asked Mattie at the end of their long day. "It's right in downtown Milledgeville on Hancock Street. The natives love it. Great oven-brick pizza, and they've got a lot of different varieties of salad."

"You betcha—love to go. Count me in. But no salads for this gal—I'm going straight for the pizza," Mattie said, grinning.

Early evening, Mattie met Sophia at the front door of the restaurant under a tall vertical sign, which said The Brick in red letters. They found a booth near the back where they could relax and talk about the week's events without fear of being overheard. After putting in their order for a large pizza with pepperoni, mushrooms, red onions, black olives, and mozzarella, Mattie said, "What did you think of our orientation?"

"To tell the truth, there were so many classes my brain shut off," Sophia said. "I'm afraid the only thing I remember is we're not supposed to tape personal memos from Caroline on a wall for everyone to read."

Mattie laughed. "So true. I have to agree. It'll be a lot easier when we actually start to work on Monday," Mattie said. "But I did learn a lot from Dr. von Brimmer's lecture yesterday when he told us about what the hospital was like at the end of the Civil War."

"Can you believe there were over five thousand patients when the war ended," Sophia said. "How do you feed that many patients, not to mention the staff. Three meals a day—where'd they get all that food?"

"They had to grow it themselves. Annie Able told me around that time, hundreds, maybe even thousands, of patients were sent out to work in the fields every day. She likes to research that stuff. She said they raised sorghum, okra, corn, soybeans, and black-eyed peas. No modern farm equipment—only mules pulling cultivators. They made their own molasses out of the sorghum. And they used the corn to make grits and cornmeal pone bread."

"I'd like to do something like that someday," Sophia said. "Not on such a massive scale, of course. I've read studies that say people feel better about themselves when they're working. Gives them self-confidence. Makes them feel worthwhile. My dream is to start up a small commune where mental patients can work outdoors and grow their own vegetables. Raise livestock. Band together and build their own houses. Be self-sufficient."

"That's a great idea, Sophia. Didn't Freud say to love and to work are the cornerstones of our happiness?"

Sophia nodded. "Maybe someday... Dr. von Brimmer's one distinguished-looking dude, don't you think? Maybe it's his salt-and-pepper beard. And he's tall, like my dad."

"Yes, he's tall, for sure. I would guess him to be at least six feet. And don't forget the bow ties. Not every man can get away with wearing a bow tie, but on him it looks, well—"

"Distinguished! Did you know he was a hero in World War II in the Philippines?"

"No, really? What happened? How'd you find out?"

"Well, he had a sister who used to live in town, but now she's moved to Arizona," Sophia said. "She was my mom's neighbor. Anyway, she told my mom that Dr. von Brimmer was part of the Bataan Death March, one of the few survivors. My mom said more than five hundred American prisoners died on that march. A Japanese soldier stabbed Dr. von Brimmer in his right leg with a bayonet for trying to give some muddy water to a dying soldier. His leg got infected. That's why he walks with a limp."

"Sounds like he got a massive bone infection from the bacteria. He probably got osteomyelitis. But he only limps a little—you hardly notice it."

"Yeah, kind of like Chester on *Gunsmoke*. I loved that show. Did you ever watch it?" Sophia asked.

"I used to watch it with my mom. Black-and-white only. After she left, my brother Wilson and I weren't able to watch TV."

"Your mother left?"

"Um, yes. In fact, she was a patient at Central State Hospital for a short while. She actually died there."

Mattie glanced over at Sophia. *Wonder how she's going to take that news? Hope she doesn't think her new friend is crazy as a loon. Crazy like her mother.*

Sophia reached across the table and touched Mattie's arm. "Gosh,

Mattie, that's a tough break," she said. "Must have been a difficult childhood for you and your brother."

Mattie nodded. "Tell me more about Dr. von Brimmer," she said, eager to change the subject.

"Sure. Okay. After World War II, when he got back to this country, he received a Purple Heart and a Bronze Star for bravery. Then he went out and married the first girl he saw. She turned out to be a real piece of work. Got into a fatal car wreck the same night she ran off with his best friend. She had taken their two-year-old son with her. They both died."

"Both of them? No, that's too awful," Mattie said. *No wonder the doc seemed so perceptive during his lecture. He's been through a lot*, she thought.

The waitress returned with their wine order. Mattie took a sip. "Tastes good," she said. "I like Chianti with pizza." She paused for a minute, took another sip and said, "Milledgeville's your hometown, right, Sophia? It must have been nice growing up in a small town where you know everyone."

"It had its ups and downs…"

The waitress moved the vase with white daisies aside and placed their pizza in the center of the table. Sophia put a piece on her plate and took a sip of her wine. "This booth is where my first boyfriend, Amos, and I used to sit on Friday nights. We were both sixteen." She pointed to a small inscription in front of her, which had been crudely carved into the surface of the rough-hewn pine tabletop. "These are our initials: *A loves S*. I like to sit here. Reminds me of him."

"What happened to Amos?"

Sophia slowly traced over their initials with her index finger. "One day he just stopped showing up for classes. Then right after that his whole family packed up and left town. I drove by his house after school. On the other side of the tracks, of course. His place was deserted. Gone. All the little kids, his brothers and sisters, gone."

"I don't understand. Why would they move so suddenly?"

"I never found out why. Never heard from Amos again. Sometimes I wonder if my mom had anything to do with it. Their leaving town so abruptly, I mean."

"You think that's possible?"

"If you knew my mom, you'd know it was possible." She took a bite of pizza. "Since Amos, I've never been able to find a man who'll love me for who I am. I want to find someone who'll love the *real* me."

At least you had a mom, Mattie thought. *She probably bought you a prom dress and matching shoes and told you what color lipstick looked good on you. And your dad—I bet he was around, too, maybe telling you to do your homework and teaching you how to drive. Two parents, both cared. You have no idea how lucky you are. Try living on a dirt farm. Try having a crazy mom who left you. A dad who dumped you.*

Mattie was aware she was staring at Sophia. What if Sophia could read her thoughts? But Sophia was leaning back against the cushions on her side of the booth, looking relaxed and happy. Mattie shook her head to clear the sad memories away.

She reached for a piece of pizza and picked off two pieces of sliced black olives before taking a bite. "Love the pizza, but I should have mentioned I'm not a fan of olives before we ordered," Mattie said. "Now, what's the story on our new psych tech, Dave? You grew up in this town, and I know his family lives here."

"There's not much to tell," Sophia said. "Dave comes from one of the most prominent families in Milledgeville. They live in an antebellum mansion on Jackson Street, the one with the white pillars and the big wraparound porch. Looks like Tara from *Gone with the Wind*. His dad is an attorney, Mr. Vickers of Vickers & Beechers, and he does a lot of pro bono legal work for the hospital. His wife is the local society matron. I actually went to Milledgeville High with Dave. It was pretty well known he didn't get along with his dad."

"Why was that I wonder?"

"I think the problem stemmed from the fact that Mr. Vickers wanted a tough-guy son, wanted him to play football and all that, but Dave refused. I remember, in junior year, Dave took a class in home economics. That about did Mr. Vickers in."

"That's such a shame," Mattie said. "Dave seems like a nice person. And I've never seen a more handsome guy. He looks like he should be posing in a black-and-white photo on the cover of *Gentlemen's Quarterly*."

Sophia laughed. "His folks would love that—they're ultraconservative."

"It's fun getting to know everyone on the staff, don't you think?"

"Sure do," Sophia said. "I've finally gotten everyone's name straight. I don't know about you, but I've had enough of orientation. I'm happy we'll start working with patients on Monday."

Mattie nodded. "It should be quite an adventure."

Chapter 7

Mattie

August 1976

On Monday, August 2, Mattie jumped out of bed at 5:00 a.m., a full half hour before her alarm went off. After showering, she hurried to the kitchen and turned on her new automatic Mr. Coffee, which she had set up the night before. The coffeepot was a housewarming gift from Aunt Tess, who had declared that as a rule she didn't believe in any of the modern electronic gadgets, but she said she would make an exception for Mattie.

Mattie stood at her kitchen counter sipping her coffee and nibbling on a piece of toast she had spread with Aunt Tess's homemade strawberry jam. She reached down and patted Sooner on his head. "The Crisis Stabilization Unit opens today, Sooner," she said. "My stomach's all jittery. Let's hope everything goes smoothly."

Sooner gave her an encouraging *"woof, woof!"*

When Mattie arrived on the unit, she found Gosia, the German nurse, had arrived ahead of her and was busy at work in the nurses' station counting the narcotics. The pharmacist from Jones building stood next to her, double-checking that the count was accurate. Mattie watched them but didn't interrupt.

Pam, the activity director, was organizing the craft supplies she had purchased for the patients. Her activity room was filled with strength-building apparatus, hula hoops, potting soil, small bottles of acrylic paint, and puzzles, all of which vied for space in the tall built-in shelves. Colorful clay pots filled with lush green plants decorated the window ledges. A forty-gallon fish tank, home to four exotic angel fish, was in the far corner of the room, resting on a black wrought-iron stand with a protective net covering the tank to prevent excessive feeding by overzealous patients. Four rectangular tables were arranged in a line down the center of the room. Each table could seat six patients.

Mattie looked around for the social worker, Sophia. Since she was nowhere in sight, Mattie assumed she was in her office. She walked down the hall to check and found Sophia sitting at her desk stapling together information packets to be given to the patients' families during the admission process. Mattie didn't take time to talk. She waved to Sophia and headed back to the nurses' station.

On her way down the hall, she passed by the linen supply room. The door was open, and she could see Mark putting away the linens, which had been sent over on a big metal cart from the Central Laundry building early in the morning. His blue button-down oxford shirt was open at the collar and tucked into his khaki bell-bottom pants. He was concentrating on his task, making sure the hems all faced the same way before placing them on shelves stacked against the wall. When he caught sight of Mattie, he turned and gave her a big grin and a thumbs-up.

Dave was checking one of the empty rooms to make sure it was supplied with soap and towels. He didn't hear Mattie approach, and she watched with amusement as he fixed the toilet roll to start in the over position, not under. Then he folded the end of the paper into a triangle.

"I don't think the patients care if the toilet roll opens under or over, Dave, but I can see you have good attention to detail."

"I just want to do a good job today. I want to make sure everyone's happy."

"That just might be an impossible task, Dave."

"I can try."

"Things will work out fine," Mattie said with more assurance than she felt. While she couldn't help but admire how handsome Dave appeared in his navy suit with matching weskit and maroon tie, she knew it would be a mess by the end of the shift. "Um, Dave, I'm afraid you might get your nice suit all wrinkled today. You'll be doing a lot of patient care, like showers and stuff. Maybe something more casual tomorrow?"

Dave looked crestfallen. "I can go home and change if you want."

"I don't think that would work. We're going to get a call for our first admission at any minute, but tomorrow—something more casual, okay?"

Dave nodded and Mattie went in search of Ben, who was staring out of a window in the solarium, all scrubbed up like it was the first day of school. He had his muted plaid shirt tucked into freshly pressed navy slacks and was sporting a brand-new pair of shiny black leather shoes. He had removed the tape from his owl-like glasses and glued the arm in place.

"Hey Ben," Mattie said. "When we get the first call for an admission would you like to come with me?"

"N-n-no. I wouldn't know how."

"There's nothing to be nervous about, Ben. I'll show you and then you'll gain some confidence before you have to do an admission by yourself. And now it's time for you to go to the break room—I've got something to give you and the other techs."

When Dave, Mark, and Ben arrived in the break room, Mattie showed them a small, square, battery-operated panic button. "It's important that each of you keep one of these little devices in your pocket at all times," she said. "The nurses will be wearing them also. If a patient is out of control, press the panic button and a buzzer will go off at the nurses' station to let the staff know you're in trouble."

"Then what happens?" Ben asked.

Mattie laughed. "Well Ben, if they're in a good mood, they'll come running to help you!"

The techs left the break room and continued their assigned tasks. Mattie kept busy trying her master key on all the locked doors on the unit: the staff bathroom, the linen supply room, the activity room, the intake room, and the patients' luggage room. She arrived back at the nurses' station at the same time as Dave, Mark, and Ben. When one of the of the three desk phones rang, Mark, the closest one to the phone, answered. "Crisis Stabilization Unit, Mark speaking." After he ended the call, he turned to Mattie. "That was Caroline. She said Gladys just phoned and can't get here until next Monday. Caroline wants you to take her place."

"Wait, Mark. You're telling me that Gladys, the nurse Caroline hired to be in charge of the unit, is not going to show up till a week from today. Not till next Monday? She's already missed the entire two weeks of orientation… and why did Caroline call from her office? Why didn't she just walk over here? Her office is only thirty feet away."

"She's probably hiding," Mark said, grinning.

At 7:45 a.m., an urgent call came from the receptionist at the front desk at Powell. "Come get this patient. Her family dropped her off at the front door and took off. She says her name is Amanda H. If I had to guess, I'd say she's having a manic episode—she's started climbing the walls."

Mattie grabbed Ben and said, "This is it—our first admit."

When they arrived at Powell, the frazzled receptionist pointed to a small holding room in the rear of the first floor. "The security guys both left her. Went to take a break. She was quiet when they left, but now she's berserk."

As soon as Ben and Mattie entered the room, their eyes were drawn upward. The ten-foot-tall brick walls were lined with rugged, irregular pieces of Lannon stone set horizontally in the wall. Every foot or so, a stone jutted out from the wall. Their potential patient, Amanda, had climbed to the ceiling, pulling herself up using the protruding stones. She was standing on a flat, outcropped stone and clutching another stone directly above her head.

Ben was rooted to his spot. He stood in the middle of the room, looking up, mouth open.

"Ben, why don't you tell Amanda about the Crisis Stabilization

Unit, where we're going to take her after she climbs down?" Mattie said.

"Um, the CSU, that's what we call the Crisis Stabilization Unit, it's real nice—you get to have pancakes for breakfast."

Mattie took a step backward, looking up. "Amanda, how are you feeling? You must be tired after your climb."

"How do you think I feel, you stupid ass? How would you feel if you had a snake in your stomach?"

"Amanda, please climb down before you fall," Mattie said. "We can talk about it."

"When hell freezes over with you in it!"

"Amanda, you have exactly until I count to three to climb down from that wall, or I'll call security, and they will pull you down."

Amanda started to cry, climbed down onto a chair, and jumped to the floor.

"Let's put Amanda in a wheelchair, Ben. That way we can make sure she doesn't try to elope on our way back to the CSU."

Ben cocked his head and gave Mattie a quizzical look. "Elope—that's what you call it when two people run away to get married."

Mattie nodded. "Right, Ben, but when we deal with patients who are trying to escape, we always use the word 'elope.' I have no idea why—the patients certainly aren't running off to get married."

The receptionist located a wheelchair. Mattie and Ben fastened the safety belt around Amanda before pushing her to Walker, then down the hall to the CSU.

After Amanda was settled in her room, Ben observed Mattie complete the admitting paperwork. "Does she really think there's a snake inside her?" he asked.

"Yep, she does," Mattie said. "But I think that's her delusional way of describing the pain she's having. Dr. von Brimmer will probably order a workup on her for appendicitis."

"You mean she's really sick?"

"Right. There's something wrong with her physically, but because she's delusional, it's hard to figure out what."

The novelty of the arrival of the first patient soon wore off. By 11:00

a.m., the staff had admitted two more patients, both male, both with a diagnosis of major depression.

Since Mattie was temporarily in charge, she needed to assign times for the staff to take morning, afternoon, and lunch breaks. Her job description also included checking that the admission orders on all the new patients' charts were completed in a timely fashion.

Dr. von Brimmer requested a surgical resident from Jones come to the CSU and do a physical assessment on Amanda. Mattie stayed by Amanda's bed during the exam, holding her hand, and encouraging her to lie still. The resident found Amanda had rebound tenderness over the right upper quadrant of her abdomen. He reviewed her admission lab work and noted a significant increase in her white blood count. He recommended Amanda be scheduled for an immediate appendectomy.

Mattie gathered the staff together for a quick update. "I just found out Amanda has been diagnosed with acute appendicitis. She will be operated on as soon as they can set up the OR for her in Jones. If she does well, she'll be back in about a week."

"Will she be all better?" Ben asked.

Mattie nodded. "After surgery, when she wakes up and finds out the pain is gone, I think her delusion about the snake will disappear. And once she returns to our unit, group therapy and medication should do the trick."

On Monday, August 9, one week after the unit opened, Gladys made her first appearance. She was an hour late and missed the report from the night shift. She wore brown Birkenstock sandals (verboten), navy jogging pants (verboten), and had a tarnished, three-strand silver necklace dangling around her neck (verboten). Her greasy brown hair looked as if it could use a good wash. Mattie's eyes were drawn toward Gladys's mouth. Four of her front teeth overlapped slightly, and pieces of her last meal were caught between the small pleats. She also had a pronounced overbite. Mattie tried not to stare.

After telling Ben to get her coffee and yelling at Anita, the Mexican cleaning lady, for not working fast enough, Gladys disappeared into Caroline's office.

"How come someone like Glad-ass got the permanent charge nurse position?" Mark asked, punctuating the last syllable of her name.

"It's a mystery to me, too, Mark, but Caroline told me—and I quote, 'Gladys is my best friend in the whole world.' I guess that says it all."

Three days after the hectic opening, the cleaning lady, Anita, rushed into the nurses' station.

"You come quick, Miss Mattie. Much bloods," she said, pointing to a patient's room at the far end of the hallway.

When Mattie arrived at the room, she found sixteen-year-old Anna, who had been diagnosed with anorexia, had taken the metal clip off a ballpoint pen, which had been given to her by a visitor. She used the sharp end to make a stab wound deep into the vein of her left wrist.

Mattie grabbed a washcloth from the bathroom and put pressure on the wound. She glanced at the door and noticed the new charge nurse, Gladys, taking a leisurely stroll down the hallway, sucking on a Tootsie Roll Pop as she walked.

"Quick, Gladys," Mattie called out. "Get us a wheelchair!"

Gladys looked into the room. She glanced at the bloody washcloth and walked away.

Minutes ticked by. No wheelchair. Bleeding continued. Anna's face had taken on a grayish pallor. Her breathing was shallow, and her pulse was a rapid 116.

Mattie gave up waiting and said, "Let's go, Anna. You can lean on me." When they were almost at the nurses' station, Anna's legs began to buckle. Mattie eased her to the floor, still holding the bloody washcloth on her wrist. Gosia saw the pair stumbling down the hall, grabbed a wheelchair, and helped Mattie lift Anna into it.

"Gosia, please take Anna over to Medical Acute Care in Jones," Mattie said. "I'll send Dave over with you. You can wait with her while they stitch her up. I'll call Dr. von Brimmer and let him know there was a suicide attempt on the unit."

Mattie found Gladys standing in a corner in the break room, munching on a chocolate-covered donut and drinking coffee out of Dave's personal Mickey Mouse mug. Mattie marched over and stood in front of Gladys, hands on her hips. "Gladys, where were you? Why didn't you bring a wheelchair like I asked you? Anna almost fainted in the hall. We're supposed to be a team!"

"I was way too busy," Gladys said. She gave her head a haughty jerk to the side, left her half-eaten donut and Dave's used coffee cup on the table, and waddled out of the break room.

Mattie was on her way to give the report to the oncoming evening shift when Caroline stepped out of her office and intercepted her. "I hear *you're* the one who left the break room a mess for three days running," Caroline said.

"The break room? Three days? I always leave it neat. Who told you that?" *Oh my God,* Mattie thought. *I bet it was the slovenly, lazy, forever-late Glad-ass, who has never picked up a dirty bowl in her life. She's the one who always leaves a mess. I've seen her take a bite out of a piece of chocolate, turn it upside down, and put it back in the box so no one can see her teeth marks in it.*

"As a matter of fact, it was my best friend, Gladys, who told me," Caroline said. "She recommended I put you on the night shift until you can learn to pick up after yourself. Therefore, you will take Nancy's place on the night shift, starting Monday. Nancy can work days."

"But Caroline, you can't do that; I was hired for days—"

"I don't want to hear any more about it," Caroline said. "Go."

"But Caroline, listen. Gladys is mad because I confronted her about how she refused to get help for that poor patient Anna, who cut her wrist. She's just doing this to get back at me."

"Nonsense," Caroline said, stomping her foot. "I've known Gladys longer than you have, and I can vouch for her character. You will work the rest of this week on days, then report for night duty on Monday."

"But next Monday's September 6. It's Labor Day. I was planning to drive down to Savannah and visit with my Aunt Tess and—"

"Right. And instead you will be working nights." Mattie watched Caroline's pouty mouth constrict into a tight line. "And, missy, you will stay on nights until you get permission from me in writing to return to the day shift. Maybe that will teach you to clean up after yourself."

Wait. Did I just fall down the rabbit hole? Stumble into the Mad Hatter's tea party? I think our supervisor's crazier than the patients! She must have bats in her belfry to think I'll go to the night shift without a protest. On the other hand, why don't I tell her I love the night shift? That should take the wind out of her sails.

Mattie sidestepped her way around Caroline. "Of course, Caroline—no problem. I'd love to work nights," she said over her shoulder before continuing on her way.

CHAPTER 8

HEATHER

August 19, 1976
Rivers Building, Ward A
Milledgeville Central State Hospital

First, I want to tell you about my teeth—or should I say lack of teeth? I'm missing my two front teeth. Makes me not want to open my mouth. No big smiles from this gal. What happened to my teeth? Well, let me set the scene. It was back in November 1958. I'd been a patient on Ward A for about six months, still hoping I could convince someone, some psychiatrist, I wasn't a maniac, that I'd been committed by mistake. Made a few friends, been quiet, followed the rules. (That was when I was my other self, the good Heather.)

Most of the attendants were okay, but they hired this new guy, Stuart. Where they found him, I can't imagine. He should have been an inmate on the male ward as far as I was concerned. Crazy as a loon.

Stuart took to agitating Jennifer. She was in her early thirties. Manic-depressive. Spent her days lying on her cot, staring at the ceiling. Stuart preferred her manic; maybe he was bored, I don't know. He watched to make sure no one on the staff was looking, and then he started in on her—called her a fat bitch, told her she was crazy and would never, ever go home. He riled her up every couple of days until she flew into a manic rage. Then he called a code and put her into restraints.

Lucinda and I took Stuart aside and had a chat. He was shocked — actually, I was too. At myself, that is. I had always been so accepting of whatever happened on the ward. But not this time. Not with Jennifer.

I told the new guy he'd better lay off.

He lost it. Said no fucking patient was going to talk to him that way. He pushed me down on the floor; I landed on my back. He knelt down, put one knee on my chest, and started hitting my face. Lucinda punched his head, pulled his hair, but nothing worked. I was able to grab his bare arm and bite down hard. Broke the skin.

The other attendants pulled him off, but the higher-ups determined I was a biter. They could have just put a sign on my back, like in *David Copperfield* or something, but instead they decided to pull my front teeth. End of story.

Every day is like the day before. Get up, make up your cot, go eat some boring food in the dining area. Breakfast, lunch, dinner, bedtime —with a lot of long hours in between. Get up and do the same thing again. Weave a basket and you will feel better. Not really, but don't I wish.

Have one too many manic episodes, and next thing you know they give you a lobotomy. Life stops then. They gave one to my friend Rosemary. She was the sweetest thing, except when she got into her rages. She would kick and scream, but she was smart enough not to bite. She was a talented pianist. Played the Grieg Concerto in A minor on the old rickety piano in the dayroom like she was playing at Carnegie Hall instead of in front of bunch of subhumans.

After her treatment, Rosemary could still play like a pro, but that was the only thing she could do. She never again put a sentence together or took care of her grooming. She no longer knew the date, time, or her name. She was hollow.

Lucinda and I passed the time by placing bets on how long our catatonic patients could stand on one foot before falling. Lucinda won by betting Rita Davis could go twenty-one hours. I bet fifteen. Rita made twenty hours. Fell flat on her face. We didn't have money for our bets, so we used promissory notes. We'd always say, "After I leave this place, I owe you ten chocolate milkshakes" (or whatever culinary delight came to mind).

Lucinda was smart, around my age. She was committed to Ward A six months before me. She told me how she stabbed her husband to death with a screwdriver.

"Him was beating up on my young 'un, Lucas, real bad, so I had to kill 'm. I's waited for the whoring bastard to get to sleep, then I's killed him," she said. "If 'n I just hurt him, I'd be a dead woman."

Her lawyer told her she was going to be tried for premeditated murder, but the clerk where Lucinda's initial hearing was held gave the wrong file to the judge; she gave him the file of a same-aged psychotic female. The judge thought he was reading Lucinda's record.

When Lucinda realized what had happened, she started to babble real loud, jump around, and punch at the air.

The judge called in a psychiatrist for a court-ordered examination. His diagnosis was paranoid schizophrenia. Lucinda was "not guilty by reason of insanity," according to the judge, which meant a one-way trip to Milledgeville.

Lucinda was happy with her diagnosis. She was glad she hadn't ended up on death row, waiting for a lethal injection.

Her sister, Adelaide, drove her two kids over from Macon to visit her every Saturday.

She cried when they left.

Chapter 9

Mattie

August 1976

Mattie decided she would handle her temporary transfer to the night shift with dignity, but a little voice in her head kept repeating, *Not fair, not fair.* After her argument with Caroline she had managed to finish her shift, but she collapsed in a heap on the sofa as soon as she got home. She hoped karma would catch up to Caroline and Glad-ass. Especially to Glad-ass.

She motioned for Sooner to jump up on the sofa beside her. "I think the only thing that'll make me feel better is to make some shortbread cookies," she told him. "Aunt Tess always made me and Wilson shortbread cookies when we felt down. Unfortunately, we're out of flour. You stay here. Be a good dog. I'm going to go next door and borrow some from Annie Able."

Annie Able opened her door and observed Mattie's gloomy face. "Honey, y'all look lower than a snake's belly," she said.

Mattie held out the empty measuring cup she had brought with her. "Do you have any flour I could borrow?"

"Sure enough do, but I'm thinking what you need is a shot of the moonshine my brother Ned brung me yesterday." She reached out, took the empty cup from Mattie's hand, and led her into the living room.

Mattie looked around the room. Two sleek Danish Modern chairs with walnut arms and legs faced a matching futon sofa. The cushions on all three pieces were upholstered with textured gold-colored material. A kidney-shaped walnut coffee table separated the chairs from the futon.

"I love your new furniture, Annie Able. When did you get it?"

"It come yesterday on a big Sears truck." She walked over to the futon, pushed down a lever on the back of it, and watched it flatten out. "If'n my kinfolk come a visitin', this here can make into a bed for 'em." She pushed the lever again and watched the futon flip back into a sofa.

"That's super, Annie Able. You'll have a place for them to sleep."

Annie Able added some soda water to the moonshine and placed the glass in Mattie's hands. "Set yourself down and tell your friend just what's a-goin' on. Drink up now. It's gonna warm up your tummy and make things seem all proper again," she said, taking a seat in one of the chairs.

Mattie sat down on the futon, took a big swallow, sputtered, and coughed. "Wow, Annie Able. This is powerful stuff!" A few moments later, she felt a warm glow descend. Her shoulders relaxed, and her breathing slowed.

"Now I just have to tell you…" Mattie said. "You won't believe what happened to me today. Caroline told me I have to go work nights because Gladys lied about me. She told Caroline I was the one who left the break room in a mess. I've only got the rest of this week on days, then starting next Monday, I've got to work the 11:00 p.m. to 7:00 a.m. shift until Her Majesty decides it's time for me to return to days."

"I know all about that there Gladys," Annie Able said. "She's a real trip. When I done interviewed her for the job, she told me she just wanted to fill out her W-2 form. Said she didn't need to be interviewed on account of Caroline already give her the charge nurse job. I wanted to tell her to fix her body up a bit—get her teeth fixed. Lordy, does that girl have an overbite. That set of choppers looks like the ones belongin' to Ned's pet donkey. But I didn't say nothin'.

Could be she ain't got money to get 'em fixed. Dentists are mighty pricey."

"You're right about that, Annie Able. Very expensive." Mattie glanced at a toy bear propped up in a maple rocking chair in a far corner of the living room. "I never saw that little fellow here before. Did you just get him?"

"Nope, I used to keep him settin' on my bed, but he wanted to come out here in the living room so he could visit with folks when they dropped by," Annie Able said. "My momma give him to me right before she died. Said he was special, and she wanted me to take good care of him." She looked away, her voice cracking as she spoke. "All the patients loved my momma, even the super-crazy ones. They called her Miz Max. She done little favors for 'em, like making cookies and setting their hair. She worked on Ward A for thirty-four years. Passed away in March. She had cancer—it was all in her bones."

Mattie got up from the futon and walked over to where Annie Able was sitting. She reached down and gave her a hug. "I'm so sorry, Annie Able. I bet she was a wonderful woman, and she loved you a lot." She stopped at the rocking chair on her way back to sit down on the futon and took a closer look at the toy bear. "Funny thing is, my brother Wilson, he used to have a toy bear just like him a long time ago when we were kids. Yes, just like that. Wilson called him Brownie Bear."

Annie Able jumped up, went over to the rocking chair, swooped the little bear up in her arms, and handed him to Mattie. "Would y'all like to hold him?"

Mattie took the bear from Annie Able and held him upright. A small portion of beige fur had rubbed off his plump tummy. His arms and legs were intact, but he was missing one of his brown glass eyes. She ran her hands up and down the fur on his legs. "This *is* Brownie. This is—was—my brother's bear," she said, almost squishing the stuffing out of him. "I'm sure of it."

"Honey, don't that beat all? Y'all recognize this little fellow? But how? I betcha there's a thousand little bears just like this here one all around, all over the world."

Mattie turned Brownie upside down and held him by his feet.

An intact line of red stitching was visible running down the inside of his right leg. "The reason I know is that years ago, when Wilson was about four, Brownie Bear got a rip in his leg. Mother told Wilson not to cry—she would fix Brownie. She put a sheet on the kitchen table, and we played like it was an operating table. Mother didn't have any matching brown thread, so she used red thread instead. Look here— you can still see the stitches."

Annie Able took a close look at the bear's right leg. "Sure 'nuff. Them stiches are still there, like you said."

Mattie took a big gulp of Ned's moonshine. "There's something I want you to know, Annie Able, but it's hard to…" She wiped a tear from her eye.

Annie Able got up, walked over to the futon, and sat down next to Mattie. "Why, honey, what's a botherin' you? Whatever it is, you know you can say. We're friends. Friends can tell each other all kinds of stuff."

Mattie took another swallow of her drink, drew in a deep breath, and exhaled. "Okay. Here goes—my mother was a patient here. My father committed her when I was little."

"Your momma was a patient at Milledgeville?" Annie Able said. She reached over and patted Mattie's hand. "Oh, honey. Bless your heart. Just bless your heart. You must've been mighty sad to be livin' without your momma."

"She died here, Annie Able. Right here in Milledgeville. Father never said how she died. Maybe an accident or something."

"So your momma, she sewed up Brownie Bear afore your daddy took her away?"

"Yes. The last time I saw Brownie was the day my mother left. She was supposed to be going for a ride in the country with my father. Wilson passed Brownie through the car window to her—he wanted his little bear to keep her company on the ride. I remember Mother gave Brownie a big kiss on his nose. Wilson laughed—he thought that was so funny. Mother never came home. I never saw her or Brownie Bear again."

Annie Able shook her head. "Well, I ain't never heard the likes. You never saw her again? That there was the last time. It sounds something awful. She went for a ride and never come back."

Mattie rubbed her temple. She could feel the first tiny twitch of a headache. "Do you know how your momma got Brownie?" Mattie asked. "Was it from a patient?"

"Yep, a patient done give it to her right when she got sick, when she was having lots of pain," Annie Able said. "I never asked her what was that patient's name. I figured, like as not, she wouldn't tell me, what with confidentiality and all."

"No way that patient could've been my mother—Father told Wilson and me she died two weeks after he committed her. So, I don't guess… I don't know what to guess. Maybe someone took Brownie when she died or something."

Annie Able looked at Mattie over the top of her glasses, which had slid a short distance down her nose. "What if'n your daddy was fibbing to you and Wilson?"

"What? I don't think so—nope, couldn't be. She died here like he said." Mattie paused. "I had no reason *not* to believe him. She's dead. At least I've always thought so, but—"

"I've got an idea—why don't y'all go on over to the library in Powell and look your momma's name up in the Big Book? It'll tell you what day she died and where she's buried."

"That's a great idea, Annie Able. I never knew such a book existed. I'll go on my next day off." Mattie rested Brownie Bear on her lap for a moment and then picked him up and gave him a hug. When she put him back in her lap, Annie Able reached over and smoothed some fur over the bald spot on his tummy.

"And honey, I want y'all to keep Wilson's bear," Annie Able said. "He's rightly yours, and I know he'll be as happy as a witch in a broom factory to be back with his kinfolk again."

"Thanks, Annie Able. You're so sweet—that means a lot to me."

"Now 'bout Caroline. It ain't fair, not one bit fair, what she done to you." Annie Able said. "But there's one good thing 'bout that night shift. Y'all will get to work with William. He's the new psych tech I interviewed last week. Cute as a bug's ear. He done wrote down on his job application he's a Black Friar."

"Black? Good. The hospital should hire more minorities," Mattie said, holding out her glass for a second shot of moonshine. Annie Able sprang up and poured another drink for each of them.

"No, Mattie, a Black Friar means a Dominican priest. They wear black robes, the kind with hoods. Think 'bout Friar Tuck. Remember? Like in Robin Hood. And William told me he's taking a year off from studying—he's trying figure out if'n he belongs back with them friars or what. But that information's confidential, just between us."

Mattie sat up in bed in the middle of the night. She couldn't remember it, but judging from her sweat-soaked nightgown, she'd knew she'd had a disturbing dream.

Even though it was one o'clock in the morning, she got out of bed and washed her hands. Then she washed them four more times. By the time she finished, she realized her handwashing compulsion had returned full force.

Her first episode had started the day after Aunt Tess rescued her and Wilson from the sharecropper's farm. At first, Aunt Tess took no notice of Mattie disappearing into the bathroom nine or ten times a day. What a lovely, neat, and clean child. But then she began to fear Mattie might have a kidney infection. That farm was a filthy place. Nasty pigs snorting, chickens running around. Maybe Mattie had caught something.

When Aunt Tess brought the subject up, Mattie hid her hands behind her back before holding them out in front of her. Aunt Tess said, "Oh my!" and promptly made an appointment for her to start therapy with the best child psychologist in Savannah. With his help, Mattie sailed through adolescence without any more episodes.

Now, her compulsion was back. Her hands still didn't feel clean, so she took her nailbrush and gave them another thorough scrubbing. She held them up in front of her face, turned them over, and examined the bright red areas. She resisted the urge to start washing them again. Instead, she slathered them in Vaseline, went back to bed, and tried to get Annie Able's words out of her head. *Can it be true? Did my father lie to me? Is my mother still alive? Lying Clive. Of course, it's possible, but what father would do that?*

Mattie arrived at work the following morning groggy from lack of sleep. She looked forward to a busy day on the unit; it would keep her from dwelling on the possibility that her mother might still be alive, and what she might discover in the so-called Big Book Annie Able had told her about.

Mattie assigned Ben to sit in on Sophia's cognitive group. When the group ended, Ben accompanied Sophia to her office to process what he'd learned. He tried to make eye contact with Sophia, but his right eye was roving in another direction. Sophia concentrated on looking only into his left eye, which was focused on her.

The first thing Ben asked was, "What's the matter with our patient named Dr. Chen?"

"What do you mean, Ben?"

"He seems so smart. He's nice to all the patients, and everyone likes him. And he always wears a suit."

"I'm glad you got a chance to sit in and observe the group today, Ben," Sophia said. "Dr. Chen was admitted because he believes he has a ferret running around in his body."

"But he seems so normal. He told everyone in the group he came from Taiwan and brought his whole family, even his grandmother, with him. He's got an important scientist job at the University of Georgia. He teaches about nuclear analytical technology—I don't even know what that is."

"All that's true, Ben. However, Dr. Chen has a fixed delusion we can't dislodge; he imagines a ferret is running around inside him—all through his lungs, intestines, and stomach. We want to X-ray him to show him there is no ferret. At first, he said okay, but when it came time for the X-ray yesterday, he said no. He was polite, but he insisted he doesn't want an X-ray."

"How come?"

"A lot of the patients are afraid of machines," Sophia said. "I'm not so sure this is the case with Dr. Chen. It's possible he's afraid, or it might be something else. Dr. Vine asked me to have a chat with him to see if I can find out what's behind his refusal."

"Like what? What do you think he'll say?"

Sophia smiled at Ben, who was, as always, eager to learn. "Well, Ben, if you're not busy, why don't you come with me to the interview. We'll ask him. We'll be very direct with our Dr. Chen."

Dr. Chen stood up when Ben and Sophia knocked on his bedroom door. "You like to come in, sit down, take a seat?" Dr. Chen asked, indicating the two chairs by the window. His bed was made, shoes placed neatly under it, and stacks of research papers were organized into two piles on his desk.

Sophia said, "Thanks, Dr. Chen. Ben and I would like to sit for a minute. We want to discuss something with you—how's everything going?"

"Everything good, no problem."

"Dr. Vine wants you to have a chest X-ray, an AP and lateral, which means anterior, posterior, and lateral. She wants to get a good look at your lungs."

"Well, here one problem," Dr. Chen said. "Ferret will know you try to show him up on X-ray. Expose him to the radiation. He will become very angry. Run every which way. Ferret will go hide way back behind spleen or liver."

"That does sound problematic," Sophia said, trying to ignore the sudden mental image she had of a ferret going on a rampage throughout Dr. Chen's body.

Dr. Chen nodded politely, first at Ben, then at Sophia. "Yes, but you understand, is not worst thing."

Ben leaned forward in his chair, making sure he caught every word.

"You give me radiation, ferret maybe die, his dead body will be in me. Dead. Dead ferret in me. Forever. Dead body forever. Maybe lying on my liver. Maybe in my intestines. Rotting. Dead."

"Please try not to be upset, Dr. Chen," Sophia said. "We understand your reluctance. You think the radiation from a chest X-ray will damage, and maybe kill, the ferret. We'll tell Dr. Vine you prefer not to go for your X-ray today." She stood up and prepared to exit. Ben stood up next to her.

"Yes, you tell to doctor. I wish to be discharged. You tell her."

"Sure. Try not to worry," Sophia said. "Ben and I will explain everything you told us to Dr. Vine."

The following day, Sophia asked Dr. Vine to hold a staffing on Dr. Chen in the conference room. Mattie asked Sophia if Ben could attend the meeting since she knew it would be a good learning experience for him. Sophia readily agreed, and at one o'clock Sophia and Ben took a seat in the conference room on one side of the long walnut table. When Dr. Vine barged through the door twenty minutes late, she said, "Where's the rest of the staff? When you phoned me, you said this was to be a staffing. I would like to have your entire staff present at my staffings. Well, let's get on with this. I'm a busy woman."

She took a seat opposite Ben and Sophia, opened Dr. Chen's chart, and began to read. "I see here that he continues to refuse to get a chest X-ray, and he's been refusing his medication." She looked directly at Ben. "What are your thoughts on this subject, young man?"

"I think we should figure out a way to get him to take an X-ray," Ben said. "What if it shows a ferret? Like a baby ferret. You never know—"

"Ben, there's no way a ferret could have gotten into Dr. Chen's body. It's a delusion," Sophia said.

"Yes, a fixed delusion, Ben," Dr. Vine said. "But we can't have our learned Dr. Chen running around the university frightening his colleagues, talking about his pet ferret, now can we?" Her lips turned slightly upward into a snide smile. Her eyes remained hard, mocking.

"I don't really know anything about ferrets except sometimes they bite," Ben said.

Dr. Vine summed up. "How about this. Why don't we do what I refer to as 'encapsulating the delusion?' I will discharge Dr. Chen if he promises me he will come to my office once a week and talk to me, and *only* me, about his ferret. He must *not* discuss the ferret with anyone at work or with his family members or with his neighbors. What do you think of that for a discharge plan?"

"Encapsulate the delusion. Good idea. Don't you think that's a good discharge plan, Ben?" Sophia said.

"R-right," Ben said. "That... that sounds like a good discharge plan, I guess."

Dr. Vine grabbed Dr. Chen's chart off the table and made a beeline out of the conference room. "Next time I do a staffing, I expect the entire staff to be present," she said over her shoulder while shoving open the door.

Ben sat glued to his seat. "Is she always like that?" he asked.

Sophia chuckled. "No, sometimes she's worse. At least this time she got it right. Why don't you come with me, and we'll let Dr. Chen know he'll be discharged today? I'll explain what Dr. Vine said about him not sharing that he's got a ferret running around inside his body with anyone except his doctor."

"Sure thing," Ben said. "We can tell him the good news—he gets to keep his delusion!"

Chapter 10

Mattie

September 1976

On her next day off, Thursday, September 2, Mattie arrived at the Central State Hospital Library on the first floor of Powell when it opened at 9:00 a.m. The lone librarian was arranging a pile of periodicals on one of the long oak tables. Bold letters on her white name tag read "Lydia."

Lydia, the librarian, Mattie thought. *That goes together nicely. She doesn't look much older than me. Wonder how long she's been here.*

"I've been working here for a year now," Lydia said.

Geez, she can read my mind.

"I'm Matilda. Matilda McAllister. Everyone calls me Mattie. I work at the new Crisis Stabilization Unit. I'd like to look at some of the old records if I could."

"I'd love to help you," Lydia said. "We don't get many visitors here —mostly people looking up data in our periodicals."

"I'm trying to find some information about my mother. She was committed here, and she died here. I'd like to find out a little more about her, like what day she died."

"I'm so sorry."

"Thanks. It's okay—it was a long time ago." *But it feels like yesterday, and it makes me very anxious to talk about it.*

"I'd like to find out her diagnosis and her cause of death. Can you show me where I can find that kind of information?"

"Everything we have pertaining to the patients is in the records room over there," Lydia said. "Most people who work here at the hospital believe there's just one Big Book, but truth is we have numerous ledgers. Unfortunately, we had to discard some of the oldest ones because they were falling apart. They were from way back when we first opened, around 1842 to 1853."

Oh no, the records disintegrated! I wanted to come back another time and find out more information about poor Tillman.

"My friend Annie Able from HR told me you are working on writing a history of Central State," Mattie said.

"Yes, as a matter of fact, I am. I didn't realize anyone was aware of my work. I find it so exciting, delving into the past. Right now, I'm researching how the hospital managed during World War II."

"World War II?"

"That was a troubling time for the institution. Most people don't realize how much the war affected this place. Almost every employee left their job between the years 1941 and 1945 to fight or help in the war effort—there were about three hundred staff left to care for more than ten thousand patients."

"Geez, that sounds awful. How could they even do that?"

"Believe it or not, the patients actually ran the institution during those years," Lydia said. "Those who were better put together took over the wards. They assigned housekeeping chores to other patients, settled disputes, and organized trips into the town of Milledgeville to buy whiskey and drugs."

"You're kidding," Mattie said. "That's all true?"

"For sure—it's all documented. I found a journal from one of the few doctors who stayed on, plus I was lucky enough to come across a patient's diary from that time period. I could go on about the history of this place all day, but I'm sure you're eager to find your mother's record. Here's the key. You have to log in and log out at the desk. Take your time. You can bring the key back whenever you're done."

Mattie paused for a moment in front of the door marked Patients' Records before unlocking it and stepping inside. She glanced around the room. Bookshelves lined the interior walls, holding thick ledgers organized according to the year. A library ladder, attached to a horizontal bar above the highest shelf, rested in the far right-hand corner. A musty smell permeated everything—no windows, no fresh air. There were two volumes for each year: *Volume One* for males, *Volume Two* for females. The volume number, along with the year, was printed in capital letters on the ledger's spine. Most of them had the year and volume number clearly marked, but on a few this information was smeared, faded, or missing.

Mattie pulled out *Volume Two, 1958*, the year she knew her mother was admitted, and blew some of the dust off of the heavy ledger. She found a partially empty shelf to rest it on, opened it with care, and began turning the pages.

Each page contained a list of fifty patients' names. Mattie read the headers on top of each of the eight columns: date of admission, age, diagnosis, last known address, ward assigned, date of death, cause of death, and marker number. She could feel her pulse racing as she turned the pages. She started by looking at the month of April. There were fifteen new admissions in April 1958; Mattie pored over each of them. *Where are you, Mother? What did they do with you? I don't remember the exact date Father took you away, but I know it was spring. The flowers were blooming, and the day was warm. Just look at the list of these poor souls. This one's from Macon. She was only thirty-four years old. Cause of death: lockjaw. They must not have given the patients tetanus shots back then—what a horrible way to die.*

The month of April produced no results; no Heather Edwards McAllister, not even one admission from Savannah.

Mattie moved on to May, scrutinizing each entry. *A lot of these patients were in a bad way*, she thought. *Dead from diseases—polio, flu, lung infections. Lots of contagious stuff. Must have spread through the wards like wildfire. Young people too. Here's one aged sixteen. From Atlanta. Cause of death: measles. What a shame.*

Mom, where are you? You've got to be here.

She went line by line, her fingers leading the way. Halfway down the page she saw it: Heather Edwards McAllister.

Date of Admission: May 15, 1958
Age: 32
Diagnosis: Mania
Address: 3002 Abercorn Street, Savannah
Placement: Rivers Building. Ward A
Date of Discharge:
Date of Death:
Cause of Death:
Marker Number:

Wait. What's going on here? I know this is my mom! Right age. I think that's the right admission date, and I know that's the right address. But the date of death and cause of death aren't here. And it says she wasn't discharged. Must be an oversight. Maybe someone forgot.

Mattie closed the ledger and locked the door to the records room. She found Lydia sitting at her desk near the front of the room. "Hi Lydia, I've brought the key back."

"Did you have any luck? Did you find what you were looking for?"

"I found my mother's name," Mattie said, her voice strained. "I know it's her—the age is correct; her address is correct. Only thing is, it says she wasn't discharged, and there's no date of death."

Lydia stopped what she was doing and looked at Mattie. "Does it say what the cause of death was?"

"No."

"That's strange. If she wasn't discharged and there's no date of death and no cause of death, it would mean she's still a patient."

Mattie considered the possibility, her heart pounding. "But my father told my brother and me she died right here at the hospital."

"The old ledgers were extremely accurate. Every entry was verified."

"But who was supposed to record the discharges or the date of death and cause of death? Maybe they forgot."

"Until ten years ago, at the end of each month, each ward secretary was required to send this library a list of all the patients they had admitted, along with those who'd been discharged, and those who had died. We'd record the patient's name in the ledger and write down the pertinent information. Now we do things differently. We've decentralized. Each ward takes care of its own records."

"But couldn't there have been an oversight back then? What if the librarian forgot to make the note? Forgot to record important things?"

"I don't think so. Librarians are pretty conscientious. They take their responsibility seriously. The ledgers were like an ongoing census. Accurate records were important."

Mattie took a step backward and stared at Lydia. "Do you think, are you saying, that maybe she's still living on Ward A in Rivers?"

"There's an outside chance she's still there, but she's probably been transferred to another ward in a different building by now," Lydia said.

Mattie could feel her body trembling. *I've missed her for so long… I missed her every day of my life. I wanted to ask her how high up to shave my legs, and are you supposed to shave your kneecaps? I wanted to find out what to do about that mean girl, Babs, when she stole my gym shoes from my locker. I wanted to ask her what to say to a boy if you like him. So many things she wasn't there for, like my birthday, and Christmas. I always put a present for her under the tree, but she never came. She wasn't there; she never opened it.*

Lydia put down the periodical she was holding, stood up, and looked closely at Mattie. "Are you okay? You're shaking. Here, let me give you a hug." Mattie nodded, and Lydia wrapped her arms around her.

Mattie tried hard to calm her racing thoughts. "I think I just need to get some air. I'll be fine."

"Do you want me to call someone?"

"No. Thanks anyway. You've been great. It was just such a shock, thinking one way all my life and then finding out it isn't true. I just need to get used to the idea."

Once outside, Mattie leaned her back against the brick building. She slid to the ground, feet stretched out in front of her. Her heart was galloping; it felt like it was thumping out of her chest. Sweat rolled down her face. She held her hands out and saw they were still trembling.

Get a grip, Mattie, she told herself. *That was a shocker. Stay still. Just let everything sink in. How can this be true? My mother's been living here all along! A patient. She's a patient. I want to tell everyone. I want to yell it from the mountaintops. I can't believe it. Almost all my life, all these years, and she's been right here. That lying Clive. He knew she was alive. How could he tell such a cruel lie to his own children?*

All I've got to do is locate her. Maybe she's walking around here somewhere. What if she's one of those ladies sitting over there wearing ten layers of clothing in the hot sun? No, of course not. Slow down. Take a breath. It's been eighteen years—is her face still like peaches and cream, the way I remember? Wait till Wilson hears; he'll be flabbergasted, like me. Like I am now.

Where to start? Simple answer: I'll go to Ward A in Rivers and ask. That's where they sent her. If she's psychotic, she might still be there. But if not, and they transferred her to another ward, I should be able to check the records and find her.

As soon as Mattie finished phoning Wilson and Aunt Tess to tell them the news, she called Sophia and Annie Able. "Guess what? My mother's not dead! It's true; she's not dead. Alive. She's living right here at Central State in one of the wards, I just don't know where," she told each of them. "You've got to come right over."

Fifteen minutes later, Sophia and Annie Able knocked at Mattie's apartment door. Mattie ushered them into the living room. After they were all comfortably seated with a glass of cabernet sauvignon in hand, Mattie told them how she had met Lydia. "She showed me where they keep the patients' records. They're in ledgers in a special room, and they go way back. I found my mother's name but no date of death. Lydia confirmed it—no date of death means not dead. Can you believe it?"

Annie Able jumped up from her seat and clapped her hands together. "Oh, hot diggity!" She reached over and pulled Mattie to her feet and gave her a bear hug. "That there's the best doggone news I ever done heard. When you find your momma, you can tell her all about Brownie Bear."

Mattie grinned and did a little dance around the room. "I'll have to pull myself together by the time I go to work tomorrow," she told her friends. "Or I won't be able to concentrate. But how can I think of anything else?"

"You'll need to make a plan for a systematic search," Sophia said, "and keep notes as you go along."

"Yes, that's exactly what I'll do. A systematic search. I'll go to Rivers, Ward A, first. Lydia said there's a chance she might still be there. I'll be able to keep my mind on my work if I have a plan. I'll write down the names of all the people I talk to. And before you know it, she'll turn up. We'll hug and talk, and it'll be like she never left."

"We're so happy for y'all, Mattie," Sophia said. "And we want you to know we're willing to help any way we can."

Chapter 11

Mattie

September 1976

Mattie arrived on the unit at 11:00 p.m. on Monday, September 6, ready for the long night ahead. She wore comfortable clothes—her favorite tan crew-neck sweater with a white blouse underneath and tan bell-bottoms. Along with a snack, she'd brought a new novel, *Roots: The Saga of an American Family*, which she hoped to start on her break. The evening shift nurses, who were about to go off duty, gave her a report on the patients, discussing their behavior problems and noting any necessary tests and treatments. Mattie took extensive notes.

The night shift techs, Peter and William, were not at the report, so as soon as it ended Mattie decided she needed to have a quick meeting with them. She found Peter at the nurses' station ordering supplies. After giving Mattie a rundown on the night shift's routine, he said, "You'll find William in the shower room taking care of old Mr. Collins. Mr. Collins has dementia—he soils his bed every night, and the only way to clean him up is to shower him."

William was standing inside the spacious shower room with the shower going full blast. He was washing down the nude Mr. Collins.

"Rub-a-dub-dub, Mr. Collins," he told the elderly gentleman. "Let's get you squeaky clean so you can have a good night's sleep."

Mattie paused in the shower doorway and watched William for a few minutes. William glanced over at her and gave an enthusiastic wave. Water from the shower was dripping down the green rubber apron he was wearing and straight into his hospital-issued, oversized rubber boots, both of which were standard wear for giving a patient a shower. The steam was causing his damp hair to curl into carrot-colored ringlets that clung to his boyish face.

"Nice to meet you, William," Mattie said, raising her voice above the sound of the running water. *Very nice*, she thought, smiling to herself as she made her way back to the nurses' station.

Two weeks prior to Mattie's first night on duty, William had applied for a psych tech's position on the CSU. He had felt a large amount of trepidation at the time. His first job interview—what should he expect? When he walked into the waiting room of Annie Able's office he could feel his stomach churn, but the minute Annie Able introduced herself William relaxed. Her smile was as wide as a barn and her welcome as warm as the colorful patchwork quilt his mother had used to cover him with at night when he was a young boy.

During the interview, Annie Able laid out the basic duties of a psych tech. He would report to the charge nurse for his assignment at the beginning of each shift. He would be expected to give direct patient care, including assisting the male patients in the shower. If a patient needed to be fed, it would be the tech's responsibility to do so. The techs were also expected to make rounds every fifteen minutes and record the whereabouts of every patient on the unit.

William and Annie Able chatted comfortably. When she asked him about his previous work experience, William told her he had never had paid employment before, but he had liked assisting the elderly priests in the seminary with their activities of daily living. Annie Able explained to William that he would not need to have an additional interview with his new supervisor, Caroline, who had told Annie Able she would no longer be interviewing any prospective night shift hires because it was a "waste" of her valuable time. This proclamation left Annie Able free to hire any psych tech she thought would be a good fit for the job. She signed William on with no hesitation; she loved his positive attitude and his curly red hair.

Mattie immersed herself in the night shift's busy work. She made notations on the charts, entered lab reports, and set up the early morning medications. Peter and William took turns making rounds, recording the whereabouts of each patient on a sheet of lined paper attached to a clipboard.

At 1:30 a.m., Mattie asked William to walk over to the ER in Jones to pick up Darryl J., a thirty-four-year-old male, who had arrived at the hospital shortly before midnight. Darryl reported he had been minding his own business, peeing behind the Salvation Army Store in town, and a man came up behind him and hit him over the head for no reason. He said he was extremely depressed and begged to be admitted.

Darryl stood five foot nine and was at least forty pounds overweight. He was wearing a long-sleeved Atlanta Braves T-shirt, jeans, and an old pair of work boots. Leftover adolescent acne scars covered both of his cheeks, and his comb-over of mousy-brown hair was in total disarray. A four-inch-square bloody gauze bandage covered the wound on the back of his head.

William reported that Darryl had become hyperverbal, talking rapidly, nonstop, during their walk over from Jones. Once on the unit, Mattie asked Darryl how he was doing, and he gave a rapid-fire response. "My friends call me Daredevil Darryl. I mean, they would call me Daredevil Darryl, if I had any friends. Or they might say Dumb Darryl. Probably Dumb Darryl because I had an affair with my best friend's wife! Yeah, they'd say Dumb Darryl, for sure." Darryl signed the Voluntary Admission Form and read and signed the Rights of Recipient. He stated he had no next of kin and denied any desire to harm himself. No red flags.

After Peter completed the body search, Mattie did a physical assessment. She removed Darryl's blood-stained bandage, redressed his head wound, and recorded his blood pressure and pulse. Darryl opened the white plastic bag he had been clutching and pulled out a pair of red-plaid cotton pajamas. "I bought these in town at the Salvation Army. I'm going to wear 'em tonight. I'm tired and my head hurts. I wanna go to bed now," he said.

Peter said, "I'll show you to you room. Your roommate, Mr. Collins, is very elderly. He's sound asleep at present, plus he's almost deaf—he won't hear you come in."

"Wait. One more thing—your institution's confidential, right?" Darryl asked. "I always heard mental hospitals gotta be confidential. You won't tell anyone I'm here, right?"

"Right," William said. "It's the law—we can't acknowledge to anyone that you're a patient here."

"Yep, state mental hospitals are tighter than the Witness Protection Program," Peter added.

Prior to Darryl's admission, he had lived with his wife, Denise, and their two sons, three-year-old Greg and four-year-old Timmy, in a brick ranch house in the Atlanta suburb of Ben Hill. Darryl was thrilled when Alex, his wife, Alicia, and their four-year-old daughter, Amy, moved in next door. The two families spent every weekend together—movie night in, barbeques, and a trip to the newly opened Walt Disney World in Orlando.

Darryl was a stay-at-home dad, which was fine with his wife Denise, who loved her job at Hi-Jacks Automotive Repair Shop. When Darryl told her he wanted to organize a meeting of all the neighborhood stay-at-home moms on Tuesday afternoons at their house, she said, "Fine. Great idea; go for it." Darryl made a flyer asking the moms to bring their kids, plus two of their kids' outgrown toys—one to exchange, the other to give to charity.

One Tuesday afternoon, Alex's wife, Alicia, asked Darryl if he would like her to stay behind and help clear up. Darryl was elated.

After they put Darryl's young sons, Greg and Timmy, and Alicia's daughter, Amy, down for their afternoon naps in the upstairs bedroom, Alicia said, "I think that's the most generous thing anyone has ever done—to collect toys for charity every week like you do."

"I've been storing them in the basement—would you like to come see?"

"Sure would," Alicia said.

The affair started in the basement laundry room with a fourteen-inch-tall donation doll, Mrs. Beasley, looking on.

A week before Darryl was admitted to the Crisis Stabilization Unit, his good friend Alex had decided it was time to organize the closet in his spare bedroom. Alex was in the middle of his cleaning spree when he found a flowery card from Darryl. It was addressed to Alex's wife, Alicia. "Hey, you sexy babe! Ditch Alex and meet me tomorrow at three o'clock at the Ramada Inn, downtown Atlanta in Capitol Park. Your Daredevil Darryl."

Alex felt his heart palpitate. He was sure it missed a beat. His wife was having an affair with his best friend and neighbor! He called a meeting with Alicia, Darryl, and Darryl's wife, Denise. "What do we need to change to make our marriages work?" Alex asked them. "Let's figure this thing out; kids are involved here."

Alicia told Alex she was fed up with all his sarcasm and all his talk about Vietnam. She pointed out the war had ended in 1973, which was three years ago already. He needed to get over it. She said she liked him because he was six feet tall, and she liked tall men with tight abs. (Except for Darryl, who was short with a paunch, but she didn't mention that.) But she said she was sick of seeing him exercise three hours every day. And she wanted him to shave off his beard—it made him look too serious.

Alex stopped talking about Nam and reduced his exercise time to an hour a day. He shaved off his beard, but he was still sarcastic.

Alicia was contrite at first, cooked Alex special meals, and brought him little surprise gifts, but soon he noticed a subtle change in her behavior. She became preoccupied, said she had to visit with her girlfriend Tracy once a week in the evening, and couldn't care less about what he liked to eat. When Alicia announced she was going to

Tracy's house for the evening, Alex followed her in his car to the Ramada Inn.

The next morning, bright and early, Alex rang Darryl's doorbell. When Darryl opened the door, Alex said, "This has to stop. I want you all to pack your stuff and get out. Move—go live somewhere else."

"I like sleeping with your wife, so I'm not leaving," Daredevil Darryl said.

Alex awakened at 5:00 a.m. the following day and hid in the tall shrubs between their two houses, waiting for Darryl to appear. At exactly 6:00 a.m., Darryl opened his front door. He yawned, pulled up his T-shirt, and scratched his hairy chest before ambling down the driveway. At the end of the drive, he bent down to pick up the newspaper.

While Darryl was bending over, Alex aimed his .45 Magnum at Darryl's butt and fired once. He missed and fired again. Darryl took off running back into the house, his belly jiggling like jelly. "Quick, Denise, I gotta leave town. Alex just took two shots at me. I need money," he said, rushing around the kitchen before stopping and grabbing a hundred dollars out of the cookie jar.

"Too bad he missed," Denise said.

Darryl slipped out his back door, jumped in the car, and raced to the Greyhound bus station in Atlanta. He was momentarily confused. Where to go? Where to hide? He had an inspiration. A foolproof plan. He would buy a ticket to Macon, Georgia, and from there he would make his way to the notorious Milledgeville asylum. He would tell them he was hearing voices. That should do the trick. It was a big place. A confidential place. He'd have a place to sleep; they would feed him, all for free. He would lie low for a while, at least till Alex came to his senses. When he got out, he would find a new wife; he would be a stay-at-home dad. He would begin all over again.

Alex followed Darryl to the Greyhound bus station and watched him climb aboard a bus headed for Macon. He tailed the bus south for an hour and a half, keeping at least three cars behind. In Macon, he was surprised to see Darryl hail a taxi.

Alex was able to keep the taxi in his sight as it made its way northeast on Georgia Route 49. *What the fuck,* Alex thought. *Where is that fat-ass going? Wonder if he's heading to Milledgeville. The asylum's near there. The Milledgeville asylum. Good thinking, Darryl, but not good enough. I learned a lot of things in Nam—one of 'em was how to track down bastards. Now I'm on a mission.*

After traveling a distance of thirty-eight miles, the taxi entered the Milledgeville city limits, where Route 49 became Hancock Street. The taxi slowed down in traffic, passing the local cinema and the historical Milledgeville City Hall before pulling into the parking lot at the Budget Inn Motel. Alex stayed out of sight while Darryl paid the driver and checked in. A half hour later, Darryl exited the motel and set off walking east on Handcock.

Alex grabbed the hammer he'd had the foresight to put in the front seat of his car and followed him on foot. Two blocks later, Darryl arrived at the Salvation Army Store and disappeared inside. When he exited, he was carrying his purchase with him in a white plastic bag.

Instead of heading back to the motel, Darryl walked into the partially wooded area behind the store. He glanced around to make sure no one was looking, faced an ancient oak tree, and prepared to urinate. As soon as Darryl was occupied with his task, Alex snuck up behind him and delivered a fierce blow with the hammer to the back of his head. Darryl fell face forward, close to the tree, his wound bleeding profusely.

Okay. Mission accomplished, Alex told himself as he walked back to his car, which he'd parked near the Budget Inn. He sat in the driver's seat, smoking Camels, throwing the butts out the window, and waited —he wanted to take one more look at Darryl's body. At 11:15 p.m., he got out of the car and strolled down Hancock Street, en route back to the Salvation Army. When he was almost at the parking lot, a siren wailed and an ambulance flew by, lights flashing. He hurried to the far side of the building and peeked around the corner. Two men were loading Darryl onto a stretcher. One of them handed Darryl his white plastic bag before they put him into the back of the waiting ambulance. *What the hell? Somebody found him. He ain't dead; I can see his arms moving. I gotta fix that.*

Inside the ambulance, Darryl begged the paramedic to tell the driver to take him to Milledgeville asylum. He explained he had real bad depression. Maybe he was even suicidal.

"Don't you worry your head none," the paramedic said. "We're taking you to Central State Hospital. That's what they call the asylum these days. Everything's gonna turn out good. We'll drop you off at central admissions in the Powell building, and after they do the admission stuff, they'll take you to Jones—it's a regular hospital right on the grounds. There's an ER there with docs who can sew up your head. My sister got herself a bad case of depression, and they fixed her up good. She was at the new Crisis Unit in the Walker building. I went to visit her. Neat place."

Darryl took a deep breath and relaxed. Perfect—he'd be safe at last.

Alex ran back to his car and managed to catch up to the ambulance just as it pulled into the parking lot of the asylum. He watched the paramedic and the ambulance driver wheel Darryl's stretcher up the steep ramp to the admission department at the west end of Powell. Alex wanted to be sure he wouldn't run into Darryl, so he waited in his car for two hours before entering the building.

"Hi, I'm Alex. I'm hearing voices. I need help. I want to be admitted," he told the night nurse on duty.

"And what are your voices saying, Alex?" she asked.

"Um, what are they saying? Um, they're saying, um, why don't you go jump off a bridge? And, oh, I almost forgot, I'm an undercover CIA operative, and the Polish mafia's looking for me."

"Okay, Alex. Take a seat. Our psychiatrist will examine you. He'll probably want to admit you to CSU for a while. Would that be okay with you?"

"What's CSU? Is that where they put people who are a little bit crazy, like if they're depressed or something or, say, like maybe they got injured?"

"Yep, CSU is the Crisis Stabilization Unit. It's for people who need short-term care."

"That's just what I had in mind," Alex said. "I mean, I'm sure those professional folks can help me get rid of the voices in my head."

The central admission clerk in Powell phoned CSU and notified Mattie that a psychotic patient, Alex K., was in need of immediate hospitalization. Peter escorted Alex to the unit at 3 a.m. After Mattie finished taking his blood pressure in the exam room, he said in a loud whisper, "I got delusions. I got voices in my head. All them Polish mafia's looking for me. All of 'em. They're hunting for me. Now. Right now. Those people don't use guns. They use machetes."

"Your blood pressure's elevated, Alex," Mattie said. "It's 188/92. How about if I give you some medication? It might help you sleep."

"Okay, but I gotta read the label on the bottle."

When Peter made rounds fifteen minutes later, he marked on his rounds board that Alex was asleep. The techs continued their night-duty tasks and Mattie settled into the rhythm of the night shift, performing a myriad of tasks—checking IVs, giving gastrostomy feedings, passing out the psychotropic drugs, and writing nursing notes on each patient's chart. There was no annoying charge nurse Gladys. No Caroline. The only drawback was that the hours were at night. All night.

Peter and William continued taking turns making rounds every fifteen minutes. At 4:45 a.m., the time Peter was scheduled to account for all the patients, he stepped into Darryl's room thinking he would find him asleep.

Darryl's roommate, the elderly Mr. Collins, was snoring loudly, but Darryl was not in his bed. His bathroom door was closed. Peter figured he had woken up and gone to use the bathroom. He knocked lightly on the door and called out, "Darryl." No response. He tried again. Nothing. The third knock with no answer alarmed him.

Peter turned the doorknob and pushed the door wide open. Darryl's body was hanging by the neck, attached by bootlaces to the light fixture in the ceiling. His eyes protruded from his dusky face, and drool trickled out of his mouth. His arms drooped by his sides. The force of the door opening had made his body sway, and his legs dangled. A straight-back chair was overturned on the floor.

Peter closed the bathroom door and walked back to the nurses' station. "Darryl hanged himself," he said in a voice just above a whisper. William and Mattie looked at each other and then at Peter.

"Darryl is hanging from the ceiling light in his bathroom," Peter said.

William walked over to Peter and clapped him on the shoulder. "Not so fast, buddy. Nice try, but there's no way that could have happened—this is one of your practical jokes, right? If Darryl really hanged himself, you wouldn't be so calm about it."

Mattie caught the glazed look in Peter's eyes. "Wait," she said. "I think Peter's in shock. Com'on, William, let's go take a look. Peter, you stay here. Sit. Wait for us."

When they got to Darryl's room, William went in first. "He's not in bed; we'd better check the bathroom," William said, pushing open the door. The thrust caused Darryl's slack and lifeless body to rotate clockwise.

William took a long step backward into the bedroom, leaving the bathroom door open. Mattie stood still, looking through the door, trying to absorb the scene in front of her. The first thought that came to her was they had to cut the body down. She rushed to the nurses' station, unlocked the drawer where the sharps were kept, and grabbed the scissors. She returned to Darryl's room and handed them to William.

William took a deep breath before walking back into the bathroom and righting the chair Darryl had used to stand on. He paused for a minute before climbing up on it and cutting the bootlaces from around Darryl's neck. Darryl's body dropped to the floor with a thud. Mattie helped William pick him up and carry him over to his bed. They stretched him out on his mattress. Red blotches were forming over his acne scars, and the hair he used for his comb-over was lying limp down the side of his face. Mattie crossed his arms over his chest before rigor mortis began setting in.

William bowed his head and said, "May heaven's gates open for you; may you find peace."

I have to focus. Got to take care of the essentials. Figure out what to do next. First, tag the big toe; next, phone our CEO, Mr. Carpenter. Document the occurrence for the uncaring Caroline. Check and see how Peter's doing.

"There's nothing we can do for him anymore, William," Mattie said. "Why don't you finish Peter's rounds, and I'll phone Mr. Carpenter and tell him there was a death on the unit."

Peter was staring at a blank wall at the nurses' station. Mattie handed him a glass of water and sat down beside him. She put her hand on his arm. "Darryl's at rest now. William said a prayer for him. I'm sorry you had to be the one to find him. Do you need anything?"

Peter shook his head.

William walked back to the station, put the rounds board on the desk, and sat down on the other side of Peter. "I finished your rounds," he said. "All the patients are asleep. Everyone's okay. How're you feeling, buddy?"

"I don't get it," Peter said, looking from Mattie to William. "If Darryl would've told me he was going to kill himself, I could have asked him to donate one of his kidneys to my cousin. She's dying, but she wants to live. And there's plenty of people who could have used his other body parts. Suicidal people only think of themselves. They never sign the back of their driver's license to give permission to have their organs harvested. I could have explained to Darryl how that works if he'd just told me his plan."

"But Peter, if you know someone's contemplating suicide, don't you think you need to talk them out of it, not talk them *into* donating their body parts?" Mattie asked.

"No, I believe it's their right to take their own life. I just wish they'd sign the back of their license first," Peter repeated.

"You sound angry, Peter," Mattie said. "That's completely normal. Those left behind often respond that way. I myself feel a deep sense of guilt. I keep going over the whole thing in my head," Mattie said. Tears stung her eyes. "I keep wondering if there was something we could've done differently. He didn't seem suicidal when we admitted him. He gave no hints at all that I remember."

William took a sip of the cold coffee he'd left on the desk an hour ago. "I was taught in the seminary suicide is a sin, but now I think it's more like the result of severe depression."

"Right," Mattie said. "And a lot of times the depression will lift with the right meds and therapy."

They sat in silence for a few minutes before Mattie got up to go to the bathroom. She quickly returned to the nurses' station. "I can't open the bathroom door," she said.

"Why, is it stuck?" Peter asked.

Mattie grimaced and sat back down at the desk. "No, but when I tried to reach out to open it, I was afraid I'd see Darryl's legs hanging down in front of me, swinging back and forth. It was awful. I just couldn't open the door. I don't think I'll ever be able to go to the bathroom again."

"Of course, you will," William said. "You'll be fine when you get home—it was a terrible night."

The hospital lawyer, Mr. Vickers, used his master key and stormed onto the unit. Mattie turned to William and Peter, who were still sitting at the desk. "I only phoned Mr. Carpenter ten minutes ago," she said. "How'd Mr. Vickers get here so fast?"

"Mr. Carpenter must have called him," William said. "It's 6:30. He's probably an early riser. I bet he was in his office over at Powell."

"Did you notify the dead man's next of kin?" Mr. Vickers demanded, the minute he got to the nurses' station.

Mattie remained seated. "He said he had no next of kin."

"Great," Mr. Vickers said. "No lawsuit."

Mattie jumped up from her chair, put her hands on her hips, and looked Mr. Vickers in the eye. "Yeah, great," she replied, her voice raised. "Great, unless you're the poor guy who's so despondent you put a noose around your neck and hang yourself. Then it's not so great."

"You do realize that the patient should never have had laces, right?" Mr. Vickers said.

"We always remove contraband from a patient," Mattie said. "It just so happens that laces are not contraband. You should know—you helped make up the contraband list, and Mr. Carpenter approved it."

Mr. Vickers spluttered. "Well, I never thought laces would be strong enough to hang someone."

Peter and William rose from their seats and stood next to Mattie. "Well, now you know," Peter said.

William put his arm around Mattie's shoulder. "Everything's going to be okay," he said. "The day shift is here. Peter and I will wait for you while you go give a quick report. Then let's get out of here— we've all had enough for one night."

When Mattie got home, she walked Sooner before lying down and trying to sleep. *Thank goodness William was right—I'm able to use the bathroom in my own apartment. But I'll never be able to forget finding Darryl's body swinging like that. Poor Darryl. He had such a shocked look in his eyes.*

The next night it was business as usual, as if nothing out of the ordinary had happened. Although none of the patients knew Darryl, the suicide was a trigger for them. Some had had a parent commit suicide, or their best friend committed suicide, or they felt suicidal themselves. Patients who reacted in any way to Darryl's death were medicated and referred to Sophia for grief counseling.

In order to avoid a coroner's inquest and possible subsequent lawsuit, Mr. Vickers advised Mr. Carpenter to treat Darryl's death as occurring from natural causes. No autopsy was performed. Darryl's suicide was swept under the rug, and the patients' schedule was maintained.

As soon as Mattie got off work each morning, she returned to her apartment totally exhausted. She often felt nauseated from being up all night. *I'd give anything for a good night's sleep. At night. Not during the day. The same hours as the rest of the working world*, she thought before falling into a coma-like sleep, too tired to even dream.

After working three long weeks of nights, she received an official memo from Caroline. "Starting next Monday, September 27, you will be reinstated to your previous psychiatric nurse staff position on the day shift."

"I had no idea that leaving nights, the dreaded night shift, would be so difficult," Mattie told Sooner that evening. "I've really enjoyed working with William and Peter. But maybe we'll be able stay in touch."

Sooner's ears perked up. He stopped chewing on his new rubber Minnie Mouse dog toy and gave a loud *"woof!"* Mattie laughed. "So, you think that's a good idea too, right, boy?" she said, scratching him behind his ears. "You're one very smart dog."

Chapter 12

Mattie

October 1976

A week after Mattie's return to the day shift, Dave was waiting for her inside the entrance to the CSU. His usually handsome baby-face skin was marred by a long, deep wrinkle across his brow.

"Dave, you mustn't frown like that—you'll get a permanent wrinkle," Mattie said.

Dave was taken aback. He pulled a small mirror out of his pocket and rubbed his hand across his forehead, smoothing out the furrow. "Okay, wrinkle's gone, but I've got to tell you something," he said. He cupped his hands around his mouth and said in a stage whisper, "Gladys has been admitted!"

"What, Dave? Are you serious? Our charge nurse Gladys?"

"Yes, Gladys. Glad-ass. She's an inpatient now. I came in early today, and the night shift told me. She was having a crazy manic episode at her house, so Dr. Vine admitted her."

"Wow. She's been admitted here, where she works? That doesn't seem appropriate," Mattie said.

The night shift reported that Gladys had spent most of the night running up and down the halls. Slept only for one hour. Refused medication. She peed on the new carpet in the far corner of the dayroom and woke up other patients by turning on the lights in their rooms.

After report, Mattie requested an appointment to see Caroline. When she arrived at her office, the door was closed. Mattie knocked; no answer. She waited a few minutes and tried again. A muted voice muttered, "Okay, okay. Come in."

Caroline was sitting behind her desk. She had bitten her fingernails down to the quick, and her wedding band and solitaire engagement ring no longer adorned her left hand. Her desk was piled high with confidential employee files, the contents spilling out and onto the floor. Used Kleenex were strewn about on top of the files. A corner of the radiologist's photo was sticking out from under the rubble.

"Sit down," Caroline said, pointing to a chair directly across from her desk. "You wanted to see me?"

Mattie picked up a bunch of papers lying haphazardly on the indicated chair, tucked them into an empty space on the nearby bookshelf, and took the seat opposite Caroline. "Gladys has been admitted, and it sounds like she gave the staff a rough time last night," Mattie said.

"Gladys?" Caroline leaned back in her chair and spoke in a monotone. "You mean the nurse, my friend Gladys? Gladys is a patient here"?

"Yes, your best friend, the charge nurse on the day shift," Mattie said.

Caroline straightened up in her chair. "Exactly when was she admitted? What's her diagnosis?" she asked in a cutting voice.

"Her diagnosis is manic-depressive, acute episode," Mattie said. "She was admitted around nine o'clock last night. I just thought you should know."

Caroline rubbed the spot where her ring used to rest. "Don't expect me to deal with that now. Can't you see I've got a lot going on?" Tears in her eyes. She swiveled her desk chair halfway around and gazed out of the window. Just as Mattie stood up to tiptoe out of the office, Caroline pivoted her chair back around and faced her. "I want you to be the charge nurse until Gladys comes back to work."

Mattie gave a big sigh of relief. *Thank goodness. I was afraid she was going to produce another one of her friends for the position.* "You're saying you want me to take Gladys's place—you want me to be in charge of the unit?"

"Yes, you. You're the one with the fancy degree, aren't you? Now leave. I need to get back to work," Caroline said, turning her chair back toward the window.

The following morning, Mattie began her new role as temporary charge nurse. Due to the established routine of the patients' day, the unit ran like a well-oiled machine. As soon as breakfast finished, the staff divided the patients into two groups: a cognitive therapy group to work on their issues or a focus group to orientate them to date, time, and person. Lunch was at noon. Following lunch, an hour was set aside for patients to go to their rooms and rest, after which there was either an activity group, or an exercise group, or a walk outside. Dinner was scheduled every day at 6:00 p.m. Visiting hours were between 7:00 p.m. and 9:00 p.m. (Patients who were not on special precautions, such as 1:1 observation for suicidal thoughts, were allowed to have visitors in their rooms.) Following visiting hours, there was a wrap-up group to process the day's events. Bedtime was 10:00 p.m.

That afternoon, Ben showed Mattie a homemade card. "Look. Gladys made this just for me," he said.

"Okay, Ben," Mattie said. "Gladys is getting more manipulative. She's only been here for a day, and she's caused nothing but havoc. This morning she called the kitchen, pretended to be staff, and told them to send her double food portions at each meal. You need to tell her it's not appropriate for her to give you a card with 'I love you' on it."

Ten minutes later, Ben scurried out of Gladys's room, holding his hands up around his head, protecting it from Gladys, who was blasting him with her pillow.

Dave and Mark walked Gladys to the seclusion room for a short time-out. No restraints—she would be free to move around the room. Mattie explained the criteria for her to rejoin the other patients on the unit: first, she must take a dose of Librium; second, she must apologize to Ben.

Mattie closed and locked the seclusion room door and returned to the nurses' station. She was able to observe Gladys's movements by glancing through the wide shatterproof window built into the wall between the nurses' station and the seclusion room. She could see Gladys sitting on the edge of the bed, staring into space. No pacing, no head banging, no peeing on the floor. A few minutes later Mattie took another look, but there was no sign of Gladys. She pressed her face right up to the window and peered through. No Gladys! *Oh my God, where'd she go?*

Mattie ran out of the nurses' station and yelled to Dave, who was standing nearby. "I can't see Gladys! I think she's done something to herself. Hurry."

Mattie unlocked the seclusion room door and raced into the room. Gladys's body was lying face up on the floor on the far side of the bed, hidden from view. A white tube sock was twisted around her neck.

I don't believe this! She's tried to choke herself to death.

Gladys's face was turning dusky; she wasn't breathing. Mattie knelt beside her and untied the sock. "Dave, go quick and call a code blue."

No pulse. Start CPR. Oh my God, I have to breathe into this woman's dirty mouth. One breath, two breaths. Start chest compressions.

The Code Blue team arrived in a matter of minutes. Mattie continued doing CPR while they set up the defibrillator. One shock later, Gladys's heart started pumping again. She began breathing on her own.

"Normal sinus rhythm," the team leader announced.

Gladys spent the remainder of the day in a bed on the medical ward in Jones, where she managed to cajole the attendants into getting her chocolate ice cream to "soothe her throat."

Later that afternoon, Dr. Vine strode into the nurses' station, picked up Gladys's chart, and banged it down on the desk. "I'm sick of that woman's shenanigans. She's constantly changing her symptoms. How can I discharge her if I can't get a definitive diagnosis? Last week she told me she was pulling out her hair, so I diagnosed her with trichotillomania. Then I find out she stole scissors from a visitor and wasn't pulling her hair out—she was cutting it out!"

Mark looked up from where he was recording the patient's vital signs in their charts. "Trichotillomania. That's considered a compulsion, right?"

Dr. Vine scowled and raised her voice. "Yes, you're right, young man. Pulling your hair out by the roots is a compulsion. Cutting your hair out is not. How does that make me look? Wrong diagnosis. I checked on her in Medical Acute Care a half hour ago, and she told me the devil made her tie the sock around her neck."

"Sounds very frustrating," Mattie said.

"Well, I know what will fix her wagon. If she wants to play that game, I'm going to send her where she'll be with bona fide psychotics."

Mattie had an inkling of what was coming. "Oh, I think she'll be okay if she stays here a while longer. Maybe some different meds?"

"No. I want her transferred to Ward A in the Rivers building. Today. Now. The minute she gets back from Medical Acute Care. I'll let the staff know she's coming."

As soon as Dr. Vine left the unit, Mattie headed to Sophia's office, a comfortable space filled with psychology books, plants, and photos of previous boyfriends. She took a seat on the sofa, waiting for Sophia to finish her social worker assessment on a new patient's chart.

"There—all done," Sophia said. "All caught up." She turned to Mattie. "You look stressed. Did something happen?"

"Well, you know Gladys tried to harm herself in the seclusion room this morning," Mattie said. "So now Dr. Vine's going to transfer her. I think Gladys's behavior was attention seeking. She didn't realize the knot would get as tight as a vise. She had both hands up by her neck when I found her, and it looked like she was trying to pull the sock off. Dr. Vine is being very harsh."

"Where's she going? What ward?"

"Ward A in Rivers."

"That'll be the end of the road for Gladys," Sophia said. "That's one of the worst regressed women's wards in the hospital. Seems punitive to me. On the other hand, a reality check might do her some good, like when you show kids the inside of a jail to deter them from committing a crime."

"I'm heading over to Rivers in the morning. I want to follow up on what I saw in the ledger—that my mother was admitted to Ward A in May 1958. Lydia, the librarian, thinks there's only a small chance that she's still there, but I want to go anyway. See what it's like. And I'll be able to check on Gladys. I wonder if Dr. Vine's version of tough love is working," Mattie said.

"You're going tomorrow? Do you want me to go with you?"

"Nope, but thanks for the offer. It's something I've got to face on my own. I don't know what I dread most—that I'll find my mom alive and psychotic, or I'll find out she really did die, and they buried her in that spooky graveyard in the woods but forgot to record it in the ledger."

Sophia gave her friend a warm hug. "Whatever happens, I'll be here for you," she said.

At 6:15 the following morning, Mattie pinned her name badge to the pocket of her blouse and clipped her master key securely onto the belt of her skirt. After leaving her apartment, she turned left past the Central Kitchen, where trucks were already unloading food and supplies at the dock. She turned right at the Post Office, a picturesque white brick building with a royal blue front door and matching blue trim around the windows. When she reached the Central State Hospital Laundry building, which stretched out over a city block, she quickened her pace, intent on getting to Ward A while the dormitory was still relatively calm and before the activities of daily living began.

As Mattie made her way along Shop Road, she could see two brick five-hundred-foot-tall smokestacks in the distance standing alongside the coal-fired power plant, which converted coal into enough electricity for the entire hospital. She turned left onto Laboratory, a partially paved, two-way country road. Sand and gravel kicked up into her shoes. Even though it was still early morning, she was hot and thirsty. After walking almost a mile, she saw the three imposing Rivers buildings sitting in a semi-circle up a hill on her right.

The Rivers buildings were constructed in 1937 on the farthest corner of the grounds near the Vinson Highway. The sole purpose of the new buildings was to provide separate quarters for contagious tuberculosis patients, who had caught the disease while living in overcrowded wards throughout the hospital. Eventually the TB epidemic was contained with new drugs. The patients who survived were deemed to be inactive and transferred back to their original wards. By 1958, the year Heather was admitted, most of the space in the Rivers buildings was designated for developmentally disabled patients with the exception of Wards A through D on the first floor of the center building, which was used to warehouse psychotic females.

The red brick on the buildings had turned dark over the years and weeds grew unchecked, giving the whole area an ominous feel. Mattie was aware the wards for the psychotic patients were in the center building, so she took a deep breath, counted to five, exhaled, and climbed the stone steps. She pulled open the heavy oak door and stepped inside to an empty cavernous lobby. A sign on the wall pointed to Ward A. Following it, she came to a steel door with a notice next to it that said "Ward A: Authorized Personnel Only."

Mattie used her master key to open the steel door. Instead of stepping directly onto Ward A, she entered a ten-foot-square cement-block antechamber with one small viewing window in the door on the opposite side of the room. She crossed the room in five strides and looked through the glass, directly into Ward A. No patients were huddled inside, close to the door, ready to elope when she opened it. All clear. She unlocked and opened the second door and stepped warily onto the ward.

Minutes after the door automatically slammed shut behind her, Mattie found herself surrounded by a semicircle of psychotic patients. *Where'd they come from? They weren't here a minute ago. This is it; I'm a goner. I can see the headlines now: Young Nurse/Counselor with No Sense Entered a Locked Regressed Mental Ward at Six Thirty in the Morning by Herself, Totally Unprotected, and Was Attacked by Twenty Psychotic Women.*

I can't back up—the door locked behind me—and I can't move forward. Wonder if it would help to scream. But it looks like nobody's here. Who's minding the shop?

Some of the women were just staring, others had their fists

clenched at their sides. An elderly patient who had managed to remove her restraint jacket flapped it around in the air. Standing next to her was a teenager with copious amounts of drool streaming down her chin. Mattie watched with alarm as the patient sucked some saliva onto her tongue and prepared to spit.

Out of nowhere, a female attendant's voice bellowed, "Y'all best let her pass." The patients parted like the Red Sea. Mattie hurried through the newly created path and came face-to-face with the night ward attendant, who was still on duty. She was standing arms akimbo, a frown on her face. Mattie could barely decipher the name written on a dirty piece of adhesive tape plastered on her chest. Emma Lou?

"Not a lot of folk come round this early," she said.

"Thank you! That really scared me. My heart's beating like crazy. I think I'll sit down for a minute."

Emma Lou smoothed out the skirt of her wrinkled white uniform and looked Mattie up and down before walking away. "You do just that."

Mattie aimed for the deserted nurses' station at the far end of the dormitory, thankful her legs would still carry her. She sat down in one of the worse-for-wear rolling chairs parked in a corner. She relaxed her shoulders and took a few deep breaths.

Two trashy paperback novels sat on the desk next to a dirty coffee cup. A half-eaten ham sandwich lay molding on top of its wrapper. Mattie scooted her chair up to the desk and pushed the sandwich off to the side. A lone cockroach scurried between the charts. She looked around, hoping to spot a list of patient names. There was a clipboard lying facedown on the desk, and she turned it over. Bingo! There it was —the patient roster. She'd found the complete patient census for Ward A.

While Mattie was sifting through the patient names, concentrating on each entry, grossly overweight Emma Lou lumbered into the station. She plunked herself down in a desk chair and reached for the ham sandwich.

"Who you lookin' for on my list?" Emma Lou said, chomping down on the sandwich.

"Heather. Heather Edwards McAllister. Do you know where she is?"

"Maybe she's here, maybe she ain't."

"You know her? Do you mean she was here? What does she look like? Is she okay?"

"First off, if she was here, she'd look like all them other so-called ladies out there. And second off, if she ain't here, it means she was transferred somewheres maybe." Emma Lou let out a loud hee-haw. "It happens like that sometimes. They just disappear."

"But I need more information. Was she in good health? Did she know her name? Did she know what day it was?"

"You sure ask a lot of questions, and I don't know the answers. Go ask them ladies out there if you're so interested. All I know is you're in my way, and I got work to do."

Mattie stood up and pushed her chair back under the desk. "I will. I'll go ask them right now. I'm sure I'll find someone who's more helpful than you are."

She stepped out of the dilapidated nurses' station into the dormitory. The room was divided into two rows of cots, forty-five in each row—a total of ninety psychotic patients. The cots were spaced roughly two feet apart, barely enough room to climb in or out of bed.

A row of clerestory windows was boarded up with individual sheets of plywood; the only light came from the bare bulbs in the ceiling. At the far end of the dormitory there was a sizable dining area, and adjacent to it was the shower room where eight patients could shower at a time.

To the right of the nurses' station, "Baby Room" was inscribed in black letters over the top of a door that had been left wide open. Several oversized, rusty baby cribs were lined up inside in full view. There were iron bars spaced about eight inches apart on all sides of each crib. A separate set of bars was clamped down like a lid across the top.

That's weird. Those things look like cages. Surely, they wouldn't keep babies in them, and, never in a million years, would anyone put an adult human in a contraption like that.

Some early risers, most of whom had slept in their housedresses, were wandering up and down the middle pathway between the cots, mumbling, swearing, and talking to their voices. A lone catatonic patient at the far end of the dorm was standing frozen in one spot, balanced on her right foot, both arms raised in the air.

Mattie walked down the center path, looking for someone, anyone, who might be together enough to tell her about Heather McAllister. Her stomach sickened at the stench of unwashed bodies and Pine-Sol.

She wandered into the dining area and meandered around the empty circular tables. Chairs lined the walls around the periphery, where a few patients lounged, waiting for breakfast. She sat down in an empty chair next to a tiny woman who was staring out into space.

"I'm Mattie," she said softly. "I'm trying to find out about a patient named Heather. She's my mother, and I've lost touch with her. Did you know someone named Heather?"

The tiny woman stared at her with glazed-over eyes before getting up and walking away.

Mattie took a deep breath and tried to picture what it must have been like for her mother living here on this dead-end street. She could see years of grime between the wide planks of the pine floorboards. No fresh air, no light streaming through the long line of covered-up windows. Mattie could only imagine the endless boredom and could feel collective crazy thoughts circling through the air. Did the patients have walks outside? Maybe. Any activities to occupy their days? No.

It's like someone rounded up ninety homeless bag ladies and dumped them here in one spot. If my mother was crazy like these women, maybe she wouldn't notice, and if she wasn't, why would she stay?

Mattie moved across the room and approached a freckle-faced teenager who appeared to be daydreaming. As soon as Mattie sat down and began to speak, the girl yelled, "Jesus saves!" and turned her chair over in her haste to get away.

Mattie stayed seated, closed her eyes, trying to think. She sensed someone standing in front of her and bolted upright in her chair. *Gladys! I almost forgot she's a patient. I can't believe Dr. Vine sent her here. I know she was hard to handle—she was acting out a lot, but Dr. Vine could've just referred her to a different psychiatrist.*

"Well, looky here. Did you come slumming?"

"I'm looking for information about someone who was a patient here."

"And who would that be?" Gladys asked.

"Heather McAllister—she's my mother."

"Your mother? Miss High-and-Mighty has a crazy mother. How about them apples?"

"Gladys, I don't want to fight with you—I just want to find my mother."

"What makes you think I'm going to help you?"

"Help me find out what happened to Heather, and I'll ask Dr. Vine to discharge you from this awful place."

"Whoa, hold your horses!" Gladys said. "Who said I want to leave? This is the best thing that ever happened to me. I've lost two pounds in two days—can't you tell?" She spun around to show off her new physique.

No, I can't tell but hey, two pounds is two pounds, and it's too early to notice a change.

"I figure if I lose a pound a day, in six weeks I'll be down to normal weight," Gladys said.

"A pound a day? That's great, Gladys."

"Don't you get it? My whole life I've tried everything, but nothing worked—my mother kept stuffing me full of pasta and ice cream. Now, no Momma—I told the staff not to let her visit, in case she sneaks me in a snack. And every patient who can stand up has to go outside every day and exercise. And here's the best part; they made an appointment for me to go to the dental clinic and get my teeth fixed. I got too many front teeth—that's why they look all crossed over. If the dentist pulls this here tooth, then the rest of them will straighten out." She opened her mouth wide and pointed to the aberrant tooth she hoped to have extracted. "And then I'm gonna get me some braces. They're only going to charge me for the supplies. No charge for the labor."

It took Mattie a minute or two to process what Gladys was saying. *Let me think—she wants to stay here, lose weight, get her teeth fixed, and become normal. I never realized how desperate she was to fit in. She's been so nasty to everyone. Maybe that was because of her negative body image. Still, it seems a little drastic. But if it works for her, well, that's a good thing. There might be a whole new side to Gladys.*

"I won't say anything to Dr. Vine about discharging you if you don't want me to," Mattie said, shaking her head and looking around the ward. "If you're sure…"

"I'm sure," Gladys said, peppy, all smiles. "Here's what I know: I met someone named Heather two days ago, but then she went poof. I remember she was a nice lady. She tried to make me feel good about being in this shithole. She told me it gets better the longer you're here. Come to think of it, she didn't seem all that crazy to me."

"Is there more you can remember? Please think. What was she wearing? Did she seem happy? Did she give any hints about being transferred?"

"Well, all I can tell you is she's about your height. Her hair's mostly gray, maybe a little brown in it. Looked stringy. She was stooped over some. Oh, and she's plump."

"Plump? Heather is plump?"

"Yeah. Plump. You know like fat, obese. Well, maybe not as fat a me but still fat."

Gladys pointed across the dorm. "See that patient over there, the big girl, standing in the middle of the dorm? Name's Bertha. Everyone calls her Big Bertha. In the 1950s, when she lived on Ward G, one of the male wards in Walker, she told everyone she was a female, but no one would listen, probably because she had a beard and big biceps. Anyway, what I heard was that one day an attendant found this bloody dick on the floor. He held it up for the men to see and asked, 'Who lost this?' All the patients, eighty-nine guys, checked their crotches—no one claimed it. Big Bertha said, 'Okay, it used to be mine, but it didn't belong on me. I'm a female.' So Big Bobby became Big Bertha. She shaved off her beard, and they transferred her here to Ward A. She's like a self-appointed mayor for the patients—settles disputes, stuff like that. She probably knows what they did with your mom."

"Gladys, how in the world did you find out all that stuff? You've only been here two days!"

A mischievous smile crept over Gladys' face. "I made friends with the night attendant, Emma Lou. You met her—she's sitting in the nurses' station over yonder. She let me read Big Bertha's chart."

"But patient's charts are confidential," Mattie said.

Gladys eyed Mattie, a sneer on her face. "Lordy Mercy—how could bad Gladys do such a thing? You're so right, Miss-High-and-Mighty. I'll never do that again. Now do you want to talk to Big Bertha or not?" Mattie was sure Gladys had no intention of giving up her nighttime entertainment of reading the other patients' charts, but she was eager to talk to Big Bertha.

"Yeah, Gladys. Let's go talk."

Big Bertha was still standing in the middle of the dorm in the wide lane that separated the two long rows of cots. A tall, once-elegant patient glided over to Big Bertha. Her full-length emerald-green satin dress swept the dust off the floor as she walked. Her face was fixed in a permanent, vacant smile—she looked as if she were smelling a rose. Her long gloves, previously white, were now a dirty shade of gray. She stopped on Big Bertha's right side.

Gladys and Mattie walked over to where Big Bertha stood, her booming voice announcing it was time for all patients to get up and get dressed. She gave Mattie an inquiring look. "You're *not* a new patient. Need something?" she asked in a deep baritone.

"Yes, I'm trying to find out what happened to my mother," Mattie said. "Her name's Heather. She lived here a long time, and I think she might have been transferred somewhere, but I don't know where. I was hoping you might have heard where she went. Any information would be appreciated. Any at all."

"This is Tulula," Big Bertha said, lifting Tulula's gloved hand in the air and giving it a big squeeze. "She's a Polish countess."

Mattie attempted a curtsy; Big Bertha looked pleased. Another patient, still wearing her threadbare nightgown, sidled up to Big Bertha. "And this here's Thelma Jean," Big Bertha said. "She's normal crazy, right, Thelma Jean?"

Big Bertha's voice boomed out over the dorm. She made a sweeping hand gesture to include the entire dormitory. "All of us—we all knew Heather." Sleepy patients pulled their blankets over their heads or sat up on the sides of their cots, ever vigilant.

"You all knew her?" Mattie asked. "How did she seem? Was she healthy? Happy? When did she leave? Where did she go?"

"We've got no idea where she went, right, Tulula?" Big Bertha said. Another squeeze. "All we know is that she ain't here. But we can show you her empty bed if you want."

Mattie's heart started to race; her knees felt weak. She said, "Her bed? Where she actually slept? I would love to see it."

Bertha, Tulula, and Thelma Jean paraded over to an empty cot at the far end of the dorm. Mattie and Gladys stayed close behind them. The cot was pushed up next to a brick wall, and an army blanket covered up the grubby gray sheet. There was a flat pillow with no pillowcase.

"This is it. Heather slept here—do you got any candy? Cigarettes?"

Mattie reached down and patted the pillow, ran her hands over the rough blanket.

"Let's go," Gladys hissed in a loud whisper. "This ain't it."

"Um, thanks, Bertha, Thelma Jean, Tulula," Mattie said. "Sorry we don't have cigarettes or candy. We have to go now. I mean, I have to go. Gladys is staying."

Mattie was sure Gladys was correct. If anyone could spot a liar, it had to be Gladys.

"But why did Bertha lie?" Mattie asked as soon as they were out of earshot.

"It's like this: they don't trust you," Gladys said. "They don't think you're really Heather's daughter. Maybe she never mentioned she had a kid or maybe they think she had a kid and the kid died. Who knows? Anyway, they protect their own. They haven't got much else, just a real sense of loyalty. It's a good sign, shows they cared about Heather. I'm sure they have a pretty good idea what happened to her, but you'll never find out from them."

Gladys walked Mattie over to the exit, maneuvering her around the catatonic patients. She waited while Mattie used her master key to unlock the door.

"Honey, next time you see this body, you won't even recognize me," Gladys said. "And ain't nobody going to be calling me Gladys, the Fat Ass, anymore."

"All the best, Gladys," Mattie said, giving her former nemesis a hug before scooting off the ward, making sure to pull the steel door tightly shut behind her.

CHAPTER 13

HEATHER

October 6, 1976
Rivers Building, Ward A
Milledgeville Central State Hospital

Dr. von Brimmer was his usual upbeat self during our "session" today. That's what he calls our meetings now—sessions.

I was wearing my favorite shawl, my only shawl. The one the patients made me when my babies, my precious Mattie and Wilson, died. It's eighteen years old now, and yep, a bit worse for wear. I won't part with it ever. Back then, when they made it, a patient named Marcia (she's dead—lung cancer from smoking all those butts) snuck in a pair of scissors, and the patients, my friends, cut up pieces of material from their clothing. Lucinda had a sewing needle hidden under a broken piece of floorboard. Bruno brought her some thread, and she sewed all the pieces together. It looks like a patchwork quilt.

"This here shawl's gonna be lookin' like Joseph's coat of many colors," she told the patients. Lucinda sure knew her Bible. "It's gonna keep our Heather all warm, inside and out."

Big Bertha gave Lucinda the biggest piece. She hacked up her neon-pink cotton petticoat she'd saved from the days when she was a drag queen, right before she was admitted. Tulula, who's a genuine countess, cut up the blue ballgown she brought with her. Tulula has no practical clothes—she always wears her old satin dresses.

Jennifer didn't have any material to give Lucinda, so she took down a curtain just like Scarlett did. It was a dark-green and kind of silky polyester that had been used to cover the window next to the nurses' station. None of the attendants knew, or cared, where it went. Lucinda made a lining out of it. Rosalind, who's not known for her loving, generous nature, brought Lucinda her only decent piece of clothing—a lace blouse with long sleeves and a collar and buttons down the front. Lucinda cut it into strips and sewed it all around, made it into a lace border.

The doc said, "Why don't you take off your shawl and stay awhile?"

I pulled it tightly around me.

"I see on your chart you were married to a man named Clive for ten years. You had two children together. Can you tell me about your marriage?"

"There's nothing to tell. I know a joke," I muttered.

The only joke I could think of was the one that used to make Matilda and Wilson double up.

Knock, knock
Who's there?
Cows go.
Cows go who?
No, cows go moo.

When I was done, he chuckled. Apparently, he had a funny bone lodged behind those big brown eyes. "That's very amusing. Where did you learn that one?"

He knew exactly where I got it from. He wanted me to talk about my kids, but I just looked away and didn't answer. He was sitting behind his big oak desk. He leaned back in his chair, ready to listen. "I understand that after you were admitted to Ward A, you had a series of wet sheet packs. Can you tell me about it? Can you remember the treatments?"

"Maybe you could just read about it in my chart," I said, in a hesitant, faltering voice.

"I'd rather you talk about it. Is there anything you remember?" His voice was calm. Persuasive.

He must be kidding. Do I remember?

It was mid-September 1958; I'd been on the ward for four months. The attendants told me I was going to have a new treatment. They said that if I would cooperate, I would get to go home. I would have agreed to anything to go see my kids. I didn't even ask what it would be like. I just said, "Yeah, sure, I'll do it."

The next morning, they came and got me. Two female attendants. They made me walk between them—I didn't struggle. I would be going home to little Wilson, my Matilda. We would hug and I'd get them ice cream and make up for all the time I'd been gone. So I went like a lamb to the slaughter. Not knowing, not wanting to know, what was in store for me.

We walked off the ward to a different building, a small one-story place down a road near the laundry. I remember looking at the big bronze letters in a plaque over the door: WSP. Wet Sheet Packs. Like they were proud of it.

Inside was one big room. There were four oversized stainless-steel bathtubs, each one sitting up high, waist level, on a separate platform. The attendants made me lie down on a table on the other side of the room. They took off my clothes and wrapped me up in sheets, crisscross like a mummy. They put on their thick rubber gloves and lifted me over to one of the tubs. It was filled to the top with ice and water. Hunks of ice, tons of ice, floating in it. They dumped me in. My head was out, but that was all. I screamed but I couldn't move; I was all wrapped up. I could feel the ice coming through the sheets. It just froze me. I slipped under for a minute, thought I was going to drown, but one of the attendants pulled me up by my hair out of the water and held me by my chin so I couldn't slide back down. The ice got into my bones, and I knew I was dying there at that moment in that cold and dark place.

I drifted into unconsciousness. It must have been fifteen or twenty minutes before they pulled me out, put me back on the table, and unwrapped the freezing sheets. They waited till I came to and carried me back to the ward.

The next day I asked when I would be released. When could I go back home? They told me the treatment didn't work, and I wouldn't be going anywhere.

"I don't remember any of it," I told the doc. Shrugged my shoulders, frowned. Decided it was a good time to pick at my cuticles.

He stared at me for a long time. Old trick. Most people are uncomfortable with long silences, so they start to babble. Not me. I could wait him out. One thing I'm really good at is waiting. After about five minutes of this stalemate, he said, "We're done for the day now, Heather."

I gave the man a toothless grin and left.

Chapter 14

Mattie

October 1976

Mattie kept close track of the staff's birthdays. While she believed any good news, such as adopting a puppy, becoming engaged, or buying a new car was cause for a party, birthday celebrations were her favorite. Mattie knew that Pam, the activity director, had a special birthday—her thirtieth—coming up on Tuesday, October 12. Mattie decided to give her a surprise party in the break room at change of shifts so the staff members from all three shifts would be able to attend.

At 2:45 p.m. on the day of Pam's party, Mattie headed to the break room to set up. She covered the table with a birthday-themed paper cloth and placed thirty small yellow candles on the red velvet cake she'd made using Aunt Tess's favorite recipe. While she was putting the Ritz crackers and pimento spread on the table, William opened the break room door and walked in. Mattie could feel her heart begin to race. *Feels like my pulse just hit 150. Gosh, I wasn't expecting him to come; I checked the schedule and saw he worked last night. Wonder if he got any sleep today.*

Before Mattie had a chance to greet William, the day shift employees came barreling through the door, ready for the party. Close on their heels were the incoming evening shift staff members. The room was full to overflowing, everyone trying to keep the noise down so they wouldn't give away the surprise.

Mattie asked Dave to go to the activity room and tell Pam she was needed in the break room right away. Dave found Pam putting Bingo cards on the tables, preparing for a late afternoon game with the patients. As soon as Dave saw her attire, he knew she suspected something. Instead of one of her usual work outfits, she was wearing a bright-red skirt and a white blouse with embroidered red pansies. She had applied a touch of mascara to her eyelashes; her bright-pink lipstick stood out against her pale creamy complexion. Dark-brown curls framed her face.

Pam gave Dave a big grin and accompanied him down the hall. When she opened the break room door, a chorus of her coworkers yelled "Surprise!" Pam caught Mattie's eye and mouthed the words, "Thank you."

After Pam blew out the candles on the cake, Mattie walked over and stood by the bookcase, enjoying the squeals of laughter that reverberated through the room when Pam unwrapped her gag gifts. William headed over to where she stood. "Great party," he said. "You did all this? The cake, the balloons, the streamers?"

Mattie nodded. "The cake's red velvet; Aunt Tess gave me the recipe. Dave helped me put up those yellow streamers. Plus, I have an ulterior motive—when I keep busy it takes my mind off my troubles."

"You have troubles?" William said. "You always seem so happy. Anything I can do?"

Mattie had no intention of disturbing the party mood by talking about her missing mother, so she said, "How are things on nights? Do y'all miss me?"

"Things actually got quieter after you left. Maybe it was you causing all the trouble."

"Not true, not true, I swear. I think it was you," Mattie said, laughing. "You know, Murphy's Law: whatever can go wrong, will go wrong. And I bet you're Irish like Murphy."

"Make that half Irish and you're on," William said. He paused and looked at Mattie. "I want to discuss something with you, but I don't want to talk about it here. Can you grab a cup of coffee with me when this is over?"

"Yes, sure thing."

When all traces of the party were cleared away, William and Mattie headed to the Walker staff cafeteria, near the back of the building. They found a booth in the far end of the room in front of an expanse of clear glass windows. Looking out, they could see a tranquil pond surrounded by tall cattails. A dozen or so orange-and-black Japanese koi were swimming gracefully around and under a manmade waterfall.

William put his black coffee and chocolate-glazed donut on a clean spot on the table and sat down across from Mattie. "You look great. What've you been up to besides working?" he said.

Mattie stirred some cream and sugar into her coffee and took a sip. "Oh, I've been playing with my dog, Sooner. I'm trying to teach him how to fetch. So far, so good. And I've spent some time visiting with my Aunt Tess in Savannah."

"Nice. I love dogs myself," William said, taking a big chunk out of his donut. "And your Aunt Tess must be happy to see you. Good donut, by the way. How come you're not eating?"

"I'm not hungry—I ate a big piece of cake."

"Me too. It was delicious. But this donut looked too good to pass up."

After a short pause, Mattie said, "You were going to talk to me about something?"

"Well, it's like this," William said, hesitating slightly, choosing his words.

"Yes?" Mattie said, nodding encouragement.

"I was doing our daily check of the patients' rooms for contraband, weed and stuff, while they were in group. I went and checked Alex's room because he was on my list."

"The patient Alex? Auditory hallucinations, Polish mafia?"

"Yep, one and the same," William said. "I searched his drawers and closet. Nothing. But when I pulled the mattress off his bed to check under it, I found a small box with this in it." He placed the box and a red button the size of a quarter onto the table.

"What was a button doing in a box under Alex's mattress?"

"I think it's from Darryl's pajamas. Those red-plaid pajamas—the ones he told us he bought at the Salvation Army. He was wearing them when he died."

"I remember. How could I ever forget? But I didn't see any missing buttons," Mattie said.

"There was one missing—the last one on the bottom. I noticed it when we laid him out on his bed."

"And you're thinking that…"

"I think Alex made Darryl hang himself, and while Darryl was hanging, Alex reached up and pulled or cut one of the buttons off his pajamas."

"What? Hold on! That's a big leap. You're saying you think Alex is a murderer? Can't be—he was sound asleep every time Peter made rounds."

"Maybe he was pretending to be asleep. Alex would have had time to sneak into Darryl's room between rounds—we only make them every fifteen minutes. And why was Alex hiding Darryl's button?" William said.

"He could've found it on the floor and planned to throw it away in the garbage."

"Or maybe he was keeping the button as a trophy," William said. "Isn't that what killers do—keep something that belonged to the victim to remind them of their kill?"

Mattie studied William's face. "I can see you're serious; you've given this a lot of thought. But that kind of scenario never entered my mind."

"And don't forget about Darryl's head injury," William said. "What if someone was following him? Came up behind him; hit him on his head. Maybe it was Alex. Maybe Alex had some sort of grudge against Darryl."

"That really would be scary," Mattie said. "I think I should talk to Dr. von Brimmer. He was Darryl's doctor, and he's also Alex's. I've never run into a situation like this before."

"Looks like it's a first for both of us," William said. "Yes, talk to Dr. von Brimmer. See what he says."

"I'll tell him we have reason to believe we're harboring a murderer on the unit," Mattie said.

"That should give him a substantial shock. Hope he has a healthy heart."

After a short pause, Mattie decided this might be as good a time as any to let William know her family situation. She took a deep breath and said as casually as she could, "My father brought my mother here to Milledgeville back in 1958. He had her committed."

"She was committed? Was she on Petition and Certificate?"

"No. Back then all a family member had to do was drop them off at the front door of Powell and tell the attendants they were crazy. That was it. No paperwork. They put my mother in Ward A in Rivers. Worst regressed women's ward in the whole hospital."

"Ward A? I don't know what to say. What happened to her? It must have been difficult for you not having your mother around."

"It really was," Mattie said. "Father told my brother, Wilson, and me that our mother died two weeks after she was admitted. We were placed in foster care on a farm up by Dexter."

"Tell me about your dad. He must have had a reason to give you up."

"He did. I think he might have had a mistress; we were probably in the way. And he had a business to run, an international business, selling women's underwear. It's called Darling Dainties. Please tell me you've never heard of it."

"I promise you I've never heard of it, and if I ever do, I promise not to let you know," William said, smiling.

Mattie grinned back at him. "Thanks, I appreciate that."

"I've no idea what it would be like in foster care. I've always been so lucky with my family. My parents were a little strict at times, but they always watched out for my two sisters and me. How were your foster parents? What do you remember about it? Were they good to you and your brother?"

Mattie looked away for a moment then back at William. *Probably not a good time to talk about the maggots in the pig's slop bucket while he's trying to eat his donut,* she thought. She plunged ahead anyway.

"The farmer and his wife were *not* nice people," Mattie said. "I think they really hated us, my brother and me. They told us they only took in foster kids for the money the state paid them, and they made us sleep in an old, rickety, leaky shed. One of my jobs was to slop the pigs. The slop bucket was usually full of flies and tons of fat crawling maggots."

William had lifted his chocolate-covered donut toward his mouth, intent on taking another bite. He paused with it midair before putting it back down on his plate.

"Maggots?"

"Yes, maggots, but that wasn't the worst. Once while I was asleep, one of the field mice got into my long hair and had a litter of baby mice during the night. I could feel them moving around when I woke up. I screamed. Wilson helped me get them out. Later that day I snuck the scissors out of the mean farmer's wife's sewing basket, went out to the shed, and gave myself a crew cut. It was the only way I could think of to keep the mice out of my hair."

William leaned back in his seat, quiet for a moment. "I guess I've been too sheltered. I had no idea people could treat foster kids like that."

Mattie glanced across the table. *Good. No judgmental look. Glad I got it out in the open. Kept it kind of lighthearted. Mother committed. I spent time in foster care. Father weird. He seems okay with it—didn't overreact. Maybe because he's used to hearing people's problems. Or maybe he's just a plain nice person.*

Mattie picked up the button and turned it over in the palm of her hand before putting it back down on the table. She looked at William. "I'll try to get an appointment with Dr. von Brimmer on Thursday—it's my day off."

"Sounds like a good plan."

"Um, actually, I know Dr. von Brimmer pretty well. He's my doctor."

"You see him as a patient? He does therapy with you?"

Mattie nodded her head. "Yes, as a matter of fact, he does. Weekly therapy. Seems I have a few issues. I have this compulsion to wash my hands about fifty times a day. Dr. von Brimmer thinks it's left over from when Wilson and I lived on the farm." She gave an involuntary shudder. "Aunt Tess found out right after I went to live with her, and she sent me to a prominent Savannah psychologist. I saw him every week for about a year, and, after that, all better. But now I've got it again. Exact same compulsion."

"That must be hard on your hands, all that washing."

"Yep, sometimes they get very sore. I've started to use Nivea Creme. Great stuff. You don't even need a prescription for it." She was suddenly self-conscious—her knuckles looked like ginger roots, rough and raw. She quickly withdrew her hands into her lap, changed her mind, and placed them back on the table. William pretended not to notice.

"What are we going to do about that?" she asked, pointing to the button.

"When Alex goes to focus group tomorrow, I'll put it back."

"I wouldn't," Mattie said. "What if he sees you?"

"Well, if I don't put it back, he's gonna know someone's got his trophy. What if he thinks you took it? He might figure out you're suspicious of him and come looking for you. If Alex could track down Darryl, he can elope from the unit and track you down."

"Okay, you're probably right. I'll tell Dr. von Brimmer you put the button back. We'll see what he advises."

William placed the button in its box, then put the box in his pocket. "Consider it done."

"Well, that said, now I've got some good news to share," Mattie said.

"Let's hear it. I'm a big believer in good news."

"I told you I thought my mother was dead. Father said she was dead, and I believed him. I never talked about her at work, mainly because it was too painful, and I didn't want to get all emotional. I thought she was buried in the cemetery in the woods. I wanted to find her grave and put a big bunch of flowers on it."

"I can understand that. And the good news is?"

"She's alive. Not one bit dead!"

"No kidding! You're saying you found out your mom is alive? That's amazing. That's *really* good news. How'd you find out, and how's she doing?"

"I found out by looking her name up in one of the old ledgers in the library. They had her name but no date of death, so Lydia, the librarian, said I could assume she's alive. According to the information in the ledger, she was assigned to Ward A in Rivers building when she first arrived, but that was eighteen years ago. Lydia told me she probably would not still be there—that she would've been transferred somewhere else by now. I decided to go myself and check. But to tell the truth, I was afraid of what I'd find. If she was still there, would she know me? If she wasn't, how would I ever trace her?"

"That's unbelievable," William said. "Your mother's not dead like you thought. It's almost like Lazarus rising."

"Last week I finally got up the courage to go to Ward A. I was hoping and praying I'd find her there." *Geez, I hope that wasn't too obvious, throwing out the word "praying,"* Mattie thought, smiling to herself. *I just want him to know I'm not some kind of heathen. Not that I've ever met a real heathen.*

"Unfortunately, I'd just missed her," Mattie said. "She'd been recently moved somewhere, but no one seemed to know where. There are more than twelve thousand patients in the hospital, right now, today, and the record keeping is, well, everyone knows it's somewhat lacking. I'm not even sure where to start looking. I feel so anxious. That's probably what triggered my handwashing compulsion."

William reached over the top of his half-eaten donut and covered Mattie's hand with his. She liked the feel of his hand on hers. Comforting, reassuring. Like everything would turn out okay. "I can't imagine what you're going through," he said. "You know your mother's alive and living here somewhere, but you don't know where. If I can help in any way, let me know." His hand lingered on hers for a moment before he moved it away.

"Thanks, William. I really appreciate it," she said. "Your turn now. You know a lot about me, so it's only fair you tell me something about yourself. Tell me about the seminary. I've never known anyone who actually lived in a monastery."

She waited while he took a sip of his coffee. "Okay, then," he said. "I guess I should start by telling you that after college I went to the Dominican House of Studies in Washington, DC. You could say that's where I became indoctrinated in the beliefs and customs of the Black Friars."

"But what was it like there?" she asked. "Did you have nice teachers? I suppose they were all monks?"

"Yes, all of my teachers were monks. Also known as Black Friars. We followed the teachings of St. Dominic, who started the order in 1214."

"And your robes look like that monk in Robin Hood."

William grinned. His green eyes twinkled. "Yep, we all looked just like Friar Tuck. My favorite teacher turned out to be Father Martin. We got off to a rough start. During our freshman year, each of the new seminarians was assigned a menial position. The monks wanted us to learn humility. I was assigned to kitchen duty. One day during freshman year, I was washing up the pots and pans when my superior, Father Martin, rushed into the kitchen. He laid a five-pound slab of meat on the butcher-block table and told me to cook it for dinner. He said, 'The prefect from the Province of St. Joseph is coming, and I want to impress him.'"

Mattie wasn't sure where this story was going, but so far she liked the sound of it. "Yes," she said. "Then what?"

"When Father Martin returned a little while later, I put the potato I was peeling down on the counter and walked over to the stove. I removed the lid from a big pot that was boiling away on one of the burners. I wanted to show him how nicely the meat was cooking. I remember the steam rose up in a big cloud. 'What have you done to my meat?' Father Martin yelled at me. 'It's *a standing rib roast*, you idiot. Get it out of the boiling water; you're making it tough as shoe leather. You're supposed to roast it in the oven. Do it now. Right now. Or you'll be scrubbing out the latrines. And I want to see you in my office this evening at eight o'clock sharp, do you hear?'"

"Oh my, William," Mattie said, shaking her head. "I would think it would be sinful to get that angry over a piece of meat."

"I thought so too. But then again, I didn't want to be scrubbing those cold stone bathrooms, so I held my tongue."

"Probably a smart move."

"That evening when I went to see Father Martin, I was totally shocked. I expected his room to be simple, unadorned, with just a cot and a desk. I knew the other monks slept on mats in cubbyholes on the third floor," William said. He paused, remembering.

"What did it look like?"

"Well, there were antique andirons in the shape of Revolutionary War soldiers standing in front of a brick fireplace. And there was a bar with lots of cans of Guinness and bottles of Christian Brothers Brandy. Expensive furniture—two sofas, plenty of chairs scattered about. The biggest surprise was that Father Martin apologized to me. Said he'd treated me badly, with no respect, which was not fitting for someone like him, who was supposed to set a good example for all the young men aspiring to a higher calling. He told me for his penance he had given himself the task of becoming my mentor and asked me what I thought about that. I didn't know what to think, so I said 'okay.' From that moment on he became my spiritual advisor and life coach. He invited me to join a bunch of six or seven seminarians who came to his study every Friday night and discussed philosophy. I loved those Friday nights. We gathered around the fireplace and puffed on Father Martin's cigarettes. We drank his liquor and discussed philosophy. The evenings always ended with a prayer."

"What an incredible story," Mattie said. She had a strong feeling it was none of her business, but she couldn't resist asking, "How come you left? Did something happen?"

William gave her an impish grin. "You mean did I steal a gold chalice or question the pope?"

"No, I was just wondering. But if you don't want to share, that's fine."

"I was kidding. Of course, I don't mind telling you. It wasn't anything dramatic. I'd finished college and was halfway through the four years of study at the seminary. One day I woke up feeling something was missing. I was twenty-six years old, and I felt like I was frittering away my life. I could feel my faith, my lifelong beliefs, crumbling. What would I do if I lost my faith? I couldn't let that happen. How could a seminarian walk around without his faith? I thought it must have been something in my dream; probably the devil tempting me. My parents would be appalled. I decided to go see Father Martin as soon as possible—I was sure he'd know what to do."

"What did he say? Was he able to help you?"

"Father Martin said I was being tested. He said it was an honor of sorts. He told me I should leave the seminary that very day and take a year off, experience life, pray, and then decide. 'Your faith will return,' he assured me. He said, 'Do good works. Remember faith and good deeds are interdependent.'"

"What in the world does that mean?"

"I had no idea. I wanted to stay and discuss that particular philosophy during one of our Friday evening sessions, but Father Martin thought it best for me to leave immediately before my faith slipped totally away."

"Geez, that's quite a story." Mattie added more cream and sugar to her cold coffee. She took a sip before saying, "I was wondering what your life was like before. I'm happy it worked out that you ended up here."

"Me too."

"Well, I'd better be getting on home now—Sooner sits and waits for me by the window." She broke into a big grin. "Of course, I think he's waiting for me, but there's a possibility he might be waiting for the treat I give him whenever I walk through the front door."

"Sounds like your pup has you trained," William said, laughing. "I have to go too. I need to get some sleep before I go to work tonight. I'll walk out with you."

Chapter 15

Mattie

October 1976

The next day at work, Mattie intercepted Ben as he headed down the hall toward the solarium to assist the patients with their breakfast trays. "Hi Ben," Mattie said. "I wanted to take a minute to talk to you about your wandering eye. The condition's caused by a weak eye muscle, and I can give you the name of a doctor who can teach you how to exercise your…" Mattie stopped talking midsentence. She looked at the object Ben was holding in his hand.

"Ben, what's that you have? I hope it's not what it looks like."

Ben held up the small, clear plastic cup with a tight-fitting lid he was holding in his right hand. It was three-fourths full of dark-brown liquid.

"Beatrice gave it to me," he said. "You know, the patient who says her husband is making a clone of her."

"Yep, I know who Beatrice is, Ben. Her husband is a nice guy, but no way is he capable of cloning his wife. Matter of fact, he's a caretaker over in the Green building."

"But Beatrice believes he's a famous scientist. Should I tell her the truth?"

"No," Mattie said. "It's never a good idea to take away a patient's delusion unless you have something better to replace it with. Beatrice needs to believe her delusion. We don't know why. It keeps her mind together somehow. Dr. von Brimmer has started her on a new med—perhaps it will help. By the way, that cup you're holding looks like it's full of diarrhea. Why are you carrying it around?"

"Because Beatrice gave it to me. I didn't want to hurt her feelings, so I just took it. She said she wanted to give me something special."

"Well, Ben, that *is* special. I would say you are a very lucky man. I'm glad you got that present, not me. Now, I suggest you go throw the whole thing in the contaminated trash and don't forget to wash your hands." Mattie was still chuckling to herself when she knocked on Sophia's door.

"Com'on in," Sophia said. "I'll just be a minute." Mattie took a seat on Sophia's sofa and tried to relax.

"All done. What's on your mind this morning?" Sophia asked.

"I had the weirdest conversation with William yesterday, and I wanted to run it by you."

"Tell Aunt Sophia all about it. You and William? What's going on?"

"Unfortunately, nothing—this isn't about me and William. It's more about Alex. William found a red button in a small box under Alex's mattress while he was doing his routine room checks. Alex was in group. He doesn't know William found the button."

"Where's it from, this button?"

"William thinks it's the missing button from the red-plaid pajamas Darryl was wearing when he hanged himself. Only now we wonder if Darryl did hang himself. We think Alex might have killed him and taken the button off his pajamas as a trophy."

Sophia frowned. "You think Alex is a murderer? That's pretty intense. He's capable, for sure. I read the results of his Minnesota Multiphasic Personality Inventory, the MMPI. It indicates he has sociopathic tendencies but absolutely no delusions or paranoia. I haven't had a chance to discuss the results with Dr. von Brimmer yet."

"I just wanted to get your input. Tomorrow's my day off, so I scheduled an appointment with Dr. von Brimmer for one o'clock. To tell the truth, I'm a little bit nervous. I want to run our theory by him, see if he agrees Alex could be a cold-blooded murderer, but I'm not sure how he'll react. I hope he'll be open to hearing me out, and he'll want to get the police involved and get an investigation started."

"Remember, Dr. von Brimmer's very conservative," Sophia said. "He's been around a long time, and he'll likely take everything you say with a grain of salt. Now, to change the subject, I'm wondering how the search for your mom is going. Any follow-up from your visit to Ward A?"

"Yep, I tracked the ward supervisor down," Mattie said. "She claimed there never was a patient named Heather McAllister on Ward A. I said she might be using her maiden name, Edwards, but she still said, 'Nope, I never heard of her,' which is bizarre because that rude night attendant heard of her. So did those patients I talked to, not to mention Gladys actually saw her."

"That really is bizarre, Mattie. Someone, somewhere, must know where she is."

Mattie woke up the following day with her stomach in a knot. She managed to eat a piece of toast with marmalade and wash it down with a strong cup of Maxwell House coffee. *Fresh air*, she thought. *Some fresh air will clear my head—I want to be able to present my case to Dr. von Brimmer in a logical manner.*

Sooner wagged his tail and sat by the door. "Stay, Sooner," she said. "You can't come with me—I've already taken you out for your walk, and I've got important business to attend to."

After giving Sooner a treat, Mattie ran down her apartment steps and made her way past the circular pond in front of Powell. She crossed Broad Street and arrived at the park, one of her favorite places —she loved strolling around the large expanse of rolling green lawn and stopping to rest on one of the many benches scattered about under the pecan trees.

On November 15,1864, two columns of General Sherman's army had marched into the asylum under the command of General Slocum and set up camp in the park. White-topped wagons stretched out behind the soldiers, with much needed supplies for their march to the sea. Hundreds of bivouacked soldiers stood around on the lawn, eating, talking, cleaning their rifles.

Sherman had directed his soldiers to forage locally but to spare the poor. Mattie felt sure the mental patients had qualified as poor. The soldiers found pumpkins, cabbages, and chickens in and around Milledgeville and brought them back to their encampment. They also dragged back farm equipment, crystal chandeliers, and silver punchbowls—anything they thought interesting. *The patients probably couldn't believe their eyes,* Mattie thought.

From her vantage point on top of the steps leading down into the park, Mattie could see the five buildings surrounding the area. To her far right, was the ivy-covered Walker building, home to the new CSU. It stood east of the park across a narrow road. Walker housed not only CSU, but a number of male wards as well. The Green building, which also bordered the park, had been built next to Walker and consisted of female wards. A pink-brick, one-story nondenominational chapel, one of the most recent buildings on the grounds, had been constructed about forty feet north of Green.

Directly across the park from Green, stood the Jones building, a fully accredited hospital with a busy surgery and well-equipped emergency room. South of Jones was an auditorium where plays and concerts were frequently performed for the patients.

Mattie walked down six cement steps and into the park. She needed a place to think. Although there were a number of patients milling about talking to their voices and smoking cigarette butts, she managed to find an unoccupied wooden bench tucked beneath one of the low-slung branches of a pecan tree. Some of the orange and yellowish-brown leaves fluttered to the ground around her as soon as she sat down. A few landed in her hair and she brushed them away. She leaned back, stretched out her legs, and watched, amused, as two playful squirrels darted about, running up and down the pecan trees nearby. A male patient, gaunt face, empty eyes, stopped for a moment in front of her bench and gave her a shy wave before moving away.

Mattie glanced at her watch. "It's almost one o'clock. Time to get going." She grinned when she realized she was talking out loud to herself. *I fit right in here*, she thought. A quick walk took her back to Powell. She proceeded up the wide concrete steps leading to the building's twin front doors, through the oak-paneled reception area and up the stairs to Dr. von Brimmer's office.

The door was partway open. Dr. von Brimmer spied Mattie before she could knock and limped over to greet her. *His leg must be hurting more today. Maybe it's the change of seasons.*

"Ah, there you are. Come in, come in. How are you today, Matilda?" Dr. von Brimmer said, using her proper name like he did during their sessions. He moved slowly back to his desk and took a seat.

Mattie sat down in the chair on the other side of the desk. "I wanted to talk to you about something that happened on the CSU," she said.

"Oh, so this is about the Crisis Stabilization Unit? Well, speak right up. I'm always here to help."

Mattie wanted to make sure she presented herself in a professional manner, not as his patient. She hoped he wouldn't bring up her handwashing compulsion.

"Now tell me, how many times have you washed your hands today?" Dr. von Brimmer asked.

"About ten times, so far."

During her weekly appointments with Dr. von Brimmer, Mattie usually dashed in and out of his office, intent on "fixing" her compulsion before she rubbed all the skin off her hands. Now she took her time and looked around the office.

Dr. von Brimmer followed her gaze. "Most people love this office, me included. It dates back to pre–Civil War. Some mighty smart people have used it to good advantage."

"It's definitely a wonderful space," Mattie said. "And I've always admired your extensive book collection." She walked over to the tall oak bookshelves and stopped in front of a photo of Dr. von Brimmer standing next to a woman holding a toddler. His arm was wrapped around her shoulder pulling them close. Affectionate. Protective. Mattie pointed to the photo. "Is that your wife and son?"

"Yes, Constance and Robert. They died twenty-five years ago in an automobile accident. Terrible accident. A head-on crash."

Sophia told me your wife was running away with another man, your best friend. Did you know? Of course, you must have. Betrayal, then death. How painful that must have been.

"That must have been awful for you."

"Yes, awful. Words are inadequate to describe my sense of loss. I still think about them every day. But come now—you didn't stop by to talk about my family. Have a seat." He pointed to the chair across from his desk. "What's going on? What can I do to help?"

Mattie sat down and folded her hands in her lap. She took a deep breath. "You know your patient Alex?"

"Yes."

"Well, a psych tech found a button under his mattress," Mattie said, pausing.

"Something tells me there is more to this story."

"Yes, it's a red button."

"And…"

"The button is an exact match to the buttons on the plaid pajamas our patient Darryl was wearing when he hanged himself," Mattie said.

"And what do you think Alex was doing with Darryl's button?"

Oh no, is this a trick question? Just answer the question, Matilda, she told herself.

"To be honest, I think your patient Alex killed Darryl. Murdered him somehow."

Dr. von Brimmer pushed his chair back from his desk, got up, walked over to the window and looked out. He stroked his beard for a few minutes before turning back to Mattie. "Whatever are you saying? According to the report I got, Darryl put the noose around his own neck, and he kicked the chair out from underneath himself."

"I'm saying I think Alex threatened Darryl with bodily harm—maybe he had some sort of weapon. He made Darryl climb up on the chair, and *he* was the one who kicked the chair out, not Darryl."

Dr. von Brimmer frowned at Mattie, who remained seated, rigid on her chair. "And how long have you had these thoughts, Matilda?"

"To tell the truth, I've been suspicious of Alex for a while. He claims he's being chased by the Polish mafia, acting all crazy, but I don't think he is. Crazy, I mean. I think he's normal, but he just wanted us to think he was crazy so he could be admitted and—"

"Why would Alex want to do a thing like that?" Dr. von Brimmer asked.

"I don't know. That's the part I can't figure out—why."

"Alex could have killed Darryl *before* he was admitted," Dr. von Brimmer said. "I would think that might have been a more expedient plan."

"I think Alex *did* try to kill him right before he was admitted. I think Alex hit Darryl on the head with a hammer or something. Darryl had a severe laceration on the occipital area of his skull when we first saw him."

Dr. von Brimmer shook his head. "Now tell me, did Darryl come right out and tell you Alex attacked him with a hammer? Darryl could have fallen, you know—hit his head on a rock."

"No, Darryl was very guarded. He didn't give any details. He was careful about what he said. He only told us he was hit from behind and he was depressed and wanted to be somewhere safe."

"Go on."

"Alex must have followed him here and pretended to be crazy so he could get himself admitted and finish the job," Mattie said.

"Getting oneself admitted to a psych hospital in order to murder someone is a bit far-fetched, don't you think?"

This isn't going well—he doesn't believe me, not one bit. "Alex thought he had no other choice. If he wanted to kill Darryl, he *had* to follow him into the CSU," Mattie said in a rush.

"Yes, go on. What's the rest of your theory?"

"That's it. Darryl thought the unit would be a safe place to hide. He thought he'd be where Alex could never get to him. Unfortunately, it didn't turn out that way."

"No, it didn't. But this is all supposition. The only proof you have is a red button, and it could have been gotten anywhere, am I correct?"

"Yes, that's correct. But what if Alex did kill Darryl?" Mattie asked. "If Alex discovers his souvenir is missing, he might think I'm the one who found it under his mattress. He might come after me next. I thought it best to have the button replaced so he won't get suspicious."

"Why would he single you out? You think Alex is going to follow you, try to harm you? You know he's locked up and can't leave."

Mattie nodded. *Next thing he'll be ordering medication for me.*

"Well, let me tell you a little about my patient's history. Maybe that will help you see him in a different light."

Mattie scrutinized Dr. von Brimmer as he leaned back in his chair. *He really looks the part. Head psychiatrist. Brown corduroy jacket. Leather patches on the elbows. Neat salt-and-pepper beard. All he needs is a pipe. His voice is so controlled. Mellow. No doubt about it; he's always the one in control.*

"I don't mean to sound skeptical, Dr. von Brimmer, but Alex has made up so many outlandish stories about his past, I'm wondering if you were able to verify his history," Mattie said.

"The information I'm about to impart to you was sent to me by a high-ranking friend of mine in the army. I asked him, as a favor, to get me a copy of Alex's military service record."

Mattie nodded. "That's great; maybe it will help explain Alex's present behavior."

"Yes, very wise of you, my dear. Our past always sneaks into our present. One of my favorite quotes is the last line of *The Great Gatsby*: 'So we beat on, boats against the current, borne back ceaselessly into the past.'"

Mattie nodded again. *Probably thinking about his own past. Never got over his wife's betrayal.*

"Ten years ago, in 1966, Alex was a nineteen-year-old recruit stationed in Vietnam," Dr. von Brimmer said. "He and his platoon buddies, led by Second Lieutenant Richardson, entered a small hamlet near Pleiku. The villagers were suspected of helping the Vietcong, so Richardson ordered his men to shoot everyone in the village. Every man, woman, and child. Alex refused and aimed his gun at Richardson. Threatened to kill him if he didn't rescind his order. The other soldiers backed Alex. Richardson was convicted in a courtmartial and Alex was sent home with a medal."

Mattie was silent for a moment. She stood up and prepared to leave. "In my mind that makes Alex even more scary. He sounds like he's capable of really hurting someone."

Dr. von Brimmer reached into his desk drawer and withdrew his prescription pad. "I'm writing you a prescription for some Librium. Why don't you call me tomorrow and let me know how you feel?" he said, walking around to the front of his desk and pressing the prescription into Mattie's hands. "Now, if you'll excuse me, I have an appointment to evaluate a female patient from one of our regressed wards. My goal is to move some of those patients to the more progressive wards. I think a more stimulating environment will help them get to their optimum level of functioning."

He walked Mattie to the door and opened it for her. "Thanks for stopping by, Matilda. Be sure to come again if you have any further problems; I'm here to help." He closed the door firmly behind her.

As she left the office, Mattie noticed an elderly woman sitting hunched over on a bench in the hallway. A tall black male attendant stood hovering a short distance away.

She's got to be from one of the regressed wards—they're the only ones who send attendants out with their patients. Must be the person Dr. von Brimmer was going to see. Hope she has better luck with him than I did.

Mattie stopped in front of the woman and spoke quietly. "Hello. Dr. von Brimmer's almost ready to see you," she said. "It's probably only going to be a few more minutes. How are you doing today?"

The patient pulled her patchwork shawl tightly around herself and looked at the floor.

"That's a beautiful shawl you're wearing," Mattie said. "It's so colorful, and it's got a pretty white lace border sewed all around it. I've never seen one like it before."

The attendant took a step closer, alert, watching. "She been a little low today, missy."

"I'm feeling okay, Bruno," the woman mumbled. "Just resting my eyes, waiting on the doctor."

Mattie smiled at them both and walked away. When she got back to her apartment, she phoned William to describe her interview with Dr. von Brimmer. "Geez, that was nothing but a waste of time," she told him. "He gave me a prescription for meds, like I was paranoid or something. I'm lucky he didn't try to commit me. Thinks I'm imagining things. He and Alex, they're in the same boys' club, only different wars—Alex was in Vietnam, and Dr. von Brimmer fought the Japanese in the Philippines."

"Don't take any chances," William said. "We know Alex is dangerous. Remember, he's capable of murder. Promise?"

Mattie tried to ignore her sudden chill bumps. "Sure, I'll be careful," she said, and hung up the phone.

Chapter 16

Heather

October 15, 1976
Rivers Building, Ward A
Milledgeville Central State Hospital

Lucinda likes to say, "Butter my butt and call me biscuit." I burst out laughing when she says that. I tried to come up with a good expression of my own, but my stuff is a little lame, like "Oh no!" or "You don't say," or "Heavens to Betsy." I guess I still have a little bit of refinement left.

Every afternoon Bruno takes a bunch of us on a walk outside. It gives us a chance to scurry around like little kids on an Easter egg hunt, looking for butts—cigarette butts—with or without attached filters. Lucinda smokes; I don't. But I'm always happy to help out.

First one to spot a butt picks it up, brushes it off, and carefully tucks it into their pocket or bag, ready to trade or inhale, whichever notion appeals most. Most of us pay no attention to the massive pecan trees or beds of rainbow-colored zinnias. We walk with eyes piercing the turf, peering under bushes, in dry birdbaths—any likely spot—ready to swoop down like a pelican and fly off with our treasure. Bruno always keeps us in line. Runs a tight ship. We listen to him and don't wander too far off course.

Today is October 15. Exactly eight months ago today, February 15, our little Nora went missing. It's a day I won't ever forget.

Nora was a patient, everybody's favorite—a thirteen-year-old beauty, a ray of sunshine. She had long blonde hair, clear blue eyes, and not the sense God gave a goose. Pretty face, no one home. Poor girl wasn't born like that. She had meningitis when she was around seven. The fever fried her brain.

Lucinda and I had had a discussion about Nora's IQ. I said her mental age was five. Lucinda guessed eight. Lucinda said she could prove it was eight because she was going to teach Nora to read. Lucinda said if Nora could learn to read, it would mean she was eight.

Lucinda sat on Nora's bed every day for a week making the "a" sound and pointing to the letter "a." Nothing. I won the bet. We agreed Nora was mentally aged five.

Watching Nora dance around the ward, friendly and nice to all the patients, made me think of my Matilda. Nora didn't look like Matilda, but she did look like she could use some mothering.

Lucinda and I made a pact to watch out for her. We made sure she had enough to eat and cautioned her not to talk to any male patients when Bruno took us outside for our afternoon walks.

One day, Nora came up to Lucinda and me and said, "I think I'm sick." She started to cry. We gave her a little group hug—me, her, and Lucinda—right in the middle of the dormitory. I remember we were standing by her cot.

"What's wrong, girl? Why you think you sick?"

Nora managed to blurt out one word. "Blood."

Lucinda said, "You get hurt? Someone hurt you? You bleeding? Where that blood? You just tell me and Miss Heather here who hurt you—we'll fix 'em good."

I had a thought. I pointed. "You're bleeding there?" Nora looked frightened, her eyes got big, and she bobbed her head up and down. Lucinda and I were relieved. We gave her another hug and told her it was normal, that it would happen once a month. She stopped crying. Lucinda left and went to her private stockpile under her bed and came back with some rags for Nora. She told her in simple terms what to do.

We told her this thing that happened was good, that it meant she was a young woman now. Nora sat on her cot while Lucinda took down her braids and tied a red ribbon into her hair. I had been saving a half-used pink Revlon lipstick I found outside on one of our walks. I gave the tube to Nora. She handed it back so I could put some on her lips.

A brilliant smile slid across her face. "I love you both," she said. "You're like my mommy and daddy."

The day Nora went missing, Bruno called in sick; he'd been out sick all week. With no Bruno to take us out on our walk, there were no butts to scavenge. This meant a lot of unhappy patients because a lot of them were having withdrawal. The other male attendants refused to step up. They said they couldn't handle the patients outside. They were right, of course.

Rosalind was having a hard time holding it together. She was a big woman, a lifer who was used to structure. She demanded her afternoon walk so she could go pick up butts. By evening she had worked herself up into a state, threatening the staff and throwing stuff.

Lucinda and I stayed clear of her. We smelled trouble coming. She was just asking to be put into restraints, and the staff obliged. Full leathers. Only thing was they were in a hurry and they forgot to check her pockets. This was on account of Rosalind was spitting wads of spittle at them, causing them to make a quick getaway.

I don't know how she did it, but when Rosalind was in the leathers she managed to get a lighter out of her pants and set the mattress pad on fire. (Lucinda and I figured she found it outside and kept it hidden in her pocket.) Miz Max smelled the smoke first. She ran around like crazy, looking for the restraint key to let Rosalind out. It was supposed to be on a special hook near the restraint bed, but it wasn't there.

She started to holler at the other staff people, "Where's the key? Where's the key?"

No one could remember. By the time Miz Max found the extra key, the fire had already worked its way through the mattress pad and singed Rosalind on her butt.

When Rosalind was in the restraint room, screaming about getting her butt burned, the other patients thought she was being tortured. They got real mad. The lesbian twins Betty and Barb picked up one of the sofas in the dayroom, and they used it like a battering ram. Broke out all the floor-to-ceiling windows. Glass went everywhere.

I guess it's lucky we're on the ground floor because about fifty patients climbed out through the broken windows and walked over jagged glass into the darkness outside. A lot of them ran into the hospital parking lot and just stood there—didn't know what they were supposed to do next. Some of them ran off to the woods. Some of them ran behind our building to the highway and flagged down passing cars.

"Com'on, Lucinda," I said, pulling at her hand. "We can get out now—you can go back to your kids."

I heard glass cracking under the patients' bare feet. A lot of them had their feet cut open, but they didn't seem to notice. There were little puddles of blood squishing around in the broken glass.

"Hurry up!" I said. "We have to go right now, this minute, before they can stop us. It's easy—follow right behind me. Step where I step."

Lucinda took my outstretched hand. She pulled me up short.

"No, can't go. Not this here way," she told me.

"Then which way do you want to go? This window's smashed all the way open. Right here in front of you. You can fit through it." Lucinda is a little on the heavy side (okay, obese), so I thought she was afraid she would have trouble climbing over the sill. "I'll help you," I told her. "This is your chance. You can go back home, back to Lucas and Sasha, like you always talked about. We can make it on the outside, if we're together."

Bedlam reigned. Staff members were blowing their whistles, screaming for order and trying to put the whole ward on lockdown. Someone, a patient, smashed out the lights on the ward. We were in total darkness, except for the moonlight. We could hear the tanker fire trucks responding to the fire alarm, sirens wailing.

"I means I can't go today. I ain't goin' go nowhere. They got bounty hunters. We gotta wait for another time. I ain't gonna go, and I ain't budging an inch."

And that was it. We held hands and fought our way back to our cots. We looked for Nora, but we couldn't find her. "She must have left. Do you think she left?" I asked Lucinda, panic-stricken.

"That young'un's like a sheep—she'd follow anyone anywhere."

"No! Not Nora. She'll never make it out there. She's just a baby. How'll she ever get back? What'll happen to her, all alone in the dark? What'll she do? How will she find food? Water? Who will take care of her?" I asked.

"They's gonna call out the bounty hunters. The bounty hunters got dogs. Hospital pay 'em six hundred dollars for every patient they bring back to this stinkhole. Bring 'em back in any shape, don't matter—they done gets their money, don't matter what the person looks like when they carry 'em back here."

"Are you saying like dead or alive? They can bring them back dead or alive?"

"More liken to be dead or raped. I heard stories, lots of stories. Them all true."

The bounty hunters rounded up most of the patients within the next few days. They did not bring back little Nora.

Chapter 17

Mattie

October 1976

Mattie and Sophia were on their way to eat lunch in the staff cafeteria when they stopped to read a flyer taped on a wall near the doorway.

"THE IMPORTANCE OF INTEGRITY IN OUR PROFESSIONAL LIVES" A LECTURE BY DR. GUY GRANT, PhD 2:00 P.M. FRIDAY, OCTOBER 15, IN THE WALKER AUDITORIUM

"Hey, that lecture's today. I'd like to go," Sophia said, placing her tray containing a healthy mix of salad and yogurt on a clean area of the lunch table. "How about you? Think you might be interested?"

Mattie sat down across from Sophia. Her tray was overloaded with the daily specials—lasagna and carrot cake. "I think what I need is a lecture on willpower," she said.

Sophia took a bite of her salad and looked across the table at Mattie. "Doesn't Dr. Guy look like Abe Lincoln, all tall and angular, with those beautiful brown eyes? The hospital's so smart to have hired him—he's a big asset to the Mental Health Management team."

Mattie laughed. "Wait. The fact that he looks like old Abe is *not* a plus in his favor. I don't think I can make it to the lecture. Sounds like you really want to go, though, right?"

"Right—you bet. Maybe I'll get a chance to talk to him afterward."

Later that afternoon, Mattie bumped into Sophia, who was on her way back from the lecture.

"How'd it go?" Mattie asked.

"Great! William was there—he said to tell you hi. He said he hoped you have had some luck in finding your mother. I told him, 'No, not yet.' Then I told him you're still looking."

"That's it? That's all he said?"

"Yep, that's all he said about you. But we talked more about Dr. Guy. William liked his lecture. I told him about Dr. Guy's latest book, *How to Maneuver through Moral Mazes.* Have you read it?"

"Not yet. Did you manage to finagle some time with Dr. Guy after his lecture?"

"No. Everyone was too crowded around him, but I think I've figured out a way," Sophia said.

"You do remember in orientation Caroline said any fraternizing with the MHM team is punishable by banishment to the night shift?" Mattie said.

"Doesn't apply to me. As a social worker, I only have to answer to our CEO, Mr. Carpenter, and I'm sure he couldn't care less. At the same time, I'm not keen on locking horns with crazy Caroline. Dr. Guy mentioned in his lecture this afternoon that he'll be out of his office all day tomorrow. He's going to give the same lecture to some new interns working over in Green. My plan is to sneak into his office and leave him my copy of a book about Alfred Adler. I'll stick a note in it with my phone number."

"What makes you think he likes Adler?" Mattie asked.

"He thinks he was one of the world's great psychotherapists, mentioned him several times in his lecture," Sophia said. "To tell the truth, Dr. Guy talking about Adler is the only thing I do remember. I sat there mesmerized. Spent the whole time staring at that beautiful man."

"Sophia, you'd really be taking a chance," Mattie said. "How are you going to pull that off without being seen? What if someone reports you?"

"I'll be quick. In and out before you know it."

"How about I cover for you? What's the worst that can happen?"

"For you, back to the night shift. Sure you're up for it?" Sophia asked.

"Yep. Sure am. And hey, that night shift wasn't so bad."

"Because of a certain former Dominican who works nights?"

Mattie laughed. "Maybe, maybe not."

"We need a plan," Sophia said.

"How about this. You let me know what time you're going to put the book on his desk, and I'll keep an eye on his office door. If Caroline walks by, I'll run over and tell her I need to talk to her privately in her office—that'll make her happy. She'll think I'm going to report someone. Then you'll have time to sneak out."

At 1:00 p.m. the following afternoon, Sophia alerted Mattie that she was ready to make her move. Mattie stood guard while Sophia stepped into the alcove that housed Dr. Guy's office. All quiet. She slid her master key into his locked office door and pushed it open. She waited a moment for her eyes to adjust to the semi-dark room before switching on the ceiling light.

Dr. Guy was sitting on the sofa on the left side of the room, directly under his laminated "Distinguished Psychologist Award." Millicent, a thirty-two-year-old schizophrenic patient, sat next to him munching on a Mars candy bar. She was totally naked. As soon as the light went on, Dr. Guy dropped his hands from Millicent's breasts.

He remained seated and stared at Sophia. His face was ashen. "I was doing therapy with her," he said.

Sophia gasped and stepped backward into the hallway. Mattie rushed over to her. "Sophia, talk to me. What's the matter? What's going on in there?"

"He's molesting Millicent. I saw him!"

Mattie stepped past Sophia and blasted into the office. She looked at Millicent, who was still sitting on the sofa, shivering and naked, flecks of chocolate stuck to her chin. Mattie could feel the rage welling up within her; it twisted in her stomach, churning, scorching. Her head pounded. Fury blinded her. She needed to stop him. Hurt him like he was hurting Millicent. Poor, mentally ill, childlike Millicent, who had enough to deal with. Now this warthog was bribing her with chocolate, touching her, violating her.

Mattie glanced at Dr. Guy's desk, which was located against the wall to the right of the door. There was a patient's metal chart lying on top of it with Millicent's name and room number on the front in bold letters. The pages detailed Millicent's life—years filled with heartache and isolation. It was the story of what crazy had done to her, what it had done to her family.

Mattie picked up the chart. She gripped it with both hands at the bottom, sandwiching the pages between the two heavy metal covers. It felt cool to her touch. She sensed an unknown force propelling her to where Dr. Guy sat, complacent, powerful, thinking he could get away with anything.

She held the chart close to her chest as she quickly squeezed between the sofa and the wall. She inched over until she was standing directly behind Dr. Guy, who was still facing forward on the sofa. Before he could move, before he could turn around, she raised the chart up high and smashed it down over his head with one ferocious blow. The edge of the metal hinge caught the side of his ear. His upper torso fell sideways, his head landing on the armrest. His eyes were wide with shock, and blood trickled down his face.

When Sophia heard Dr. Guy's loud groan, she rushed back into the office. She saw Mattie raise her arm again, bent on bringing the chart down on Dr. Guy's head for the second time. Sophia ran over and grabbed Mattie's arm. "Stop it, Mattie!" Sophia said. "Get control. You're going to kill him!"

"He deserves it. Look what he's making this poor schizophrenic girl do."

Sophia took the chart from her hands. "Take a deep breath. Let security handle it. They'll turn him over to the Milledgeville Police."

Millicent stood up and said in a faltering voice, "Dr. Guy told me if I let him do stuff, he'd send me home to my children."

Dr. Guy lifted himself back into a sitting position and wiped the blood off his ear with his hand. He pointed to the quivering Millicent.

"Don't listen to her. We all know she's schizophrenic. She's confused. She doesn't know what she's saying. It's all her fault."

"Dr. Guy—if I can even call you a doctor—this young woman is the victim. You are the perpetrator, and you'll have plenty of time to think about that while you rot in jail," Mattie said.

Sophia grabbed a Kleenex and wiped the chocolate from Millicent's face before retrieving her undergarments and rumpled blouse off the floor. "You *will* get to go home soon, Millicent, I promise you," Sophia said. "You're getting a little better every day. But Dr. Guy can't help you go home. Dr. Vine is your doctor. She's the only one who can write your discharge order."

Sophia helped Millicent get dressed, put her arm around her shoulder, and walked her back to her room. Mattie dashed back to the nurses' station and phoned hospital security and Dr. von Brimmer. Then she disappeared into the staff bathroom and feverishly scrubbed both her hands.

When Sophia got back to the nurses' station, she found Mattie rubbing Nivea Creme on her reddened skin. "I think we both could use a little refreshment," Sophia said. They walked down the hall to Sophia's office. Mattie made herself comfortable on the sofa while Sophia reached into her bottom right-hand desk drawer and brought out a bottle of Baileys Irish Cream. She poured each of them a small glass and sat down next to Mattie.

"What a prick Dr. Guy turned out to be," Sophia said. "I can't believe I ever thought he was so fantastic."

Mattie took a sip of her Baileys. "My nerves are shot—I guess I still have some anger issues," she said. "Thanks for grabbing the chart from me before I killed the bastard."

"Judging from the whack over the head you gave him, I'd say yes, you have some anger issues. Not that he didn't deserve it."

"I've been seeing Dr. von Brimmer. You might have noticed I wash my hands a lot."

Sophia nodded. "I noticed you go to the bathroom about ten times a day, but to tell the truth, I thought you had a weak bladder."

"Nope. Bladder's fine. I'm in there washing my hands. It's a form of compulsive disorder. Dr. von Brimmer thinks it's because of my time slopping the pigs—I never feel clean. Anxiety makes it worse. Now I can tell him I also have unresolved anger. It'll give us something else to work on besides my compulsions."

"How long have you been hanging on to all that anger? When did it start?"

"I first remember getting that angry when Wilson and I were sent to the farm. The farmer sent us to a rural country school near Dexter. I was in fourth grade; my brother, Wilson, was in first. He was brilliant, but because he couldn't, or wouldn't, speak, everyone treated him like he was an imbecile, even his teachers. At lunchtime, a bunch of the older kids at school used to form a ring around him, call him a retard, and poke at him with sticks to try to make him talk. Then it was time for me to charge in, fists flying, to rescue my little brother."

"That must have been hard," Sophia said, pouring them both another Baileys.

"The bullies cleared out, but they always came back. On the school bus, on the playground. There was no letup until Aunt Tess found us at the farm and brought us back to live with her in Savannah."

"Everybody's got something to work on. You have compulsive issues, and it looks like anger issues, but not to worry. I think you fall into the 'normal crazy' category."

"'Normal crazy'? Can there be such a thing?"

"Of course. You just want to be careful you don't step over the line."

"That's always been one of my fears—that I'll end up on the other side of the keys."

Sophia sipped her drink. "Not a chance. You're very grounded, stable for the most part. You know what you want out of life. Now let's talk about me—my favorite subject, as you might have noticed," she said, smiling brightly. "I have absolutely no judgment when it comes to men. I'll never find anyone—no soul mate for me. Or as Annie Able says, 'There's no lid for my pot.'"

"Well, Sophia, the good thing in all of this is that you caught Dr. Guy before he could hurt anyone else. He'll never get work in this field again. And there will be someone for you, Sophia. You just need to be patient."

Mattie awoke on Saturday, the first day of her weekend off, filled with a sense of dread. She had tossed and turned most of the night, nightmares of Dr. Guy invading her dreams.

To make matters worse, she couldn't shake her thoughts. *What if I never find my mother? What if she has to live out her years wandering around the hospital grounds like thousands of others, like an unloved, unwashed bag lady? Maybe I'll go see Aunt Tess. I know she'll give me a warm hug and some good advice. Just what I need.*

Sooner was overjoyed at the prospect of spending two days with Annie Able. "Be a good dog while I'm gone," Mattie told him. "Auntie Annie Able's going to make you some homemade doggie biscuits, and you might even get to lick the bowl."

On her drive to Savannah, gloomy, overcast skies turned to rain, echoing Mattie's inner turmoil. When she arrived at Aunt Tess's house, she found it still enveloped in the morning mist. The pink begonias and Moroccan ivy, which usually overflowed the wrought iron window boxes, had succumbed to the chilly October weather.

Mattie could smell the gingerbread as soon as she opened the front door. It was Aunt Tess's special recipe, used for those occasions of boyfriends acting badly or job layoffs. Apparently, being unable to find one's lost mother also qualified.

The smell drew her into the kitchen. After giving Mattie a warm hug, Aunt Tess added boiling water to the loose tea leaves she had measured into her antique silver teapot. She placed the teapot, along with cream and sugar, on a lace-covered serving tray. Next, she cut two pieces of gingerbread cake and placed them on her best Wedgwood dessert plates. She poured a generous amount of lemon sauce over each piece.

"Matilda, my dear, why don't you take the gingerbread into the living room and put it on the coffee table? I'll bring the tea. Come, Albert." Aunt Tess had named her obese English bulldog Albert after her late husband, whose ashes she had disposed of in the city garbage dump. While she was delighted to have seen the last of her loathsome husband, she was very fond of his replacement, who lived for her cooking.

Aunt Tess took a seat on the Chippendale sofa next to the fireplace. Albert plodded over and lowered himself—plop—onto the oriental carpet in front of her. "Since you mentioned on the phone you are distressed about your missing mother, our dear Heather, I thought this would be a perfect occasion for gingerbread cake and lemon sauce," Aunt Tess said. "For the gingerbread, I like to use fresh ginger. It makes all the difference."

Whenever Aunt Tess presented a favorite dish, she liked to discuss the ingredients she used, including the cooking or baking directions. Wilson and Mattie planned to write her recipes down someday and compile a book, but for now Mattie had to deal with other issues.

She eased down into one of the two wingback chairs opposite Aunt Tess and helped herself to a plate of gingerbread. "Just delicious," she said, allowing the slightly tart lemon sauce to rest on her tongue for an extra moment before swallowing. "It's the pièce de résistance."

Aunt Tess smoothed her wavy gray hair, making sure the bun she had positioned on the nape of her neck had no flyaway strands. She took her glasses off for a moment, blinked a couple of times, and peered at Mattie. "Oh dear, Matilda, you look exhausted," she said.

Mattie nodded. "I do feel exhausted. There was an incident at work—I caught our psychologist molesting a female patient."

"Oh, my, my, my. How absolutely terrible. I never dreamed such a thing could happen. By a psychologist, no less. That poor girl. I believe that's a criminal offense, and I hope he spends a long time in jail!"

"Yes, he will for sure. The hospital's lawyer, Mr. Vickers, is going to press charges on behalf of the patient. At first, I was angry, but then I found the whole thing very depressing. Being able to trust people is very important to me. But mostly I'm exhausted because I can't find my mother, Aunt Tess. She has to be living somewhere in the hospital, but I can't find her. I know she's there; I can feel it. I walk around the grounds every day after work, peering at every old lady I see, wondering if she could possibly be my lost mother."

"Your mother was—is—a lovely lady. Remember I told you and Wilson I met her once when I walked over to your house on Abercorn before you were born? Such a kind person. I wish I could say the same of my brother, Clive. But let's put that aside for now. I have an idea. Quite a good one, I think."

Mattie stopped eating her gingerbread and looked across the coffee table at Aunt Tess. "What is it?"

"My plan is a simple one—we could offer a reward. I have funds set aside that I received when Albert died. Luckily, he passed on before he could drink all our money away. And it's only fitting he should do some good from the grave. Heaven knows he did little good while he was alive."

Mattie studied her aunt's face. Smooth brow. Gentle, loving smile. "You'd do that for me, Aunt Tess? For Wilson and me?"

"Of course, that and so much more. Do you think a reward for information of, say, two hundred dollars would be enough?"

"Oh yes. For sure—that would be great! You know that old photo I have of her—the only photo—I can use that to make up a flyer with her date of birth and a description of her. Then I'll Xerox a bunch of copies."

"She might have gone a bit gray by now."

"You're right, Aunt Tess. Gladys told me her hair has turned gray, and it's kind of stringy. She said she's about my height, plump, and a little stooped over."

"Remind me again who Gladys is, my dear."

"She was the charge nurse on my unit until she started acting a bit crazy and got sent to Ward A in the Rivers building. When I visited Ward A, I met up with her. She told me she'd recently met a patient named Heather, but she hadn't seen her for a few days. The patients pretended they had no idea where Heather was or what had happened to her."

Aunt Tess nodded. "Of course. Gladys. Now I recall."

The front door slammed and Wilson charged into the room, his cheeks red from his run. "Saw your car in the drive, Sis. I'm leaving to go back to school tomorrow; glad I caught you. What's going on? Is the Crisis Stabilization Unit closing? Did you lose your job? Is everything okay?"

"Everything's fine," Mattie said. "The unit's going strong. Matter of fact, we've been open for two and a half months now, and we're constantly filled to capacity. Truth is, I was feeling a bit down about not being able to find our mother, but Aunt Tess just told me she's going to put up a reward for information. Two hundred dollars! Isn't that wonderful, Wilson? Now I'm sure something will turn up."

"Really Aunt Tess?" Wilson said. "That's very generous of you." Aunt Tess patted the sofa beside her. Wilson walked over, sat down, and picked up her hand. He held it for a moment before giving it a gentle kiss and placing it back in her lap.

Mattie flashed them a warm smile. "Yes, thank you, Aunt Tess, a million times over. Wilson and I will never be able to repay you for all you've done for us."

"Nonsense," Aunt Tess said. "Taking care of you both was one of the best things that ever happened to me. From the moment I laid eyes on you, everything in my life changed for the better—you managed to bring love and laughter into my house. I should be thanking you." She fingered the string of pearls that rested on the collar of her pale-blue sweater and paused to take a loving look at Mattie and Wilson before placing her hands back in her lap. "Now then, children," she said, "There's something I need to tell you."

"What is it, Aunt Tess? You look so worried," Mattie said.

"I hate to be the bearer of bad tidings, but some detectives came to the house last week. They told me your father's going to be spending a long time in the federal penitentiary in Atlanta."

"Oh no, Aunt Tess," Mattie said. "But why? What in the world did Father do? Do you know any more about it?"

Wilson got up from the sofa and paced back and forth in front of the fireplace. "I never expected anything like this," he said. "Where were the detectives from—the Savannah Police Department?"

"No, they were investigators from the Inspector General's Office. They told me the charge against Clive was for mail fraud. I hadn't had any word from him in quite a long time, and now I know why. And can you believe that Albert didn't even bark when the detectives rang the bell? He's supposed to be a watchdog, for goodness sake, and he didn't even wake up from his nap." Albert looked up at Aunt Tess.

"He heard his name, so he thinks it's time for a treat," she said, smiling down at her beloved, indulged pet.

"Do you know how long his sentence is?" Wilson asked.

"Yes, I thought it quite long. The judge sentenced him to twenty years, with two years off for good behavior."

"Eighteen years," Mattie said. "He'll be locked up for eighteen years." *Mother was committed eighteen years ago. Wow. Hard to believe. That's some mighty powerful karma.*

"But why did detectives come here, Aunt Tess? What did they want with you?"

"They were trying to find out if I knew his wife, a lady named Baby Bun. They told me they were doing a background check on her. They wanted to ascertain if she was involved in the crime in any way. I believe she was the same young lady Clive brought to dinner last July. I made jambalaya. For dessert I made key lime—"

"Did you just say Father's wife? He married Baby Bun?" Wilson said, his voice rising.

Aunt Tess reached up to touch her pearls. "Yes, and I thought it quite rude that he never invited us to the wedding. We are family, you know."

"Did they say any more about his crime? What kind of mail fraud? What did he do exactly?" Wilson asked.

"According to the investigators, Clive sent thousands of letters to people in three different states pleading for donations to help the poor souls who lost everything when hurricane Belle hit our coastline three months ago," Aunt Tess said. "He collected more than fifty thousand dollars, and can you believe, he spent all that money on himself and Baby Bun."

"Mail fraud," Wilson said. "Mail fraud. That's big. I think since President Ford declared Belle a natural disaster, it's called a federal crime. Stiff sentence."

"The detectives said he spent most of the money on gambling and fancy cars. Baby Bun was the one who called in an anonymous tip. The detectives knew it was her because they traced the call; it was made from their house."

"I bet he never knew Baby Bun turned him in," Wilson said. "If she was involved, if she had any knowledge of what Father was doing, I'm sure she covered her tracks. She'll be squeaky clean. And now, since she's his wife, she'll get to take over the Darling Dainties business."

"Yes, you're right, dear boy," Aunt Tess said. "The detectives told me she acted all innocent when she walked alongside Clive all the way up to the prison gates. Clive was yelling the whole time that he was innocent but, of course, no one believed him."

"I drove by that prison once; it's enclosed by a forty-foot wall," Mattie said. "Why do people do such things? He didn't need the money. I just don't understand it."

Aunt Tess's eyes became misty, and she brushed away a tear. "It pains me to say it, but your father was like that when we were children. He stole from the poor box at the Methodist church. He didn't need the money then either—he just wanted to prove he could do it."

"That's so sad," Mattie said. "What a wasted life."

"Now, let's not talk about this any longer," Aunt Tess said. "Let's enjoy our time together. Matilda, be a dear and go into the kitchen and cut your brother a big slice of my gingerbread. Give my boy some extra lemon sauce too."

"Of course, Aunt Tess," Mattie said. "Your gingerbread cake with lemon sauce always makes things seem a lot better."

Chapter 18

Mattie

October 1976

By late October, the silver maple trees on the hospital grounds had turned into a kaleidoscope of color. Brilliant orange, red, and yellow leaves fluttered to the ground or clung to the branches of the soon-to-be-dormant trees. The cooler weather energized Mattie. She spent long hours after she finished working tramping around the hospital, going from ward to ward, showing the photo of her mother and telling her story to whoever would stop and listen.

Mattie made out the assignments for the day shift each morning at work as soon as she finished listening to the night report. Following the report, Mark retrieved the four-shelved metal cart, full of the breakfast trays for the patients, from outside the locked CSU door where it had been parked by employees from Central Kitchen. When he pushed the cart down the hall to the solarium, hungry patients heard it rumble by their rooms and formed a line behind him. The sight reminded Mattie of the Pied Piper.

Mattie liked to eat with the patients whenever possible—it gave her a chance to interact with them. Before sitting down to eat, she helped Mark take the breakfast trays off the cart and distribute them to patients who were seated randomly at the round tables in the solarium —no assigned seats. When Mark and Mattie finished giving out the trays, they located the two trays on the cart marked "For Staff Breakfast" and carried them over to a table where patients sat eating. There were two empty spots. Mark asked the patients if it was okay to join them. Minimal mumbled response. Mark and Mattie each took a seat.

The patient to Mattie's right was thirty-seven-year-old Margaret D. She had been picked up three days ago by the police, babbling and incoherent, as she stumbled out of a bar in Milledgeville. Mattie watched her shovel a bagel, cereal, and a croissant into her mouth at a rapid pace, washing the food down with swigs of decaf coffee. Mattie stopped eating her oatmeal long enough to say, "Slow down a little, Margaret, so you don't choke."

Mattie turned to Harriet, who had been diagnosed with postpartum depression. Tears were running down her face. "Harriet, you need to eat at least five bites," Mattie told her. "After that, you can leave the table."

Elderly Mr. Collins was sitting to Mark's left. Mark knew from the way Mr. Collins's teeth were flapping they were not his own. "After breakfast, we have to find your *own* set of teeth, Mr. Collins. How'd you sleep last night?" Mr. Collins answered with a song, a very loud song: "The old wooden bucket; I couldn't help but fuck it."

Mattie struggled not to laugh. Mark was able to suppress a smile, but his eyes twinkled. "Not now, Mr. Collins," Mark said. "That song is not appropriate at the breakfast table."

Dave hurried into the solarium and walked over to where Mattie was sitting. "There's a patient waiting on you in the intake room. The tech from central admissions just walked her over." Mattie excused herself, got up from the table, and put her tray with the half-eaten oatmeal and toast on the cart before starting down the hall with Dave. "What's her name, Dave? Who came with her—any relatives?"

"Name's Marybelle S. Her husband came with her. His name is Geoffrey, and he's not one bit friendly."

Mattie gathered the necessary paperwork before heading to the intake room, a sparsely furnished eighteen-by-twenty-foot space with no windows—a holding tank of sorts. There was a round table in the middle of the room with four chairs circling it. The only décor was an acrylic painting of three white egrets taking flight across a coastal marsh at sunset.

As soon as Mattie opened the door, Marybelle stood up. Her wrinkled beige-linen pantsuit hung loosely on her bony frame. Worry lines marred her forehead, and newly shed tears were smeared on her cheeks. "What's going to happen to me?" Marybelle asked, her voice tremulous. "I've been here three times. *Three times.* I've had to leave my husband and little girls for weeks on end. Nothing works. I've tried, really tried, but it's a compulsion. I can't stop. None of the medications worked. Here, take a look." Marybelle pulled off one of her bright-yellow mittens. Her middle finger was oozing blood—she had chewed it halfway into the nail bed. There were little bits of yellow wool stuck to the wound.

"I see your point, Marybelle," Mattie said, trying to ignore her queasy stomach. "The minute we're finished here, we'll get a bandage on that wound."

Marybelle's husband, Geoffrey, who had been hovering nearby, took a step forward and stood next to his wife. He glared at Mattie. His teeth were clenched, his eyes narrowed. "I want my wife to get shock treatments," he said, his head bobbing as he spoke. "That's the only thing that'll cure her. Dr. Vine said she's got dermatophagia. That's why she chews her fingers. She needs some shock treatments. I'm sure they'll fix what's ailing her." He gave a phony ha ha and walked over to the far side of the room and stood, arms crossed, under the painting of the egrets.

After Marybelle signed the Voluntary Admission Form and completed the other paperwork, Mattie asked Geoffrey to wait in the intake room while she escorted Marybelle down the hall to the treatment room. Once there, Mattie did a body search and took her vital signs. She asked Marybelle to sit on the examination table while she bandaged her bloody fingers.

"I feel like I got to know you a little during your other admissions, Marybelle," Mattie said. "This time feels different. Your nails are much worse, and you've lost a lot of weight. Why don't you tell me what's going on—your husband seems so angry. Not like the last time you came. Are you having a lot of stress at home? Taking care of your two young daughters must be quite a challenge."

Mattie waited patiently while Marybelle looked down at the floor. A minute later, she raised her head and looked Mattie in the eye. "You're right," she said. "Geoffrey *is* furious with me. It's nothing to do with my girls—they are who keep me sane."

"And he's furious because…"

Marybelle's facial muscles relaxed. "It's a relief to tell someone," she said. "He's furious because I had an affair. A short affair. It started about two months ago. Geoffrey's mother, of all people, saw me in the passenger seat of a man's car—the man I was having the affair with. She followed us to the motel and, of course, she wasted no time in telling Geoffrey. I broke it off the next day, but I feel so bad. So guilty. That's why I didn't argue with him about getting shock treatments. He wants to punish me. I know that. But I figure it's a small price to pay for getting our marriage back together."

"Actually, it's a big price to pay, Marybelle. From what I've observed, only elderly people with severe depression get good results from ECT. You'll end up with a massive headache, short-term memory loss, and a lot of confusion. And your compulsion won't be any better. It might make Geoffrey feel like he's gotten even by punishing you, but it won't take away any of your guilt. What you need is a good therapist and a stress-free environment."

"Really? You don't think I should go through with it?"

"I can only say, if it were me, I'd run the other way. Maybe you can take your girls and go live with your mom for a while. Our social worker, Sophia, does private counseling. She'd be a great help to you."

Marybelle took Mattie's hands in hers and held on tight for a moment. "Thank you. I'll think it over. I'd better say goodbye to Geoffrey now. He's not a very patient person."

Mattie was delighted to see both Mark and Ben sitting in the break room when she went to eat her lunch. She loved talking to the techs. They spent most of each day working closely with the patients, and they usually had interesting insights into their behavior. She took a seat and spread her food out on the table—a tuna salad sandwich with

Velveeta cheese on Wonder Bread, a Hostess Twinkie, and a piece of pecan pie. "I'm starving. I didn't get to finish eating breakfast with the patients this morning because I went to do an admission on a new patient. Her name is Marybelle, and I remember her well—this is her third admission."

"Recidivism," Mark said, taking a big bite out of his ham on rye. "Three or more readmissions, and you call it recidivism."

Mattie nodded. She decided to start on her dessert first and popped half the Twinkie into her mouth.

"I feel kind of sick," Ben said.

"Sick, Ben? What kind of sick? Maybe you're coming down with the flu or something," Mattie said, licking her lips.

"Nope. Not that," Ben said. "I feel sick to my stomach because I saw Marybelle's fingers right before lunch. Now I can't eat the peanut butter and jelly sandwich my mom made me this morning. She used Jif, the crunchy kind—it's my favorite." He held up two smashed pieces of white bread glued together with a blob of peanut butter and jelly. The jelly dripped down the side. "See, I haven't even taken one bite."

"That's good peanut butter, Ben," Mark said, giving Ben a thumbs up. "You know the saying, 'Choosy mothers choose Jif.' Marybelle's fingers are gross, but I got used to gross stuff when I traveled in Australia. Our guide used to eat live insects, the crawling kind, for breakfast."

Ben pretended to poke his finger down his throat and made a fake gagging sound.

"I got a chance to read some of Marybelle's chart," Mark said, munching away at his sandwich. "Dr. Vine wrote in her progress notes that she's considering ECT. Looks like Marybelle's husband is pushing for it."

"Oh," Ben said. "My parents and I went to see *One Flew Over the Cuckoo's Nest* two months ago. It showed all about shock treatments."

"Well, it's really not quite that barbaric in real life, Ben," Mattie said. "Here's what usually happens: Gosia walks the patients who are scheduled for ECT over to Jones early in the morning. They have a special ECT room set aside. She starts the IV and attaches the electrodes to the patient's head. Then the anesthesiologist puts the patient to sleep before the treatment starts. They usually get a series of eight shocks on the following Mondays, Wednesdays, and Fridays."

"I was doing some research recently," Mark said. "I found out the only way to know if the electricity has surged through the patient's body is to look for the patient's toes to bend up and back to the top of the foot and for the toes to fan out."

"Right," Mattie said. "That's the Babinski reflex."

"A long time ago, back in the '50s, they didn't use any anesthesia," Mark said. "As soon as the doc pressed the ECT machine's on button, the patient shot up into the air. They looked like they were levitating."

"What does levitate mean?" Ben asked

"Means they defied gravity, like they were floating for a second. A lot of times, they came crashing back down on the bed so hard they broke their back or their legs. And, picture this, the electricity made their hair stand on end."

"No way!" Ben said.

"I wonder why her husband wants her to have ECT," Mark said. "He must think it's some magic cure for dermatophagia."

"What's that? I never heard of that," Ben said.

"That's her diagnosis," Mark said. "It's a compulsion to bite your skin."

"Marybelle's husband wants her to get ECT because he's furious at her for having an affair," Mattie said. "He was hurt, and he wants to hurt her back. I think he sees ECT as a fit punishment for her transgressions."

"You're kidding," Mark said.

"That's plain mean," Ben said. "My dad always says that if you do something mean, then something mean will happen back to you in the future."

Mark said, "Your dad was talking about karma, Ben. That's just how it works. Of course, we'll never know if karma gets Marybelle's husband. When she's discharged, we'll lose track of them both."

"The good news is I think Marybelle will refuse to sign the consent form," Mattie told the techs. "Then there's nothing anyone can do to make her go through with it. I told her it would be helpful to get out of her stressful situation and get into some individual therapy with Sophia."

"That sounds like a good idea, Mattie," Mark said. "I can't believe there are people like her husband in this world who seek to harm another person for their own gratification."

"I can believe it," Mattie said. "But I wish I couldn't."

After lunch, Mark and Ben went to spend time with the patients. Mattie joined Gosia in the nurses' station, where a pharmacist from Jones was discussing the side effects of a new medication, the benzodiazepine called clonazepam.

Dave rushed up to where they were standing. "Sorry to interrupt," he said, "but I need to tell Mattie something." He turned to Mattie and wrung his hands. "Mattie, you won't believe what I just saw! I have to tell you. You'll never believe it. Guess, just guess."

Gosia glared at him and put her hands on her hips. "We listen about new drug now. Better for you to talk later."

Mattie told Dave she would meet him in ten minutes in the break room. When she arrived, Dave was sitting at the table in front of a plate piled high with chocolate chip cookies. He was arranging them into little stacks, each stack three cookies high. He waited for Mattie to sit down next to him, eager to build suspense. "Here, try one of these cookies," he said. "They're yummy—I made them myself."

"Thanks, Dave, but I'm not hungry now."

"Well, are you ready for some news? I saw Bernard in the woods this morning. He was with Caroline. I didn't realize he's such a thin dude till I saw his legs poking out from behind a big oak tree."

"His legs were poking out behind a tree? You're talking about the Director of Mental Health Management Bernard Bellini?"

"Yes. Him. Bernard. He's way too thin. He should stop jogging so much and eat some carbs. I could make him one of my whipped cream and meringue Pavlovas—my creation won second place in the Baldwin County Fair last year."

"Tell me again—where did you say you saw Bernard and Caroline?"

"I saw them out in the woods, not too far from the old cemetery.

And..." He repeated the word twice. "And..." Dramatic pause. He leaned over toward Mattie and whispered, "They were doing *it*."

"*It*? No, you must be kidding."

"*It*," he said, beaming. "You know, *it*. Bernard and Caroline."

"That's unbelievable. I thought Caroline hated the MHM team. She told the staff not to dare to fraternize with them. Are you sure of what you saw?"

"Yep, I'm sure. I saw part of a plaid blanket and Bernard was on top of—"

"That's okay, Dave. I don't want those details to get lodged in my psyche, or else every time I see Caroline that's all I'll picture. What I need to know is what time of day was it, and what you were doing in the woods."

"I went outside around eleven o'clock to check on Barbara Anne," Dave said. "She had two teenage friends visit her yesterday, and I saw the three of them huddled together in a corner of the solarium, like they were up to something. After that, she asked Dr. Vine to give her a grounds pass so she could walk around outside and get some exercise. But I figured one of her friends had snuck in some weed, and she was going to go have a smoke in the woods."

"Keep going, Dave. What happened next?"

"I peeked around the tree to make sure it was them, then I turned around and left. I really like Caroline's toenail polish—I think it's called Mighty Red Tomato."

"Do you think they saw you?"

"Nope. They were totally concentrating. No one usually goes near that area. There are ghosts in the cemetery. I just happened to be there because I was looking for Barbara Anne."

"Dave, you do realize there aren't any ghosts in the cemetery, despite what you may have heard from other people, right?"

"*Maybe* not any ghosts, but that place is very spooky."

Mattie said, "We have to keep this between us. We'll agree to keep this quiet for now. Okay?"

Dave put his index finger up to his lips. "Yeah, quiet. We should keep quiet."

"And did you find Barbara Anne?" Mattie asked.

"She wasn't even in the woods—she was walking around in the rose garden. I asked Pam to do a body search after Barbara Anne got back inside. Pam said Barbara Anne was clean. I did a room search but nothing turned up."

"Excellent job, Dave. You're very observant, and you have a good rapport with the patients."

"Does that mean I can have a raise?"

Mattie laughed. "Nice try, Dave. I just approved you for a raise two weeks ago. Surely you haven't forgotten already. Now isn't it time for you to make your rounds?"

Mattie found Sophia in the hallway by the solarium, talking to an autistic twelve-year-old female who was admitted for chasing her mother around their dining-room table with a butcher knife. Mattie walked over to where Sophia was standing and took her aside for a moment. "When you're done, can you meet me in the conference room?" she asked in a low voice. "I need to tell you something in private."

Mattie waited for Sophia in the empty conference room. Sophia arrived about five minutes later.

"You'll never believe what Dave just told me," Mattie said as soon as Sophia stepped inside and closed the door.

"What? Did something happen? Tell me, what's going on?"

"He told me he saw Caroline and Bernard together in the woods this morning."

"Together? Were they making out?"

"Well, according to Dave they were doing more than making out."

"More? Dave saw them?"

"Yep. Behind a big oak tree. He said, and I quote, 'They were doing it.'"

"No, you must be kidding!"

"That's exactly what I said!"

Sophia pulled out one of the conference room chairs and took a seat. Mattie sat down next to her.

Sophia turned and looked at Mattie. "I've been meaning to tell you, I've got *my* eye on Bernard. But you mustn't say a word, okay?"

"Uh, I was just telling you, Caroline's already got Bernard,"

Mattie said. "The woods, remember? Anyway, he's way too thin for you. Shakespeare said to beware of a man with a lean and hungry look."

"Shakespeare's dead," Sophia said, grinning. "That doesn't apply in today's world. Lean means sexy. I think Caroline's ego's bruised because of the radiologist. I heard he ran off with the X-ray tech from Jones."

"But the X-ray tech's a male."

"Apparently he swings both ways. Caroline wants a temporary fix. Obviously, she and Bernard have a physical thing. She probably flashed him and he was mush. I want the whole package: Bernard, big house, three kids. I've decided I like the fact he was ingenious enough to create a firm like MHM all by himself. Important image. Smart, sophisticated, assertive and—"

"You've forgotten one small thing—the guy's married," Mattie said.

"Nope, not anymore. I heard he filed for divorce," Sophia said. "I know he uses people, and he's manipulative. But I can change him. Give me a couple of months and he'll be a whole new man. Gentle and caring."

"You know, you can *never* change another person. You can only change yourself."

"That mantra's for other people; I'm giving it a try."

Mattie nodded. She decided to change the subject. "By the way, how did Alex do in your cognitive group this morning? I'm still concerned about him. Even though Dr. von Brimmer doesn't think he's dangerous, I certainly do."

"Alex talked a lot about Vietnam," Sophia said. "He said at night the Vietcong would sneak into the American camps, plant booby traps, and escape through a bunch of underground tunnels. The mission of Alex's platoon was to track the Vietcong through the jungle. He said the whole time they were afraid they were going to get ambushed and stabbed to death."

"Do you believe his account?" Mattie asked. "Could be all fantasy. He tells lots of stories."

"Actually, I do," Sophia said. "He almost lost it when he was talking about getting ambushed by the Vietcong. He was shaking all over."

"Well," Mattie said, "that kind of experience could account for Alex's aggressive behavior. In report this morning, the night nurse, Nancy, told us Alex was kicking the wall in the solarium around 2:00 a.m. for no reason. He stopped when William and Peter confronted him. He might not be crazy, but he sure is angry."

"I talked to Dr. von Brimmer briefly yesterday," Sophia said. "I asked him when he plans to discharge Alex. He told me he thought everyone was overreacting, and he has no plan to release him anytime soon."

That afternoon, Mattie notified each staff member on duty they needed to go to the conference room at 2:00 p.m. for an urgent meeting. After everyone arrived, she asked them to take a seat around the long table—she and Sophia had something important to discuss with them.

Once everyone was seated, Mattie began. "I want to let you know a half hour ago Alex signed a Five Day Release Form. All of you realize what that means: he wants to leave and he's adamant about it."

"You mean that after his five days are over, he'll get to walk off the unit, just walk out the door?" Ben asked.

Sophia said, "Not exactly. It doesn't mean he can walk out, free as a bird, in five days. Five business days, that is. Dr. von Brimmer wants Alex to remain on the unit and get treatment. However, Alex is determined to leave right away, and that's why he's signed a Five Day Release Form. It means in five days Alex will have a court hearing in front of a judge."

"Do we have to take him to the Baldwin County Courthouse in town for the hearing?" Dave asked.

"No," Sophia said. "The judge will come here to the Crisis Unit to hear the case. As soon as the proceedings are over, that same day, he'll make the decision as to whether Alex stays or goes. If Alex can show the judge he's normal, the judge will order him to be discharged immediately. But if Alex can't show he's normal, the judge can commit him for up to ninety days. If that happens, his status will change from voluntary to involuntary."

"How does that impact the staff?" Mark asked.

"Alex might be afraid the court hearing won't go his way, so he might try to elope before it happens," Sophia said.

"I'd like to see him gone, but we want to do it the right way," Mattie said. "It's our job to make sure he doesn't leave the unit before his case is heard. I'm wondering if the judge will decide if he is mentally ill or just—"

"Or just an angry guy?" Mark asked. "I'd vote for that."

"Bottom line here is that all of us need to be on the lookout for Alex trying to elope," Mattie said. She decided not to share her suspicion that Alex might have murdered Darryl, but she wanted everyone to know he was potentially dangerous. "If you see him hovering by the doorway, looking like he's going to make a run for it the next time the door is unlocked, call security right away. Remember, Alex fought in Vietnam, and he has a lot of leftover anger in him. Don't take any chances."

When the meeting was over, Mattie returned to the nurses' station. She sat down to write a narrative report on Alex's chart regarding his aggressive behavior at breakfast that morning. Alex had taken Mr. Collins's bowl of oatmeal off his tray and thrown it on the floor. Plastic bowl, no one was hurt, but Alex had had no provocation. His volatile behavior was upsetting the other patients.

The following day at work, Mattie and Sophia made plans to go to the staff cafeteria for their three-dollar Friday special lunch: meatloaf and gravy, mashed potatoes, green beans, and peach cobbler for dessert. As soon as they walked off the unit, Sophia turned to Mattie. "Guess what? Bernard phoned me last evening and invited me to go to the American Conference of Hospital Managers in Aspen next week."

"I'm happy if you're happy, but what if Caroline finds out?" Mattie said. "She's crazy about Bernard—she's been following him around like a lovesick puppy. Remember how Dave said she met up with him in the woods? And Caroline told me that she and Bernard are having a private meeting this afternoon in his office to discuss the unit finances."

"Caroline's definitely going to find out," Sophia said as they headed toward the cafeteria. "Today, as a matter of fact. Their meeting this afternoon is *not* going to be about finances. Bernard told me on the phone last night that he's going to tell her that their little affair is over. Done. Kaput."

"Well, good luck to him on that," Mattie said. "I have a feeling she won't be too thrilled."

"You're right—she'll probably have a conniption fit."

When Mattie and Sophia returned from lunch, there were two more admissions waiting to be processed. By early afternoon, every bed on the unit was occupied. The staff stayed busy making rounds, conducting groups, and generally keeping order. Mattie passed Sophia in the hall. "I forgot to ask you what day you and Bernard are leaving on your ski trip."

"We're leaving this Saturday," Sophia said. "I'll have Bernard all to myself for one whole week. I'll get in some skiing while he goes to his lectures during the day, and in the evenings, we'll be able to relax in front of the fireplace in our suite. I'll tell you all about it when I get back."

"Very romantic," Mattie said. "I'd better go. I'm a woman on a mission. I need to find Dave and ask him to spend some time with Mr. Collins."

"I saw you've confined Mr. Collins to his wheelchair," Sophia said. "That should slow him down a bit. Has he been sneaking into the other patients' rooms again, trying on their teeth?"

"Even worse," Mattie said. "Dave told me he had to fish Mr. Collins's own set of choppers out of his toilet bowl this morning. Dave helped me get a restraint jacket on him so he can't tip his wheelchair over. His dementia's getting worse; he's not orientated to person, place, or thing."

"When you do find Dave, you might want to mention our Mr. Collins is in bad need of a diaper change," Sophia said.

"Will do."

As Mattie continued toward the solarium at the far end of the hall, she peeked into various patients' rooms thinking Dave might be in one of them. No Dave. She passed Mr. Collins sitting in his wheelchair in the hallway near Caroline's office. His chin was resting on his chest, and he was half asleep. *Sophia's right. Poor Mr. Collins is in definite need of a diaper change.*

Mattie found Dave in the solarium where he was watering the remains of a golden pothos climbing plant. Earlier in the day, one of the teenage patients had broken off three of the eight-foot-long vines from the center post, braided them together, and used them as a jump rope.

Dave listened attentively while Mattie explained the Mr. Collins diaper dilemma. He said he'd be happy to help; he was very fond of Mr. Collins. On her way out of the solarium, Mattie noticed Caroline entering the unit through the rear door. *I don't believe this—our supervisor using her master key to sneak onto the unit. That door is only supposed to be used to evacuate he patients in case of a fire. I bet she just left her meeting with Bernard.*

Even though Caroline had her head lowered when she scooted past her, Mattie could see her facial muscles were taut, her eyes were bloodshot, and tears dripped down her cheeks. She charged toward her office, passing Mr. Collins in the hallway still half-asleep in his wheelchair. After sniffing the air a few times, she gave him a big heave-ho, causing his wheelchair to careen erratically down the hallway. She opened the door to her office, stormed in, and slammed it shut.

Mattie rushed over to Mr. Collins and grabbed his wheelchair before it hit a wall. She pushed him to a quiet spot in the solarium and patted his shoulder, aware he was unable to comprehend a word she said. She glanced around to make sure they were alone before speaking. "You must excuse Caroline's behavior, Mr. Collins. I think she just found out she's not the one who's going to be taking a trip to Aspen with Bernard Bellini. It looks like she's not taking the news very well. Between you and me, Mr. Collins, I think Bernard's a real bastard."

Chapter 19

Heather

October 31, 1976
Rivers Building, Ward A
Milledgeville Central State Hospital

Today is Halloween. Said so on my calendar—last day of October. No one mentions Halloween here. They think we have enough scary things going on in our brains without that. The leaves are changing color outside; I can see them through the windows. If you stare out the windows too long, you'll get medicated for being in a "fugue state." That's some mental condition they thought up.

Studying the red-and-orange leaves made me think about the last Halloween I spent with Wilson and Matilda. Wilson wanted to be a train engineer, so I made him a little costume—an apron with gray-and-black stripes, and a matching cap with a train logo on the front. My Matilda was a ghost—white sheet with the eyeholes cut out. I haven't held a pair of scissors in eighteen years.

I saw Dr. von Brimmer again today. He had my chart on his desk and was thumbing through it when I shuffled into his office. Bruno waited for me outside. You can't go anywhere without an escort, like they think you're going to try to make a run for it. The doc said, "How are you today, Heather?" I responded by muttering, head down.

One thing I've learned over the years is how to play stupid. Stupid is a safe place. Hear no evil, etc. The only way to survive. People assume you're not all there if you put your head down and talk to yourself. Works every time. It helps to spit on the floor once in a while, too. Shows you have no social conscience. Try not to get it on your shoes, though. I've taught a couple of my friends on the ward this trick.

Dr. von Brimmer put my chart down and looked at me. "I want to recommend you be transferred to another ward. One with some activities you can do to keep busy. You'll get more time outside. Would you like that?"

I told him no. Said I was okay where I was.

"I need you to talk to me, Heather. Tell me about the time Clive came to visit."

I wanted to tell him if he was so interested, he could read about it on my chart. I decided to stay silent.

"Heather, you need to trust me. Tell me what happened." Cajoling. Persuasive.

I snuck a look at him. He was sitting behind his big-ass desk, toying with my chart, toying with my life. I'm in this straight-backed chair like a little schoolkid in front of him.

I mumbled that I didn't feel like talking.

"I need you to take your hand away from your mouth so I can understand you," he said. "Please repeat what you said."

"I don't wanna go anywhere," I said.

He looked at me a moment too long. Next thing I knew he was up and out from behind his desk. He pointed to the brown leather sofa on the far wall. It looked all Freudian-like.

Not on your life. No sofa, no analysis, no sharing.

He walked around to where I sat, took my hand, and walked me over to the sofa. I sat down. He pulled a straight-backed wooden chair right in front of me, sat in it facing me.

"You don't have to lie down," he said. "I just want you to sit here and talk to me."

"What about?"

"Okay. I've played your game of stupid long enough. I know that you know how to hold a conversation. You know a lot of things; one of them is how to act dim-witted. You learned how from the patients on the ward, right? Am I on the right track?"

I took my time, fingered the brown leather. It was like alligator skin—rough and worn in places, smooth as a baby's skin in others. Baby skin. Wilson's baby skin. Bubbles in the little tub. Splashing. Rubber ducky.

I looked him in the eye and said, "Okay, Doc. Yes, you guessed it. I *can* hold a conversation. I can also recite the Gettysburg Address, tell you there are 5,280 feet in a mile. You want to hear the periodic table? Want to hear me count backward from a hundred by sevens? Would that make you happy?"

"You sound angry, Heather." Always the shrink. Repeat the obvious.

"Yeah, angry." I got up from the designated seating arrangement and paced around the room. "Angry? *Angry?* Yes, when I bother to feel anything."

"And where does that anger come from?"

"In the first place, I don't know anything that's going on in the world. Who's the president? What's happened to America while I've been in here?"

"There's a Republican president in the White House now; his name's Gerald Ford. We can talk politics next session if you like, but today I want you to tell me about Clive. I know he dropped you off here in 1958; it's on your chart. There's a record of your admission and a detailed account of how you were detained. What I don't understand is why you chose to remain silent all these years, take on a mental patient's personality, instead of trying to convince the staff you were okay. I have a feeling it had something to do with Clive's visit. Let's see, he had you committed May 15, 1958, and his first and only visit was in December of that year. What happened when he came to see you?"

I sat back down on the leather sofa. He leaned toward me in his chair like he cared or something. I have a hard time when people are nice to me. Do okay when they are distant or hateful—that puts my back up. I get angry and I can cope. Kindness makes me vulnerable. Like I want to cry. Criers don't survive. Better to stay angry.

I decided to get this over, give Dr. B. what he wanted so I could head back to my ward. I wanted to talk to Lucinda. Ask her why she thought the doc was playing with my mind. Maybe he was doing a case study on me. Going to write me up in some psychiatric journal: "Patient Survives Eighteen Years in Regressed Mental Ward by Playing Dumb."

Pacing helped. If I was going to spill my guts, I needed to pace. I got up and walked over to his bookcase, turned around, and looked back at where he sat.

"Clive? You want to know about Clive? He came one day, just like it says on my chart. It was a couple of months after I bit the attendant. The staff had made it clear there was no discharge in sight for me. Bruno told me I had a visitor. I had never had a visitor, not one, since I was committed. I looked a little disheveled, my hair was thinning—probably from a lack of vitamins, or maybe I was getting alopecia from the stress, I don't know. Anyway, I allowed myself to get excited. Lucinda combed my hair and lent me a brooch she had stolen from a visitor. I remember it had little amber stones shaped in the form of a butterfly. Wings, it had wings. That's how I felt that day. Like I had wings; like I could fly. A visitor. Some of the patients gathered round, wished me well. 'Who is it? Maybe someone from your church.'"

"'Maybe,' I told them. 'Maybe.'

"Bruno, God bless him, he must have sensed something was wrong. He told me not to fret if things didn't turn out the way I was expecting. 'Nonsense, Bruno,' I said. 'I have a visitor. My first. What could go wrong with that?'"

Dr. von Brimmer nodded and said, "Go on." He's a good listener, but then he's trained to be. He didn't try to take notes or anything, just sat there and listened. I braced myself for what I was going to say to him.

"My visitor was waiting in the closet-like place the visitors use," I told him. "They don't need much space, because like I said, there are never many of them. Bruno asked me if he could come into the room with me. I told him okay. When we opened the door, there he was, Clive, that bastard who dumped me in this place. Bruno put his hand on my shoulder to steady me. For a minute I thought Clive had come to say he was sorry. He was going to tell everyone it was a big mistake; he was going to figure out a way so as I could go back home to my kids. 'I have some bad news to tell you, my dear,' he said.

"A million scenarios went through my mind, like when you're drowning, I guess. I asked him, 'What bad news? Are Matilda and Wilson okay? Are they hurt?'

"'The bad news is that the kids are dead,' Clive said. 'Our house burned to the ground. Looks like Matilda was using the stove,' he told me. Still it didn't register. 'Dead?' I repeated. 'Matilda using the stove?'

"'Yep, proper little housewife, just like her momma. The firefighters said she was trying to cook dinner for her little brother.' Those were his exact words.

"'Cook dinner for Wilson? She was cooking dinner for Wilson?'" I tried to process what he was telling me.

"Then it came to me. Dead. Both dead. All I lived for—to get out, to be with my kids. Make them brush their teeth at night, give them hugs, ask 'How was school today?' Gone. No more. Even if I got out of this hellhole, they wouldn't be there. They were gone.

"How could I mourn my babies if I couldn't see their graves? When they put Matilda in her coffin, was she wearing her white pinafore? The one with the lace around the bottom. And little Wilson. In the ground? I had Wilson's bear, but nothing of my darling girl. I wanted a bow from her hair. How could I mourn my baby girl if I had nothing of hers to hold?

"I remember Clive told me they died of smoke inhalation. He shoved some papers at me and told me to sign so he could collect insurance money on the house. He said, 'If you're too insane to sign, I'm going to sign them for you.'

"Bruno got real upset when Clive said that. He told Clive to look at what he'd done to me. Said there was no way I could sign any papers. Then he told Clive he'd better be leaving. Let me rest. Bruno asked Clive if he was sure about the young'uns. He said, 'Them's both dead? You see their little dead bodies?'

"I screamed, 'Noooooo,' and rushed, head down, at Clive, the force of my body shoving him up against the wall. I tried to scratch his face, claw it. Screamed more. 'Why was Matilda cooking? Why were they home alone? Where were you? Why weren't you taking care of them? You bastard, you bastard.'

"Bruno pulled me off. I think Clive left then. I collapsed on the floor. Bruno must have helped me back to the ward. I remember Lucinda handed me Brownie Bear, and I crawled onto my cot. The patients all came by and stood by my bed. Bruno started to sing 'Swing Low, Sweet Chariot.' Only the chariot wasn't coming to carry me home. It carried my babies home. How could I live without them?

"The patients hummed while Bruno sang; his voice carried over the whole dormitory. Even the staff stopped to listen. It was as mournful a song as I'd ever heard. Everyone just stood there, circling my bed. Grieved with me, for me. Like my loss was their loss—I covered up my head and sobbed.

"The patients, they came to see me every chance they got, taking turns, giving me little tokens. Big Bertha pretended to swallow her pill, but she cheeked it instead—took it back out of her mouth when no one was looking. She gave it to me so I could rest. I remember Thelma Jean brought me a red-and-white piece of peppermint hard candy she stole from a staff member.

"After about two weeks or so, Maxine came and sat by my bed, took my hand. 'We're your family now, Heather,' she said. 'All of us. Everyone here.'"

"'You'll be my family?' I asked her."

"'Right,' Maxine said, patting my head like I was an infant. 'And I'll pray for the day to come when you'll stop grieving. I'll pray for you to find peace,' she told me."

"'I'll never leave here, Maxine,' I said. 'There's nothing for me in the outside world. My children are gone, my house is gone. This will be my home forever.' She made me eat some soup she brought from home. That's all I remember."

I stopped pacing and sat back down on the sofa. Dr. B. handed me a clean linen handkerchief from his pocket, all ironed and folded neatly.

It had been a long time since I had held a linen handkerchief. I didn't want to blow my nose on it.

"Go ahead—you can keep it; it's yours," he said.

Mine. All mine. Good. I figured I would wash it and give it to Lucinda. She would be able to use it to trade for some trinkets.

Dr. von Brimmer got up and walked over to his desk, picked up his prescription pad, wrote something, put the pad down.

I sat there coming to grips with my memories. Trying not to be so vulnerable. Trying to get that chip back on my shoulder.

The doc walked over to the door, opened it, and told Bruno I was ready to go back.

"And please ask the nurses to start Heather on this new prescription," he said, handing Bruno a piece of paper.

"Let's see what new pills the nice doctor done ordered for yous," Bruno said as he walked me back toward the ward.

He unfolded the prescription note and read it out loud. "One set of front teeth for Heather McAllister. Please ask the dentist to send the bill to me. Signed: Dr. von Brimmer."

"Just you looky here at this. That there doctor just ordered yous a new set of front teeth. You's gonna get your teeth back, and the doctor, him's gonna pay for 'em. Can you rightly believe that?"

I could not.

Chapter 20

Mattie

October 1976

Mattie looked forward to the fourth Wednesday of each month when a prominent psychiatrist would attend one of the weekly staff meetings and give a lecture on modern psychiatric practices. As the Director of Mental Health Management, Bernardo Bellini, or Bernard as he liked to be called, believed it was his place to introduce the speaker. He used the occasion to tell his captive audience what a good job he was doing managing the CSU.

Bernard made no secret of his goal to constantly keep the unit filled to capacity with patients in crisis. A full unit meant job security for Bernard. No patients, no job. Bernard made a point of wooing the local doctors, encouraging them to admit their mentally ill patients to the unit. It was rumored he offered them two-night stays in swank Atlanta hotels, female escorts included, if they would admit three patients a month.

On Wednesday, October 27, the monthly psychiatrist's lecture was scheduled to take place at 10:00 a.m. in the solarium. When the Walker building was constructed in 1860, the space now called the solarium, was a dormitory, known as Ward G, home to ninety psychotic male patients. Now, as part of the new CSU, the large solarium did double duty: it was the room where the current patients ate their meals and the room where the staff meetings were held.

During the period when Ward G was being repurposed into a solarium for the CSU, the extensive expanse of windows was scoured to remove years of grime, and now an abundance of light shone into the room. The wide pine floorboards, installed by slaves, had been milled from the heart of hundred-foot-tall yellow longleaf pines, growing rampant in forests spread out across southeast Georgia at the time. The floor had been given a new life with a good scrubbing and an application of linseed oil.

An old storage room at the far end of the solarium, which had previously held equipment for Ward G, had been cleaned out and remodeled into a small kitchen, containing a sink and refrigerator, holding juice, milk, and ice cream for the patients. The door was fitted with a lock to prevent patients from wandering in and helping themselves.

At 8:30 a.m., Mattie walked down the hall to the solarium to check in with Ben and Dave and make sure everything was ready for the lecture. She found them moving about between the tables, encouraging some dawdling, depressed patients to finish their oatmeal, toast, and scrambled eggs.

Mattie nodded to the techs. "When you're done helping the patients with breakfast, can you move the tables to one side and set up the folding chairs for the lecture?" she said.

Five minutes before the meeting was scheduled to start, most of the staff had taken their seats. Mattie found an empty aisle chair in the second row. As soon as she sat down, she saw Bernard enter the room and walk up to the podium. He was wearing a dark-gray gabardine suit with a black shirt. The suit drooped over his tall, thin frame. He ran his right hand through his black hair, which looked as if it had been doused with olive oil.

A few minutes later, Caroline rushed into the room. She barreled her way down the first row of chairs, stepping on several peoples' toes as she went, heading for Ben's seat in the middle of the row. When she got there, she leaned down and mouthed, "Move!" After Ben obeyed her command, she seated herself in his empty chair, a few feet away from the podium where Bernard stood looking out over his audience.

Mattie smiled to herself as soon as she saw the internationally renowned adolescent psychiatrist, Dr. Lovett, walk into the solarium. *He looks like he's about to go sailing*, she thought. He was wearing a navy-blue sportscoat with gold embossed buttons, a white cotton turtleneck, and spotless white pants. Mattie took in his square jaw, high forehead, and slightly lopsided smile. Judging from the way his hair was starting to gray at the temples, she guessed his age around forty. Plus, she knew he was wearing bifocals—she could see the horizontal line.

Dr. Lovett strolled over to the podium and shook hands with Bernard. "Welcome, Dr. Lovett," Bernard said. "Our staff is looking forward to your insight into how to handle troubled, acting-out adolescents. We're hoping you'll have time for questions and—" Bernard stopped mid-sentence. He'd caught sight of the lovely Sophia, who sat in a center seat in the fourth row. He acknowledged her with a wink before continuing his introduction.

"I know you'll want to pay close attention to what Dr. Lovett has to say," Bernard told the staff. "He's discovered a revolutionary new method of treatment for adolescents. If you'll excuse me now, I'm afraid I have another meeting I must attend."

Mattie's attention was drawn toward a commotion in the middle of the first row. She watched Caroline jump out of her seat, knock over an empty chair, right it, and continue on her way—hot on the trail of the disappearing Bernard.

As soon as Bernard left the solarium, Dr. Lovett walked away from the podium and over to the kitchen. He stood in front of the door for a moment before asking Dave, who was standing nearby, to open it with his key. Dave complied. Dr. Lovett stepped into the kitchen. The audience craned their necks to see what he was doing. *Maybe he's thirsty*, Mattie thought. *Maybe he's planning to help himself to some of the patients' orange juice.* But when he pushed a patient out of the small room in a wheelchair, Mattie and the rest of the staff gave a collective gasp.

After this dramatic reemergence from the kitchen, Mattie watched Dr. Lovett propel his patient to the front of the podium. He gave her wheelchair a tap with his foot. Jana's head didn't move—it was permanently fixed in the facedown position, her neck muscles atrophied from years of staring at the ground.

"This is sixteen-year-old Jana W.," Dr. Lovett said, turning her wheelchair so his audience could view her posture from the side. "What happened to this poor young girl, you wonder? Was she in an auto accident? Was she born like this? No! What you see here is the result of poor parenting. So, what does she need? Reparenting. She needs reparenting," he said, pausing long enough to let his words sink in. "Now I'm going to tell you some of her history. Bear with me—you need to know at least part of it if you're going to be able to help her.

"Jana was ten when her mother, Beverly, married Suehail, a wealthy businessman from Beirut, Lebanon. He disliked Jana on sight, and he wasted no time enrolling her in boarding school. On her first night away from home, Jana wet the bed, a practice that the school would not tolerate. 'We will find another school,' Suehail told Beverly. 'She will soon outgrow her enuresis.'

"A series of boarding schools began. Jana was enrolled, Jana wet her bed, Jana was sent home. After some searching, Suehail found an expensive alternative school for disturbed adolescents in the Colorado mountains. The staff put Jana in a wheelchair, pushed her into the dining room, and told her she could not leave until she ate her lunch. Jana refused. They left her sitting in front of her food until it was time for her next meal. She refused that meal also and every meal after that.

"Eventually, one of the doctors on the staff inserted a gastrostomy tube into her stomach, and the staff poured pureed food down it three times a day. They still kept Jana in a wheelchair; they tied her to it, in fact. Not that she tried to get up. She spent her days hunched over, staring at the floor. That is the reason her head is now in this position." Dr. Lovett circled Jana's chair and pointed to her neck. "As you can see, her muscles will no longer hold her head up. Her head is frozen in this downward position."

Mattie raised her hand. "Dr. Lovett, I was wondering if Jana's mother ever went to visit her. She must have missed her mom a lot, don't you think?"

"Yes, of course. Mothers and daughters belong together. But

Beverly is not a strong woman, and her husband has forbidden her to see Jana. Told her it's for Jana's own good. Last week Suehail insisted that Beverly sign full custody of her daughter over to me.

"Now if no one else has a question, we will proceed to reparent Jana. Our goal is to make her feel loved and secure. We want her to thrive just like she would have done if she'd had proper parents in the first place." He pushed Jana's wheelchair aside, stepped in front of the podium, and surveyed his audience. "I would like a volunteer to assume the role of Jana's mother. Who's up for the challenge?"

Dr. Lovett's gaze fell upon the German nurse, Gosia, who was sitting, ramrod straight, in the sixth row. Her face had developed a deep-red flush, the result of a full-blown hot flash. She raised her right hand to her face in an attempt to wipe away a trickle of sweat, which was dripping from her brow down onto her cheeks.

Dr. Lovett said, "Excellent, we have our first volunteer. What's your name, my dear?" he asked, straining his eyes to read Gosia's name tag.

"Gosia, I am Gosia. But this I cannot do," she said. "I know nothing about what you say is this reparenting."

"Let me explain," Dr. Lovett said. "It works like this: Jana will become like your biological child. It will be exactly as if you have given birth to her. You will develop an exceptionally close bond with Jana. You must take her back to her infancy days by feeding and clothing her, as if she were your newborn baby girl. You will hold her and give her milk out of a baby bottle. You will cuddle her and change her diaper like she is a little baby. This is what we mean by reparenting—Jana will have a new mother, and you are it, Gosia. You are the one!"

Gosia rose to her feet. "Th-his... it cannot be t-rue," she said, looking around the room.

"Also, be aware that this is a long-term commitment. I expect Jana will be here for at least six weeks," Dr. Lovett said.

Gosia plopped down in her chair and sighed. "Six weeks here? I should do the diapers and baby bottles for six weeks?"

"Yes, six weeks should do the trick. Just look at this poor girl! Now, we need a new father." Dr. Lovett pointed a finger at Mark. "What about you over there, young man?"

Mark folded his arms over his chest and leaned back in his chair

"No," he said. "No way. And to be clear, I don't believe we should be feeding a teenage girl with a baby bottle."

Good going Mark, Mattie thought. *Stand up for what you believe. I'm not sure what to think; maybe it'll work. All I know is I can't stand seeing that poor girl like that.*

Dave called out from his seat in row five, "I'll do it. I think it'll be a fun experiment. Count me in. I'm ready."

"Thank you, young man. My sense is that you will make a wonderful father for Jana. But I want to point out to all of you, this is *not* an experiment. I have seen documented results, and all of them have been positive."

He looked out over his audience, nodding his head. "Good. Yes. Okay. New parents are Mommy Gosia and Daddy Dave. I will meet with you both in the conference room in one hour. Thank you all for your time."

Gosia began her mommy duties the very next day; Mattie couldn't believe how quickly she got into the role. On a daily basis, she propped Jana up on a pillow, insisted she drink formula from a bottle, and turned her on her side to burp her. She brought her new baby rattles and a teething ring. In the evenings, she returned to the unit to read *Goodnight Moon* and tuck her in.

The physical therapy exercises, hot packs, and massages to release Jana's atrophied neck muscles were successful, and once again she became capable of holding her head up. Dr. Lovett removed her gastrostomy tube, and Jana began taking food by mouth. Gosia introduced her to a variety of Gerber junior baby food and taught her to feed herself with the silver-plated spoon she bought for her. As the days progressed, Gosia weaned Jana off the bottle and gave her milk in a sippy cup.

Several weeks after the reparenting program began, Mattie walked into the break room hoping to take a few minutes to regroup from an intense morning on the unit. She was surprised to see Gosia cutting generous pieces of apple strudel and putting them on pretty paper plates. To Mattie's knowledge, this was the first break Gosia had ever taken. She was one of the hardest working people on the unit; she never slowed down, not even for a minute.

"Gosia make strudel for staff," she said. "You sit here now, eat this."

"Gosia, that looks beautiful, almost too good to eat," Mattie said, taking a seat at the table. "And I've been meaning to tell you how impressed the whole staff is with Jana's progress."

"Yes, no more catheter. I take it out, and now my Jana, she urinates in toilet, not in bed. Soon I will teach her to make strudel with me, both of us together, like I make with my mama when I was a young girl in Germany. I bake it many layers."

Boy, I've never heard Gosia so chatty. And she's stopped wearing her laced-up granny shoes. It's bright clothing now—flowered skirts and matching blouses. No more scowling; smiles all the time. Makes good eye contact too. A real transformation. Motherhood must agree with her.

"Me too, Gosia. I used to bake with my mother—we made sour cream pound cakes. Did your mother come to America with you?"

"No, she did not come. She died in France when war was over."

"Your mother died *after* the war?"

Gosia stopped cutting the strudel and sat down next to Mattie. "Yes. We live in Cologne. In Germany. After war ended, much confusion. Many people looting. And the soldiers, the American soldiers, would shoot them, but then the soldiers start to loot and my mama said it was too dangerous, and it was time to leave our homeland and go to her sister's house in Detroit. In America."

"Well, that was a big decision, but I understand why your mother wanted to leave."

"Mama said the streets in America all paved with gold. She said to me, 'Come my little Malgosia.' We hold hands and go with many other people. We will walk all across Germany and walk in France to Paris. In Paris, we will get visa for to go to America."

"Your mother called you Malgosia? Is that your real name?"

"Yes, of course. My name. Mostly it is for Polish people, but my mama like name Malgosia."

"Were there lots of people on the road to Paris?"

"Yes, thousands. More come every day. They walk, like us, to Paris. We want to leave the shooting and get visas to come here to America. When we get hungry, we dig the potatoes from fields. Rotten potatoes.

At the night we stop. We lie down on ground and mama tells me stories about America. No bombed-out buildings in America. Such a fairyland. Then she coughs and spits up blood."

Mattie took a careful look at Gosia. She felt like she had never really seen her before. *What she must have gone through and still kept her sanity.*

Gosia had tears in her eyes. "We get to refugee camp outside of Paris. We sleep in cots. There is food, but mama cannot eat. All day she coughs, spits up blood. The doctor comes every day. Then one morning, I wake up and see blood clots all over on her sheets. On the floor by the cot, more blood. I step in blood. I hold her hand; it is cold like ice. I beg the doctor to fix her, make her wake up. But he said it was too late for her—she had TB, he tells me. She hemorrhaged. I did not know what he was saying to me. Then he says she is dead. She will not wake up. They bury her behind the big tent. I pick some flowers for her grave."

Mattie reached over, took Gosia's hands in hers, and held on to them for a moment. "Gosia, I'm so sorry. What a sad story. But how did you get here? How did you get to America without your mother?"

"A Red Cross lady, she help me. She get visa for me and come with me to Detroit. My mama's sister greet us and says I look just like mama. There is plenty to eat in America at mama's sister's house, but I can tell you, the dirty back streets of Detroit are not paved with gold."

"Oh Gosia, I never knew. I had no idea," Mattie said.

"It was a long time ago. Now everything is okay. Your mama is alive still?"

"Well, my father said she died here in Central State right after he had her committed."

Gosia raised her eyebrows and started to speak. Mattie was sure she was about to ask her a question, but she paused instead. "I know, it's confusing," Mattie said. "My mother was a patient. She was committed in 1958 when I was eight years old. I thought she died here, but I looked her name up in the library records and found out she's alive."

Gosia looked stunned. She inhaled a big gulp of air and stared at Mattie for a moment. She exhaled and said, "What do you say? Your dead mama is not dead? Oh, how can such a thing happen? Such joy. A miracle!"

"There's more to the story," Mattie said. "You see, I know she's alive, living here in the hospital, but I can't find her."

"Your dear mama is lost? Gosia will help to find her. Jana will help. We will look. We will find her. Such excitement. Such a good thing."

"I xeroxed a bunch of flyers with an old photo of my mother on them," Mattie said. She got up and walked over to the bookcase and removed a manila envelope she kept on the middle shelf. She pulled out a bunch of flyers and gave them to Gosia. "You can take these—I have more. I've started to give them out to all the ward supervisors in case they've seen her. I left a few copies with the secretary in Jones. You never know, but I'm hoping."

Gosia studied the photo for a few minutes. "You and your mama look like the same," she said. "But your mama has curls in her hair, you have the short, straight hair."

"Yes, but that's an old photo of her. I have reason to think her hair isn't curly any longer—it's long and stringy. And mostly gray with a little brown."

"Eat the strudel. I need to work now. Jana and me, we will go outside later. We will look everywhere for your mama."

Mattie left the break room shortly after Gosia, still thinking about Gosia's story. *Boy, you never know what people have lived through or are still going through,* she thought. *My life's been easy compared to hers.*

Mattie continued to walk down the hall, preoccupied with her thoughts, when she ran into Dave. "You know how I volunteered to do the reparenting for Dr. Lovett?" he said. "I'm supposed to be Jana's daddy, but I've been shut out. Gosia never lets me hold Jana or feed her some baby food. Jana needs a father too. Do you think I should talk to Dr. Lovett?"

"Actually, it would be best if you talk to Gosia," Mattie said. "She's the one who's taking over. If that doesn't work, you need to follow the chain of command."

"You mean I should talk to Caroline first, then Dr. Lovett? I can't talk to Caroline. She refuses to take appointments to see anyone."

"Well, Dave, I have a feeling you and Jana's new mother can work things out. You probably just need some couples' counseling," Mattie said.

Dave's handsome face broke into a big grin. "Not on your life."

Mattie stopped in at the activity room, hoping to find Pam and tell her how much she appreciated the decorations she had helped the patients make for Halloween. Pam was happy to see her. She showed Mattie the pumpkins the patients were busy embellishing with black markers.

Pam and Mattie stepped a few feet away from the group for a minute. "You've done a fantastic job with all the decorations, Pam," Mattie said. "The orange-and-black crepe paper you taped to the solarium walls looks so cool. I love Halloween. When I was little, my mother used to make our costumes. I was usually a ghost, and I remember one year my mother sewed my little brother a train engineer's outfit."

"That's a nice memory about your mom," Pam said.

Mattie caught sight of a mound of shredded newspaper piled mile-high on Pam's desk. "What are you going to use all that newspaper for, Pam?"

"That's for our next project. We're going to mix up some flour and water in a bucket, dip the newspaper strips in it, and make a papier-mâché man. Central Kitchen is sending us a bunch of fruits and vegetables and we're going to totally cover his body with them." Pam giggled with delight, picturing the finished project.

"Wow—that sounds impressive. How tall is he going to be?"

"About six feet. We're going to put lettuce all over his torso and arms and legs. Then we'll cut up some slices of cucumbers to make his eyes, and we'll use the long green stalks from the spring onions for his hair. Strips of red-pepper for his mouth. We'll hoist him up on an IV pole in the hallway so the visitors can see him."

"What a great idea, Pam!" Mattie said. "You could call him Harvest Man. I bet it'll take the patients' minds off their troubles, at least for a little while."

Chapter 21

Mattie

November 1976

Jana continued to make steady progress. By the end of November, her long auburn hair had regained its luster, and her complexion had taken on a ruddy glow. She learned to walk without assistance. Gosia gave her a small cupcake with chocolate icing to celebrate.

The day following this milestone, Gosia finished distributing the medication early and asked to talk to Mattie alone for a minute. They walked to the empty conference room together, and as soon as the door closed behind them, Gosia announced that she'd come up with a wonderful plan—she was going to ask Dr. Lovett to discharge Jana to her care so she could adopt her darling child. They would make strudel together and go to the park. Jana would attend a neighborhood school and tell Gosia all about it when she came home each afternoon.

Gosia made an appointment to see Dr. Lovett the next day. She explained that she had learned to love Jana while she was caring for her. She thought of Jana as her biological child. To Gosia's dismay, he informed her that he had no intention of releasing Jana to her care. He planned to retain full custody.

Friday afternoon, Gosia took her time setting up her 1:00 p.m.

medications. She stood by the medication cart, which was parked in the far corner of the nurses' station near the narcotic cabinet, and sniffled, stopping every few minutes to wipe her nose with her starched white hanky.

Mattie walked over to her and put her arm around her shoulder. "I'm guessing you heard some bad news about your request to adopt Jana, right?" Mattie said. "Your meeting with Dr. Lovett didn't go well, did it?"

Gosia lowered her head and started to cry. Mattie took her hand and once again led her into the conference room.

"Here, have a seat," Mattie said. "No need to cry, Gosia. I believe the problem is that Dr. Lovett thinks he's found the golden goose."

"What is this 'golden goose'?"

"Well, it means that Jana could make Dr. Lovett famous. If he keeps Jana in his custody, he can document her behavior and publish an article about his successful reparenting case in one of the psychiatric journals."

"Oh, this not so good for me and my Jana."

"You and Jana have been out searching everywhere for my mother. You've been showing the patients the flyer with her photo on it, trying to get information about her. Now it's my turn to help you."

Gosia wiped away her tears with her hanky. Her face lit up. "Tell me this thing. How I keep my Jana?"

Mattie explained to Gosia that she and Jana could go to court and have Jana declared an emancipated minor by a judge. Even though she was just sixteen, Jana would legally become an adult; she would be able to make her own decisions. Dr. Lovett would no longer have custody of her.

Gosia happily filled out the forms and coached Jana on how to respond to the judge. She told her to let the judge know she'd have her own bedroom when she lived at Gosia's house, and that she would be able to make money working on the weekends at the local German bakery."

At the Court Hearing, which was held on the unit, Jana was proclaimed an emancipated minor, capable of providing for herself. Dr. Lovett discharged her the same day "against medical advice." She walked out of CSU holding her new mother's hand. When they got home, Gosia and Jana baked Mattie a big, flaky, golden-brown apple strudel.

When Mark made rounds on the unit on the evening of November 28, he could find no trace of Alex. Mark concluded Alex must have mingled with the visitors and slipped out the door with them when the visiting hours were over. After notifying security, Mark phoned William and asked him to check on Mattie, who had been the subject of one of Alex's tirades the day before. He also asked William to meet with him, Dave, Ben, and a couple of security guys as soon as he left Mattie's apartment. "We've got to go find this Alex guy. He's trouble," Mark told William.

Shortly after 9:00 p.m., Mattie said, "Sooner, I can tell you need to go outside, but where in the world did I put your leash?" Sooner wagged his tail in anticipation.

Mattie made a quick search of the apartment. "Okay, No leash? We can deal with that." She ran down the back stairs; Sooner bounded down a half step behind her. As soon as they reached ground level, Sooner raced around looking for a stick. He picked up a short, dried-up branch, brought it to Mattie, and dropped it at her feet.

"Okay, Sooner," she said. "I can see you want to play, but I'm too cold—I forgot my sweater. Of course, you have a fur coat on but..." Mattie stopped midsentence.

Sooner dropped his stick and moved in front of her. He smelled the air. Mattie heard a guttural sound come from deep within his chest.

Alex edged out from behind the building.

Mattie froze.

Alex held a toothbrush in his right hand pointed straight at Mattie. The bristles were still attached to one end; the other end was filed to a sharp point. With his weapon held high, Alex took a step toward Mattie. Before he could strike, Sooner pulled back into a springing position and lunged, knocking Alex to the ground. Alex landed on his back, rolled over, got up on his feet, and took off running toward the woods. Sooner barked and gave chase.

Mattie picked up the toothbrush Alex had dropped, stumbled back to her apartment building, and slumped down on the first step.

Oh my God. That maniac was trying to kill me. What if he stabbed my carotid? I could've bled out. He was going to use a toothbrush. A toothbrush, for God's sake! She looked down at the weapon in her hand. *Boy, that was a close call. If it weren't for my dog, I'd be dead. Stabbed to death. I can see the headline: "Escaped Mental Patient Stabs Unsuspecting Milledgeville Employee to Death with a Toothbrush." I won't tell Aunt Tess; she'll think all her worries are coming true.*

Mattie's heart was racing. She took a few deep breaths, then exhaled, trying to get it to slow down. Sooner trotted back to Mattie and dropped a piece of denim at her feet. She sat up and looked at it; picked it up. "Good boy, Sooner—you took a bite from his butt."

Moments after Mattie and Sooner retreated back inside her apartment, William knocked on the door. After ascertaining it *was* William—not Alex circling back to do her harm—she opened the door wide and stood there trembling.

"What's the matter, Mattie? You look terrified."

"Alex tried to kill me!" Tears began flowing down her face. "You were right about him. I was so scared, but I tried not to show it."

"It's okay," William said, stepping inside and putting his arm around her shoulder. He led her to the sofa. "You're going to be fine. You've had a shock. Sit down, I'll get you a drink. Water? Or maybe something stronger? Do you have any whiskey in the apartment? That should settle your nerves."

She stopped crying; her voice quivered. "Water would be fine."

William walked into the kitchen, poured a glass of cold water, and sat beside her while she took a big gulp.

"Best to take small sips," he said. "Now, tell me what happened."

Mattie nodded her thanks. "I took Sooner outside. I couldn't find his leash, so we ran down the back steps. Alex was waiting around a corner, and he jumped out and tried to stab me with a toothbrush!"

"You're kidding—a toothbrush?"

"Well, it wasn't the end with the bristles. He sharpened the other end with something; I don't know what he used. Maybe a sharp rock. It had a real point on it. If it weren't for Sooner, I'm sure he would have used it on me. He had this mean look in his eye like he wanted to hurt me. And he would have if Sooner hadn't jumped on him and knocked him to the ground."

Mattie put her water down on the coffee table and leaned back against the sofa pillows. Sooner dropped a chewed-up tennis ball on the floor in front of her. She watched it bounce away.

"I've got to get going," William said. "I only stopped by to warn you Alex eloped. Sorry I'd didn't make it here in time. Mark, Dave, Ben, and the security guys are waiting for me at the fire station. We're going to search the woods for Alex. Do you think you'll be okay?"

"I'll be fine. I feel better already. I'll lock the door and have some wine."

"Good plan. We might have to search all night—however long it takes. Can I borrow Sooner to help track?"

"Of course. Sorry I can't find his leash, but he knows how to heel, and he'll follow all your commands. Oh, and one more thing: he took a bite out of Alex's behind." She handed William the piece of denim.

"Thanks. This will help—good job, Sooner," he said, patting him on the head.

William gave Mattie a quick kiss on the cheek. "Be sure to lock the door the minute I leave. Come Sooner. Let's go find Alex."

The next morning, Mattie tried to keep busy while she waited to hear from William. Since she had the day off and Sooner wasn't home, she decided it would be a good time to remove his paw prints from the linoleum floor in the kitchen. She was in the midst of giving the floor a once-over with a wet mop when the phone on the kitchen counter rang. She carefully crossed the wet floor and picked up the receiver.

"Hi, Mattie. It's William. I'm calling from the General Medical Hospital in Macon. I'm in their ER. Something's happened, and it's not good."

"Hold on a minute, William," she said, turning the volume down on the radio next to the phone. "Did you just say you're in the emergency room?"

"Yes, right," William said. "General Medical in Macon. Alex impaled himself on a grave marker. He fell right on top of it. Went straight into his chest—almost all the way through him. Blood everywhere. He's bad off. I don't think he's going to make it."

"Hang on. I can get there in half an hour."

When Mattie arrived, she found William sitting outside the hospital, hunched over on a bench near the entrance to the emergency room. His face was an eerie gray color, and there were dark circles under his eyes.

Mattie brushed some withered leaves off the bench and sat down. "William, what in the world happened? How did Alex get impaled? Did he trip and fall or something? Tell me everything you know."

William lifted his head and looked at Mattie. "We searched until midnight, then we went home to rest for a few hours. I took Sooner back to my place with me, got him settled. At daybreak, Sooner and I met up with security and Mark, Dave, and Ben. We searched for about two more hours, way back deep in the woods. The others stopped to rest, but Sooner and I kept going. I wanted to search around the graveyard. We walked a long way, following the trail. When we finally got to the outskirts, I heard a noise like someone walking, stepping on branches. Sooner started barking."

"Yes. Then what?"

"Alex heard him and took off running right through the middle of the cemetery. He was jumping over vines and fallen tree branches. He splashed through a bog with about a foot of standing water in it. Tons of mud. Got all over him. He was able to avoid all the markers he could see—the ones that are triangular-shaped on the top. What he couldn't see so good were the older markers, probably from way back when the hospital first opened. They're thin and rusty and look like sticks poking out of the ground."

"What happened next?" Mattie asked. "Where did he fall?"

"He jumped up on a big log and stood on it for a second. Then he turned around and looked back to see how close Sooner and I were getting. When he turned forward again, he must've lost his balance.

He fell facedown off the log and landed on top of one of those old markers—the thin ones. It went right into his chest. Impaled him. Sooner and I ran over to try to help. Luckily, Mark, Dave, and Ben were heading our way. They heard me yell. Ben ran back and told the fire department. They came right away, put Alex on a stretcher, and carried him back to the ambulance. The ambulance brought him here to Macon General Medical because they knew this ER is a designated trauma center."

"Geeze, you must be exhausted, William. What a night."

"Yeah, I'm tired. Still trying to process what happened. After things calmed down, Mark took Sooner back to his place. I told him I'd pick him up later. Dave and Ben went back home."

"Wow," Mattie said. "There are no words. What a terrible way for Alex to die."

"Well, he's not exactly dead," William said. "At least not yet. When the ambulance drivers wheeled him inside on a gurney, he still had that rusty marker sticking out. They can't remove it until they get him to surgery."

"Okay, you stay here. I'll go check and get an update."

As soon as Mattie entered the ER, she looked around to get her bearings. She spotted a nurse standing by the central desk. "I'm the charge nurse from the Crisis Stabilization Unit at Milledgeville," Mattie said. "Would it be okay to visit with Alex for a few minutes?"

"Sure, we're trying to schedule him for surgery."

"What's the holdup?"

"We're waiting for the surgeon on call to answer his page. Alex is down there on your left."

Mattie slipped in behind the heavy denim curtain that surrounded Alex's bed. He was lying on his back, his body rigid. An iron marker, about twenty inches long, stuck out of his bare chest. He turned his head toward Mattie and spoke in a low voice. "They gave me a shot. Good one, too. Stopped the pain. Made me feel drunk."

"You feel drunk?"

"Yep, drunk. Look what happened to me. You done this; it's all your fault. And that mutt of yours took a hunk out of my behind."

"Me? My fault? You're the one who tried to attack me, Alex. I've always treated you with respect, and you tried to kill me. How does that make it my fault?"

Alex turned his head away. "Fuck you. Leave me alone. I wanna die in peace."

"I'll leave, but first I want to ask you something. Everyone thought Darryl committed suicide, but you killed him, didn't you?"

A nurse pulled back the curtain, glanced at them, and left without comment.

"Okay," Alex muttered. "If you must know, I did make that bastard hang himself. Told fat ass if he didn't jump, I'd cut his throat. Showed him the razor."

"But how did you get a razor? We did a thorough search when you were admitted."

Alex tried to laugh, but it sounded more like a croak. "You guys missed it—I had it all taped up next to the seam inside my jeans. I made Darryl climb up on the chair. I kicked it out, and he went swinging. Go tell the nurse I need more medication—I'm dying."

He started a cycle of deep rapid breaths, which gradually decreased, followed by a short period of apnea—no breathing at all. Then the cycle started again—more deep rapid breaths.

Cheyne-Stokes respiration. He really is dying. He's almost gone for sure.

She reached for his wrist, tried to find a pulse. Nothing. She pulled back the curtain and yelled for someone to bring the crash cart. Alex exhaled one last breath.

The nurse arrived with the crash cart within seconds, the ER doctor close behind her. "We can't use the defibrillator on someone with an iron stake in his chest," he told Mattie. "And if we pull it, he'll bleed out. Won't work."

Mattie gripped the side rails on his bed and stared down at Alex's body. The doctor pointed to the monitor, which was emitting a long, loud tone. "And now he's got a flat line. He's gone, I'm afraid. The injury was too catastrophic. He had a lot of internal damage."

"Yes," Mattie said. "There was way too much damage…"

"Are you a relative?" the doctor asked.

"No. I was acquainted with him, but I didn't really know him until a few minutes ago."

The ER nurse put five absorbent pads under Alex's back to soak up the blood before pulling the marker out. She covered him with a sheet and tagged his big toe.

William was still sitting outside where Mattie had left him. "What's happening? How's Alex?" he asked.

Mattie sank down on the bench next to him. "I can't believe it. Alex died while I was talking to him. Never got to surgery. I should feel something I guess, but I'm just plain numb. Maybe I'm even glad he's dead. Is that wrong?"

"No, that's normal," William said, turning toward her. "He was a threat to you while he was alive. We both know he was capable of murder."

"What I don't understand is how he turned out like that. A murderer. He smuggled a razor on the unit—it was taped next to the seam inside his jeans. He said he told Darryl if he didn't jump, he would cut his throat."

"He told you he had a razor taped inside his jeans? After he took them off, I should've turned them inside out. Lesson learned. I'll do that next time, for sure. But I hope there's never a next time. Not like this.

"I want to ask you something, Mattie. When you were in the ER with Alex, did you notice the number etched into the shaft on the top section of the marker? It was a little hard to read, but it's there, I saw it."

"No. Was I supposed to?" Mattie said. "All I saw was a lot of blood and a man dying in front of me."

"Do you remember telling me what Annie Able said about Tillman? How he was the first patient to arrive at the asylum? How his family carted him here in a wagon?"

"Sure, I do. Tillman died at the hospital and was buried in the cemetery 133 years ago."

"You told me Annie Able said that 'Number One' was written on Tillman's grave marker."

"Wait," Mattie said. "Are you saying 'Number One' was written on the marker imbedded in Alex's chest? I never thought to look for a number."

"Yep, that's what I'm telling you."

"No! No way. The marker that tripped Alex was Tillman's marker? It was the one on top of his grave? I can't believe it. I wonder if Tillman reached up and grabbed Alex's foot? But, of course, that's impossible," Mattie said, shaking her head.

"Impossible," William said.

"Right. Of course not. Unless you believe in ghosts."

"No ghosts."

After a moment of silence, Mattie said, "Just coincidence?"

"Just coincidence."

"We should go talk to the social worker who covers the ER," Mattie said. "We can give her Sophia's number. Alex told us when we admitted him that he had a wife. I believe he said her name was Alicia. And he had a young daughter. He said they lived in Atlanta, but he wouldn't give their address. The two social workers can work with the police to try and find them."

"Good. The family will be able to arrange for burial."

"And they won't have to spend the rest of their lives wondering what happened to him," Mattie said.

They stood up, ready to leave. Mattie rubbed her forehead, trying to forestall a full-blown headache. "Let's go pick up Sooner," she said.

"Yeah, good idea. I think we'll both be happy to put this whole sad episode behind us."

Chapter 22

Heather

November 20, 1976
Rivers Building, Ward A
Milledgeville Central State Hospital

Around noon today there was a big commotion by the front door. I ran and found Lucinda.

"They done brought our little Nora back," she told me. "Them bounty hunters. They just pushed her through the door and went off."

"Where could she have been all this time?" I asked.

Nora walked to her old cot in the middle of the dorm. No one had been assigned to her bed because everyone knows Ward A is a one-way street. We hardly ever get new patients in here, and no one ever gets well enough for discharge. It's like the little brown box Clive used to put down on our kitchen floor to trap roaches. It had "Roach Motel" written on the top in red letters. There was only one way in— through a tiny door. The advertisement said, "The roaches crawl in, but they don't crawl out." On the other wards it's different. You have a chance to leave one of them if you take your meds and "show promise."

Nora lay down in her bed and pulled the sheet up to her chin. Her lovely blonde hair had been cut short and uneven, like a whisk broom.

She had a healed scar running down her face, stretching from the corner of her right eyebrow to the right side of her cheek, all the way to her neck.

Lucinda took one of Nora's hands and said, "Child, what them men done did to yous?"

No answer. Tears formed in her eyes and dripped over the scar. Lucinda wiped Nora's eyes with the corner of the sheet.

I sat down on the floor next to her bed and took her other hand. We stayed with her till she drifted off to sleep.

Lucinda and I went to the far end of the dormitory and huddled, talking low. Not that any of the patients could understand what we were talking about, but you never know.

"She looks god-awful, Lucinda," I said.

"We done got a problem. That ain't extra fat you see on that child. She gonna have a baby."

"Can't be."

"Is so—Lucinda knows these things."

I was stunned. "But when? Who would have done that to our Nora? Where do you think she's been?"

"The bounty men got her. Been messin' with her. Pretended they just now found her. I'm gonna get their asses."

"There's too many of them, Lucinda. You don't know their names."

Lucinda's face turned into granite. She spoke through gritted teeth, "I's can find out. I's got my ways."

That did not shock me—I knew she spoke the truth.

"But Lucinda, if she's pregnant they'll take the baby and put it into foster care," I said. "Or maybe they'll sell it. The baby will never know its sweet momma."

"Then we's gotta make sure that don't happen. We can birth the baby right here, then sneak it out of this place and give it to my kinfolk to raise. They can bring that young 'un with 'em so it can visit with its momma when they's bringing my Lucas and Sasha to visit with me."

"But Lucinda, I won't know what to do. I've never seen a baby get born except my two, and they don't count because I was mighty distracted."

"Well, you's in luck now 'cause I knows a lot about birthin', and one thing I knows is we's got about six weeks, maybe less, to get ourselves all organized."

"But Lucinda, don't you think the staff will guess?"

"She's small, that young 'un. We find her a couple of them big-size housedresses. An' ain't you never paid attention to how they never pay attention? All but Bruno and Miz Max, and she done died, gone to heaven, and Bruno, he married to my sister Adelaide."

"I almost forgot. Bruno is a fine man."

"Yes, ma'am. And that fine man, he gonna help us get our supplies. We's gonna need lots of stuff for the birthin'."

I asked her, "What stuff?" My brain was racing. I should get some toilet paper to write a list on. "What about the boiled water?" I asked. "How are we going to get some boiled water?"

"You just stop that worrying now, Miss Heather," she said. "Let Lucinda here do the worryin'. What yous gotta figure out is where we's gonna find a container to put the messy part in, the part that comes out right after the baby."

"You mean the afterbirth?"

"Yep, the afterbirth. Every new momma has an afterbirth. We needs to plan on how to get rid of it without no one seein'."

I pictured the whole scene—Nora in labor, not understanding what was happening. New baby all pink and crying. Afterbirth.

"I don't think we can pull this off, Lucinda. A lot of things could go wrong and—"

"We's gonna need a sheet so we can tear it up and make Nora a breast binder. That's so her milk don't come down. We's gotta get some rubber to put over her bedsheet, keep it clean. We's gonna need warm water and a washcloth to clean up the new young 'un and a little blanket to wrap it in after it gets born."

"Okay, okay," I said. "I'll make a list. I'll find what we need." I figured we'd have enough time. Six weeks to beg, borrow, and steal the birthing stuff.

Our baby, Nora, was going to have a baby.

God help us all.

Chapter 23

Mattie

November 1976

Mattie found Dave sitting alone at the table in the break room, taking a short respite from his morning activities. She took a seat across the table from him. "Hey Mattie," Dave said. "I just finished with Mr. Collins's morning care. I changed his diaper, gave him a shower, and helped him eat breakfast. It seems to me his dementia's getting worse."

"You're right about that, Dave. We've tried lots of different meds on him, but he's not getting any better. I hate to interrupt your break, but I need to talk to you about something."

"Does my dad have anything to do with it?"

"No, Mr. Vickers knows nothing about this. Not yet anyway."

"So then, what's up?"

"Well, I was walking down the hall yesterday, and I passed Jason's room," Mattie said. "His door was open, and I noticed you were sitting way too close to him on his bed."

"I was doing some Gestalt therapy," Dave said. "I was telling him to pretend to put his mother in an empty chair so he could yell at her and tell her how she messed him up."

"Dave, I know you mean well, but only social workers, nurse

therapists, and psychologists are certified to do individual therapy with the patients. Jason's an adolescent, which means he's very impressionable. You could have led him down the wrong path or opened up a Pandora's box you couldn't control. And by sitting so close to him, you gave him the wrong message."

Dave averted his eyes. "Sorry. I was just trying to do my job."

"I've also noticed you walk down the hall with him, laughing and joking," Mattie said. "He sits next to you when you do your current events group. You even wait for him while he goes to the bathroom. The other patients are beginning to notice."

Dave stood up, his shoulders drooped, and he looked as if he were going to cry. He swiped at his eyes, just as the tears started. "I have to go now and check on Mr. Collins," he said, walking out the door without looking back.

Later that afternoon, Mattie answered a phone call at the nurses' station.

"I'm Jason's mother. I'm calling to tell you to keep that psych tech of yours away from my son."

"Which psych tech? Did something happen?"

"Dave, the tall one. The good-looking one. The one with perfect skin," Jason's mother yelled. "Jason came home on a two-day pass—Dr. Vine wants to see how he'll adjust when she discharges him next week. I went to wash Jason's jeans just now, and what do you think I found in his pocket?" She didn't wait for Mattie to answer. "I found a note from Dave. He invited Jason to meet him in Central City Park tomorrow afternoon. Said he wants to discuss something with him. My son is an underaged adolescent. You people are supposed to be helping him. Jason is—well, he's confused. Yes, confused about things, certain things. Like I said, Dave's a terrible influence. In fact, I think you should fire him."

Mattie tried unsuccessfully to figure out her next move. Irate mother, Dave's daddy, who happened to be the hospital lawyer. She needed to get some perspective; she needed to talk to Sophia.

Mattie quickly completed the staff schedule she'd been preparing and walked down the hall to Sophia's office.

"You look like you're having a bad day," Sophia said. "Have a seat—tell me what's going on."

"Well, to start with I accidentally stuck myself with a needle about an hour ago—rammed it right into the bone of my thumb."

"Ouch! I bet that hurt. How'd it happen?" Sophia said.

"I was trying to give a shot to an agitated patient, you know, Bob P. He was just admitted around noon yesterday—he's got so many tattoos you can't even see his skin."

"I'm familiar with Bob; I did his social history last evening."

"I don't know if you noticed, but he had a stud in his tongue," Mattie said. "We had to get it out before we sent him for an MRI. Did you hear they've got a brand-new MRI machine over in Jones? First one in the state of Georgia. I read in the guidelines that the magnets in it are capable of pulling a metal stud right through the patient's tongue."

"I did see his stud. By the way, Dr. Vine told me she doesn't think much of the new MRI machine," Sophia said. "She called it a 'newfangled' invention. She said it will never catch on."

Mattie chuckled. "I personally think the MRI is here to stay."

"So, go on," Sophia said. "How'd you get the needle in your thumb?"

"Just as I started to inject the medication, Tattoo Man jumped a mile and the needle went into me instead of him. When Mark saw the needle and syringe sticking out of the bone, waving in the breeze, he fainted clear away!"

"No! He fainted? Is he okay? He looks like such a strong, macho guy. Can't picture him fainting."

"Yep. He went down like a ton of bricks. Gosia was happy though—she got to use that new bottle of smelling salts she'd been saving for such an occasion."

"I've read that needle sticks are the most frequent of all hospital accidents. Sounds very painful."

"All better now. Didn't even need a Band-Aid." Mattie held up her thumb for her friend to see. "Now Sophia, if you have a minute, there's something I'd like to run past you."

"Of course. Be happy to help."

"I know you've been working with Jason in your adolescent group."

"Yes, a very troubled young man. He appears to be having an identity crisis."

Mattie nodded. "I got a call from Jason's mother. She told me she found a note from Dave in her son's jeans."

"I knew Jason had a pass to go home for a couple of days. Matter of fact, I suggested it to Dr. Vine. We need to see how Jason interacts with his family. What did Dave's note say?"

"It said for Jason to meet him in Central City Park, downtown Milledgeville, tomorrow afternoon. Dave knows the rule about not meeting our patients off unit while they're still under our care."

"Right. Meeting a patient *following* discharge doesn't break any rules but seeing them when they're still hospitalized jeopardizes the professional staff/patient roles."

"But here's the thing," Mattie said. "I've already talked to Dave once about how he needs to have clear boundaries with Jason. I don't know whether to give him another warning or just go ahead and report him to Caroline. What would you do? I'm on the fence."

"First, thing I'd do is have a drink of sherry—helps with processing." She reached into her bottom right-hand desk drawer, pulled out a bottle of sherry and two dainty crystal sherry glasses, and poured some of the deep-amber liquid into them After they'd both taken a sip, Sophia said, "Now let's look at the situation logically. These are the facts, as we know them: one, Dave's a handsome dude; and two, he wants everyone to think he's heterosexual, not homosexual."

"How did you come up with that, Sophia? I agree he's good-looking. He could have posed for Michelangelo's statue of David. But just because he's handsome doesn't mean he's gay."

"You might have noticed he plucks his eyebrows," Sophia said. "But it's a lot more than that. Remember when he produced a photo of his supposed girlfriend at one of our orientation sessions? I don't think he even had a girlfriend. I think it was just a photo of a girl he had found lying around somewhere."

"But he said his girlfriend had been raped. Surely, he wouldn't lie about that," Mattie said.

"The rape part never happened because he never had a girlfriend," Sophia said. "I'm sure, looking back, it was just a made-up story. He told me that he was going to marry the girl in the photo. He was trying to spread the word he was a sensitive, heterosexual male."

Mattie shifted her position, tossing the possibility over in her mind.

"More than likely the reason for the cover-up is because of his family," Sophia said. "If he announces to the world he's gay, it'll be very difficult for them. Small town; lots of gossip. And added to that, Dave might think his daddy will reject him, maybe even cut him out of his will."

Sophia got up from her desk and paced for a few minutes. "Your options are limited. I think you have to inform Caroline. She's still your supervisor, even though she's not too well put together. And I have a hunch that Jason's mother won't let this go. She's probably on the phone right now to our CEO, Mr. Carpenter, accusing Dave of all kinds of things and telling him you did nothing to prevent it."

"I guess I'll try to get an appointment with Caroline," Mattie said. "I might need another glass of sherry first. Do you have any idea what it's like to deal with that woman?"

"It's the best option for you and for Dave," Sophia said, pouring them both another glass.

"You're right of course. The part that's clear to me is that Dave has stepped over the line, and if I don't say anything it means I'll be giving my silent approval to his actions. But I want to let Dave know first—I'll explain why I have to report him."

Mattie found Dave sitting in a chair next to Mr. Collins in the dayroom. Although Mr. Collins couldn't understand a word Dave was saying, he frequently reached over, nodded his head, and patted Dave's arm. Mattie asked Dave to meet her in the conference room as soon as he finished interacting with Mr. Collins.

When Dave arrived in the conference room, Mattie asked him to take a seat. "There's something I need to tell you," she said.

Small beads of sweat ran down Dave's chiseled face. He sat down and looked across the table at Mattie.

"Dave, it's come to my attention you planned to meet Jason at Central City Park tomorrow. We need to talk about it."

Dave clenched the arms of his chair. "How'd you find out? Did Jason say something? I told him not to tell. People might not understand."

"Dave, we're talking about you meeting an adolescent boy while he's out on pass," Mattie said. "I can't ignore this situation. I have to report you to Caroline."

Dave gave Mattie a long, pleading look. "Are you going to tell my father? I don't know what I'll do if he finds out."

"Mr. Vickers won't hear about it from me, but I can't guarantee he won't find out if Jason's mother decides to contact Mr. Carpenter. You know our CEO would go straight to your father's office. I can't tell you how sorry I am, Dave," Mattie said.

Dave stood up, turned away from Mattie, and walked out of the conference room without looking back.

Mattie decided to wait until the next day to approach Caroline. When she arrived at Caroline's office, she knocked twice before Caroline said, "Come in."

"Caroline, it's almost dark in here," Mattie said after her eyes adjusted. "Do you mind if I turn on the light? I need to talk to you about something."

"No. No light. Say what you have to say and leave. Can't you see I'm busy?"

Mattie debated whether to move some of the papers off the only chair in the room and take a seat, but she decided against it—she wanted to make a quick exit.

"Caroline, it's come to my attention that our psych tech, Dave, has been—well, he's... he invited a patient, an adolescent boy named Jason, to meet him tomorrow while Jason's supposed to be home with his family on a therapeutic pass."

"So?"

"We have a policy that clearly states staff members must not have contact with our patients when they are off unit on a pass. I'd like you to talk to Dave and tell him his behavior is not acceptable."

Caroline waved Mattie off with her ringless left hand. "I have no intention of talking to him. I'm way too busy. Close my door on your way out."

After work that day, Mattie decided some fresh air would help her think about how to expand the search for her mother and what to do about Dave. She walked over to the park and sat down on her favorite wooden bench. She pulled her thin navy sweater tightly around her shoulders and looked up at the clear-blue November sky.

It's cold today—what was I thinking? Should've worn my heavy jacket. I've got to figure out what's the right thing to do about Dave. I don't want him to lose his job. He's so good with the patients. They love him, and that counts for a lot. Caroline's no help. Looks like the radiologist's taken off. No surprise there. Funny thing is, I could almost feel sorry for Caroline, if she wasn't such a—

Mattie's thoughts were interrupted by Dave, who appeared in front of her bench, completely out of breath. His light-brown hair, usually flawlessly coiffed, was in disarray.

"I need to tell you something," he said, panting, face flushed. "Now, before I lose my nerve. I'm gay. I'm a gay man. You're the first person I've told. Please, please don't judge me. It's who I am. I'm gay. There, I've said it."

"Dave, come sit down," Mattie said. "You're all out of breath. I'd never judge you. It takes real courage to own who you are. I'm honored that you confided in me. Sit here and let's talk. Why now? Today? Such an important decision. I'm really proud of you."

Dave sank down next to Mattie, a big grin of relief plastered on his face. He turned toward her. "I want to say I'm sorry. I'm going to apologize to Jason's mother. I'll explain to her I didn't mean anything, and I won't see her son again."

"That's a good idea, Dave. That should appease her. I'm sure she doesn't want any publicity, and if she was thinking of suing, your apology should take that off the table."

"You were right to report me," Dave said. "But I want to explain it isn't what you think. I didn't encourage Jason—he's way too young for me. Jason wanted to talk to me. He kind of knew I'm gay like him. He said there was no one else he could talk to about it, and he thought I would understand. I made a bad decision to say I would meet him in the park while he was on pass, but I thought it would be easier for him to talk to me there. I want you to know the truth."

"I'm glad you told me," Mattie said. "It puts a whole new light on the situation. I thought perhaps you were gay, Dave, but I didn't know for sure. I'm happy there was nothing going on with Jason. It's good you came to talk to me."

"Jason wants to tell his family, but he doesn't know how. I encouraged him to just do it, come right out in the open. The problem is, I'm scared to do that myself. I want to talk to my dad, tell him I'm gay, but I'm afraid to. I'm in worse shape than Jason, and I'm a lot older than he is."

Mattie reached over and patted Dave's hand. "It might not be as hard as you think, Dave. I bet your dad already has some idea, and if you bring it out in the open it might make things better between you."

"You think it might? You think it would be for the best? My mother probably will understand, but my dad… I don't know, he might get mad."

"He might. Or he might get mad and get over it. You're his son; he loves you."

"Thanks, Mattie. Thanks for listening," Dave said. "I'm going to go home now. I think I'm going to tell my mom first and then my dad. Wish me luck."

Mattie leaned over and gave Dave a big hug. "You have a lot of courage, Dave," she said. "You'll do fine."

Chapter 24

Mattie

December 1976

After accepting the social work position at the hospital in July, Sophia decided to move back to Milledgeville, her old hometown. She bought a stately Victorian on Liberty Street and spent her free time renovating it. She had new bathroom fixtures installed and updated the kitchen. The oak floors had been stripped, stained, and sealed. Fresh paint in every room. Total bathroom remodel. New electrical wiring. With the modernizations complete, Sophia thought this would be a perfect time to have a party—she loved to entertain, especially during the holiday season. She placed an invitation on the bulletin board in the CSU break room inviting the staff to attend a Christmas party beginning at 6:00 p.m. at her home on Saturday, December 18.

Three days prior to the party, Sophia began decorating her living room. She covered a five-foot-tall live tree, which she'd managed to maneuver into a sturdy stand, with twinkling lights, silver bows, and two dozen handblown Polish ornaments. She used a stepstool to hang a fresh sprig of mistletoe in the center of the curved white archway separating the living room from the dining room. When she finished, she poured herself a glass of cabernet and stepped back to admire her handiwork.

On the day of the party, Sophia picked some stems of bright green holly with red berries from her garden and arranged them in a basket in the center of the dining-room table. She walked into the kitchen, picked up the phone, and called Mattie for the third time that day. "Tell me the truth. Do you think Bernard will remember my party's tonight? What if he forgot the date? He signed up to come to the party, but do you really think he means to attend?"

"He'll be there, Sophia. It's going to be a fun party."

"But he hasn't said boo to me since we got back from Aspen. Well, he did wink at me once in that staff meeting, but I've waited by the phone for hours and he hasn't called or anything. I thought we had something. He kept telling me what a wonderful time he was having when we went away. Maybe I just missed his call, and he didn't leave a message on my answering machine and—"

"He'll be there, Sophia. Take my word for it."

At exactly six o'clock on the day of the party, Mattie stood on Sophia's front stoop holding a bowl of crab dip and a package of crackers. She reached for the brass door knocker and rapped twice. Sophia threw the door open, delighted her friend was the first to arrive. She put her small white poodle, Samantha III, down on the floor, reached out, and gave Mattie a warm hug.

Philippa, an employee of Milledgeville Amazing Maids, stood at the far end of the foyer near the staircase, ready for the festivities to begin. She had squeezed her voluptuous figure into a lacy black-and-white maid's uniform.

"Philippa," Sophia said, "please take Mattie's crab dip and crackers to the kitchen."

"Hey, Sophia," Mattie whispered when the Amazing Maid was out of earshot. "Did you call an escort service by mistake?"

"It'll be okay, I think," Sophia said, laughing. "I just want her to make my guests feel comfortable."

"Beautiful necklace," Mattie said. "Is it new?"

Sophia reached up and touched her necklace—two stunning diamonds in a vertical platinum setting. "Bernard gave it to me while we were in Aspen," she said. "The diamonds mean present and future."

As the guests started to arrive and began mingling, a trio of local musicians set up their instruments in a corner of the living room and began playing selections from Debussy on viola, flute, and harp. A buzz of conversation and occasional exuberant laughter filled every room.

Mattie noticed they were getting short on ice. She opened the kitchen door and came face-to-face with Philippa scooping her fingers into the crab dip, then sucking the flavors off each finger before dipping in for more. Mattie backed out of the kitchen and went to find Sophia to report the maid's unsanitary culinary practice. She spotted her standing by the front door, staring vacantly at it. "Come back to your guests, Sophia," Mattie said. "Either he'll come or he won't, but watching the door doesn't help. And you have to do something about that maid; she's double dipping in the food—with her fingers."

Mattie could see Sophia had no intention of deserting her post, so she wandered into the dining room where she caught a glimpse of William. She watched him walk to the far end of the table and reach for a wheat cracker. Before he could immerse it in the crab dip, Mattie walked up behind him. "I wouldn't eat that dip if I were you. You've got no idea who's been poking their germy little fingers into it." William spun around to find out who was being so officious. His eyes lit up when he saw it was Mattie. He gave her a big grin. "I was hoping you'd be here. I wanted to ask you if you'd had any luck locating your mother."

"No, not yet. I'm becoming more anxious every day that she doesn't turn up," Mattie said. "Aunt Tess gave me two hundred dollars to offer as a reward for information, but it didn't help. Not one response. My friends and I have put up tons of flyers with an old photo of her on it, but so far, no luck. I've been going a little crazy lately thinking of all the awful things that might have happened to her. It almost seems like she disappeared into thin air."

"We know that's not possible—she's got to be somewhere in the hospital."

"Right, but maybe the staff took her and they're hiding her and doing secret experiments on her, like in an underground laboratory," Mattie said. "I know they used to do all kinds of stuff to the patients without their permission, like dunk them in ice water, or give them toxic medication in douches, or give them nauseants to make them throw up."

"I didn't know they did that stuff to the patients."

"Yeah, it's true. I ran into Lydia at the hospital library last week, and she told me about the research she's been doing. She found out doctors and nurses used to try to cure primary syphilis, that's when a patient first gets chancres—those terrible skin lesions—by injecting the syphilitic patient with malaria. The malaria killed most of them. And according to Lydia, one hundred and twenty-one lobotomies were performed in Jones. She also told me in the operating room in Jones, the doctors used to do this thing called surgical removal therapy. They'd cut out part of the poor patient's large colon because they believed there was a sort of sepsis in the colon, and it was the focal point of mental illness."

"That sounds barbaric; like medieval torture," William said.

"Yes, and have you noticed all the patients from the wards shuffling around the park outside with the whites of their eyes, the sclera, all turned yellow? That's because they were given tons of Thorazine pills years ago. Like it was candy. Now they have permanent liver damage."

William moved closer to Mattie, put his arm around her shoulder, and patted her gently. "You've got to stop this line of thinking, or you're going to make yourself sick. Nothing like that has happened to your mom—those experiments took place over fifty years ago."

"You're right—my thinking *is* getting a little bonkers. Mother must've gotten lost in the system. Maybe her paperwork was misplaced when they transferred her. I do try to think of her being happy—visualize the moment when I find her."

"Good. That's real good. Keep picturing a positive outcome. Is there anything I can do to help?"

"No. Not unless you know a special prayer for lost mothers."

"Well, you're not ready for Saint Jude yet—he's for hopeless cases. Let's try Mother Teresa. She's a nun in Calcutta, and she's been doing a lot of miracles lately. I'll ask my Dominican friends from the seminary to put in a good word for you. They pray a lot—every day, in fact."

"That would be much appreciated, William. I can use all the help I can get. Oh, did Peter come with you? I wanted to introduce him to Annie Able. I bet she and Peter would hit it off."

"Unfortunately, Peter couldn't make it—he's scheduled to work tonight. Maybe another time."

Mattie excused herself. "I'd love to stay and talk some more, but I need to find Sophia."

Sophia was alone in the kitchen, standing by the sink, her shoulders slumped.

"He said he'd come, and he will," Mattie told her friend. "Just be patient."

Half hour later, Sophia was back at her post by the front door. Loud rap. Sophia swung the door open wide—no waiting for Philippa. "Bernard. At last. Come right in. Let me take your jacket."

"Thank you, Sophia. Love your outfit," he said, his eyes taking in her red satin minidress. "You look ravishing."

Sophia tossed her head of loose blonde curls and turned to the party guests in the immediate area. "The Director of Mental Health Management Bernard Bellini has arrived," she said.

As soon as Bernard stepped into the foyer, a thin, stylishly dressed female appeared behind him. The woman stepped inside, latched onto Bernard's upper right arm, and held on tight. She was wearing a diamond necklace exactly like the one Bernard had given Sophia, but the woman's pendant had three, not two, diamonds in it —past, present, *and* future. "This is my wife, Serena," Bernard told the small number of guests who remained nearby. He helped her off with her coat and passed it to Philippa before strutting into the main part of the house as if he owned it. He checked out the music trio and nodded his approval at the array of food covering the dining-room table. Serena tagged along behind him.

Sophia tracked down Mattie, who was chatting with Pam, Gosia, and Jana in the sunroom. She tugged on Mattie's arm and took her aside. "Please, please, please can you get that witch away from Bernard so I can talk to him alone?" she pleaded.

"Sure. Give me a few minutes," Mattie said. "She might be in need of a maid. I'll recommend Philippa."

Sophia peeked around a corner in the living room where Serena and Bernard stood talking. She watched Mattie walk up to the couple and chat with Serena for a few minutes before leading her into the kitchen to meet Philippa.

Sophia dashed over to Bernard. "Quick. Come upstairs," she said. "I'll be waiting for you in my bedroom."

"With all these people here? In the middle of your party?" he asked. "Of course, I'd be delighted."

"No, I mean I want to *talk* to you," Sophia told him.

Once upstairs, Bernard launched an offensive. "You've no cause to be upset. I brought Serena so she wouldn't get suspicious. I want to ask you an important question."

"You said you were getting a divorce! And you bring your wife when you're about to propose to me?"

"What I'm proposing, my beautiful Sophia, is for you to move into my apartment in Atlanta. It's newly decorated in white and gold, and it's near Piedmont Park."

Some of the guests were walking around the second floor on a self-guided tour. Sophia suggested to Bernard that they move their conversation into the master bath for privacy. She opened the bathroom door and saw the half-naked outlines of Mark and the Milledgeville Amazing Maid, Philippa, embracing inside her new European-style, floor-to-ceiling glass enclosed shower.

Sophia took a step back. "Oh no!"

Mark slid open the shower door and popped his head out. "Sorry, I forgot to turn the lock."

Sophia told Bernard to come with her to the balcony off the master bedroom. She closed the French doors behind them and faced Bernard. "You're telling me you want me to leave my house, move into your apartment, and become your mistress?"

"Only until my divorce comes through. As soon as it does, we'll get married."

"And how long might that be? A year? Two years? Ten years?

Never? You can't be serious. And what's with the necklace? You bought her a necklace exactly like mine, only bigger."

"Yes, but I've known her longer."

"That's not good enough, Bernard!" Sophia stepped over to the edge of the balcony, undid the clasp on her necklace, and hurled it over the black wrought-iron railing. "I want you to leave my party," she said, storming back into the bedroom. "Leave now, this minute. Don't ever come near me again, or your wife will hear about what you're doing."

She ran downstairs, picked up Samantha III, and waited. When Bernard arrived back in the foyer, she put Samantha on the floor and pointed. The pedigreed poodle danced around for a minute before grabbing the bottom of Bernard's left trouser leg. Bernard shook his leg up and down and hopped around on one foot. Samantha held on tight, growling and snarling. A small group gathered to watch the performance.

Sophia called Samantha off.

Philippa, who had been watching with amusement, handed Bernard and Serena their coats. Bernard hobbled over to the front door and pulled it open. Serena followed him out, not stopping to say goodbye.

After the guests went home, Sophia and Mattie picked up the dirty dishes and carried them to the kitchen. "I thought it was a marriage proposal, not a mistress proposal," Sophia said. "Now I'm sure I'm destined to live my life alone."

"At least you were able to find the necklace you threw over the balcony."

"Yep," Sophia said. "It was worth crawling around in the bushes for. I'm going to have the diamonds reset into a dinner ring. Bye the way, Philippa told me the reason she had to leave early was because she had another engagement—one that paid better."

"Wonder what that was," Mattie said.

"I think I know. I was arguing with that jerk Bernard, and we went into the master bathroom to get some privacy. Mark and Philippa were in there, almost nude, standing in my shower."

"No! Mark and Philippa?"

"Yep, those two."

"Was the water turned on?"

"Nope, dry run."

"Looks like Philippa took you seriously when you told her she should make your guests feel comfortable."

"I didn't mean *that* comfortable," Sophia said. "But I do have to admire someone who puts her heart into her job, goes that extra mile."

"I have to agree," Mattie said. "Apart from Bernard, it was a great party, Sophia. And it's good you found out what he's really like before you got more involved."

"Yep, I'm totally done with Bernard. I think he and Caroline deserve each other."

Gosia had requested time off to spend Christmas Eve with her daughter, Jana, so Mattie scheduled herself to work from 1:00 p.m. to 9:00 p.m., which would enable her to cover a portion of both shifts. At five o'clock, she took a phone call at the nurses' station from Mr. Vickers.

"There was an accident," he said, his voice quivering. "Dave, my son, Dave, won't be coming to work tomorrow. Or maybe ever."

"Mr. Vickers, please, try to tell me what happened."

"The police said he was heading north on Route 441 up by Lake Sinclair. They think he swerved to miss a deer, and he wrapped his Ferrari around an oak tree."

"That's awful, Mr. Vickers. Where is he now? How bad are his injuries?"

"His face... His right cheekbone's shattered, and his jaw is broken in two places. They're going to wire it shut."

"What about the rest of him?"

"Bad. His legs won't move. Arms either. He's got no feeling in them. The doctor told me he'll be a quadriplegic if he makes it. His hip's shattered. Spleen's ruptured."

Dave's mom was sobbing in the background. "I have to go. My wife needs me."

Mattie called an impromptu staff meeting in the conference room. "Dave's been in an accident," she said. "His face is smashed up and he's got internal injuries, but the worst thing is, if he pulls through, he'll spend the rest of his life in a wheelchair. He's a quadriplegic."

"A quadriplegic?" Ben said.

"Means he can't move his arms *or* his legs," Mark said.

"And it happened on Christmas Eve," Ben said. "What a terrible Christmas."

"It *is* terrible," Mattie said. "Just awful. But we'd better get back to our patients now—Christmas Eve is a sad time for most of them."

Is my mother sad? I wonder what she's doing right now. Is she sitting alone and bored somewhere with nothing to do? Is she remembering when there were four of us, when we were a family? She made pot roast every Christmas Eve for our supper. Wilson and I would open our gifts from under the tree... Tears stung Mattie's eyes. She struggled to focus on the present, stay busy. She decided to help Mark round up patients for the Christmas Eve group.

Mary Duggan, the daughter of one of the surgeons from Jones, had accepted Mattie's invitation to visit CSU on Christmas Eve and play her violin for the patients. After the patients finished eating dinner, Mark asked them to attend the group in the solarium. Eight patients showed up. Mattie helped Mark arrange eleven chairs in a circle—two for staff, one for Mary Duggan, and the remainder for the patients.

When the patients were seated and settled, Mattie and Mark took their seats in the circle. Mary lifted her violin from its case and tucked her chin into the chin rest. She hesitated a moment, picked up her bow, and began playing "Away in a Manger." The sweet sound of her violin permeated the solarium. At the end of the piece, everyone clapped. Mary looked around the group and gave each person a shy smile.

Mattie glanced over at Mark, who sat on the edge of his chair, watching the lovely Irish-looking lass. Mark caught Mattie's eye, smiled, and gave her a quick thumbs up.

A patient named Esther stood up and glanced around the group. Her wrists, which she had cut with a razor prior to admission, were heavily bandaged, her arms hung loosely by her sides. She looked over at Mary Duggan. "I know a song," she said. "Can you play 'It Came Upon the Midnight Clear'?"

Mary Duggan nodded. Her long auburn ringlets bounced up and down as she picked up her bow. Esther began to sing; she had the voice of an angel. The familiar words of the hymn rang out and filled every corner of the room. "… peace on the earth, goodwill to men, from heaven's all-gracious King."

The patients stopped fidgeting; sat up straight in their chairs. Everyone was still, listening. Mattie closed her eyes. She stopped thinking about the past and worrying about the future as the peace of Christmas gently settled over each of them, easing their pain, and bringing them comfort.

Chapter 25

Heather

Christmas Day, 1976
Rivers Building, Ward A
Milledgeville Central State Hospital

Nora's baby was born last night. How we pulled that off, I'll never know. I was nervous, let me tell you, but good ol' Lucinda was as calm as a cucumber. I asked her how many times she had helped birth a baby, and she said about a hundred. No wonder she was so calm.

"Miss Heather," she said, "our Nora is 'bout ready to give birth, and we's gotta decide what time that baby comes. Won't do no good to have a crying baby come out in the middle of the daytime. Staff will grab on to that young 'un and just haul it away to the orphanage."

"But what can we do, Lucinda? We can't just decide we want the baby to be born at night. Babies come whenever they're ready."

"You's right, Miss Heather—yous don't know nothin' about birthin' babies."

"You're playing like this is *Gone with the Wind*?"

"'xactly right. And you's Prissy." She let out a loud hee-haw, slapped her behind, and said, "Butter my butt and call me biscuit."

"But Lucinda…"

"Stop your frettin', Miss Heather. Lucinda here done got things figured out. Adelaide, yous knows—my sister Adelaide—she got a friend working for a baby doctor. She gonna ask her friend to borrow me some Pitocin and a syringe with a needle. Pitocin shot starts up the labor pains right away, maybe in one hour. Maybe less."

"But Lucinda, how in the world are you going to smuggle in Pitocin?"

"When Adelaide brings my Lucas and Sasha to visit on Saturday, she'll sneak them supplies to me. All's we gotta do is bide our time, give the shot, and yep, them contractions will start right up. Nighttime. Daytime. Whatever time I's give the shot."

We figured Christmas Eve would work best. We knew only one staff person would be assigned to work the night shift on Christmas Eve on account of the holiday. Bruno signed up to work like Lucinda told him.

We waited until most of the patients were in bed asleep. Around 9:00 p.m., Lucinda and I got up from our cots and walked over and woke up Nora, all gentle like. She gave us a sweet smile. "Nora, guess what?" I said. "You have a little baby in your tummy." I used the words "in your tummy," trying to keep it simple. I didn't want to go into the exact anatomical location. Nora knew where her tummy was.

Nora clutched her stomach. She said, "How's the baby going to get out?"

I looked over at Lucinda then back at Nora. "It's gonna be a surprise," I told her.

Nora got very excited. "The little baby—it'll be like a present, right?" she asked. She had no earthly idea that her attackers caused her pregnancy. She thought the baby inside her just happened—a miracle as it were. We didn't set her straight.

"Me and Miss Heather is gonna help yous get your baby," Lucinda said. "Lucinda here is gonna give yous a shot in your butt." Nora looked at Lucinda. Turned over on her side like Lucinda told her. Never let out a whimper. Blind trust. Wish I could trust people like that.

I could hear the rest of the patients whispering to each other about Nora. Heard them say the word baby.

Rebecca was one of the lucky patients—she got visitors. Last week I asked her to try to get her visitors to bring in a rubber sheet for me because I was starting to wet my bed. Everyone knows that you can be sent to a worse ward for that (could there be a worse one?). I could've told Rebecca the truth, but she rambles a lot. She might have told her relatives about Nora. Funny, I never told a lie in my life before I came here. Anyway, Rebecca believed me. She got all manic and told her kinfolk it was an emergency: "Heather is peeing all over herself." Next visit they smuggled in a small rubber sheet, the kind like they use in hospitals. We put the rubber sheet under Nora.

Rebecca walked over to Nora's bed and tried to fluff her pillow, but it was long past the point of fluffing. Flat as a pancake. She walked away and returned with three pillows she had slid out from underneath the heads of sleeping patients. She was lucky they didn't wake up and punch her. She stacked the three flat pillows under Nora's head.

Having babies of your own, like when my Matilda and Wilson were born, is not a bit like watching someone else's baby getting born. To be honest, I was very squeamish at the thought. I pictured the worst—baby getting stuck in the birth canal; blue baby with cord around its neck, not breathing. I said "ummm" to calm myself. I wanted to be a good midwife's assistant.

Lucinda crushed up a pill between two spoons and mixed it with some watery orange juice she had saved from breakfast. She told Nora it would make her relax, but then she whispered to me, "Honey, that pill will make her forget she had birthin' pains—better that way. Adelaide brung it when she brung the syringe."

The Pitocin worked fast. About an hour after Lucinda gave Nora the shot in her butt, the labor pains started fast and furious. Nora tried to be a trooper; she grabbed my hand and held on tight. Her face was dripping sweat. I wiped it off with a corner of the sheet.

It turned out to be a mercifully short labor. Around midnight Lucinda said, "Look. See? Baby's head's crowning." I really wasn't that anxious to look. But when I did, I saw the baby's bald little head showing in the birth canal.

I kept on holding on to Nora's hand and told her to bite down hard on a piece of wood I'd picked up outside. She gave a big push.

Muffled scream.

The baby was born.

Lucinda beamed. "Ain't no sign of tearing," she said.

The baby looked a little dark—not real blue but not pink either. And it wasn't crying like it should. Lucinda worked fast. She turned the baby over and swept her little finger into its mouth to get rid of the mucus. When she turned it back over, it let out a cry. Everyone standing by Nora's bed clapped, including Bruno.

I watched, amazed. Lucinda laid the baby on Nora's tummy. She tied two pieces of string about an inch apart on the cord close to the baby's body. She cut through the cord between the pieces of string with a sharp stone she had found outside and scrubbed clean. That woman sure knew what she was doing.

I was standing by, holding a basin of warm water and the towel I had washed a dozen times to make it soft. Lucinda used it to rub the bloody mucus off the baby's skin. She wrapped the baby in one of Bruno's old soft flannel shirts and laid her in Nora's arms. Nora's face was pale; she had lost her pink-cheek glow. Her hair was still damp with sweat. She looked exhausted but happy.

"You's got yous a girl baby, Miss Nora," Lucinda said. "What you want to name this young 'un?"

"My own baby, my baby? Is she really mine?" She looked at Lucinda. "Lucinda. I'll name her Lucinda."

I saw a tear spring to Lucinda's eye. She wiped it away.

"That's a great idea, Nora," I said. "We can call her Lucy for short. Would you like that?" I asked, giving her hand an extra squeeze.

"Yes. I would like that. Little Lucy. She's so small. I love her."

I had found a container for the afterbirth, just like Lucinda had asked me to. It was a big burlap trash bag—Bruno got it from Adelaide, who got it from the folks she cleaned house for. Lucinda held little Lucy while Bruno lifted Nora up out of bed like she was a rag doll. I whipped off the soiled rubber sheet from underneath her and replaced it with the clean cotton one I'd stolen off the laundry cart.

I threw the rubber sheet and the afterbirth in the trash bag. Bruno would dispose of it later.

"Tomorrow we gotta get the breast binder on her afore her milk comes down," Lucinda said. Bruno had gotten hold of one for us—we didn't ask him where he found it.

Lucinda propped Nora back up on the pillows and tucked little Lucy in next to her. "Nora, child, some yous friends want to pay yous a visit. They got gifts for the baby. You okay with that?"

"I would like that, Lucinda," Nora said.

Big Bertha walked over to Nora's bed. Big Bertha's two cohorts, Tulula, the Polish countess, and Thelma Jean, who was normal crazy, came with her. She never went anywhere without them.

"We have come from the Orient bringing gifts for the new King," Thelma Jean said. "I have gold." She laid a spit-polished quarter on the sheet next to Nora.

"The baby's a girl, Thelma Jean," I told her.

"Like me," Big Bertha said. She laid her favorite rag doll on the pillow beside Nora's sweet face.

Tulula reached down, took Nora's right hand, and put a solid gold bracelet into it. Beautiful. Must have been left over from her countess days.

After they left, Lucinda explained to Nora step-by-step what would happen next. "Bruno, he's gonna take the baby to my sister, Adelaide. She's gonna rear her up for yous. Every Saturday they gonna bring the baby here, and yous gets to hold her, and when she gets bigger, yous can play with her."

"Play with her? I get to play with her?"

"Yes, Nora, on Saturdays you will get to hold Lucy," I said. "Then when she gets bigger, you can play with her."

Nora took this well—she didn't know any different. I wanted to explain that Adelaide had a wet nurse lined up for Lucy and that tomorrow we were going to wrap her breasts tightly so her milk couldn't come down. But I knew she wouldn't understand, so I just let it go.

Bruno came in with a basket. Not exactly a Moses basket, but it was the biggest one he could find back among the rushes in the basket-weaving room. I placed Lucy in the basket, on her back, all wrapped up snug. She turned her little head to the side and fell asleep.

Bruno carried the basket around the dormitory, stopping where small clusters of patients who were still awake stood talking. Little Lucy slept through the patients' tears as they reached out one by one, touched her perfect, round little face, and patted her through the warm flannel shirt.

A half hour later, when everyone had had a chance to see her, Lucinda lifted the baby from her basket and let Nora hold her one more time.

It was 1:00 a.m. on Christmas Day.

Lucinda put Lucy back in her basket and tucked her in. Bruno took her through the door, off the ward, out back to where Adelaide waited.

The place seemed empty without her.

Chapter 26

Mattie

January 1977

On the first day of 1977, Mattie walked down the CSU hallway looking for Mark. She peeked into the activity room, the break room, and the seclusion room. No Mark. As she proceeded down the long hall, she wondered what it was like when ninety psychotic males lived in the space. This had been the Walker building's old Ward G. She knew from what Gladys had told her that Big Bertha once lived here when she was Big Bobby. Did he walk down this same hallway on his way to the dormitory, which the CSU patients now used as the solarium?

Mattie had seen twenty or so large rusty iron rings on the floor when she'd toured the unit with Caroline last July. The workmen had yanked them out of the walls and heaped them in a pile in the hallway. Mattie was aware that human beings had once been chained to the rings for weeks, or months, or years at a time. For the patient's safety, maybe. Or maybe for the safety of the staff. Maybe both.

Mattie reminded herself that there were no medications to calm the patients back in 1884, the year the Walker building was completed. She shuddered, grateful she lived in the era of liquid restraints, the new, powerful, modern medications.

Mattie found Mark in the laundry room, loading the cart with clean towels he planned to distribute to the patients. "Happy New Year, Mark," she said. "How was your New Year's Eve? Did you stay in or go party?"

"As a matter of fact, I asked Mary Duggan to go to a friend's house with me."

"Ah, Mary, our Christmas Eve violinist. And? Never mind—that grin you're wearing says it all. I came looking for you to tell you that you're responsible for new admissions today. You have the honor of admitting the first patient for the year 1977. She just arrived. Her name is Heidi G., and she's a transfer from Manor House Nursing Home. She's waiting on you in the intake room. The ambulance driver, his name's Anton, is staying with her right now."

Mark gathered the paperwork together and walked into the intake room. "Hello, I'm Mark," he said, addressing both Heidi and Anton. "Heidi, I'm going to ask you a few questions, we have some forms to sign, then I'll show you around the unit. How does that sound?"

Heidi looked up at Mark from where she sat at the table, but she did not answer.

"She doesn't talk," Anton said.

"A medical condition?"

"Nope, she cut her tongue off. She held it out with a washcloth and sliced most of it off. Blood everywhere. Her roommate, one of our elderly patients, had a heart attack when she saw Heidi's tongue lying on the floor. She thought it was jumping around."

Mark recoiled a step, a movement unnoticed by Heidi. "Geez," Mark said. "That really happened? I probably would have had a coronary too."

"She's also blind. Pulled her right eye out when she was sixteen.

She put her finger into her eye socket and pulled it out. The left she did last year. Same deal; pulled it out. It was on her cheekbone, just lying there. The doctors couldn't reattach it, so they removed it and put in a glass eye to hold the space open."

"Okay. That's a lot of info. Anything else you want to share?" Mark said.

"She's usually agitated, so we medicate her a lot. Oh, and she's got an older brother named Fredrick, who's pretty involved."

"So, she's blind and mute, but she can still hear?" Mark asked.

"You got it."

"I think this is what's known as a 'dump,'" Mark said.

"Right," Anton said, edging toward the door. "We thought you might refuse to take her if you knew her history. Heidi's your problem now—we deserve a rest."

"Wait a minute, Anton. Can she walk? Can she use sign language? Can she go to the bathroom, or does she use a bedpan? Can she feed herself?"

"It's all in her chart," Anton said. "See ya." He did a quick dodge around Mark and bolted for the door.

When Mark finished the admission, he settled Heidi into room 102, the room closest to the nurses' station. Late morning, Mattie was sitting in the station, writing narratives in the patients' charts when a loud, god-awful screeching sound flooded the unit. She jumped up and raced to room 102 in time to see Heidi wailing and kicking the wall. She took her hand and led her to her bed. Heidi lay down, turned her back to Mattie, and curled up in a fetal position.

Mattie knew there was nothing the matter with Heidi's hearing, so she said, "I know how frustrating it must be for you not being able to talk, so I've arranged for a sign language teacher to come work with you in the morning. Her name is Mrs. Bean. You will learn how to make signs into Mrs. Bean's hand, and then Mrs. Bean will tell everyone what you're saying. She will be your voice. You won't have to make that noise anymore—you'll be able to use sign language so you can ask for what you need."

Mrs. Bean, a warm, matronly lady, spent six hours a day on the unit for the next two weeks teaching Heidi how to communicate by making signs into Mrs. Bean's palm. After Heidi became proficient, Sophia suggested that Heidi attend her cognitive group.

Mrs. Bean said she would be "tickled pink" to attend the group and relay to everyone what Heidi was signing into her palm. After the group ended, Mattie walked down the hall to Sophia's office to get a progress report. "I can only stay for a minute, Sophia," she said. "I just want to find out how Heidi did in your group this morning?"

"Well, for her first group, she was awesome. She was able to express herself with Mrs. Bean's help. She signed something I find very interesting. She said two ugly, scary gargoyles had appeared in her bathroom mirror and instructed her when and how to remove her eyes. Mrs. Bean relayed all this to the group."

"I bet that freaked them out."

"No, actually they were very supportive. I think it made their own troubles seem trivial. Anyway, the gargoyles whispered in Heidi's ear that if she didn't want to talk about what happened, she should cut off her tongue. So, she did exactly what they told her; she took a knife and cut off her tongue. She also mentioned she does not hallucinate anymore. She said the gargoyles are gone. She thinks the new medications made them leave."

"Yeah, Dr. von Brimmer put her on a hefty dose of Haldol. And Cogentin, if she needs it for side effects. But I have to say, I'll never look at a gargoyle the same way again. I thought they were supposed to keep bad spirits away."

"Right, but in Heidi's case, they *were* the bad spirits. I still need to talk to one of her relatives to get a social history," Sophia said. "I saw her brother Fredrick from a distance. He looks kind of promising and not just for a social history."

Mattie laughed and nodded her encouragement. "He meets your tall criteria, and by all accounts he's very intelligent. I heard he owns his own business, Eco Green Edible Bog Plants, Inc. He's a 'save the planet' type, in a good way."

"Eco-Friendly Fredrick—I like that," Sophia said. "I'm going to try to schedule an interview with him later this afternoon."

"That's great, Sophia. When you're done talking to him about Heidi, you can ask him about himself."

"The problem with all the other men I've met is they look at me like I'm some sort of trophy—a dumb blonde for them to show off. If I put on some yucky clothes, no makeup, and pull my hair back in a bun, do you think Fredrick will see me for who I really am?"

"That's a great idea, Sophia," Mattie said, getting on board with

Sophia's plan. "He won't focus on your looks—he'll get to know the real you. Remember the brown lace-up granny shoes Gosia used to wear? Maybe you can find a pair of those?"

Sophia laughed. "That might be stretching it a bit."

Just past noon the next day, Sophia looked around the unit for Mattie. She found her in the solarium talking to Mrs. Wentworth, an amiable, down-to-earth grandmother, who had been admitted two weeks prior with a diagnosis of major depressive disorder.

"Now, Mrs. Wentworth," Sophia heard Mattie telling the patient, "you know you're a diabetic. You took another patient's lemon meringue pie off the food cart. It will put you in your grave. Your blood sugar was 485 this morning."

"Then I'll die happy," Mrs. Wentworth said, gulping down the remnants of the pie. She handed her empty plate to Mattie, who put the plate on the food cart.

Mattie and Sophia walked over to a quiet corner of the solarium, away from the patients, and took a seat at one of the empty tables.

"I wanted to let you know my social history interview with Fredrick yesterday went really good," Sophia told Mattie. "I wore my plain-Jane clothes, like you and I talked about. First, Fredrick told me all about Heidi's childhood. She was perfectly normal up to the age of seven, but then she began to disintegrate, lost some of her motor skills, cognitive skills, and her ability to socialize. Became psychotic. She was diagnosed at age eight with Heller's syndrome."

"I didn't know about the Heller's syndrome. It wasn't in the chart Manor House sent over. That's pretty rare, isn't it?"

"Yeah, and really rough on the family. Fredrick said her teenage years were a nightmare."

"I can imagine they were."

"After that part of the interview was over, the family history part, we discussed a lot of other things. It was so comfortable just being with him. He's so relaxed, and he's got a great sense of humor. We didn't finish talking until six o'clock."

"Wow," Mattie said. "Sounds like he might be a keeper."

"And at the end of our meeting, he asked me out. He's going to be waiting for me today when I get off work. Five o'clock, right outside the unit. We're going out for dinner. Not coffee in the cafeteria. Dinner at the Tic Toc Room in Macon. What do you think of that?"

"I think that's wonderful! And I've heard great things about that place—it was a speakeasy for a while, then a nightclub. And I think that's where Little Richard got his start."

At 4:45, Sophia disappeared into the staff bathroom, taking with her the small overnight suitcase she'd brought to work. When she reappeared, she was wearing a sleek black jumpsuit, a sterling silver necklace, and three-inch-high stilettos. She had applied a bright pink lipstick and soft blue eye shadow, which brought out the blue and green flecks in her hazel eyes. Her light-blond hair fell softly around her shoulders.

As soon as Sophia left the unit, she spied Fredrick sitting by the door, reading the latest issue of *Mother Earth News*. He paid no attention to the striking beauty who walked over to his chair and stopped in front of him.

Fredrick glanced up. "I'm waiting for the social worker, Miss Sophia," he said.

Sophia gave him a big friendly smile. "Then wait no longer. It's me, Sophia."

"Sophia?"

"Right. Me. Sophia," she laughed. "Time to go. It's a half hour drive to Macon, and I'm starving."

Mattie was delighted to see how well Heidi responded to treatment. A volunteer from the American Foundation for the Blind came to visit and brought her a walking stick. Heidi used it to go on walks outside with Pam's activity group. When Mrs. Bean was not with her, Heidi would print what she wanted on a piece of paper and hand it to someone nearby.

On the day of Heidi's discharge, two male attendants from Manor House Nursing Home pushed an empty gurney through the CSU door. They lowered it close to the floor to make it easier for Heidi to climb aboard. One of the attendants raised the head of the gurney to a forty-five-degree angle; the other folded back the sheet and fluffed the pillow.

Heidi used her walking stick to guide herself down the hallway. She extended her hand and touched the gurney before sitting down. Once she was comfortable, she swung her legs up and leaned back against the pillow on the headrest.

Her sightless eyes stared straight ahead. She paused and signed into Mrs. Bean's hand, "Did someone named Anton come from Manor House?" Mrs. Bean asked the question out loud for Heidi.

"Yes, Heidi. It's me, Anton. I've come to take you back."

Heidi broke out into a big grin. "I bet you all missed me, right?" she signed to Mrs. Bean, who relayed her message.

"You betcha." Anton took her hand and held it for a moment. "You look great, Heidi. A hundred percent better than when I left you. Nice to see you smile. We'll be back at Manor House in no time." He fastened a safety belt over her waist, raised the gurney back up to regulation height, and snapped the side rails up into place.

Heidi looked around as if she could see. Patients walked up close to the gurney, patted her arm, and wished her well. Martin, a gruff, heavy-set patient, handed her a bunch of fern fronds he had picked from a potted plant in the solarium. He took Heidi's hand and kissed it. Mattie watched the tears flow out of the glands in Heidi's upper eyelids and roll down her cheeks. Heidi sensed Mattie was close by. "Tell Mattie I need a hug," she signed to Mrs. Bean.

Mattie leaned over, hugged Heidi, and whispered in her ear, "Everyone's going to miss you."

The two attendants wheeled Heidi out of CSU and pushed her through the front door of the Walker building. They carried the gurney down the steps and hoisted it into the back of the ambulance, which they had left parked in the street in front of the building. Anton sat in the back next to Heidi. The other attendant jumped into the driver's seat, blasted the siren, and drove the ambulance back to Manor House.

Mattie made her way past fussy children, hungry diners, and waiters carrying trays, to a quiet booth near the back wall of The Brick where Sophia and Annie Able were waiting. She greeted them warmly, slid into the booth, and made herself comfortable. The three friends ordered a bottle of Chianti to share.

Sophia took a roll from the breadbasket, tore off a small piece, and dipped it into the shallow dish of olive oil and pesto. She took a nibble, put the bread back on her plate, and gave Mattie and Annie Able a dreamy smile. "I never ever thought I'd find someone who's so romantic," she said. "Yesterday, he bought me six red roses, and Valentine Day's not until next month."

"Can we assume you're talking about Fredrick?" Mattie asked with a big grin. "And do you want to tell your friends any more details regarding exactly *how* romantic he is?"

Sophia shook her head. "Nope, can't say that I do. You'll have to take my word for it."

Annie Able leaned across the table and took Sophia's hand. "Fredrick's a good ol' boy. It's great you two done met up with each other."

"Thanks, Annie Able," Sophia said.

"Did you tell your folks about him yet?" Mattie asked.

"Not exactly. Not *all* about him. I just told them the part about how he owns his own business but not what kind of business. Fredrick really believes in what he's doing—he's trying to make the planet green—and I didn't want my parents to ridicule him for his effort."

"Wait till they hear he raises bog plants," Mattie said, reaching for a piece of crunchy calamari.

"Holy moly! He could've been owning a hog business, not a bog business," Annie Able said. "They ought to be happy that he ain't. Hogs smell something fierce."

"Here's the best part: Fredrick and I are going to start up a bog farm," Sophia said. "He owns forty acres near the Oconee River, and he's going to figure out how to flood ten of the acres by piping in water from the river."

"A bog farm, Sophia?" Mattie said.

"Yep, and we'll employ mentally ill people to work for us," Sophia said. "Fredrick and I will teach them how to raise their own food and build their own houses. We'll help them become self-sufficient."

"Sophia, that's wonderful! It's just what you've always dreamed of doing," Mattie said. "And you're on the right track. I read somewhere that millions of people in Third World countries get their nourishment from the rhizome of a bog plant called taro."

"You lost me there," Annie Able said. "What's a rhizome, anyways?"

"It's a big bulb growing underground, and it looks almost like a potato," Sophia said. "You can mush it up, pound it flat, and make a kind of bread with it. Fredrick's been experimenting with making cookies. And soup. Very nourishing soup."

Annie Able licked her lips. "Sure would like to give that cookie recipe a try," she said.

Chapter 27

Heather

February 18, 1977
Rivers Building, Ward A
Milledgeville Central State Hospital

I went to see Dr. von Brimmer again today. Bruno walked me over. The doc smiled when I walked into his office. I smiled back—a big toothy grin to show off my new front teeth.

"Amazing difference," he said. "How do they make you feel?"

"Like a princess," I said. I was being sarcastic, but he didn't notice.

"You look wonderful. And I have another surprise for you. There's a new dress and some makeup in the bathroom over there." He pointed to the door near the window. Has his own bathroom. Big shot, I guess.

I went into the bathroom, like he told me. The dress was hanging up behind the door. Pale-blue linen sheath, no belt. Matching blue pumps. Nylons. Silk lingerie. I stood in front of the full-length mirror, thinking. I took the dress off the hanger and carried it out to where he was sitting at his desk, waiting on me.

"Are these things supposed to be for me?" I asked, holding up the dress.

"Are they not your size?" he asked.

"I don't need your charity," I said. "I'm not one of your psychological research experiments. Are you trying to find out what happens when you treat a patient like they're normal? Are you writing up my response? Planning to publish? Well, write this up: Heather won't play; she likes it how things are. She can take care of herself just fine."

He got up and planted himself right in front of me. "I can see how well you take care of yourself. You live in deplorable conditions on a back ward in a state mental hospital, and your brain is turning to mush from lack of use. You call that doing okay? Well, I don't. Now go put on the dress. Try the makeup. Do it for yourself, not for me. And to answer your question, no, I'm not doing research on you, and if I were doing research, I'd find someone who doesn't have such a large chip on her shoulder."

"I can't wear this—it wouldn't be who I am," I said, holding out the dress for him to take back. He shook his head. "It'll be who you'll become," he said, and took my hand and led me back to the bathroom.

The bathroom was big, over a hundred square feet, I reckoned. Lots of gold. I opened the back buttons of my grubby, dowdy housedress and let it slide to the floor. I felt the silk underwear, put it on. I slipped the linen dress over my head and looked in the mirror. Gave myself a big smile. I loved looking at my new front teeth. I looked human again.

Shoes were an exact fit. *How'd he know my size? Did he just guess, or are my feet the same size as his dead wife's? Maybe these are his dead wife's clothes? What if I'm wearing a dead person's clothes? Lucinda would be horrified. Bad omen. Should I ask him? Do I care? A new dress is a new dress.* I scrunched up my face. Where in the world could I wear it? To dinner in the solarium? Menu: soybeans and collards.

I twirled once to see the back. Perfect. I picked up the medium beige liquid foundation, smoothed it over my face. Blush, lipstick—I put them on. Wet my hair a little and patted it down in place. When I looked in the mirror again, the old Heather looked back at me. I went out to the office. This time, Dr. von Brimmer was sitting on his sofa, relaxed, waiting.

"You look like a new woman," he said. I smiled in spite of myself.

"Two questions: First, did these clothes belong to your wife? And second, where do you think I can go wearing this stuff?"

"To answer your first question, no, the clothes are *not* from my wife; they're new for you. And second, what if I were to write you a pass, and we go for a walk to the rose garden?"

I thought, *Why not? What the heck! It's not like I'm busy doing anything.*

Bruno was sitting on the bench outside the doc's office, waiting to walk me back. When I stepped out of the office in my new blue dress, he didn't recognize me. Didn't know who I was. He looked around. "Where Miss Heather?" he asked Dr. von Brimmer, who was standing right behind me.

"It's me, Bruno," I said. "I'm Miss Heather."

I could tell he was shocked. He took a step backward and stared at me for a minute. Then he burst into one of his ear-to-ear smiles. I have to admit I was pleased.

Dr. B. said, "We're going to go for a walk, Bruno. I'll drop her off in Ward A in an hour or two."

He took my hand. Said he didn't want me to fall down the stairs in my new shoes. He didn't let go while we walked. Felt good. Warm and strong.

We sat down on a weathered wooden bench and looked out over the garden. The roses were gone, cut back for the winter. Only clumps of short, dead-looking stems remained. I told him I felt like the dead bushes—ugly with sharp thorns.

He said, "Nature provides the roses with thorns to protect the delicate flowers. They look dead now with their unsightly brown stems, but, come spring, they'll bloom again. They'll be even more beautiful. You'll see masses of pink old-fashioned David Austin roses, and the breeze will carry their scent all over the hospital grounds."

I let him know how isolated I felt, asked him to tell me about what had happened in the outside world while I was shut away on Ward A.

He told me about how President Kennedy was assassinated and how he once got to meet Dr. Martin Luther King. He told me there had been a war going on in a far-off place called Vietnam, but the last of the American troops had come home in 1973. He said it had been an unpopular war, and when the soldiers returned, they were shunned and forgotten.

"I was in a war, you know," he said. "World War II. I was captured in the Philippines in 1942. A Japanese soldier stabbed me in my right leg with a bayonet while I was trying to give my sick friend a drink of water. Dirty, muddy water."

"Your friend, was he okay?" I asked.

He didn't answer for a while. "No. His name was Ian. We were on the Bataan Death March together. I lived, he died. We were both nineteen."

He talked about the Watergate scandal, and how President Nixon had resigned, and how Vice President Ford had taken over. He told me about a new kind of music called disco and about the new Atari games that were coming out.

When we returned to his office, I went into the bathroom, took my new dress off, and put it on the hanger. Kept the silk slip on. It felt good under my housedress. The doc walked me back, like he said he would.

That evening, same as every evening, Lucinda and I sat on the edge of our cots, facing each other, and replayed our whole day, blow by blow. Our cots are so close together that our knees almost touch. I told her about Dr. B. taking me to the rose garden. We talked about how Big Bertha started a food fight at lunch—mashed potatoes splattered all over the dining room. And black-eyed peas. And some slimy okra. The attendants made the patients get down on their hands and knees and clean it up.

When we were done talking, Lucinda tensed up. "It's gonna be tomorrow," she said, a big tear rolling down her face.

I asked her what was going to be tomorrow, but I already knew. Tomorrow was Monday. The Insulin Therapy Group was scheduled to start on Monday. Six patients, including Lucinda, had volunteered to go the basement of Jones for a new experiment.

"I's leaving tomorrow," Lucinda said. Another tear. "Gonna make my break around eleven when we's scheduled to go out walkin'. Bruno told Adelaide to wait up for me on the side of the highway."

"But what if the group leader tries to follow you—bring you back?"

"Can't happen. If'n he starts a chasin' me, then all them other folks he's watchin' gonna skedaddle every-which-a-way."

"But you'll need a car," I said. "How will you buy a car? If you get a car, where will you go? The bounty hunters will hunt you down. I'm worried sick, Lucinda."

"Ain't no need to fret, now—Bruno and Adelaide done got me a car. They's packing us up some food. Me and Lucas and Sasha's headin' to kinfolk in Mississippi."

I moved over and sat on the cot next to her. I touched my cheek to hers. Our tears mingled and fell on the bedsheet. I shifted back over to my cot and pulled out a small, oval-shaped stone from under my bed. It was worn smooth. I found it outside when Bruno took us on one of our walks.

I scooted back over to Lucinda's cot and pressed it into her hand. "If you need me, Lucinda, all you have to do is rub on it," I told her. "And I'll be there. I promise. In your mind, of course, but I'll be there. We can never be apart if you keep the stone."

She kissed it and clutched it in her hand.

"I got something for y'all," she said, handing me a small package wrapped in some discarded paper forms from the nurses' station. I opened it slowly. *Is this really happening? Is my best friend in the whole world leaving tomorrow?* Inside the paper was Lucinda's photo of her kids, Sasha and Lucas. They were looking at the camera, smiling. Sasha had her arm draped around Lucas's shoulder. It was the photo she'd kept taped to the head of her cot for the past eighteen years. She kissed it each morning when she woke up.

"I can't take this, Lucinda. It's too precious. Your kids. You lived to see your kids."

"Don't need it no more. Them two will be with me all the way to Mississippi."

"Thank you, Lucinda," I said, running my hand carefully over Sasha and Lucas's faces. "I'll take good care of it."

We fell asleep holding hands across the space between our cots.

Chapter 28

Mattie

February 1977

Mattie and Sophia were relaxing in Annie Able's living room on Friday evening following a busy week at work. Annie Able had prepared a mixture of onion, artichoke, and parmesan cheese, piled the mixture on toast, and placed it under the broiler until the tops were golden brown. After her creation had cooled down, she cut each piece into triangles.

"This is so delicious, Annie Able," Mattie said, reaching for another piece.

Sophia nodded agreement. "Have you ever thought of opening up a catering business? Talent like this should not be wasted."

Annie Able glowed. "Thanks, y'all. Matter of fact, I've been a thinkin' on it," she said.

"That's wonderful, Annie Able. I bet you'd be very successful," Mattie said.

Sophia sipped her margarita. "I saw Gosia walking around the grounds yesterday," she said. "She was showing some patients a flyer with a photo of your mother on it, Mattie. One poor woman, who looked like a bag lady, was lying on a bench, totally covered up with newspapers. Gosia made her sit up—she wanted to see if she matched the photo."

Mattie shifted her weight, trying to find a comfortable spot on Annie Able's firm-cushioned futon. "Yep, Gosia's been out every day," Mattie said. "Doesn't seem to bother her that it's the middle of February and very nippy outside. She puts on her winter jacket, and off she goes. She always takes Jana with her."

"Yeah, the problem is most of the patients walking around outside are on passes from the wards," Sophia said. "Not many of them can process what Gosia is saying. But all of us, all your friends, are committed to helping you search, Mattie."

"Thanks so much. I can't tell you how much I appreciate it."

"That's what friends are for," Annie Able said.

"Now I need your opinion about something," Mattie said. "I spotted Caroline stalking Bernard."

Annie Able gasped. "Stalking? That little lady could get herself into a mess of trouble."

"She and Bernard were having some sort of affair, but now Bernard's ignoring her. And she's mad, real mad," Mattie said.

Sophia scowled and took a big gulp of her drink. "What a snake in the grass that Bernard is. Y'all remember how he asked me to be his mistress?"

"Yep, that was a Christmas party we'll never forget!" Mattie said, grinning at Sophia. "Tons of drama—you and Bernard, Mark and Philippa. A memorable event, for sure. But, Sophia, you were able to move forward, get on with your life. Caroline just sits in her office all day and mopes. When she does venture out, you should see her—she wraps herself up in a bath blanket, slams her office door, and she's off to hunt for Bernard. The staff has to take cover or get trampled."

"Where did she follow him to this morning?" Sophia asked.

"The library in Powell," Mattie said. "I was in there doing some research. When I looked over at the window, I could see her peeking through it, looking straight at him. He didn't see her because he was too engrossed in talking to the new assistant librarian, who looks about nineteen. Way too young for him."

"That should really set her off," Sophia said.

Annie Able chuckled. "I bet she had a hissy fit."

"What was it you were researching, Mattie?" Sophia asked

"I was looking for info on a condition called Morgellons. I was hoping to find it listed in the *Diagnostic and Statistical Manual of Mental Disorders*. The DSM-II. We'd admitted a patient who told us he had Morgellons. He insisted he had parasites crawling out of his skin. I wanted to find out more about it."

"My understanding is jury's still out on whether it's a delusion or a physical thing," Sophia said. "There's a theory floating about that parasites get into the soil on our farms and from there into the crops. When people eat the food, the miniscule parasites enter their bodies. Then they crawl out through the patient's skin and form patches with lots of black fibers in them. Some psychiatrists swear it's all a delusion, but lots of scientists insist it's parasites or some type of mite."

Annie Able's eyes widened and her mouth fell open. She pushed her glasses back into position on the bridge of her nose. "I sure do admire y'all mental health people, havin' to deal with the likes of that!"

"You're right, Annie Able," Mattie said. "It does get gross at times, for sure. But back to Caroline. Do you think we should do something? It's hard to stand by and watch a human being disintegrate like that. Wasn't long ago she was prancing around on those red heels, telling everyone she was married to a doctor. Now, she can't even make eye contact, let alone run a busy psych unit."

"I don't think counseling will help at this point—she's way too angry," Sophia said. "Let's wait and see what happens. I believe in natural consequences. She's making some bad decisions, and at some point she'll have to deal with the consequences of her actions."

Mattie was standing near Caroline's office the following morning when she saw her open the door and peek out. *Wow*, Mattie, thought. *I'm standing so close I could touch her, but I don't think she even sees me.*

Caroline walked past Mattie, off the Crisis Unit, and out of the front door of Walker. She made her way to the employee parking lot and looked around. When she spied Bernard's car, she walked around to the driver's side and etched a long, deep scratch on the car door with her set of house keys, which she'd brought along for that purpose.

At noon, Mr. Carpenter summoned Caroline to his office in Powell. Caroline pushed his secretary aside and stomped into the room. Mr. Carpenter and Mr. Vickers loomed in front of her. Bernard and a uniformed policeman were standing to the right of them.

"What's going on?" Caroline asked. "Why are all of you looking at me? What the heck is that policeman doing here? I haven't done anything."

"We have a witness who saw you scratch Bernard's car door with a screwdriver this morning," Mr. Carpenter said.

Caroline stamped her foot and screeched, "You people are so dumb. It wasn't a screwdriver; it was a key. Just a plain old key!"

"You're admitting you caused damage to this man's vehicle?" Mr. Vickers asked.

Caroline pointed at Bernard. "Yes, he deserved it. And that's not all I want to do to him," she said, taking a step forward. "We were having an affair, a great affair, but he dropped me like a hot cake."

"Hold it right there," Mr. Carpenter said. "You're lucky, very lucky, that Bernard's agreed not to press charges. Regarding your employment, I am offering you a position as a psych tech on the Crisis Stabilization Unit. If you refuse, you will be terminated immediately with no severance pay."

"But... but females can't be psych techs."

"That's a misconception. I'm sure you'll be able to do as good a job as any male."

"Who'll take my place as supervisor? I ran that unit. There's no one good enough to take over."

"Matilda McAllister will be the new supervisor," Mr. Carpenter said. "Matter of fact, now that I'm thinking about it, we will eliminate the charge nurse position. Merge the two jobs. Matilda McAllister will be both charge nurse and supervisor. That will save the hospital a whole person's salary each year, money better spent on hospital improvements. Her references show her to be well educated, organized, and efficient. I believe she'll be more than equal to the task."

Caroline took a minute and studied each man's face. Considered her options. "Okay, have it your way. I'll take the psych tech position," she said in a more subdued tone. She turned on her heel and prepared to leave.

"Wait—there's one more thing," Mr. Carpenter said to her retreating back. "You must agree to stay away from Bernard. No contact whatsoever. Am I clear?"

Caroline turned back around and faced Mr. Carpenter. She shot a scornful look at Bernard. "Why would I want to go near that scum?" she yelled, slamming the door behind her as she left.

After Caroline finished her high-level meeting, she zipped home and discarded her stilettos and fancy skintight clothes. She put on a plain blue blouse, a white sweater with buttons down the front, tan pants, and black flats. An hour later, she was back on the unit. She glanced down the hall and saw Mattie helping Ben push a heavy laundry cart toward the linen room. She hurried and caught up with them.

"Here, let me do that," she said to Mattie. "I'm your new psych tech."

Mattie stopped the cart, took a step backward, and stared at Caroline, taking in her easy smile and new ensemble. "You're telling me you're no longer the supervisor?" Mattie said. "You're a psych tech now? When did that happen? Who'll take your place?"

"It happened about an hour ago. Mr. Carpenter called me into his office. Said I could leave with no pension or take a psych tech position. I chose the latter. And you'll take my place. You'll be the new supervisor. If you agree, that is. You'll probably get a call from him any minute."

"I'm the new supervisor? But who'll take over as charge nurse?"

"No one—Mr. Carpenter eliminated the charge nurse position to save the hospital some money. Now we're only going to have a supervisor, and that's you."

"You're sure?"

"Positive. And hey, don't feel sorry for me. To tell the truth, I'm relieved. No more hospital politics. No more responsibility. I get to relax and be with the patients."

"There's a lot going on," Mattie whispered to Sophia when she passed her later in the hall. "I'm going to get the supervisor job, and Caroline's turned into a psych tech. She's reinvented herself!"

Mattie asked Caroline if she felt comfortable giving Kenny R., who had burned out his esophagus by swallowing Drano, a gastrostomy feeding. Caroline readily agreed; she told Mattie she had learned the procedure years ago when she was a student nurse.

Caroline found an IV pole in the linen room, rolled it into Kenny's room, and placed it next to his wheelchair. She peered at the short ten-inch soft rubber tube, which poked out of a hole in his stomach. Several thick black retention sutures attached the tube to his skin around the stoma, the opening where the tube entered Kenny's stomach. *Good. Starting to heal. No sign of infection. I can do this,* she told herself. *Take it step by step.*

Caroline hung a bag full of bright green, nutrient rich, pureed food on the IV pole. *Yuck. Looks like a bag full of glop,* she thought. After unclamping the short tube coming out of Kenny's stomach, she attached the long tube descending from the bottom of the feeding bag to it. The green liquid began to snake down the tubing, right into his stomach. When the last drop was finished, she flushed the tubing with sterile water and wheeled him out on the unit.

Mattie was aware Caroline had sailed through her first assignment, so she decided to ask her to assist Pam with the afternoon activity, a bread-making class. Caroline said she would be delighted to help. She knew the activity would give Kenny a chance to socialize, so she pushed him down to the solarium to join in the class, chatting with him the whole time.

"I really, really want to help the patients make bread," Ben told Mattie. "My mom taught me how to knead and stuff. Making bread makes people feel good."

Mattie smiled and nodded. "Ben, the job's all yours."

Pam covered five of the tables in the solarium with clean sheets, and Caroline hummed while she sprinkled flour over them to prevent the dough from sticking once the patients started the kneading process. A small cloud of white flour dust rose toward the ceiling.

Five female, depressed, elderly Italian patients, excited at the prospect of making bread, joined in the activity, talking to each other in their native language. Caroline encouraged them with the only Italian she knew, "*Buona, buona. Migliore*; you're the best."

As soon as everyone was busy kneading (the Italian ladies were already proficient; they had perfected the skill in childhood), Ben walked over to where Caroline was standing. "You seem so different, Caroline," Ben said. "You even dress different. Now you seem normal like everyone else. But do you miss being the boss, when everyone had to do what you told them to?"

"Nope, I don't miss it a bit, Ben. When I was supervisor, I had to play the game—know who to suck up to. There was no one to watch my back. I like this a lot more—taking care of Kenny and the others. I'm done with all that corporate-world stuff."

"And one more thing, Caroline. I keep wondering where Gladys is. Everyone knows she's your best friend. Is she coming back here when she gets out of Ward A?"

"No, she won't be coming back," Caroline said. "Dr. Vine discharged her a few days ago. I haven't seen her, but I heard she lost a lot of weight and got her front teeth straightened. She's going to start a private counseling business teaching overweight people how to lose weight and get healthy."

"But she would have to be nice to people and stuff."

"Yep, apparently from what I've heard she's nice as pie now."

Kenny noticed Pam had become engaged in a discussion with a patient. He could see she had taken her eye off the bread knife—it lay on the table, unattended, behind her. He looked around to make sure Caroline and Ben were still talking at the far end of the solarium before maneuvering his wheelchair up to the table. Moving at lightning speed, he grabbed the knife and cut the stitches that held his gastrostomy tube in place. With a gasp of pain, he pulled the tube out of his stomach and threw it on the floor.

Caroline saw Kenny in her peripheral vision. She rushed over and yanked the knife out of his hand. Blood oozed from around the wound. She reached down and picked up the tube. "What do you think you're doing, Kenny? What were you thinking? Now, you're going to have to get a new tube inserted. Ben, run down the hall and get Mattie. Tell her what happened."

"Okay. Sure. I'll go get her."

Caroline turned to Kenny. She knelt down next to him beside his wheelchair. "Why did you do a thing like that? You knew it would have to be put back in."

Kenny put his head down. "I'm sorry, Caroline."

She was attentive, concerned. "But why?"

"I drank the Drano because I wanted to kill myself. My wife was jumping the janitor," Kenny said. "My wife's Italian. When she's excited, she talks fast in Italian like those lady patients. I don't want to eat through a tube sticking out of my stomach. I want to taste the bread. I miss my wife."

Caroline stood up and patted him on his shoulder. "I know this is hard for you to believe right now, Kenny, but one day you'll wake up in the morning, and you won't miss her as much."

"I won't miss her as much?"

"Right, and you'll be able to pick up the pieces and start over."

Ben rushed back to the solarium, followed by Mattie. He wheeled Kenny to the exam room where Mattie placed a piece of sterile gauze over the wound. Mark took Kenny over to the surgery department in the Jones building, where a surgeon prepared to insert a new G-tube.

Dave was sitting in his wheelchair on the sidewalk near the Walker building, waiting to intercept Mattie as she left work for the day. He was attended by a broad-chested, gorgeous hunk of a man, Sylvester, who fussed over Dave, tucking a fur quilt around him so it covered his paralyzed legs.

Dave's once-handsome face was asymmetrical. His fractured left cheekbone and jaw had both healed, but his right eye was about a half inch higher than his left. When he saw Mattie approaching, a lopsided smile lit up his face.

"Dave, how are you?" Mattie asked, reaching down to give him a hug. "We've missed you around here."

"I wanted to stop by before and say hi to everyone, but I, well, I just wasn't up to—"

"That's okay, Dave," Mattie said. "I know everyone understands."

"Look at me. This is why I don't want to go inside," he blurted out. "I know people will stare at me. And I was afraid you wouldn't recognize me, Mattie. Most people don't. Maybe I need a little more surgery." A tear rolled out of the corner of his eye. Sylvester bent down and wiped the tear away. He produced a cool cloth and gently ran it over Dave's face.

"No, Dave," Mattie said. "I knew right away it was you. Why don't you introduce me to your caregiver?" Dave flashed another crooked smile and said, "This is my partner, Sylvester. My dad introduced us. Can you believe that? Dad knew exactly who I would like to be my caregiver. He knew exactly who would make me happy."

"Dave, that's wonderful," Mattie said. "It looks like you've gotten what you've been looking for all your life. I'm really glad. You deserve to be happy."

"Will you tell everyone I said hi? I'm not ready to visit with the other people yet, but maybe soon."

"Of course. I'll let everyone know."

"We have to go now. Mother's having a formal dinner for us tonight. For Sylvester and me. Kind of like a coming-out dinner. It takes me a long time to get ready."

"That's good, Dave. I'm glad you stopped by, I really am. Come again soon. Okay?"

"Sure. Okay, I'd like that."

"Bye now," Sylvester said as he turned the wheelchair around and whisked Dave away.

Chapter 29

Heather

March 22, 1977
Rivers Building, Ward A
Milledgeville Central State Hospital

Lucina left this morning. When we woke up, we acted all casual—we didn't want to call attention to ourselves. I was able to give her a quick hug before she went out the door, heading toward freedom and a new life. "Goodbye, dear friend," I whispered. "Godspeed. I'll remember you always." Our tears mingled for the last time, and then she was gone.

I ran back to my cot, started crying my eyes out. I wanted to cry away all my sorrow. I pulled the threadbare blanket up over my head and sobbed into my pillow. I felt only despair.

At ten o'clock, Bruno came and got me. Gently pulled the covers back. Gave me some tissues. "Miz Lucinda wouldn't want you to grieve for her, Miz Heather. Another door's gonna open for you, just wait and see. You's a strong lady. A fine lady. I'm gonna walk you over to see that doctor now."

When we got to Powell, Bruno knocked on the doc's door and

stepped back. He would sit in the hall for an hour and wait for me till I was done. What a patient man he was.

The doc told me to take a seat on the sofa. His voice was gentle; he seemed glad to see me.

"How are things with you today, Heather?"

Dr. von Brimmer always starts out like that: "How are things with you today, Heather? Do you have anything that you'd like to share?"

I flashed my new pearly whites at him and said, "I'm okay, I guess," and walked over to his sofa and sat down. I never lie down, like his other patients. I like to sit very prim and proper. Ladylike.

He pulled up a chair and sat down across from me. I looked at my hands. Pushed back the cuticle on my index finger. Bit the nail on my thumb.

"It seems like you've got something on your mind, today."

"Um…"

"Why don't you tell me about it? Maybe I can help."

I looked him in the eye. *What the heck?* I thought. *Maybe he can.* "First, you have to swear to me that this session is confidential. You can't write about it in my chart or tell anyone."

He looked at me and nodded. "We've been over this before. You can trust me. This session is confidential. Between a doctor and a patient."

Should I take a chance?

I took my time, looked around the office. The afternoon sun was coming in through the floor-to-ceiling windows. I studied the tendrils of ivy curling around the panes.

"I'm worried about Lucinda."

"Tell me about her again," he said. "She's your best friend, right?"

"She's my best friend, but there's a bunch of us who hang out together: Sad Sue—she's the one who never stops crying. And Happy Helen."

"Happy Helen? There is such a person?"

"Well, she's not really happy. She can't help laughing. You could tell her a massive meteorite was about to hit the town of Milledgeville, and she would burst out laughing like a hyena. Not that I've ever heard a hyena. We call her Happy Helen."

"Sounds like Helen might be a hebephrenic."

"What's that?"

"It's a formal thought disorder. A form of schizophrenia."

"Whatever she's got, she sure can play cards—the four of us play almost every night. Me, Lucinda, Happy Helen, and Sad Sue."

"I thought cards were forbidden on your ward."

"You're right. No card playing allowed," I said. "That's why we have to play at night. Sad Sue smuggled them in. She just kept crying and begging till her family gave up and brought them. After the lights go out, we wait until after the attendant makes his rounds, and we jump out of bed. We go sit on a blanket in the corner and play Texas hold'em. Sad Sue's brother taught her how, and she showed us. The attendants, they make rounds every hour on the hour, so when it's time for them to come back, we jump into our cots and pull the sheet up. When they leave, we get up and finish our game."

"And that's what you want me to keep confidential?"

"Well, no, there's more. I wanted to tell you that we know how to sneak outside."

"And how do you accomplish that?"

"The lock on the back-exit door is easy to pick. Sad Sue uses a bobby pin to open it. We walk single file out the door and go outside and collect stuff. Like pretty rocks and trinkets and stuff."

Dr. von Brimmer knitted his brow, then relaxed and chuckled.

"So, you pick the lock with a hairpin?" he said. "How come all of you don't run off?"

"I don't want to leave, Sue and Helen are in no shape to leave, and Lucinda believes the ghosts from the cemetery are roaming around and might grab her."

Dr. B. leaned toward me and looked me in the eye. "Heather," he said, "if I didn't know better, I'd say you were using avoidance behavior." He sat back in his chair and waited. "Now why don't you tell me what's really going on? You said you were worried about Lucinda." I shifted my position on the sofa. *It's now or never.*

"Lucinda volunteered to take part in a trial using insulin to fix psychotic patients. It's called the Insulin Therapy Group. Started today

—Bruno walked her over to Jones early this morning to join up with them."

He nodded. "Can you tell me more about it?"

"She's not diabetic or anything, but she'll get injected with insulin every day for six weeks. The staff separates the bunch of them from the rest of us while they get experimented on. They put them on another ward. No one knows where it's at—it's secret. They get extra food, healthy stuff, and they have to exercise a lot."

"What's Lucinda in for? I mean, what's her diagnosis, do you know?"

"She's not really crazy, if that's what you mean. She got mixed up in the system. Looked like she was heading to jail for stabbing her husband with a screwdriver—he was beating up on her kids. But a clerk gave the judge a psychotic person's paperwork by mistake. The judge thought it was Lucinda's file and ruled she was unfit to stand trial. I think the clerk was a relative of hers, but that's beside the point. So she got sent here instead of jail. Her commitment was different than mine; she was in for being criminally insane. No release for her ever. Her family lives two towns over. They come visit every Saturday. Bring her kids, Sasha and Lucas. They're getting big now."

"You've been friends a long time?"

"Eighteen years. Her kids were babies when I got here. She helped me get used to everything. The ward, the rules. She always had my back, looked out for me. We looked out for each other. But I don't understand about the insulin treatment. Sounds so dangerous."

"It goes like this," the doc said. "Lucinda will be injected with eighty units of regular insulin. The staff will wait for her to pass out, which is what happens when your body has too much insulin. When her blood pressure drops very low, to around 80/20, they'll give her IV glucagon to bring her back to a conscious state. The purpose of the treatment is to shock her mind back to normal, but in Lucinda's case, she was never mentally ill in the first place, so all she'll get out of it is a lot of confusion."

"Does it hurt?"

"She'll perspire a lot; her face will flush. She'll have extra saliva. But as for actual pain, no, I don't think that part will be painful. After

"Discharge me? Live on your farm? Do you have any cows?"

He laughed. "There are four cows—Bessie and Bella and Clarabelle and Penelope. But the cows would be in the barn. You'd live in the farmhouse and have your own room, of course."

"I love cows—I learned how to milk them when I lived on the farm with Wilson."

The idea churned around in my brain. "I wouldn't be your patient anymore?"

"No, you'd be my friend."

I looked into the eyes of one of the kindest men I had ever met.

"Not doctor and patient. Just like regular people?"

"Right, just like regular people."

"And could I grow flowers—maybe plant a gardenia bush?"

"Of course. The soil is wonderful. You could grow lots of flowers, vegetables too."

I couldn't sit still. I stood up, paced in a circle. Stopped pacing. Could I? Should I? My mood became a thousand times lighter. I laughed, totally delighted. I could picture it. Me, the farm, cows, flowers.

"I can write you a discharge from Ward A tomorrow," Dr. von Brimmer said. "You will no longer be my patient. I will not be your therapist."

"Tomorrow?" I said. "As soon as that?"

"Yes, tomorrow, March 23. Would that be okay?"

"I'll be ready tomorrow. Tomorrow will be perfect."

"Tomorrow it is."

Chapter 30

Mattie

April 1977

Sophia's office door was open. Mattie hesitated at the doorway.

"Hey, Mattie. Com'on in," Sophia said as soon as she spied her.

"You look pale. Something the matter?"

"No. Well, yes, maybe. It's just that I'm feeling so bad. Dave stopped by to say hi yesterday. He was in a wheelchair—he couldn't even lift his hand to wave goodbye."

Sophia put her arm around Mattie's shoulders. "Here, sit down for a minute."

"I can't stay. I have to get back out on the unit. But I'm constantly replaying the whole Dave thing in my head. To tell the truth, Sophia, I'm thinking about quitting. I can't seem to focus at work. What if I give a patient the wrong meds or something? What if I kill someone? I wouldn't be able live with myself. Maybe I should go work in a flower shop."

"Nonsense. The thing is you need to take better care of yourself. Maybe some guided imagery, or hey, what about yoga? Meditation? Anything that will decrease your anxiety so you can concentrate. Why not take a couple of days off? Forget about looking for your mother and forget about work for a while. Have some fun. Invite William out for drink."

"Invite William out for a drink?"

"Yes, William. And to refresh your memory, he's that cute redheaded Irish-looking guy, who helped you solve a murder," Sophia said.

"You're right about the Irish. He's half Irish, he told me. But asking him out for a drink seems, well, a little forward."

"Okay. How's this—invite him over for dinner."

A slow smile slid across Mattie's face. "I could do that—invite him for dinner. I wonder if he'd come. I haven't seen him lately, and he missed the last staff meeting. Might be a lost cause."

"Not so fast. He's probably just shy. The poor guy's been shut away for most of his life."

"You're so right, Sophia. Dinner. But spaghetti and meatballs are the only dinner things I know how to cook. And to tell the truth, I'm not so great at that."

Sophia laughed. "Remember it's the thought…"

"Thanks, Sophia. I always feel better when I talk to you. Having William over for dinner will take my mind off other things. I'll call him tonight."

That evening, Mattie took a long, hot bath to plan her strategy. *I won't harp on my missing mom, tell him how it's driving me crazy. I'll be lighthearted, go with the flow. I'll need to buy some ingredients in the morning.* When she finished her bath, she phoned William. He said, "Sure, I can come for dinner. It's my night off, and I love spaghetti."

Early evening the next day, Mattie showered, shampooed, and dried and fluffed her hair. She applied lipstick, a touch of mascara but no blush—her cheeks were already bright pink. She slipped into her forest-green tunic and a pair of jeans. Black leather platform heels completed her outfit.

Now I'm ready to tackle the kitchen. Apron on. Right. Don't panic. All is well. First put some water on to boil, then shape the meatballs. Next, make the tomato sauce.

While she was shaping the meatballs, the doorbell rang. *Can't be William—way too early.* She glanced at the kitchen clock. *Oh no, it must be William. Geez, I've got tomato sauce all over my white apron, and my makeup's running down my face. He'll probably turn around and go home.*

She grabbed a kitchen towel, wrapped it around her hand, and used it to open the door. William stood there, big smile on his face, holding up a bottle of Silver Oak Napa Valley Cabernet in one hand and a bag of Perfect Pup Dog Treats in the other.

"Something for you, something for Sooner," he said.

"But which one is for me?" she asked with a playful grin.

"The one that says Perfect Pup, of course."

"My favorite. Come on in. As you can see, I'm not quite ready."

William walked into the kitchen just in time to rescue the pasta water, which was on the verge of boiling over. "Here, let me help," he said as he moved the saucepan to an unlit burner.

"That's music to my ears," Mattie said. "I can't decide what I want to do with the meatballs—fry them in a pan or roast them in the oven," she said while washing her sticky hands in the kitchen sink.

"Here, you sit." William said. "I'll pour you a little wine, and you can watch while I finish up." He directed her to a chair at the kitchen table.

Can this be true? Handsome, smart, and knows how to cook?

William reheated the pasta water to a boil and submerged the spaghetti in it. He chopped an onion and sautéed it in olive oil. When the onion softened, he added mushrooms, a splash of the Napa Valley Cabernet, and two medium-sized cans of crushed tomatoes. Using the palm of his hand as a measure, he stirred in some oregano, basil, and thyme. After browning the meatballs in a separate frying pan, he added them to the sauce and let the mixture simmer. He drained the spaghetti and put it in a bowl with an small amount of olive oil before dipping a spoon into the rich sauce and bringing it over to Mattie.

"Here, taste this," he said.

"Delicious!"

After dinner, they carried their wine into the living room and sat down on the sofa; Sooner lay down on the carpet at their feet.

"Sooner loved those Perfect Pups," Mattie said.

"It was nice of you to share."

"I like to be generous."

William was silent; he shifted his position. "Ah, I was in the seminary for a long time…"

"I remember you telling me. You went to high school in Wisconsin, and after college you went to the seminary at the Dominican House of Studies in Washington, DC."

"Um, yes, right. We studied philosophy *and* political science *and* comparative religion. We played sports a lot, but we never learned about, uh, you know, girls."

"Well, let me start by telling you we don't bite. At least most of us don't. And we like to process a lot. Nothing is ever cut and dried, like with guys."

"Nothing?"

"Pretty much nothing. Like our relationship, for example."

"Our relationship… you want to process it?"

"Of course," Mattie said. "It goes like this: We're friends. We've been through a lot, what with the murder and everything, but it's also like we're not going anywhere. At least not together. You only have a year of freedom, then you need to make a decision. The outside world is tough. We need good people on the inside praying for us. I think you'll make a great monk, William."

"I told you how my faith disappeared while I was in the seminary," William said. "Poof, gone, just like that. When Father Martin advised me to take a year off, I didn't think I would ever regain that peace that comes in believing in something greater than you are. But now, when I'm with you, God's in His heaven and all's right with the world. I find myself believing again."

"I don't know what to say to that, William. If something were to happen to me, would your faith disappear? I don't want the responsibility of knowing your faith is dependent upon me being around."

"That's not it at all," William said. "Knowing you is just a bonus. My faith comes from within. When I walk around and see the faces of the mentally ill and what they suffer, I believe God has them under His wing. His special people. I can actually feel God's presence at Milledgeville."

"Or under Her wing. Who told you God is a guy?"

"Propaganda from the seminary," he said with a chuckle. He scooted over on the sofa until he was within a few inches of Mattie. "I've missed seeing you for the past couple of weeks. I wanted to call you, ask you out, but I didn't have the nerve. So, now you have it—I can't picture living my life with you not in it. I—"

Mattie jumped up. "Would you like some more of the cabernet? The Napa Valley you bought tastes great."

How can I even be thinking of falling for this monk person? You're not supposed to be flirting with monks. But what if he leaves the monks? What if...

William stood up, took Mattie's hand, and guided her back to the sofa. "No thanks, but I'm glad you like it," William said. "I had no idea what to bring. I asked Mark. He recommended it."

"I think Mark knows his wine."

"There's something I've been wanting to say, but I don't know how," William said as soon as they were seated again. "The problem is, I don't have any idea how to proceed with you. All I know is my heart beats faster when I hear your voice. I'm forever wondering what you're up to and hoping to catch a glimpse of you at work. When other high school students were in their locker rooms talking about girls, I was studying Plato. As you probably guessed, I've never kissed a girl. I don't know if I should ask your permission or—"

"You don't need to ask permission." Mattie took William's hand and guided it to her cheek. He touched it, looked into her eyes for a moment, and pressed his lips to hers.

Nice. So gentle. I've just kissed a monk!

William leaned his head back on the sofa, took a deep breath, exhaled, and smiled. "That was amazing. Now I understand what they were talking about." He sat up straight and faced Mattie. "I'd like to do it again, but first I want to tell you something. Regardless of what happens with us, I've decided *not* to return to the Dominicans. My mentor, Father Thomas, is helping me apply to Rome for a dispensation from my vows."

"You already took your vows?"

"I've only taken vows to be a transitional deacon. It's a two-stage process: first, you become a deacon, then you take your final vows at ordination. Being a deacon means I can do baptisms and marriages, but no saying Mass, performing confirmations, anointing the sick, or hearing confessions."

"And you're applying to the pope to undo your vows?"

"Yes. Right. Should take about a year. In the meanwhile, I'm going to study clinical psychology, maybe get my doctorate. It's the best way I can think of to help the mentally ill."

"You're *not* going back?"

"Definitely not going back. Free as a bird."

"Then I'd like to do that again. The kiss… It was so nice. Your first kiss, and it was with me."

"Good, I need more practice." William embraced Mattie in a warm hug and then leaned down and kissed her forehead, eyelids, and cheeks.

"You learn fast," she said, grinning ear to ear. "But wait, I have something I want to ask you. I ran into Dr. von Brimmer at work yesterday. He apologized for not trusting my judgment about Alex. I let him off the hook, told him it would be hard for anyone to believe there was a cold-blooded murderer on the unit."

"Hey, that's good news. He apologized."

"Yep. And to make it up to me, he invited me for dinner on Saturday. He told me I could bring a guest, and I was wondering if you'd like to go with me. He said he loves to cook, and I can see you're a good cook, so I thought, well, maybe…"

"That's this Saturday, April 23?"

"Right."

"I'm not scheduled to work that night, so I'd love to come."

"Okay. Dinner will be at 6:30, he told me, so if you get to my place at about 5:15, we'd have plenty of time to walk there. Dr. von Brimmer lives in a farmhouse about a quarter mile from my apartment. And maybe we can take a detour so I can see the cemetery where Tillman's buried. I'd like to put some spring wildflowers on his grave."

"Of course. I don't think Tillman gets much company. I'm sure he'd like us to stop by."

Mattie turned toward William and giggled. "Great, all settled. Now, let's get back to practicing."

Chapter 31

Mattie

April 1977

Mattie woke up early Saturday morning and jumped out of bed. *Wait, not a workday. This is my day off, and William and I are going to walk over to Dr. von Brimmer's farm for dinner. Yay! It's going to be a great day.* She hummed a little of ABBA's "Dancing Queen" while she made coffee, tidied up the apartment, and brushed Sooner until his bronze coat gleamed. She spent the afternoon organizing the large array of photographs she'd taken while tramping about on long walks with Sooner, exploring the coves and inlets around man-made Lake Sinclair near the town of Milledgeville. She pasted them into an album, ready to share with Aunt Tess and Wilson.

When the doorbell rang at 5:15 p.m., Mattie nearly tripped over her feet in her haste to get to the door, but before opening it, she stopped, inhaled deeply, and counted to ten. "Hello, William," she said, welcoming him with what she hoped was a calm voice.

William stepped inside and brought out a bouquet of sunflowers from behind his back. He smiled and handed them to Mattie. "I'm working on becoming a romantic," he said.

"You're doing an excellent job; they're beautiful."

Sooner followed Mattie into the kitchen and gave her a beseeching look while Mattie quickly arranged the flowers in a porcelain vase. "Nope, not this time, Sooner," she said, bending over and patting him on his head. "We're going to stop by Tillman's grave and then head over to Dr. von Brimmer's for dinner and, sorry, I can only take one guest."

William and Mattie headed down the apartment steps and walked to the periphery of the woods. William pointed to an overgrown trail. "Look, Mattie. There's the path." They hiked along it, focused on reaching the graveyard, skirting over moss-covered rocks and fallen logs. Thirty-foot-tall stately oaks formed a canopy overhead, and the delicate fronds of the woodland ferns created a blanket of green in all directions. Mattie stopped to pick wildflowers along the path, intent on placing them on Tillman's grave once they reached the cemetery.

After fifteen or twenty minutes, they reached a meadow teeming with wildflowers—Virginia bluebells bobbing their sky-blue heads, trout lilies with their delicate speckled leaves, and white shooting stars, looking like small sparkling lights.

"The cemetery is on the other side, just past those trees," William said. "Com'on, I'll show you where Tillman's buried." He looked at the wildflowers Mattie was scrunching in her hand. A wide grin broke out on his face. "You can put what's left of them on his grave."

"They do look kind of sad. I hope Tillman will appreciate the thought," she said.

The moment Mattie caught sight of the cemetery, she stopped, stunned. "Oh my goodness, William. It's much bigger than I imagined!" she said, inhaling the smell of bog vegetation, where pools of water had formed swampy areas, filled with decaying leaves, noisy bullfrogs, and submerged plants. Vines grew rampant along the ground and up the sides of Southern live oaks, Spanish moss dangling from their branches.

William maneuvered around numerous graves until he reached a mound of dirt close to the center of the cemetery. He shuddered. "Here it is," he called out. "Tillman's grave. Right on the other side of this log —the one Alex fell off. The marker's gone, of course, but I'm sure this is it."

Mattie made her way over to where William stood and knelt down close to the center of the grave. After brushing away a small pile of dried-out leaves, she placed the wildflowers on the mound. *Here you go, Tillman. I bought you a bunch of spring flowers I picked by the trail in the woods. Sorry they're a bit wilted. I wanted to say thanks for tripping Alex. And don't tell anyone, but I do believe in ghosts.*

"I feel bad for Tillman," she said, standing up. "He had a rough journey."

Dusk was beginning to settle in as they left the cemetery, heading toward the farmhouse. A slight breeze caused Mattie to pause. "Let's stop for a minute, William," she said. "It's almost the end of April and I thought it would be much warmer by now. I'm a little chilly; I'm going to button my jacket."

William turned toward her and took both her hands in his. "Nervous?" he asked. "Your hands are trembling."

"No—well, maybe just a little. I'm not sure why. We're just going for dinner."

As soon as they rounded the next bend, a two-story white-frame farmhouse with a wide wraparound porch came into view. A wooden swing hung in the front yard by two thick ropes from the branches of a gnarled ginkgo tree. Beyond the farmhouse was a red dairy barn, bordered on both sides by clumps of towering Austrian pines. A few small areas of the original gray barnwood peeked through the red paint.

"Looks like a Currier and Ives painting, don't you think?" Mattie asked.

"That I do," William said, taking her hand and giving it a reassuring squeeze.

As they approached the farmhouse, a black-and-white border collie appeared from around the corner and wagged his tail in welcome. They petted his long, silky coat before walking up the front steps and ringing the doorbell.

When Dr. von Brimmer opened the door, his face lit up. "Come in, come in. So glad you can join us." He asked his guests to step into the spacious front foyer and turned toward William. "You must be Mattie's friend William," he said, shaking William's hand. "Good to meet you."

Dr. von Brimmer patted the front bib of his pink gingham apron, which covered his tweed sport coat and fine-wale dark-brown corduroy pants. He chuckled and pointed to the ruffle on the bottom. "This is a tribute to my feminine side. My fiancée insists I wear an apron when I help her cook," he said, untying the ribbons in the back. He hung the apron on a coat hook near the front door and led Mattie and William into the spacious living room.

"Fiancée? I didn't know you were getting married," Mattie said, following behind Dr. von Brimmer.

"I proposed yesterday, and I'm happy to tell you that she accepted," Dr. von Brimmer said. "She's in the kitchen right now, putting the finishing touches on her specialty: a sour cream pound cake with a lemon glaze."

"Congratulations," William said.

"Yes, that's wonderful," Mattie said.

Dr. von Brimmer invited Mattie and William to take a seat on the blue damask sofa near the fireplace. He sat down in one of the wingback chairs across from them and stretched out his aching leg.

Mattie looked over at Dr. von Brimmer. "I remember when I was a little girl, I used to help my mother in the kitchen," she said. "We made sour cream pound cakes together. It was my mother's favorite."

"That's nice to hear," Dr. von Brimmer said. "An excellent way to bond with a parent. I'm sure my fiancée will share her recipe with you. She's very generous. I think you two will get on well."

Dr. von Brimmer looked at William. "I understand you like to cook."

While William was describing his early forays in the Dominican Order's kitchen, Mattie relaxed, relishing the moment, only half listening as William and Dr. von Brimmer discussed the best wine to add to coq au vin. She inhaled the aroma of the upcoming dinner wafting out from the kitchen and smiled to herself.

Dr. von Brimmer turned toward Mattie. "Now tell me, how are you getting on?" he said. "I've heard good things about your work on the Crisis Stabilization Unit."

"Thanks, Dr. von Brimmer; I appreciate that. It's a lot of responsibility, but I love it. As for how I'm getting on—remember, I told you in one of our sessions how I discovered my mother was alive? Well, I've been going crazy trying to find her."

"She doesn't mean literally crazy. Just a figure of speech," William said.

Dr. von Brimmer gave a hearty laugh. "Of course, of course. Just a figure of speech. And I imagine William is a great support to you."

"Oh yes, he's been helping me look, and so have my other friends. I had an old photo of my mother, and I made up a flyer. We've been showing it around everywhere."

Dr. von Brimmer glanced toward the kitchen. "Here comes my lovely bride-to-be," he said, rising from his chair to greet her. William and Mattie stood up and walked over next to Dr. von Brimmer, eager to meet their hostess.

"So sorry to keep you waiting," she said, removing her apron and placing it on a nearby table. "I had to finish putting the glaze on my pound cake. Welcome."

She held out her hand to William. "I'm William," he said, shaking hands. "This looks like a neat setup you have here, what with the barn, farm animals, and everything."

"You're very kind to say so," she said, giving William a gracious smile. "And yes, we both love the farm. I've started a garden, all kinds of vegetables, including asparagus. And herbs. Mint grows especially well here. I have to laugh at myself—I thought I could tame it, but it's taking over the entire backyard. Now, tell me the truth—do you like pot roast?"

"My favorite."

Dr. von Brimmer gestured toward Mattie. "And this is our new Crisis Stabilization Unit supervisor. I've heard she's doing a great job managing the unit. But that's only to be expected—she's very experienced in her field."

Mattie turned toward Dr. von Brimmer's fiancé, taking a moment to admire her elegant ensemble—a deep-pink silk jumpsuit, which accentuated her slim silhouette, a white shell necklace and matching earrings. Cream pumps. *That jumpsuit looks like it could be a Pierre Cardin. I saw one like it in Cosmopolitan. Wonder if she's from Milledgeville. Bet she belongs to the Women's Society.*

"Thank you," Mattie said. "I'm M—"

"That's a charming locket you're wearing," her hostess said, looking straight at Mattie. "I had a locket like that once. Yes, I had one exactly like that."

"Oh, I thought this was a one of a kind," Mattie said, reaching up to her neck and covering the locket with her hand.

"Do you have photos in it? I did. I had a tiny photo of each of my children. I can't believe how similar it is."

"There are miniature photos of me and my brother. One of us on each side," Mattie said. *Why is this woman so focused on my jewelry? She couldn't have had a locket like this. Why would she say that? Maybe she's just trying to make conversation. I should be polite; after all I'm a guest here.*

"Would you mind if I took a look? I'd love to see your photos."

"They're not much to look at—they're real small. They were taken when we were kids. And I don't take it off."

"But I would love to see such cherished mementos."

Mattie's stomach churned, and her head began to pound. *Why is she so insistent? Should I say, "No way"? That would be rude. Now what? I guess I'd better let her see it. Maybe she'll move on to something else.*

Mattie tried to unfasten the locket, but the clasp was stuck. William moved over and fiddled with it for minute or two. The locket slid off into Mattie's hand.

"Here," Mattie said. "The hinges are a little rusty. Open it. You'll see the photos of me and my brother."

"What's your brother's name?"

"Wilson. His name's Wilson."

"Wilson? Your brother is Wilson?"

Heather held the locket carefully in her hand, looked down at it, slipped her fingernail under the edge, and opened it up. "These photos... This *is* my locket!" Still holding the locket, Heather backed over to the wing chair and grabbed it to steady herself. She stood perfectly still for a moment, staring at Mattie. "You're my Matilda, my darling Mattie. It seems impossible to believe, but I'm your mother, Matilda. I'm your *mother*."

"My mother? No way! You're making that up. And don't call me your darling!" Mattie could feel waves of rage creeping up through her body. *What is it I'm I supposed to do when I feel like I'm losing it? Oh yeah, take deep breaths. Count backward from ten. Don't think that's going to work.* "And I'd like you to give me my locket back right now," she yelled.

Dr. von Brimmer raised his eyebrows, causing two deep furrows to appear in his forehead. He looked at Mattie and shook his head. He started to say something but stopped.

Don't give me that disapproving look of yours, Dr. von Brimmer. About time you came off your high horse. Your fiancée is not my mother. And you're not the one in control for a change. Keep watching. I might just haul off and give this impostor a good slap.

"You're *not* my mother!"

"But I am! I know I am," Heather insisted.

"My mother was a patient. Not just a regular patient—she was a *committed* patient," Mattie said, her voice shrill, loud. "You've *never* been a patient. You've probably never even been inside *any* of the wards. Patients don't know how to be gracious like you. They don't have poise like you. And they certainly never wear classy clothes and nylon stockings. Why are you saying that? Is this some sort of trick? A test? Maybe a prank? How can you stand there and claim you're my mother? No way! You can't be... Liar, liar!" she screamed.

William walked over and put his arm around Mattie's shoulder. "Let's go out on the porch and talk about this."

Mattie pushed his arm away. Took a step backward.

Dr. von Brimmer reached down and rubbed his old leg injury. He walked over, stood beside Heather, and looked directly at Mattie. "I urge you to talk to William. Let's give each other a little space. Talk to William. He seems like a sensible person."

"No, I want to go home. Now. I don't like liars."

"Please, Mattie," William said. "Let's just talk outside. Then you can decide what you want to do."

Mattie took a deep breath, exhaled slowly. "Okay, William," she said, her voice almost back to normal, "I'll talk to you, but there's not much to talk about." She cast a dismissive look at Heather and pushed open the front door.

Chapter 32

Mattie

April 1977

Mattie walked across the porch and stood beside one of the tall white posts next to the steps. She gazed out over the farm. The border collie that had greeted them on their arrival nudged her leg. Mattie reached down and patted his head.

William walked over and stood beside her. Mattie looked up at the stars. "Do you have a favorite month?" Mattie asked him. "May is mine. April showers, then May flowers."

"But that's not what we're going to talk about. We need to talk about what happened just now."

Mattie turned away from William and rested her forehead against the post. "That woman is *no way* my mother," she said, her voice subdued. "Gladys told me my mother has stringy, gray hair, she's stooped over, and she's fat. That skinny woman is not my mother. No, never. I have to keep on looking. That's not her."

"Maybe she changed her hair color, got a new style—women do that, you know. And maybe she's standing up straight because she's feeling good about herself. And she could've lost weight by eating healthy farm food and working in the garden.

"You were very angry in there. I think it's from years of suppressing pent-up feelings of abandonment. But consider, those people meant you no harm."

Mattie jerked around to face him. "So now you're my therapist? Save it for the patients. I thought you were my friend."

"I am your friend, Mattie. That's why I'm out here. I want you to take a step back and look at what you're doing."

"You're saying you believe her, William? You're thinking it's true? I should have known. You believe in miracles—loaves and fishes, walking on water. But not me. I believe in reality. And the reality is that it's not possible for that woman to ever have been a patient on Ward A."

"You're afraid," William said.

"What, afraid? Of course, I'm not!"

"You're afraid that if you believe her, and it turns out *not* to be true, you'll lose your mother all over again."

"And you really think that woman's my mother?"

"I'm just saying to give her a chance. Let her explain. You walk away now, and it will be harder and harder to come back. You'll come up with all kinds of reasons to believe she's an impostor. But is that fair? No. Not to you, not to her."

"Okay, let's get this over. I just want to find out who she is and why this big charade," Mattie said.

Back inside, Mattie took a seat on the sofa, and William sat down beside her. Dr. von Brimmer and Heather, who had been standing by the fireplace deep in conversation, sat down in the chairs across from the sofa. Mattie shot them a defiant look.

"We're so pleased you decided to stay, Mattie," Dr. von Brimmer said. "I feel sure we can get to the bottom of this. Let's try to sort the whole thing out."

"I would like nothing better than to believe I've found my long-lost mother," Mattie said, looking straight at Heather. "But it doesn't add up. I know for a fact my mother was a mental patient in the worst female ward in the hospital. It holds ninety patients, most of them psychotic. You couldn't have been a patient there. You're too well put together. You're neat, well-groomed, and well-spoken. I feel like you and Dr. von Brimmer are playing a trick on me for some reason. Maybe a test to see how much I know about mental illness. Is that it? A test of some sort?"

"No, Matilda," Heather said. "This isn't a test. It's real, I'm real." She stood up and began to pace. "When Clive drove me to the asylum eighteen years ago, he lied to the attendants. Told them I was crazy. When I realized what was happening, I screamed like a banshee, ran around in circles, and banged my head against the visitors' desk. They thought I was insane and put me in a straitjacket and carried me to Ward A. I guess I really did go kind of crazy; I became so depressed. Clive came to visit me that December, right before Christmas. He told me you and Wilson died in a house fire. Smoke inhalation. I believed him—I thought you both were dead. I was grief-stricken. There was no motivation to leave, so I stayed."

"You're trying to tell me you went from Ward A to this?" Mattie said.

Heather stopped pacing and stood next to the fireplace. She looked at Mattie. "Yes, I did. I swear I did. Ten months ago, last July, I started seeing Dr. von Brimmer for therapy, and he brought me out of myself. Gave me this life, a reason to live. Why would I make up such a story?"

"I don't know. People lie."

"Clive lied. Your mother does not lie. I think I saw you once, you know," Heather said. "It was a while ago, before I got my new front teeth. I was on my hands and knees scrubbing the floors over in Powell. You were walking down the hall and stopped for a minute. You seemed so kind, like you wanted to help me. You asked me what ward I was from. I thought to myself, 'She's probably around the same age my Matilda would be if she were alive. Maybe she would have looked just like that. So pretty, so confident.'

"I remember I didn't want to take my hand away from my mouth to answer you. Didn't want you to notice my front teeth were missing. I figured you'd know why, and I didn't want you to be scared. You smiled down at me. After you passed by, I kept on scrubbing. And crying. Scrubbing and crying. So they took me back to Ward A. I never forgot."

"You were that washerwoman?" Mattie said. "That was you? I remember that moment. I told my friend Sophia about it. I can't believe that was you. You look so different, like another person."

"I *am* a different person. I've walked through the valley and come out the other side, thanks to Dr. B.," Heather said, smiling and nodding toward him. "He's been teaching me how to conduct myself in the modern world. Like *Pygmalion*. You know, *My Fair Lady*. Professor Higgins?"

Mattie shot a quizzical look at Dr. von Brimmer, who was following every word. She turned and looked at William. He moved closer to her on the sofa and reached over and took her hand.

Dr. von Brimmer stood up, walked over to the fireplace, and put his arm around Heather's shoulder. "Everything Heather is telling you is correct," he said. "I discharged her on March 23. Let's see— today is April 23, so that would make it exactly one month ago today. I invited her to come and live on the farm—I had an extra bedroom, and I knew she would benefit from being here. During the past month we've fallen in love, and I'll be the happiest mortal on earth the day she becomes my wife."

"But I went to Ward A last October hoping my mother might still be there," Mattie said. "The attendant and the patients said they didn't know where she was. They said she might have been transferred somewhere. And later I asked the ward supervisor—she said she'd never heard of a patient named Heather McAllister."

"I can shed some light on the ward supervisor business," Dr. von Brimmer said. "When I discharged Heather to my care, I asked the supervisor to keep it under her hat. I was afraid if word got out, people might not understand the relationship Heather and I enjoyed at the time was purely platonic."

"When you went to Ward A in October, I *was* still a patient," Heather said. "Believe me, I remember those times well. The morning you came, I must have been off the ward. Sometimes an attendant would take a bunch of patients outside real early in the morning to pick up trash—it was kind of like being on a chain gang."

"Why didn't the patients tell me the truth?"

"They were suspicious of you. They knew you couldn't be my daughter because they knew my daughter had died in a house fire."

"Heather told me she had had two children, but her chart indicated they were dead," Dr. von Brimmer said.

"Don't you see?" Heather said. "The patients were trying to protect me. They never told me about your visit."

"And that rude attendant, Emma Lou. Was *she* trying to protect you?" Mattie asked.

"No, it was plain as pie Emma Lou didn't know if I was a patient or not," Heather said. "She didn't know what patients were outside doing garbage pickup, and she didn't care either, not one bit."

Heather said, "Matilda, do you remember when you used to sit at my dressing table at our house on Abercorn, and I would stand behind you and comb your hair? Wilson used to sit on the floor by us, playing with his little bear."

"His little bear?"

"Yes, he called him Brownie Bear," Heather said. "He gave him to me in the car that day—the day Clive took me away. Said Brownie Bear wanted to go for a ride with me, so I took him. I kept that little bear with me always. But when Maxine got sick, she had cancer, I gave Brownie Bear to her. Maxine was an attendant on Ward A. So good to me—so good to all of us on the ward. I wanted to give her something special to comfort her; something to hold on to when the pain got bad. I gave her Brownie Bear. I gave him away."

Mattie sat like a frozen statue on the sofa. "Wilson's bear," she said. "Wilson gave him to our mother. I saw him myself. He handed Brownie to her through the open car window. We knew Mother would come back. We sat by the front door and waited till it got dark, then Father came home without her. He said, 'Your mother's going to live somewhere else. In a mental hospital. She's never coming back. Go to bed.'"

Heather left Dr. von Brimmer's side and walked over to the sofa. She stood in front of Mattie and held out her arms. Mattie turned her head toward William, who nodded to her. Mattie hesitated for a moment before taking Heather's hands in hers and standing up.

"This isn't a dream?" Mattie asked, facing Heather. "It feels like a dream. You're my mother?"

"Yes, for sure. Your mother."

"William, it's my mom. My mother—she's here. I found her. She came back. Look, Dr. von Brimmer, it's my mom. I can't believe I found my mom!"

Mattie put her head down on Heather's shoulder. Heather wrapped her arms around her.

"It's been so long," Mattie whispered, tears of joy streaming down her face. "I've missed you so much. Every day since..."

"Me too, my darling. Me too. If you only knew how much," Heather said, taking a handkerchief from her pocket and wiping away Mattie's tears. "Let's sit down. I've got so much to ask you. I need to know about Wilson. He's okay too? There never was a fire, right? Tell me where you both went and how you survived. And Aunt Tess—such a kind person. Is she well?"

"You two talk; you've got a lot to catch up on," Dr. von Brimmer said. "William and I will serve the dinner. The pot roast must be ready by now. Okay with you, William?"

"Sure, lead the way."

After everyone was seated at the dining-room table, Dr. von Brimmer uncorked a bottle of Dom Pérignon. "I was saving this for a special occasion, and what could be more special than this? I would like to offer a toast: To two wonderful people who have found each other again after eighteen years of separation. Here's to my lovely Heather, who hung the moon, and to her daughter, Matilda, whose bright smile brings out the stars."

Sooner danced around the apartment the following evening, holding his Minnie Mouse toy in his mouth. "Not now, Sooner," Mattie said. "I can't play now. Annie Able and Sophia are on their way over. Wait till they hear our good news."

When Sophia and Annie Able arrived at Mattie's door, she gave them each a hug and ushered them into the living room, where she had set out a chilled bottle of Moët & Chandon Imperial Champagne on the coffee table, along with three champagne flutes.

Sophia and Annie Able took a seat on the sofa. Mattie sat in a chair across from them. "Champagne!" Sophia said. "I bet I know what's going on—William proposed?"

"Wrong!" Mattie said. "Something better."

"Wait. Something better than a proposal? Then I bet you done got a million-dollar inheritance," Annie Able said.

"Wrong!"

"Mattie, you're bursting at the seams! You have to tell us right this minute," Sophia said. "If it's not William and it's not a million dollars, it's got to be something about your mother, right?"

"Right. My mother! I found her."

"No! You found her?" Sophia said. "Where? Where in the world was she? Was she living on one of the wards?"

"I'm so tickled for you," Annie Able said. "Now tell us all about it. Don't dare leave out one little word."

Mattie began talking with a great burst of energy. "You'll never believe it. Remember, I told you William and I were invited to Dr. von Brimmer's farmhouse for dinner last evening? We got there around 6:30. His fiancée was out of view, still in the kitchen, cooking. He told William and me he'd just proposed to her the day before."

"That must have been a surprise," Sophia said.

"Yes, for sure. Anyway, this woman was in the kitchen fixing pot roast and her special sour cream pound cake. When she walked into the living room, I didn't recognize her—not then. I just thought she was like a regular person, Dr. von Brimmer's fiancée. She noticed I was wearing my mother's locket."

"The one you buried in the pigsty—the one you saved?" Sophia said.

"Right, that's the one. She looked at me kind of funny and said she used to have one like it. I took it off to show her, and she held it for a minute. She knew exactly how to open it. After she saw the photos of me and Wilson, she told me it was *her* locket, and I was her daughter Matilda."

"No! That's unbelievable. But did you recognize her?" Sophia said.

"What did she look like? The patients age quickly because they don't take care of themselves. Did she act like a patient?"

"That's the whole thing," Mattie said. "She didn't look or act like a mental patient at all, so I told her I didn't believe her; I didn't believe she was my mother. But William talked to me on the porch, and he told me I should listen to her story. I did, and boy, was I shocked. My mother knew all about Brownie Bear. We ended up hugging and laughing and having a wonderful meal together."

"Wait," Sophia said. "You're saying Dr. von Brimmer discharged your mom, and she went to live with him?"

"Yes, but she had her own room. Dr. von Brimmer said they were just friends at first, but then they fell in love."

"After a patient is discharged, they're free to do whatever they like," Sophia said.

"Aww. That's so sweet," Annie Able said. "And there's a president for a doctor a marryin' a patient."

"A president? Oh, you mean a precedent," Mattie said. "How did you find out? I don't think a lot of people know that."

"The librarian, Lydia, told me," Annie Able said. "She said it happened about the early 1930s, but I forgot the doctor's name. I recollect Lydia said probably the patient was normal. She thinks her family wanted to get rid of her, so they dumped her at the asylum. Lydia said that used to happen a lot."

"No one can get away with railroading people like that in this day and age," Sophia said. "Anyone who would like treatment in a mental health facility can sign in using the Voluntary Form, but no one can be held against their will unless they are examined by two physicians within twenty-four hours, who both believe the patient is a danger to themselves or others."

"Yes, and one of those physicians must be a psychiatrist," Mattie said. "It's a good thing the law was changed so no one else can end up the way my mother did."

"Did the happy couple fix on a date?" Annie Able asked.

Mattie poured the champagne. "It's going to be at the farm in June. Not sure of the date yet, but y'all are invited, of course."

"Wonderful! Can't wait," Sophia said.

"I just done figured it out—your momma, Heather, was the patient who give Brownie Bear to my momma," Annie Able said. "She must have kept the bear to herself all those years, but when my momma got so sick, she give Brownie to her."

"Yes, you're right, Annie Able," Mattie said. "My mother explained to me how she gave Brownie to Maxine because she wanted her to be able to hold on to Brownie when she was in pain. My mother said holding on to him was what helped her all those years."

"The patients on Ward A, they was like family to my momma," Annie Able said. "She would've been happy as a tick on a dog, if she knew you got your momma back again."

Mattie went into the kitchen and brought out a plate of goat cheese and fig hors d'oeuvres to serve her guests. She filled each of their glasses with champagne.

"Let's have a toast" Sophia said "To the future bride and groom. Every happiness."

"Every happiness," they repeated, clinking their glasses together and enjoying the taste of the bubbly liquid.

"And here's to family and friendship," Mattie said, topping off their glasses.

"To family and friendship," they repeated.

"And Mattie, honey, you've just got to give me your recipe for these goat cheese thingamajigs," Annie Able said. "They sure as heck are delicious."

Chapter 33

Heather

April 24, 1977
The Farm

I guess you could say yesterday was *more* than an okay day—it was a ten-star day, the best day of my life! I found my children. Yep, not only found them but found them all grown up and beautiful.

Last night, Dr. B. invited this young lady and her boyfriend over for dinner. When I stepped out of the kitchen to meet them, I saw she was wearing my old locket. I almost grabbed it right off her neck because my first thought was that it was mine; it belonged to me. (Dr. B. says I will have these aggressive tendencies for a while.)

The young lady turned out to be my daughter, Matilda. People mostly call her Mattie now, for short, but I still like to call her Matilda. She saved my locket by burying it in a pigsty when the Georgia Family and Children Services people took her and my little boy, Wilson, to live on a farm. What a girl. What courage, what stamina.

Tomorrow will be another ten-star day. Wilson's driving here to the farm to see me. Matilda tells me he's turned into a fine young man. He's going to bring Aunt Tess. She was kind to me—came to visit me once when I lived on Abercorn Street. She tried to warn me about her brother Clive. I should've listened.

After dinner, we all sat in the living room and talked till midnight. Matilda told me Clive had told everyone I was legally dead. That's like having a divorce, I think. Dr. B. says we'll get a lawyer to figure it out. My Matilda also told me Clive was locked up in the Atlanta Penitentiary. It's got forty-foot walls all around the outside. She said he's going to be there for a long time. I tried not to look too pleased, but I secretly hoped it would give him time to think about all the suffering he had caused. And Matilda told me about how Aunt Tess took care of her and Wilson, and how many times she and Wilson talked about me —they tried hard to remember every little thing I ever said or did.

My daughter sees me as a classy lady, and I try to live up to that image. I take time to fix my hair, and I don't cuss anymore, not that I was ever that much on cussing. I don't reach across the table, grab a bunch of food, and stuff it into my mouth. I try to remember all the good manners I learned in Miss Elizabeth's Private School. But sometimes I get into my old ways. I see a pretty trinket on the ground outside, pick it up, and hide it under my pillow. Only now my pillow isn't flat. It's plump and pretty with red roses all over it. Matching sheets too.

When I moved my few pitiful possessions into Dr. B.'s house, I was confused. Like going to a different country, where I didn't know the customs. The kitchen stove and refrigerator were a funny green color, avocado. And there was an orangey-colored fondue pot sitting on the counter. I had no idea what it was for. Everything was so fancy. I was afraid to try to cook, but Dr. B. encouraged me, and pretty soon it all came back to me.

I spent the first two days in the old claw-footed bathtub, just soaking and washing my hair with Suave shampoo. I took so many baths that Dr. B. told me it was time to stop. Said I was getting obsessive.

I said, "I have to wash off the smell. Can't you smell it? I smell like the ward."

He said, "No, my dear, you smell lovely, like lavender."

What a gentleman. How lucky I am. I don't know how to drive. Clive believed that a man should do the driving, but I'm going to take lessons. And money? I have to study about how to manage it. I'm used to bartering for everything or having it provided to me. But I'm sure I'll catch on soon.

Matilda's going to help me plan my wedding. It'll take place next month, in June. (Dr. B. bought me a proper calendar, with photographs of lovely flowers on the top of every page.) We're going to set up a gazebo in the north meadow under the oak tree, and after the ceremony, the reception will be in our house. Drinks on the porch. Matilda said her friend Annie Able is starting a catering business, so we're going to ask her to be in charge of the food.

Dr. B. is going to write a day pass for all the patients who would like to come: First, Rebecca, she got the rubber sheet for Nora; then there's Big Bertha, used to be Big Bobby, and her cohorts Tulula—she's the countess—and Thelma Jean. I can't forget Sad Sue, Happy Helen, and Jennifer—she's the one I got my teeth knocked out for—and, of course, Nora. I'd like to have something special for them, something they wouldn't usually get to eat, like grilled hamburgers and watermelon.

Little Lucy's five months old now. Adelaide takes her to visit with Nora every Saturday. Turns out the baby's half black, half white. Kind of a blend, like Lucinda and me. Adelaide's going to bring her to the wedding.

Matilda's inviting her friends from work. She told me all about them. Dave, he was a psych tech, but he's in a wheelchair now. His caregiver and partner, Sylvester, will bring him. And there's a German lady, Gosia. Matilda said that after World War II was over, Gosia walked across Germany holding her mother's hand. She'll probably bring her adopted daughter, Jana.

And Caroline's invited; she used to be the supervisor. Mark—he's a very smart psych tech—is going to come, and he'll bring his girlfriend, an Irish girl named Mary Duggan. And Matilda told me she's going to invite a very shy psych tech named Peter. Matilda worked with him for a few weeks on the night shift. She wants to fix him up with Annie

Able. Matilda thinks they'll be perfect together. Lots more, too, but I don't remember their names.

Matilda's boyfriend, William, is going to pronounce us "man and wife." He said he can still marry people because he has to stay being a monk until the pope gives him a "dispensation." I'm not sure what that is exactly—I'll ask Dr. B. about it. Wilson's going to be the best man, and Matilda will be my maid of honor. I'm going to ask Bruno to give me away. Dear Bruno. What can I say about a man who was my father and my brother? A good man; they come no better.

Matilda wants me to meet her friends Sophia and Annie Able. She told me all about them. She said they both helped search for me, and she said Annie Able's momma was Miz Max, the best attendant on the ward—maybe in the whole hospital. I loved Maxine.

I'm going to invite Matilda, Sophia, and Annie Able to lunch one day next week. Matilda's dog, Sooner, can come too. Matilda says he's very loving, and he can fetch, sit, lie down, and roll over. She said, "Someone threw him out of a car window like he was trash." Guess there are a lot of malicious people out there, like Clive, for example, but I try not to think about him.

Matilda told me a secret. Mothers and daughter do that—tell secrets. She said, "Look at my hands, Mom. When I woke up this morning, I didn't run into the bathroom to scrub them first thing. I think I'm getting better. I don't feel anxious anymore now that I've found you." Then she kissed me on the cheek.

Matilda asked me if I had some friends for her to meet, so I told her, "My only friend is Lucinda."

She said, "That's great. I bet she'd love to come to the wedding."

I said, "She would, but she's not here anymore."

Matilda said, "Oh, she died? I'm so sorry."

"She's not dead, just far away," I told her. "She was admitted as being criminally insane by mistake. It meant she would never have been able to leave the hospital, so she arranged to escape when she volunteered to take part in a clinical study. The patients in the study were allowed to go for a nature walk, and Lucinda left the group and ran over by the highway. The group leader couldn't follow her or else all the other patients might have taken off. When Lucinda got to the highway, her sister was waiting for her in a car. Then Lucinda and her two kids, Sasha and Lucas, headed for Mississippi."

Matilda said, "I would have loved to have met her. Sounds like an interesting person and a good friend."

"Yes," I said. "A good friend. I got a postcard from her a few weeks back. It was from Jackson, Mississippi. She said her car broke down in Birmingham. She, Lucas, and Sasha had to hitchhike the rest of the way to Jackson. Asked for food from the farms, slept in barns, or on the ground at night. I think she's happy now. She's started a new life with her kids."

"Like you, Mom," Matilda said. "She started a new life, just like you."

I haven't got it all figured out yet, why bad things happen to good people. If someone were to ask me, "Are you bitter?" I would say no. Bitterness gets in the way of things—things like love and kindness and understanding.

If I could rewrite my life script, would I? Yes.

Are there things I'm grateful for? Yes. Like finding my children and meeting Dr. B. And for dear friends, Lucinda and Maxine and Bruno. There's Nora. And Nora's baby… Lots of things.

Would I wish what I endured on another living human? No. (That's not exactly true. I would have wished it on Clive.)

It's late now, almost midnight. Dr. B.'s already asleep. I'm going to go lie down next to him, put my head on the pillowcase covered with roses, and dream of dancing among the stars and playing on the moon.

The End

Afterword

The exodus from the great state hospitals began in the mid-1980s. Today, most of the buildings that once teemed with thousands of patients lie empty and abandoned. One might wonder what happened to those patients who left the only life they had ever known, the only place they had ever called home. They had never held a job, paid a bill, never shopped for food, or cooked a meal for themselves. In theory, the patients removed from the institutions were supposed to be cared for by regional mental health centers. Some were sent back to their "loving" families, who had once been overjoyed to get rid of them. The majority had no families, no friends. Many, if not most, couldn't cope on the outside—they ate out of garbage cans, lived on the streets, committed suicide in record numbers.

A few of the institutions were bought by investors, who through herculean efforts were able to preserve the historic buildings. An example of this is the former Traverse City State Mental Hospital in Michigan. This magnificent building was designed by nineteenth century psychiatrist Dr. Thomas Story Kirkbride, who believed patients deserved "cheerful landscapes and handsome architecture." It has been repurposed as condos in The Village at Grand Traverse Commons.

Afterword

Milledgeville Central State Mental Hospital said goodbye to the last of its patients in 2010. It is now possible to tour the grounds by foot or by car, no ticket or pass is necessary. However, going inside the buildings is prohibited with the exception of the first floor of the antebellum Powell building. The remainder of the buildings are too dangerous to enter—caved-in ceilings, collapsed roofs, debris on the floor, broken windows, overturned sinks, rust-eaten tubs, and fallen light fixtures.

Although the bodies of the estimated twenty-five thousand patients who died at the Milledgeville asylum have not been recovered, the Georgia Consumer Council managed to locate two thousand iron grave markers scattered throughout numerous graveyards on the property. They placed the markers in long, neat lines in a beautiful, eerie space in the Cedar Lane Cemetery on the corner of Lawrence Road and Central Shop Road. When you pass through the iron gates, you can follow the gravel path to the crest of the hill where a life-size bronze angel looks out over the cemetery and acts as a perpetual guardian.

No Crisis Stabilization Unit ever existed in Milledgeville Central State Hospital. There was never a Ward A in Rivers or Ward G in Walker. Patients were not contained in a holding room in the main floor of Powell, although they were admitted through Powell in an area set aside in the far west wing. The Jones building did have a fully-equipped surgery and state-of-the-art medical equipment—it serviced not only the patients at the asylum but the townspeople as well. The iconic eatery, The Brick, is still located at 136 West Hancock Street in downtown Milledgeville, but it didn't open its doors until 1993.

Mattie, her family, and coworkers came to life in the imagination of the author. However, the world of the mentally ill, as they experienced it, is an accurate reflection of the times.

If you do get a chance to tour the asylum grounds, walk by the picturesque train depot, where steam locomotives once lumbered along a branch of the main railroad line, carrying workers and visitors to and from the town. Check out the Central Kitchen building, which served an estimated fifty-two thousand meals a day. And if you have time, stroll over to the Rivers building, located near the end of

Afterword

Laboratory Road, and glance up at the first-floor windows. Close your eyes for a moment and imagine. When you open them, look again. You might catch a glimpse of Big Bertha roaming the halls with her cohorts Thelma Jean and Countess Tulula trailing along behind her.

Some say their ghosts still walk the halls of the infamous Ward A.

A Note From The Author

The inspiration to write *Milledgeville Asylum* came to me in the early '60s, when I was a student nurse at St. Louis State Psychiatric Hospital, completing my psychiatric rotation. A recently admitted patient approached me, telling me she didn't belong in the hospital, and begging me to help her escape. She swore her husband hated her and had placed her in the hospital against her will. My instructor explained the patient was paranoid—her chart confirmed this—but a little voice inside me kept asking, "What if she's telling the truth?"

Following graduation, I took a position as a public health nurse in rural Georgia. One of my first referrals was from Milledgeville asylum, requesting I follow up on a husband and wife team, both schizophrenics. It was believed they were living somewhere within the forty-square-mile territory I traversed daily in my trusty old car, wearing my navy-blue public health nurse suit and carrying my doctor's bag full of medical items. I located the couple working as caretakers at an overgrown, forgotten plantation—the old Merck mansion, whose heirs were fighting over ownership in the courts.

The couple was delighted to show me around the mansion—a magnificent oak staircase, fourteen bedrooms, and priceless antiques. They indicated living on the "outside" was very hard, spoke longingly of Milledgeville, and wondered if they might be able to return. (Their plea reminded me of the 1966 French movie, *King of Hearts*). I added the couple to my caseload and visited them weekly until vandals set fire to the mansion. After the fire, I was unable to track them down, but I remembered how they had considered Milledgeville their home.

I vowed one day to write a novel based on the female patient I had cared for at St. Louis State Hospital, who, for all intents and purposes, appeared totally sane. And I knew Milledgeville would be the perfect setting.

Thank you for reading *Milledgeville Asylum*. I would appreciate it if you would post a review on Amazon. And please send any questions or comments to the author at annoleary2@yahoo.com.

Acknowledgments

Thanks to Maririta Hicks, Lee Heffner, Ellen Winkler, author Rachael Wright, the late Marcus Trower, Carolyn Hays, proofreader Marla Markman, Bryan Canter Interior Layout Consultant at Telikos Publishing, and all my wonderful coworkers, friends, and family who encouraged and supported me during my journey.

A huge shout-out to Beverly Ehrman (https://beediting.com), copy editor extraordinaire, who polished the manuscript and made it shine. And to Emily Heid (www.BootstrapBooksPublishing.com), who was always at my side, using her expertise to help me navigate through the complex world of publishing.

About the Author

Ann O'Leary was born in Tenby, Wales, and came to the United States as a child with her mother and brother. After becoming a naturalized citizen at age eighteen, she attended St. Joseph Hospital School of Nursing in Memphis, Tennessee. During her three-month psychiatric internship at St. Louis State Hospital, she developed a lifelong love of working with the mentally ill.

Upon graduating from St. Joseph, Ann worked in varied areas of nursing including public health, newborn nursery, surgery, pediatrics, emergency room, numerous medical-surgical floors, and one nursing home before deciding to return to her first love: psychiatric nursing.

After obtaining a Bachelor of Science from the University of St. Francis in Joliet, Illinois, and a Master of Science from National Louis University in Chicago, she assisted with the opening of the DuPage County Crisis Stabilization Unit in Wheaton, Illinois. She was subsequently hired to work at an in-patient hospital Behavioral Health Department before accepting the position as charge nurse on the evening shift in a busy psychiatric ward at a prominent Illinois hospital.